ICEBORN

THE SEABORN CYCLE SERIES

Seaborn
Iceborn

MICHAEL LIVINGSTON
ICEBORN

BOOK 2 OF THE SEABORN CYCLE

HEAD
of ZEUS

An Ad Astra Book

First published in the UK in 2025 by Head of Zeus,
part of Bloomsbury Publishing Plc

9 7 5 3 1 2 4 6 8

A catalogue record for this book is available from the British Library.

ISBN (PB): 9781035905805
ISBN (E): 9781035905775

Typeset by Siliconchips Services Ltd UK

FSC
www.fsc.org

MIX
Paper | Supporting
responsible forestry
FSC® C171272

Printed and bound in Great Britain by
CPI Group (UK) Ltd, Croydon CR0 4YY

Head of Zeus Ltd
First Floor East
5–8 Hardwick Street
London EC1R 4RG

WWW.HEADOFZEUS.COM

Prologue

When the Aluman Awoke

It was still strange to walk through the high halls of the Spire. It felt wrong. Menes wasn't sure it would ever feel right.

He had no memory of a time when he wasn't aware of the slender tower that sat beside the mouth of the harbor. He'd grown up in the Mother's City, after all. The Spire was as natural to his world as Myst Wera's mountains, its surrounding sea, its docks, and its domed palace of the Stone.

He just never dreamed he'd go there.

The evokers kept men as guards, of course. They did it for the same reason that men like him filled the ranks of the Stoneguard: men were weak of mind but strong of back. But even the guards of the evokers were never allowed beyond the first level of the magickers' high tower.

Yet here he was: Menes, captain of the Stoneguard, walking down a hallway close to the top of the Spire, where its beacon of fire seemed to feed the very clouds.

One of his most trusted men stood before the door ahead

of him, a golden cloak draped over his shoulder, starkly contrasting against his gray tunic. He had his long spear standing upright in his other arm—or as upright as any of them could manage in the tight corridors of the evokers. Casting with Char, Menes had noted, apparently didn't need the room that spear fighting required.

The man's eyes widened a little to see his captain approaching.

"The room has not been entered since I left?" Menes asked.

The man's helm moved in a crisp nod. "This man assures you it has not."

"Good," Menes said. "See to it that I'm not disturbed."

The man saluted, then rotated aside to allow Menes to unlock the door and step into the room. Once inside, the captain carefully closed the door behind him.

The room was a mess, the kind of disorder that would have seen a man in the Stoneguard flogged. But this room hadn't belonged to a true man, much less a member of his beloved Stoneguard. This was the room of a scholar, one of the cut-men.

As a young man, long before he was captain of the Stoneguard, Menes had gotten into an argument in a dockside bar over whether a cut-man was really a man. Over ale, a dockworker had insisted that a man born a man was a man whether or not he still had his eggs. Menes had disagreed, and the fact that a cut-man had been allowed a room so far up within the secretive Spire seemed now to prove his point—men weren't allowed up in the Spire, but a scholar like Tewrick was.

Menes removed his helmet and set it on one of the stacks

of papers beside the door. He smoothed his hair, then his brown beard. He sniffed at the air inside.

Fire.

It was a distant smell, but he could still sense it. It had been an evoker's fire, he was told—a fire created three months earlier, on the very night that the Windborn had attacked the Spire and murdered his High Matron.

None of it made sense, but then, he hadn't been here that terrible night to make sense of it. Against his advice, the High Matron had chosen to meet the Windborn emissary in the Spire—the one place that he and the men of his Stoneguard could not protect her. That an evoker's fire had burned part of a scholar's room seemed one of the least strange things about what had happened.

And yet it was the scholar who'd been on his mind ever since. A little man, as most of the cut-men were. A man of books and letters. Insignificant in the scheme of the world. But he'd left with the Hero of the Harbor, Belakané, after a new High Matron had been chosen—one to replace her dead mother.

Strange and strange again.

"Tewrick," he said, repeating the scholar's name to himself as he started making his way through the shelves of papers and books. "What part did you play?"

Menes instinctively didn't trust scholars. So while it had bothered him that Bela had left the city so soon after the death of her mother, it had bothered him far more that the little cut-man had gone with her—on a mission in search of a myth.

The captain stopped at a shelf, frowned as he idly thumbed through the papers there.

They'd find Ealond, Bela had said. They'd undo the magick that kept the fabled alumen alive.

The alumen. The mechanical men who'd nearly destroyed their ancestors back on the First Isle. The mechanical men who, even now—so Bela said—attacked the Windborn, who then attacked the Seaborn in turn.

It was like the blocks that Menes used to line up when he was a child: push the first one, and it would tip into the next, which would tip into the next and the next, and soon they'd all be falling.

The alumen were the first block. Stop them, and Bela would stop the Windborn and Seaborn from going to war.

Except the alumen were a myth. Or at least he'd always thought so.

Menes walked to the balcony at the end of the room. Its doors were shut, so he pushed them open to the midday light.

The Mother's City stretched out below him, bundled up against its crescent-moon bay. On the opposite side of the waters, the Stone sat calm and resolute. His home.

It all looked different from such a height. Everything seemed so much smaller—everything, that is, except the growing fleet of ships that filled the bay. Its size, he was certain, could only be appreciated from on high like this. Hundreds of masts crowded the harbor, drawn from every Seaborn port.

Belakané meant to stop a war with the Windborn. A fine plan if it worked. But the new High Matron wasn't waiting to find out if it did. She meant to win the war by striking first.

All they needed to know was where to go. Where did the airships come from? Where was the Windborn home?

Menes inhaled the high, clean air, then turned back toward the room. The last time he'd been there, he'd thrown a sheet over the hulking mass just inside the balcony. He pulled it away now.

The aluman was broken in two at the waist, its lower half nothing but a tangled mess of cables. Even so, it was nearly his own height—a broad-shouldered wedge of metal plates whose silver finishes were scorched with black burns. One arm was gone, the other folded out so that its clawed hand could tap and scratch upon the stone floor. Moving that one hand was all it could do now, and although it disgusted him to speak with such an unnatural thing, Menes had learned to communicate with it. A click for a yes. A scratch for a no. It was simple.

"Hello, Asryth," he said.

Its neckless head was badly cracked, making its skeletal visage more frightening. But one glass eye still worked. It flickered to life, a pale blue of powers that he did not understand. Its one hand flexed as it awoke, clawing across the stone.

The scholar had kept a table in this part of the room, and Menes pulled out a chair to sit behind it, facing the metal thing that shouldn't have been real. He took a deep breath, collecting his thoughts. It had taken time to get the information that the High Matron required, but he'd been a patient man.

"You've told me so much, Asryth," he said. "We know where the land of the Windborn is now. I suppose I should thank you."

The light in the aluman's eye burned steady. A razor-tipped finger lifted and tapped down to the ground.

Click.

Yes.

Outside, white clouds drifted eastward. Below them, the sails of a growing fleet waited to follow.

"I think you know we mean to invade, to defeat them. In weeks, we will set sail."

Click.

Yes.

He stared at the unblinking eye. "I feel I owe you one final thing more," he said. "A final truth. You are an abomination. You should not be. And if Belakané fails to close the portal—if she fails to end the magick that gives you life—we will send another. After the Windborn fall, we'll use their captured airships if need be. I don't know if you feel, but if you do, I hope you are afraid. Because we will not rest until the power that drives you and your kind is cut off once and for all."

He stopped speaking. Asryth's dim blue eye seemed to glow brighter for a moment. And then that single finger moved across the ground, scraping against the stone.

No, it said.

No.

I

The Sea of Ice

Bela awoke in the night, and for a moment, she didn't remember where she was. Her skin had been hot with a sweat beyond her spent passions, but her breath rose as fog in the frigid air of her cabin.

Her cabin. Yes, she thought, her eyes making out the familiar details of the walls around and ceiling above. The *Sandcrow*.

So very far from home.

Nestled in her arms, Oni stirred and shifted at Bela's movement. The loose curls of the shipmaiden's long black hair had spread out across Bela's chest—darker against her more olive tones than they were against Oni's brown skin—and as Bela shivered awake, some of the stray strands tickled at her nose.

As quietly as she could, Bela huffed the hairs away, then stared up at the frost-covered boards in the night, wondering if she could possibly go back to sleep.

And with dreams of fire, did she want to?

After a few minutes, Bela sighed and slipped a leg free

of the thick wool blanket that was bound up around them. Oni seemed to smile in response, and her cheek settled further into Bela's shoulder. She purred with sleep.

Bela smiled too. She'd long known that Oni's devotion was far more than the duty owed by a maiden to her shipmistress. But it still pleased her to see the happiness writ so plain on her sleeping face.

But Bela couldn't stay in bed all night. Memories of the war had her awake now. And she wasn't about to spend the remaining long hours of the night being a pillow.

Carefully, she hugged her maiden, feeling the tight cords of her muscled back as she rolled her over and slipped her arm out from beneath the maiden's head. When Oni eased back into the warmth of the blanket, Bela shifted it up around her, tucked her in.

Free from the blanket and her maiden's arms, Bela swung her feet to the fur rug on the floor and stood, naked to the cold air. She stretched her limbs in the small but comfortable cabin that was her home.

Not for the first time, she found herself bothered by the lack of a rolling sea beneath her feet. She was Seaborn. Her life had been the sea. Even before she became mistress of the *Sandcrow*, she had experienced happiness only when she'd ridden the waves and known the rise and fall of the Mother Sea like her second breath. The stillness of the room this past month—the unrelenting immobility of the ship around them—made the world seem off-balance and wrong.

Bela shivered, the cold sliding over her skin beginning to override her body's heat. As quietly as she could, she gathered up her clothes and put them on: the sea-grayed shirt and pants that she'd worn since she was salted, then the layers upon uncomfortable layers needed to fight back the horrifying cold of the Sea of Ice.

They'd come a long way from the warm and sandy shores of the Fair Isles.

Taking one last look at the beautiful Oni sleeping, Bela pulled on her boots and stepped into the corridor, then up the stairs and out into the bitter night.

The four lanterns strung about the deck illuminated a pool of frozen white around the ship. There was so little to see, but Bela knew that even the sun when it rose would bring nothing more to their view. The world around them, once a terror of waves, had become an endless blank canvas.

If Tewrick was right, no one had seen anything like it in a thousand years.

Malaika was on watch, and Bela saw her standing against the frost-painted mainmast at midship, a black figure against the pale beyond. For a moment, the fog that was rising around the grizzled woman made it appear as if she was smoking through some of the last of her prized stash of shred, but when Bela came down from the rear deck, she could see that it was only the steam of her breath.

Malaika looked over at the movement and nodded. "Mistress."

Her nod was curt, hardly a proper mark of respect for the shipmistress of a vessel—any ship, but certainly not one so magnificent as the *Sandcrow*—and for a moment, it crossed Bela's mind to reprimand her. But the night would be long and cold, and she saw no sense in adding to the woman's discomfort. She knew, too, that Malaika was surely holding back much more that she wanted to say. More than any of the sparse crew they still had left, Malaika had not been quiet about questioning the sanity of their mission. And now that the winter's frozen sea had locked them all in place, she'd come to have a kind of morbid humor about what she saw as their inevitable demise.

Bela would never say it out loud, but she suspected the woman was probably right.

The ice floes that had locked them in, that had stormed up against their sides as the snows spun and the sea went white with freeze, had been grinding against the *Sandcrow*'s hull for weeks. The ice had even broken through in places, leaving poor Sanyu to work ever harder at keeping the ship afloat in one piece. And winter would last many months more.

"Had yourself some sport," another voice said from the dark.

Bela caught what looked like a smirk on Malaika's face as they turned in the direction of the sound. "Onyeka," Bela said, nodding respectfully at the older woman's approach. Few of the salted women had wanted the evoker aboard for the voyage. Magick, they thought, had no place on the waves of the world. Bela had been nervous, too, especially after the betrayal by one of her order had cost Bela's mother her life. But there was no question that her magick had been useful more than once.

"Heard your rubbing all the way up front," Onyeka said. "Woke me up."

Malaika had turned to look back out at their blank surrounds. "Jealousy is a terrible thing," she muttered.

Onyeka's eyes narrowed on Bela, as if she were expecting her to reprimand the salted woman for her disrespect.

But Bela ignored it. "It's no doubt for the best that your

devotion to your magick takes away the distraction of such things."

The evoker's expression showed she wasn't certain if Bela was mocking her or not. "So it is. Distraction with the Char is death."

Bela nodded, though, of course, she didn't know from her own experience. To the women who could ingest it, the Char opened them to the ability to weave. It brought them magick. But everyone knew the stories of the evokers who, in haste or hope or fear, took too much at once.

Their deaths, the stories said, were the same as those who had tried to ingest the Char and failed: contorted agony and bloody screams. Bela knew the sight of that pain. Her mother had breathed in the Char that night. She'd breathed it in, and the result was so terrible that Bela had taken her life to end her pain.

Onyeka stifled a yawn in the cold air.

"I am sorry to have woken you, though," Bela said. "You need your strength."

It was no mockery. The evoker's magicks had brought them heat on the coldest of nights and shattered shafts of ice when they'd burst through the hull. Her presence might've made life aboard the *Sandcrow* difficult for Bela at times—to command magick, as the saying went, was to command the world—but Bela couldn't question her usefulness as the winter had set in. And there was no greater truth than the fact that what was useful was prized. It was the way of the Seaborn.

Onyeka sniffed and straightened her back. "I'm strong enough still, girl."

Bela gritted her teeth and nodded to the woman's authority.

Malaika sighed. "I miss the sun." It wasn't a complaint, just a statement of honest truth.

"The sun and palm-shaded sand," Bela said, smiling. "I'm not meant for this cold."

"No one is," Onyeka said.

Bela expected a rejoinder from Malaika—likely something about the unspoken truth that the ship wasn't built for it either—but the woman was staring out into the night. Her shoulders had tightened.

"What?" Bela asked.

"I don't—" She shook her head as if she were trying to make sense of what she'd seen. "I—I thought I saw something."

"Nothing lives here," Onyeka said. "Nothing."

"We do," Bela whispered.

Malaika pointed a grubby finger out into the night. "There!"

The word had hardly left her lips when there was a roar upon the cold air, and a white shape surged into the feeble light of their lanterns.

The evoker yelled. The white thing sped closer, a four-legged run, then leaped up and onto the deck. It roared again, and beneath its obsidian eyes were long teeth, pearl white against black gums. Daggered claws slashed through the air, and Malaika's blood arced across the decking—hot red on frosted white.

The veteran sailhand was falling away. The mouth of teeth turned to Bela. It roared, and its breath smelled of old fish.

A bear. White as snow, and bigger than any two of them.

In the corner of her vision, Bela saw the glitter of gold

flecking the air. Char. Thank the Mother, the evoker actually had her pouch with her. Bela could envision Onyeka inhaling the shimmery yellow haze, then twitching her old fingers through the rest of the falling cloud to thread it and weave it into raw power.

It would be a beautiful sight, she knew. But she didn't turn to look. Without thought, her hand found the cutlass at her hip, and a moment later, she was holding the familiar weight of a claw of her own.

The bear roared again.

This time, Bela roared back.

2

The Hunters

As the world awoke, Alira was already on the move, high above the jungle floor, hurrying along the thick branch of a mature Furywood tree. The slanting rays of sunlight that pierced the canopy threw splashes of brightness upon the bark, and she bounded between the trees—the leather beneath her feet arching with each step, helping her find her grip and balance on the ancient wood.

Not so long ago, she'd been Seaborn, a woman of the waves, and she would have found the height dizzying, the massive trees impossible, the run along such branches incomprehensible.

But she was Stormborn now, a huntress of the trees. And her prey was close.

She didn't need to look around her to know the pace of the others. She could sense them in the shake of the branches, the rippling of the leaves, the flight of the birds. So her eyes looked only to the pools of light and—far below—the darting shadow of a deer in flight.

In truth, the animal ought to have been dead minutes

ago. Kora had nocked her arrow and drawn back her bow, had readied for her first kill while Alira looked on proudly. But the young girl had hesitated. Despite her training, her arrow went high. Spooked, the deer had run, and the chase had begun.

Alira glanced quickly to her left, where Kora was keeping pace upon a closely parallel branch through the trees. It was the first time that Kora had worn the full garb of a huntress: the loose brown trousers tucked into tall, turned-down leather boots; the sleeveless green shirt with a leather band supporting her growing chest; the branches lashed together like plates upon her forearms. Her hood had fallen back from her brown hair as she ran. Alira could see that the girl's face was taut with shame and anger—the same look, Alira was certain, that she'd held herself when she'd gone high on *her* first hunt.

Alira sensed the narrowing of the wood beneath her feet and so looked forward again, her eyes searching through the maze of branches and leaves ahead.

There.

Her hands instinctively went to her back, feeling the bow that was slung there, making certain it was secure. About the only thing more shameful than missing a shot would be losing a bow on the run.

The deer flashed through a pool of light below, and Alira smiled. It was tiring. They were getting closer. Kora would have her chance again.

Alira grinned in anticipation. This time, Kora's arrow would fly true. Of that, there was no doubt. The orphaned girl was already a better shot than her teacher ever would be; the bow was a comfort for her. Alira sensed it every time she watched Kora focus and loose a shot. The release of the string released horrors and nightmares—the dark memories of what she'd seen when the Bloodborn had slaughtered her family. Alira couldn't imagine what it must have been like—the screaming that Kora would've heard as she'd fled into the trees, the guilt of knowing she'd survived. Alira was still haunted by what she and Whéuri had found in Kora's small farmhouse.

Ten more paces onward, bow secured, Alira kicked off from the branch she was on, leaping out over a fall higher than the mast of the tallest ship.

For a heartbeat, she was flying, sailing in the sky. Then her outstretched hands hit a draping vine, her fingers caught and gripped it, and her body pulled it taut as she swung down onto the branch of another tree farther ahead.

Her feet touched. For a moment, she crouched to hold her weight and balance. Then she was up, letting go of the vine, padding onward. The other hunters found their own places around her. Some above. Some below. Kora alighted just paces behind her on the same branch.

Ahead, Alira could see where the thickening branch of this Furywood tree met its wide trunk—just one of a ring of branches that grew out from the same height. A crowning, the Stormborn called it. A ring of growth that appeared every ten years.

Back among the even larger trees of Anjel, the Stormborn built their homes and shops around the crownings, the doorways lining wooden walkways that were woven into the very life of the trees. There were no such walkways here, but the gathering of the branches against the wide trunk made a kind of platform just the same. Once the branch nearest on the right had closed to within reach, Alira leapt for it, taking only two steps closer to the main trunk before she leapt for the next branch—leap by leap, making her way around the tree.

Behind her, a bird called in the distance.

Then, there was the gentlest sound of joy from her left, and Alira glanced in that direction just long enough to see Kora flashing out of sight on the other side of the mighty tree trunk.

A race?

Alira smiled, let only one foot remain on the next branch before she jumped off it. Then again.

Again.

And just before she reached the branch that extended out toward the deer's wake, Kora leaped in front of her.

More birds were calling. An insistent sound.

Kora looked back, a wide grin on her face, and she nearly ran into Whéuri, who suddenly dropped down from the heights above, shaking the branch as she crouched into her landing.

The Stormborn woman had one hand up.

Kora skittered to a halt and crouched beside the older huntress. Alira did the same. "Something's wrong," Whéuri whispered.

Alira had seen the Stormborn woman worried before. The tension of her body and the intensity in her voice were like that now. But worse. Scared. And she had never seen the older woman, the leader of the hunt, close to being out of breath.

Like all of them, Whéuri had been running with her face guard—a fence around her collar made of upright oak branches lashed together with sinew cord—lowered upon her green shirt. But now she flipped it up into place, reaching one hand around her head to cinch it tight about her neck. She raised her hood, too, so that only her eyes were showing in the half-light.

Alira followed her lead. The scent of oak filled her lungs as she moved it up before her face and tightened it. Kora, wide-eyed, didn't put her guard up immediately, but when Alira nodded toward it, she did so quickly.

Whéuri gave them an approving nod, then peered up to their right and pursed her lips to make the sound of a birdcall through the trees.

A call echoed back; then a shape passed down through the branches and landed beside them. It was Whéuri's man, Bryt.

"You saw it too?" His voice was hushed. His mask and hood were already up.

Whéuri nodded, made another birdcall. Two trills of a redbird. It meant the end of the hunt. Trills answered back from the trees around them. Shadows receded, leaving them alone. Kora's shoulders fell.

Whéuri and Bryt didn't move, though, so neither did Alira and Kora. The four of them crouched together on the wide branch, Whéuri and Bryt staring down into the darkness near the base of the tree—not where the deer had disappeared.

Alira felt Kora's unspoken questions, but she had no answers to give. And while she might be the young girl's teacher, she knew better than to speak out of turn in front of her own teacher. Instead, she just watched Whéuri. How the woman almost imperceptibly shifted the weight between her legs as she crouched, keeping one ready to spring at any moment. How she flicked her eyes in a watchful, careful circuit without ever losing focus on the object of her attention below.

So when Whéuri unclasped the bow from her back, Alira did the same, and Kora followed her too. They might not be able to see what the huntress saw—or even hear what she heard—but they knew enough to be ready.

Minutes passed. The jungle seemed quiet. Finally, Whéuri gave a nod to Bryt.

The man, his own bow still on his back, slid down off the branch, using his last grip on its stony bark to swing himself down to another branch below. Level by level, he dropped toward the ground, his passing marked only by the occasional shifting of leaves and the scattered moments when he didn't disappear against his background.

Whéuri watched Bryt descend. The older woman's eyes twinkled with the passion that Alira had more than once heard them share.

Learning that a woman could enjoy a man for something more than his necessary seed of breeding was among the hardest lessons Alira had been made to learn among the Stormborn. It was unheard of elsewhere in the Fair Isles. One of the last things she'd said to her friend Bela—just seconds before a surprise Windborn attack destroyed their ship, killed everyone aboard, and brought Alira here to this island by the grace of the Mother Sea—was that women weren't meant to be with men outside of begetting. Bela had been telling her a story of seeing such a thing, and Alira had felt her friend's secret yearning for it, but she'd told Bela it was wrong. Whéuri and the Stormborn had welcomed

Alira, had taught her to leave her past behind and look only to the future, but that night—that look of pain in Bela's eyes—was something that she could not forget. Especially now, when she saw how close Whéuri could be with Bryt, how different things were among the Stormborn. Bela would have been happy here, Alira thought, except she knew her friend would never leave the sea. Bela was Seaborn more truly than anyone she'd ever known.

Her friend had saltwater in her veins.

Kora shifted on the branch, the bark making a scraping sound beneath her feet. Alira's eyes snapped up to her, and Whéuri's did too. They couldn't see her face behind the wooden guard, but Alira didn't doubt that her cheeks were red.

"Things don't feel right. Look at the tree," the older huntress whispered, and she flicked her gaze back down toward the jungle floor. Bryt was nearly there.

Alira looked down too. As it approached the earth, the trunk of the Furywood tree was like a tower wall. At its base, its great roots had cracked the earth as they spread out, as if the tree was the arm of Father Sky, reaching down from on high to grip the earth, its fingers clutching deep. For a moment, Alira almost opened her mouth to say that she saw nothing wrong—it looked the same as the many other mature Furywood trees on the island—but then she noticed that fronded plants were growing on some of the burled knuckles of those godlike fingers.

Alira had learned that there were certain plants that could take root upon Furywood saplings and kill them. For the Stormborn who called the tall trees home, one eye was always on the watch for such harms, and a knife was always ready to cut them back if spotted. But all those that Alira had seen were thick, choking vines. Nothing with fronds. And nothing on a mature tree such as this.

Bryt was perched just above the fronds now. His eyes looked from them to the dense pack of the surrounding jungle. He made a birdcall—a high tone, falling away.

Whéuri nodded, hooked her bow onto her back once more. As Alira and Kora did the same, the older huntress gave them a nod and then slipped down to a lower branch. Moments later, Alira and Kora did the same. Whatever was growing upon the tree's roots—whatever might be out there—they would see it soon.

3

The White Beast

The bear lunged for Bela, its jaws wide.

She leaped back, away from the snap of its teeth, but the pounding of the bear's weight on the boards made the deck bounce as if it had been wave-struck. It pitched Bela off-balance, but she still managed to twist away from a quick swipe of the beast's claws—a strike intended to take out her gut.

The wood under her heaved, but Bela widened her stance as if the ship were in a storm, and she swept her sword out in an attack of her own. The blade cut through the cold air, ran a red gash across the top of the bear's forearm.

It roared in pain and surged at her again.

She once more twisted out of reach of its gaping maw, but when the next claw swiped at her, Bela's foot hit a coil of frozen rope and had nowhere to go. The claws missed her, but its arm did not. It punched her shoulder, and the weight of it bounced her backward like a toy boat caught by a cresting wave.

Her fingers, numb from the cold, lost their grip on the

sword. The steel skittered across the deck. Her back hit the raised frame of the cargo hatch as she flew, and it slammed her against the wood. She slid across its frozen top, splayed out across the surface, pitching frost.

Her momentum stopped when her feet hit the other side of the hatch. She coughed frigid air into her lungs and looked back. The wood of the hatch beneath her bent with the extra weight, but it didn't give way.

Onyeka's skin was gently aglow from the Char. Her eyes were half-closed, and her fingers were rippling through the air, weaving with invisible strings. Malaika was on the deck, her eyes wide as she clutched at the torn line across the front of her chest. She was covered in blood.

The beast had turned back at them, but when it reached for the fallen woman, its paw was struck away like a fly cast aside by some mighty, unseen hand.

The bear snuffed, roared, then tried to leap upon Malaika instead, but Onyeka's weaving tightened. Bela could actually see it now: a wall of air made visible as it arose from the deck, pulling with it a fine mist of frost. The wall took the bear's weight, held it, and then threw it backward.

Right at Bela.

She cursed, kicking against the smooth boards under her back, and she just managed to roll herself off the cargo hatch the moment before the beast hurtled into it.

The hatch had held her weight, but that was a feather compared to the bulk of the massive bear. The cold boards snapped and shattered into splinters. The animal fell through. It roared as it bounced down into the hold of the ship.

The hold where the rest of the crew would be sleeping.

Bela's sword hadn't gone far. She slid through the frost, grabbed it, then glanced back at Onyeka and Malaika. The evoker was kneeling, gold upon her skin, weaving across the fallen woman's wound. Already, the skin was pulling back together.

Bela thought for a moment of leaping down through the open hatch after the bear, but she knew it was folly. She'd break a leg at best.

Weeks earlier, she had ordered the *Sandcrow*'s foredeck ladder sealed to preserve what warmth they had belowdecks, so she now had to run toward the wider doors at the quarterdeck. Shoving through them, she dashed right, taking the stairwell down to the level of the main hold.

The walls around her echoed with the screams of her crew and the deep, throaty noise of the angry beast.

It had been only seconds since the bear had crashed through, but when she swung around the stairs toward the cargo hold, all she saw was devastation. The animal was in a blind rage in the tight space. Hammocks that had been slung along the walls were tattered. Shiphands who'd been asleep in them were dead or dying. No one in here was armed—no one had a reason to be—and the women stuck in the cramped space had nowhere to run.

We are what we can do.

The old adage came to Bela's mind like a voice from another room. It was a truth, perhaps the strongest truth, that bound the Seaborn each to each: what was useful was prized. A woman was what she could do.

And Bela was the shipmistress of the *Sandcrow*.

This is what I can do.

She didn't stop. She didn't even hesitate. Raising her

sword, she ran screaming into the space, shouting at everyone to run even as she slashed her blade across the thick white fur on the back of the beast.

The bear screamed—there was no other word for the sound—and a red line stained its back. Then it was turning, lumbering around, trying to reach her.

Bela danced away, trying to keep behind it.

The bear swung around, its body crashing into deck supports and fracturing them.

Looking past its bulk, Bela saw at least two women limping away, heading for the stairs. Beyond them was Oni, flying down the stairs with a sword in her hand. She shoved the two wounded women behind her. "Mistress!"

"Here!" Bela shouted.

Between them, the animal turned its attention to the newcomer. It threw a mighty paw at Oni, but she ducked the blow.

And then, in the midst of the chaos, Bela saw him. Tewrick. The scriptkey. The one man on the ship.

He must have been sleeping in a corner of the room when the bear came crashing down. The little bald man was huddled there now, not ten feet from Oni, his eyes wide in fear, hugging his satchel to his chest as if the books inside might protect him.

Though she knew little of such things, Bela was certain they would not.

"Oni!" Bela shouted. "The scriptkey!" She darted around one of the bear's kicking legs and slashed again at its back, hoping to get through to its spine. Or at least get its attention.

The animal roared in response, and in lumbering rage, it again tried to spin around.

Oni moved quickly. Bela saw her run over to the little man, grab him by his slight shoulders, and unceremoniously heave him toward the stairs.

His bag fell from his hands as he stumbled away. He screamed in horror—a pathetic, weak sound—and reached back for his precious books.

"Cockless fool!" Oni yelled. She slapped him away and shoved him onward.

But it was too late. The bear had already scented the scriptkey's fear. Forgetting Bela, it lunged back in the other direction. Oni cursed, rolled out of the way. Tewrick scrambled backward, just out of its reach.

Bela lunged, too, and her sword plunged deep into the monster's extended leg.

The blade bit nerve, and the beast reared up in anger and pain. Its head crashed into the ceiling, raining down frost and splinters.

Then, when it brought its weight down, the impact knocked Bela off her feet.

She fell back against the hard floor—and heard, deep in the ship below her, the sound of wood breaking. The sound of water. Then new screams from belowdecks.

The bear lifted up again, deliberately smashing into the deck above. Weakened by the cold, a line of planks snapped and swung down. Biting air washed over them.

The boards fell at an angle, making a kind of ramp back up to the top deck. The bear lurched toward it, claws scraping and then hooking into the wood.

The ship trembled, wounded.

Bela got to her feet, but then she hesitated, caught between her concern for the sounds belowdecks and her desperate desire to kill the rampaging beast before it could do even greater damage.

Suddenly, Onyeka was there, atop the ramp. Bela's heart soared, but then she saw how the evoker's fingers twitched and flexed with the magick of weaving—but not with the expected grace. Something was wrong. There was panic in her eyes.

The bear lunged upward. Its open mouth, full of teeth and stench, caught the old woman by the neck. Her scream was wet and short.

In one massive bound, the animal carried the evoker out of sight. A moment later, the ship shook with the weight of it jumping down for the ice.

Then the *Sandcrow* quivered again, groaning in death.

Oni got to her feet beside Bela. Her eyes took in the gore of the savaged women that surrounded them, the open cold where Onyeka had stood. She looked down as if she could see where the frigid water was breaching the hull belowdecks. Each was a horror. Together, they were almost inconceivable.

"Well, shit," the shipmaiden said.

4

A Shattered Tree

Whéuri had already reached the ground by the time Alira and Kora dropped down from the lowest of the tree's massive branches. She and Bryt stood beside one of the exposed roots of the Furywood, staring at a rounded burl at the base that was as wide as they were tall. The strange, fronded plants were growing in a circle around the top edge of it, almost like a leafy crown.

"I've never seen such a thing," Bryt whispered.

None of them had. The plants were like squat, trunkless palms, their fronds growing in bunches. Alira reached out and touched the leaves on one of the stiff stalks. They were sharp at the edges, like thin green blades. It reminded her of something she might've once seen, but she couldn't remember where or when.

Whéuri's eyes, visible over her face guard, were uneasy as she looked around at the surrounding jungle. "This isn't right."

Bryt knelt down, lowered his guard, and pulled back his hood for a closer look at where the plants met the

Furywood. "The burl's been split." He pointed, and Alira could see the vertical lines running down the sides of the rounded knuckle of wood. They looked like scars, once-open wounds that had been filled up with the new growth of the strange plant.

"Are the plants splitting it?" Kora asked. Even as she said it, her tone made clear what a preposterous notion that was. Furywood had a strength like stone. Alira had seen that herself when she and Bela first came to Myst Mahaki with the crew of the *Black Crow* to watch the Furywood reaping. Even snapped open and fired by the lightning of the god of storms, the tree trunks were dulling the axes they'd been using to fell and plank them.

Bryt shook his head. "The lines are too straight."

"Tools did this," Alira said.

"But if we didn't do it," Kora said, her voice already starting to shake with the answer she suspected, "then who—?"

"Bloodborn," Whéuri whispered.

Alira, pulling her attention from the Furywood burl, saw that the older huntress had her bow out, and she was staring at another group of trees, growing in a pool of light. They were the size of Furywood saplings—the height of a tall woman—and they had the upright stance of those great trees, but their branches were far more tightly bunched. They were lined up across a gap in the Furywood canopy.

Alira swallowed hard.

They were lined up. Straight. Evenly spaced.

Wild-born trees didn't grow like that. Planted ones did.

Whéuri had silently nocked an arrow. Alira did too. Her mind flashed with how Kora had stumbled out of the jungle, covered in the blood of her family.

"We should leave," Kora begged. "Alira, please."

"A shattered tree, a hearkened sea," Whéuri whispered. "A tattered sail, a hardened gale."

Alira blinked, caught between her fear and her confusion. "What? A shattered tree?"

"A Stormborn prophecy," Bryt said from behind them.

Whéuri nodded slowly, then froze, her head cocked to one side. "Mother! Their leaves are glowing." She was still looking at the planted line. She took a step toward them.

It was true. The leaves of the trees were white under green, but where their pale undersides were visible, the white was shot through with a faint yellow glow, as if their veins were filled with molten gold.

Bryt was still kneeling, still examining the base of the frond plants where they'd been grafted into the Furywood. "There's something else on these roots here. A fungus, maybe?"

He was reaching out. Alira was staring at the glow of those distant leaves. How familiar it was. How it reminded her of Mabaya, the evoker on the *Black Crow*—how she'd glowed each time she'd inhaled her precious Char to weave her magick.

Alira's heart stopped.

The rootfields behind the gates of the Spire. Where the evokers gathered the Char that made their magick. *That* was where she'd seen fronds like those grafted onto the root.

Alira spun. But Bryt had already touched the yellow dust that grew along the roots of the fronds. He'd already brought it up to his face. "No!" she shouted.

But it was too late. Bryt had sniffed at it, breathed it in.

As a child, Alira had dreamed of being an evoker. She'd counted down the days until her twelfth year, when a sybyl would come and cast the Char-weaving to judge her womb and her will. For nights on end, she'd made the same prayer to every goddess and god of the Nine—that her womb would be found unfit for begetting in the Hall of Matrons, and that her will would be found worthy for the life of an evoker in the Spire. The sybyl had agreed, and so she'd been given the Trial of Light. But it had taken only a heartbeat to learn that she was incapable of magick, that she was a mundane. When the sybyl gave her a tiny bit of Char, when Alira breathed it into her lungs, the pain had burst through her like an eruption, as if the sun itself had exploded behind her eyes. She'd screamed for hours.

The sybyl had offered up only a few specks of the fine golden dust for the Trial. That was all. Hardly even enough to see.

Bryt inhaled far more.

He snapped backward, contorting as if a line between his heels and the back of his head had been suddenly pulled taut. His mouth flexed to the sky. He screamed, and it was a sound ripped from his soul.

Startled birds rattled from the trees. The whole jungle seemed to shudder in shock.

Whéuri spun around, dropping her bow and reaching back for him—reaching for her love—but Alira saw that Bryt's fingers were still dusted with the golden Char. And there was so much more of it upon the roots of the fronded plants beside him. Holding her breath, she grabbed his shoulders and yanked him backward, away from the Furywood burl. As his arms flexed and whipped in agony, she rolled past them to grab the dusted hand. The fingers clenched like claws, but she shoved them into the dirt.

Whéuri was there. She slid to the ground above him, her eyes over his. "Bryt," she kept repeating. "Bryt."

He didn't seem to hear her. His eyes were wide, the whites shot through with pink. He choked air through his screams, coughed a spray of blood across Whéuri's face guard.

"To'whir's mercy," Kora mumbled. She was backing away in shock.

Whéuri, even in her horror, knew enough to try to hold her man down, to keep him from hurting himself. She threw her weight down on his shoulders, pinned his head between her thighs to still his thrashing.

Alira, once she was sure his hand was free of the Char, flipped herself over his kicking legs to do the same, though in her heart, she knew it didn't matter. Not with what he'd taken in.

Whéuri looked up at her, an agony of confusion on her face. There were no evokers among the Stormborn.

"Char," Alira said.

"Char?"

Alira nodded to the yellow dust on the plants. "Seaborn evokers use it. No one else can."

"Magick," Whéuri said.

Under their hands, Bryt stopped screaming and clenched his jaw against the pain. The sound of teeth striking teeth was a hideous crack.

Whéuri's eyes whipped over to Kora. "Your bow! Bring it here!"

The command snapped the girl from her own horror. She darted forward, holding out her bow.

The older huntress, fighting Bryt's bucking shoulders, gestured toward his face with her chin. There were tears in her eyes. "Wedge the grip into his mouth."

"Wedge—?"

"Between his teeth! Give him something to bite on!"

The younger girl knelt beside him, stretched the bow over his face. It took all three of them to pry his jaws apart. His teeth and gums were smeared with red.

He bit down on the bow, wailing through the wood.

When their eyes met, Alira knew Whéuri's unspoken question. She shook her head. "Nothing we can do," she whispered.

Whéuri nodded. She flipped down her face guard and bent her trembling mouth toward his forehead. Her lips moved in words that were only for him.

Kora stood, stepped back—out of fear or out of respect, Alira didn't know. Still holding Bryt's legs, she closed her eyes and turned her head away, to give them what privacy she could.

As she did so, she heard a new sound. A sound she'd heard only once in life—though far too often in nightmares since. Behind Bryt's screams, there was laughter in the woods. An animal sound, but a woman made it. Alira knew.

The laughter was answered by another. Far off. But coming closer.

Alira's eyes shot open. She looked at Kora. The girl had heard it, too, and she was backing toward the Furywood tree, her eyes panicked like a cornered animal. She'd heard the sound on the night the Bloodborn slaughtered her family.

"Run," Whéuri said.

"We can carry him," Alira tried.

Whéuri shook her head. "You know we can't."

"Come with us, then." Alira, reluctantly, started to rise.

Whéuri smiled through her tears. "You know I can't." She shifted around Bryt, easing her body down to replace Alira's weight. He shook and struggled in his agony, but he didn't writhe away.

"Please," Alira said as she stood. "Please."

"Take my bow," Whéuri replied. Her voice was calm. Certain.

Alira looked at the weapon on the ground. "You'll need—"

"Only my knife." The huntress was lying over her man now, her eyes looking into his, searching for him past the screams.

Alira picked up Whéuri's bow. She looked out in the direction of the laughter, expecting to see the Bloodborn already floating out of the shadows. Whéuri's hand suddenly snatched at her ankle, making her jump. "Remember this," the huntress said.

A shattered tree, a hearkened sea,
a tattered sail, a hardened gale,
and the gale scattered sail and sea.
A scattered hour, a sharpened power,
a battered land, a blackened hand,
and the hand shattered land and power.

Alira nodded. "What does it mean?"

Whéuri let go of her ankle. "You may find out." The huntress, Alira saw, had her knife out of its scabbard. "Now go, Alira Stormborn," she said. "Go and remember."

5

River of Mist

The metal man in the river was a perfect match for Shae's mood. A heavy mountain fog had settled in over the rolling waters, but she could still see the thing standing there, waist-deep in its cold flow, frozen mid-stride. Same as ever. The aluman had gone where it wasn't meant to go, and now it was stuck there.

Just like her.

Little rocks, beaten to smoothness by the water, lined the river's edge. Shae squatted down and pushed her fingers through them. At last, she found one she liked. Round and flat. Just the right size. She picked it up and balanced it in her grip. Like the air, it was cold in a way things never were in the Fair Isles. She stood, thought for a moment about how the stone's chill seemed to lessen against her skin but would, after she'd thrown it, leave her hand colder when it was gone. Then, cocking back her arm, she spun it over the stream. It bellied off the placid area behind a rock where fish liked to feed, skipped into the air, and plinked into the aluman's face.

The metal made a hollow ring. It didn't move.

Same as ever.

A dog barked in the village that spread out along the river behind her. It was a lonely, disembodied sound in the fog, and it did not improve her spirits.

Shae took her time gathering up a few more stones—time was one thing she had in abundance now—then she sat down on a wide boulder that stuck out from the riverbank. Below her feet, a few brown-backed minnows darted anxiously in a shallow eddy.

Watching the fish twist and turn—free to move yet not free to leave their little pocket of water—she felt a rising anger, not for the first time, that Kayden Mar had taken her aboard the Windborn airship as it had fled from the Spire. She was the Bone Pirate, by the gods. She belonged in a ship upon the warm blue sea, a world away from this cold stone seat.

In the first days, when she'd realized what he'd done, how he'd brought her across the uncrossable ocean to his home, she'd screamed out the rage.

Now, months later, helpless, she skipped another stone across the water.

It hit the same spot on the aluman's frozen face. Perhaps a little harder than the first one, though it made no difference. The stone tumbled down into the water and disappeared. If she ever ran out of rocks to throw, Shae knew there were hundreds of them now piled around the metal man's feet.

She would've died. That was the truth of it. Mabaya's magick had choked the life out of her. She'd been minutes from the Mother's Embrace. But Kayden had used the handcannon she'd found and thrown to him. He'd killed the old evoker, and by taking her aboard the airship, he'd been able to save Shae's life. For all that, she was now a prisoner among his people, the Windborn, and all this damnable solid land. And the worst of it was that a part of her felt like she *owed* him for it.

The next stone made a very loud sound indeed.

"Thought I'd find you here."

Shae had already cocked back her arm to throw the next rock. She paused on hearing Kayden's voice, squeezing the stone in her hand as if it were clay that she could mold through her fingers. But like the frozen aluman, it didn't change. She took a breath, then spun the rock out into the fog. It hit the water and immediately sank.

"Ta'moa's tit," she cursed.

"Sorry," Kayden said. His voice was quiet, so very different from the tone of authority he'd had when she'd first met him aboard his airship. He'd been a captain then, a commanding presence with the mysterious power of the twin handcannons at his hips.

But of course, that was before he'd had to blow up his airship to keep it from falling into her hands. Before he'd let his crew die.

"You were right," she said. "I'm here." She stared out at the spot where the stone had disappeared. Keeping her voice flat and calm was harder than it ought to have been.

"Yeah," he said.

She didn't turn around, didn't look back up the bank to where he'd be standing. Instead, she rummaged through the stones at her side until she found another that felt right.

"I remember when that one came," he finally said.

Shae didn't need to ask what he was talking about. Even if the fog hadn't seemingly cut off the rest of the world, the aluman dominated the otherwise-quiet stretch of river; the half of it that still rose above the water seemed almost as tall as a woman. On a far warmer day, months ago, she'd swum over to it, gone under the water to examine it. She'd seen that its feet—if she was going to compare the metal thing to a woman's anatomy—were strangely long, and that it actually stood on a wide pad of clawed metal that might've passed for toes. In all, its plated legs looked, she thought, like the strong hind legs of a horse, built for both power and springing speed. The Bone Pirate who'd raised her had taught her to go for her enemy's joints in a fight—"Attack the knees," the old woman had often growled—but the aluman wasn't a woman. Its joints were like thick hinges, metal on metal between the shields of its thighs and shins. Its body was short compared to its legs. Like a plated fish, it was covered in a series of interlocking metal sheets that grew outward with its thickening chest, building up to armored shoulders that were just wider than the extended joints of its massive hips. Its arms were long enough to reach its knees, and they ended in hands with two fingers and two thumbs. What passed for its head, staring sightless at them, seemed half as big as it should've been, and it was sunk down into its shoulders. It had two circles of glass where its eyes ought to have been, and holes and a slotted metal grill for its nose and mouth. Looking at its face, it seemed almost a mockery of a woman's. Like a metal skull.

As Shae stared out at it, she heard Kayden scrambling down the embankment, getting closer. "How long ago?" she asked.

"It was … ten years now, I think." His boots crunched the dirt and stones. "I never told you about it?"

Shae shook her head. "You didn't."

"Used to be a couple of farms on that side of the river." His voice seemed more confident now that he knew what he was going to say. "We'd spent a few months digging new ditches to get the water around them, but the ditches weren't finished yet. A couple of families decided to move over there anyway, though. Young couples, newly married. They couldn't wait to get started in their new lives together."

Shae, staring out into the fog beyond the aluman, nodded her head. Marriage was a new concept for her. There were no such compacts among the Seaborn, much less between the women of her pirate crew, but she was pretty sure she understood it now. She'd even ceased shuddering when she saw men and women together in the village—or when she saw how Kayden would look at her sometimes.

"Anyway, the aluman came in the night," Kayden continued. "We eventually tracked the path it took. Figured out it had swung down from the Gap and been turned back by the defenses on the road across the Greensward. It doubled back for some reason, came up the valley toward town."

Still holding the rock she'd picked up, Shae narrowed her eyes at the massive thing in the water. "No one saw it?"

Kayden walked out onto her boulder and shifted his holstered handcannons so he could sit down just a couple of feet away. He sighed, and his breath came out in its own fog—something else that was new to her. "Didn't see many alumen around Felcamp back then. So the town wasn't really keeping watch. Alumen were still mostly on the other side of the Pillars."

The Pillars. Shae instinctively looked up from the river, but the thick fog blocked her view of the distant peaks to the east. They were there, though, a long chain of them, jagged and sharp as sharks' teeth, taller than anything Shae had ever seen. Not even the Mother's Mount reached so high into the clouds. If Kayden's airship hadn't carried her over them, she'd have believed that they held up the sky.

Kayden started to reach over to take one of the stones from the pile she'd made, then stopped. "May I?"

His uncertainty made her turn to look at him. When she'd first met him, he'd been wearing a crimson shirt, emblazoned with the symbols of his command. But he wasn't a captain anymore. He looked little different from most of the men in Felcamp: woolen trousers, leather boots, a furred coat over a brown, hooded tunic. He'd probably had the hood pulled up against the cold as he'd looked for her; pulling it back had left his dark hair in need of a comb. The fog around them made his skin seem paler than usual, but it set his dark eyes into sharp contrast.

He tried a smile, and though the corners of his mouth hinted at the brash man he'd been, his dark eyes expected failure—and were too ready to accept it.

She hesitated, then held out the stone she already had in her hands. She told herself it was weighted wrong for her fingers.

Kayden took it with genuine relief, then skipped it over into the chest of the aluman. The clang set the dog in town barking again.

Shae frowned and quickly picked up another stone. She threw it, and hers hit too.

"Nice one," Kayden said.

"Did it kill many people?" Shae asked.

Kayden looked back to the aluman. He swallowed hard.

"Three. Could've been worse. A lumicker happened to be working on the lines guarding the bridge that night. With those down, the aluman could've walked right into town, killed us all. Thank the gods it tried to cross the river instead."

"They're not very smart."

"I'm fine with that."

They sat for a while. The water made hollow, tinny sounds as it ran around the waist of the dead aluman. Shae could see how the fog was clinging to its cold silver skin, rolling and coalescing into rivulets that ran down to fall from the sharper joints. "Did you see it that night?" she finally asked.

"Folks knew when the screaming started. The bells were ringing. My father and I were with some of the first men across the bridge, and we saw it coming out of one of the farmhouses. It ripped the farmer in two. As easy as you or I would pull meat from the bone."

"They're that strong?"

Kayden didn't answer. When she turned to look at him, she saw that he was staring out into the fog beyond the aluman.

"What—?"

He held up his hand. "Shhh. Listen."

Her heart skipped a beat. As she turned to follow his gaze across the river, she expected to hear footsteps, heavy and hard upon the earth. Her hand instinctively went to the two halves of the blowreed pipe that hung beside the spyglass on her belt—the only objects of her former life that had crossed the sea with her—despite knowing that the poisoned fangs, which had been so effective as darts in pirate raids, would be useless against an aluman.

But then she heard the sound more clearly. A humming, low and steady. A sound she knew, or thought she should know.

Kayden stood, and she did too. He looked up into the foggy air.

The needle point of an airship pierced the cloudy banks of fog, and its long, sleek body seemed to push through the widening opening it had made. It loomed over them, and the wooden ship that was slung beneath it came into view. A moment later, the cloud roiled as the spinning blades along its sides cut free of the fog. Its engines, like everything else powered by the lumick technology of the Windborn, glowed pale blue. Beyond the hum of the blades, Shae could now hear the calls of the men upon the airship's deck, wearing uniforms like the one Kayden had once worn.

Kayden's neck craned as it passed over them. He suddenly gasped. "Gods, it's from Silverhall."

"How do you—?"

"The silver lines." He pointed, and she now saw that there were three bands of silver slashed across the side of the wooden hull.

"The silver means it comes from Silverhall?"

"It means it belongs to the king," Kayden said. He shook his head as if waking from a dream. He turned and hurried off the boulder. "We'll need to go," he said over his shoulder. "They'll land at the mooring field, which won't leave a lot of time to make the house presentable for him. Gods, Mother is probably already screaming at the servants."

He was almost to the rise of the embankment when he stopped and looked back to her. She hadn't moved. "It's the king," he said. He walked back. "He's going to want to see you."

"See me?" In the first months, many of the Windborn had pressed her for details on her life in the Fair Isles. They saw her as the enemy, a source of information. But for all that they might've wanted to, they'd never tortured her. Kayden's father, Lord Mar, had pointedly put her under his protection. She was grateful, but she'd always known his protection only went as far as his authority. The lord of Felcamp answered to the king in Silverhall, and if the king should want to do something more with her …

Kayden seemed to read her thoughts. "It's going to be all right. You've got to trust me."

And she'd never given them much information. Certainly not what they would've wanted. Whether they believed her or not, she told them the truth: she didn't know the inner workings of the Seaborn court. She didn't know their politics or their aims or their response to the Windborn airships. She was a pirate, nibbling on the edges of society. She knew as much of the Seaborn as a shark needed to know of a pod of seals: how to survive by finding and picking off the weak ones.

"Shaesara." Kayden held out his hand to her. "You must trust me."

She knew there was nowhere she could run, nowhere else she could go. She knew, too, that Kayden would want to protect her, that no matter what was going to happen, he was going to try. And that, she thought, was at least better than swimming without a shore in sight. "I trust you," she said.

She reached out and took his hand. And when he looked into her eyes, she tried to smile in the way she thought he would like—tried to smile like it was actually true.

6

The Hunted

They ran.

Alira didn't know where they were going, but she knew it was away from the Bloodborn—away from Bryt's haunting screams.

They had to dodge and weave between trees, crash through drapes of vines and walls of brush and branch. Alira's arms were laced with cuts. And even with the guard up in front of her face, she could still feel the sting of sweat running through the tiny scrapes across her brow. Her eyes blurred with tears from the pain, but she ran. She ran and she did not look back.

Not until Bryt's screaming suddenly stopped.

She'd pushed Kora ahead of her when they'd fled, but the sudden silence made the girl stumble to a halt. Alira stopped too. Panting, crying, they looked back through the thick jungle. There was nothing to see but the jumble of green and shadow and the unmistakable signs of their passing.

"Gods," Kora gasped. "Gods, they'll find us."

It was true. A Stormborn child could track such a trail.

Alira's chest constricted with fear, but her fist tightened on Whéuri's bow, which she'd been carrying in her hand. What would the huntress do?

Kora's eyes somehow caught the movement. It choked something in her. "Whéuri. What about Whéuri?"

"She's dead," Alira said. Saying it made her want to throw up, but if it wasn't true yet, it would be soon enough. She flipped the bow around her body to free her hands. "They're both dead."

Kora's eyes were full of shock and horror. She shook her head and put her hands to her ears as if that would make it all go away.

Alira ignored her for the moment. There was no outpacing the Bloodborn. She knew that. When she and Bela had been attacked those many months ago, the Bloodborn woman had used some kind of magick. For all Alira knew, they could move the trees themselves, as Mabaya once had. Or burn a hole through them, as Tukaha had done before she'd been killed by the woman.

That meant they needed to hide. Somewhere.

Her eyes darted, searching the shadows. At last, her gaze fell upon a wide Furywood trunk not far away that was draped with enough vine to let them climb to its first crowning. Not much. But a start. They'd be harder to track off the ground. And they'd have better positions if it came to a fight.

"Up," she said, turning to the girl. She reached out and grabbed Kora's shoulders, shaking her so that she'd focus on the moment and not her fears. "We've got to climb up."

Kora was wide-eyed and weeping, but finally she nodded.

"Hurry," Alira urged, and she pulled her toward the tree, trampling through the brush. There was no sense trying to cover their tracks here. The Bloodborn would know where they'd gone. Their only hope was that the monsters couldn't follow.

They had just reached the trunk of the mighty tree when a scream pierced the air in the distance behind them. A sound of incomprehensible pain. A sound that came, Alira was sure, from Whéuri.

Kora started to climb, and Alira followed close behind, gripping and kicking her way up the bark and vines.

When Whéuri didn't scream again, Alira said a silent prayer that she'd taken a Bloodborn bitch with her into the final dark.

They reached the first crowning, and they made quick work of cutting the vines they'd climbed. Then Alira pushed Kora to climb farther up to the second crowning. There, she pointed to a wide branch-path that led not away from the Bloodborn, but back toward them.

Kora shook her head in fright, but she knew enough not to protest aloud.

Alira leaned to her ear, their face guards touching. "They'll assume every other direction but back," she whispered. "Slow and silent. Back and up, by whatever path least likely to leave a trace."

The girl was frozen for a moment, and Alira put a hand on her arm and squeezed it with a reassurance she did not feel.

Kora nodded. Then, to Alira's relief, she padded forward along a branch in perfect, trackless silence.

They were three trees back and two crowns farther off the ground when they saw the Bloodborn moving below.

Kora, slipping along the branch ahead, saw them first. She stopped in mid-step and melted down into a crouch, little more than a bump in the wide wood. Alira did the same, slipping Whéuri's bow off her back in the same motion.

It took Alira only moments to track Kora's gaze and spot the shapes moving below.

There were a dozen of them: black shapes moving in a line, following the path that their crashing run had made. Their heads moved side to side in a careful watch. Their inhuman laughter was no more. They moved like shadows of wind-touched trees. Silent as ghosts.

The Bloodborn would see where the trail ended. The only question was what they would do then. What they *could* do then. Could they climb as Stormborn huntresses did? Could they fly?

Alira's hand once more tightened on the grip of Whéuri's weapon. If the Bloodborn *could* fly, then by the goddess, she'd grant one an arrow straight to the chest. She'd make Whéuri proud.

Kora made the gentlest of clicks, the sound of a bird's beak pocking wood. When Alira looked over, she saw the girl gesture toward the last of the Bloodborn.

The woman was carrying something, but it was hard to see it clearly. Something small.

No bigger than her fist. Alira narrowed her eyes, trying to make it out.

Then the Bloodborn passed through a pocket of open space. The light glinted and shined off the thing.

A crystal. And not just any crystal.

Soulglass.

Alira was sure of it. Twice previously, she'd seen one.

Just hours before the bombs of the Windborn took Bela's life, they'd gone with the evoker Tukaha into an ancient temple, and there they'd taken such a crystal—moments before a Bloodborn magicker had attacked them, murdered the evoker, and nearly killed her and Bela. Later, after the Windborn had destroyed their ship and left Alira stranded here on Myst Mahaki, she'd seen Bryt and Whéuri recover another soulglass from the temple. She'd never known what it meant, what it was, but she knew it was important to them. She'd seen how the Stormborn elder, Amaru, had lifted it up as if it were beloved.

"Take peace," Alira whispered, her words no louder than her breath given voice. They were the elder's words, what Amaru had said as she'd held the soulglass before her people. "All find rest."

"All find rest," Kora breathed.

Like hidden hawks, the two of them watched from their high perches while the Bloodborn moved on out of sight.

Only when they were gone did either of them move. Kora went first, uncoiling herself from her position on the branch and carefully creeping forward to the next Furywood crowning. There, she slunk in silence to the other side of the trunk, putting one more shield between them and the departed Bloodborn. Alira followed and found the girl crouched on a branch, leaning back against the trunk. Kora's eyes were closed. Though she made no sound, tears ran down her cheeks.

Alira got down beside her, wiped the tears. When more came, she opened her arms, and Kora fell into them. The girl made no sound as she mourned. It wasn't the first time that she'd had to wail in silence.

Alira wanted to cry, too, but she somehow felt Whéuri's eyes upon her, the rebuke of her dead teacher. Giving in to the emotion would be letting go of her control, and she couldn't afford that now. So she held Kora close as she cried, held her as she thought a mother would. And as she held her, she looked past her, out at the jungle, thinking about what to do next, looking for signs of life.

Kora stilled, sniffed, and took a shuddering breath. As her back stiffened, Alira let her go, let her straighten up. She looked into the girl's eyes. They were reddened from crying, but they were determined.

Alira nodded, squeezed Kora's shoulder, and then stood. She looked back in the direction that the Bloodborn had gone. There was no movement still.

Kora stood beside her. "What now?" she whispered, leaning close.

Alira blinked, then gestured in the direction of Bryt and Whéuri.

"Back?"

"I have to know."

Kora nodded, and in silence, she tiptoed along the Furywood branch in that direction.

They'd been in a race before, full of life as they'd run through the trees, almost heedless of their heavy steps. Now every movement was calculated, and death hung over them like a thick fog that had to be pushed through by sheer force of will.

Before, they'd been hunting. Now, they were hunted.

Moving so slowly, it took them an hour to cover the distance that their earlier panicked run had managed in mere minutes. The sky, when they glimpsed it between trees, had begun to darken. A storm was coming.

Kora, moving ahead, was the first to recognize where they were. She settled down along a wide branch, exactly where they'd crouched with Whéuri when they'd looked down and first seen the strange growths upon the Furywood's roots. Already it seemed a lifetime ago.

Thunder shook through the jungle. Distant but looming.

Alira reached Kora, took a deep breath, and looked down—down the long lines of the enormous trunk, down to the wide roots gripping into the earth, where the Char dusted the plants that had been grafted into those great fingers of living wood, where Bryt had inhaled that horrible yellow dust and Whéuri had pulled her knife as the Bloodborn had come.

The clearing was there. It was empty.

7

The Ship's Death

Her black-booted feet on a sheet of endless white, Bela watched her ship die.

It wasn't what she was supposed to do. She knew that. A mistress was meant to go down with her ship.

Helm to the end.

She'd been an unsalted girl when she'd first heard that phrase. It was one of the earliest memories she had. She was a mere stick of a thing back then; that she'd become Belakané, the Hero of the Harbor, wasn't something she could've imagined. The *Windborn* were nothing anyone could've imagined. She'd been just Bela, just a girl who desired the sea. Other girls dreamed of children or magick, and prayed to the Nine in hope. Her friend Alira had been like that; all she'd ever wanted was to weave the Char dust. But not Bela. She'd dreamed of wind and sail. When the evoker came to judge their womb and their will, Alira had taken the test and nearly died. Bela walked herself to the ashmarker that very day. He'd cut the first tick of a wave under her right eye, filled it with the heated dust of crushed bark. Many of the older girls who'd done it had bitten their cheeks or fought the restraints as the darkness seared into their flesh, black on black. Some of the weaker ones had even screamed, and they'd been ashamed.

Bela hadn't moved. She hadn't screamed out. Not for that first tick, and not for the swirl and all the waves that had come after.

Ashmarked or not, she'd been too young to be salted back then. So she'd tended the supplies in a warehouse near the Merchanter's Maze. That early memory was there. She'd been counting off stores of dried pork against white marks on the stocking sheet when one of Domina Bibsbé's crews returned from the sea. A hull at harbor could be a time for raucous laughter and delightfully foul speech—every palm-shaded girl and boy learned it early—but the crew that filed into the great storeroom that day did so in silence.

They'd lost someone. Even then, Bela knew the signs.

Their shipmistress had taken her position before them, uncovering her head in respect as the old domina limped out from her office to hear their report and let them pay their respects to her. Bela could see a glimmer of tears tracing through the knots of tattooed sea that swept up from the woman's cheek to break above her eye. Domina Bibsbé saw them, too, and her shoulders hunched as if they already felt the weight of the news that was being delivered.

Stocking sheet forgotten, Bela had slipped between barrels to get close enough to listen.

It was the Bone Pirate, of course. They'd all known the skull-masked woman had been haunting the southern isles. In shaking words, the shipmistress told how the domina's eldest daughter had been at the helm of one of the half-dozen rumrunners in convoy when the Bone Pirate's damnable hull had crossed their wake. The domina's eldest daughter was a brave woman—Bela had met her once before, and even as a child she'd recognized the qualities that would make her a fine mistress—and she'd ordered the other runners to full-sail ahead. Even as they bolted, though, the young woman had flipped her own rudder, cutting a frothing line through the waves in order to broadside the Bone Pirate and give the others time to escape.

A gamble. A good chance well taken.

A loss, though. The Bone Pirate had been ready, and she'd struck first. When the killing was done, the pirate had captured her prize.

Domina Bibsbé had listened, staring at the ground. Her eyes had glinted wet in the lanterned dark. She'd looked so much older in that moment. "And what of my girl?" she'd asked, her voice quiet.

The shipmistress had tried to speak but failed. So it was her maiden who did. The rumrunner's second in command took two steps forward, bowed to the pained old woman, and whispered the bitter truth.

"With the ship," she'd said. "Helm to the end."

The domina had nodded then. And when she'd at last looked up at them, there was pride mixed with the loss on her face. "A strong girl. A good girl," she'd said. "Helm to the end."

A mistress goes down with the ship. Old Domina Bibsbé had known it, and her young daughter had known it—Mother hold her soul. The rumrunners in that room had known it. Even the Bone Pirate would have known it.

Helm to the end.

And yet now, a black dot on a white expanse, Bela stood and watched her *Sandcrow* die. No mistress at her helm. No one in her belly but the dead.

Of the half-hundred crew who'd crowded her decks when they left Myst Wera, only seven of them were left. They stood in a ragged and silent line, close beside the jumbled crates and bags that they'd salvaged while they could.

Like the others, Bela rubbed at cold, numbed arms. The blue sky—a welcome break from the weeks of blizzard—teased a warmth it didn't provide.

A horrible, discordant song marked the ceaseless pressures that grappled her ship in its death throes. The low moan of twisting timbers. The higher scream of her keel catching and scraping on the bone-hard ice. A mid-range of snapping wood amid the wretched groans. A few of the crew shuddered visibly when the mainstay finally snapped with a boom.

"She's going," Malaika said. The grizzled woman had been predicting the vessel's demise since they'd first been locked in ice. But if she felt any satisfaction in seeing it come true, she showed nothing of it. Her long braids of black hair shook as if she wanted to reject the very notion of what they were seeing.

Three more crashes drummed like thunder.

"Bulkheads," Neka said. The tall woman had a reddish tinge to the curls of her hair. Its contrast with her paler skin marked her as one of the Kubwa people, stronger and hardier than a shorebreak. But even her voice was hardly audible, like the whisper of a loved one's disease. "Not long now."

The *Sandcrow* shifted as she drank deep of the icy water below. The new weight rotated her backward against the white plain. A shower of splinters vaulted up from her foredeck to crash down into the frozen landscape.

"Mother," Malaika croaked. "She's breaking up sure now. She'll go down by halves."

There were a few nods and hushed whispers of agreement from some of the others, but the crew members quickly fell back into their mutual silence as they watched their only hope of returning home be shredded piece by fracturing piece in the unforgiving floes.

Another shower of splinters from the deck, and the *Sandcrow* rolled even farther back into the waiting white, exposing more and more of her hull to the sky.

The sight of her underbelly was obscene, and Bela looked away across the stretch of endless white that just weeks earlier had been a deep and driving sea. For a moment, she thought she could see movement out there, a white rise shifting upon a white sea, but then it was gone.

Alone.

Bela's eyes turned to the sky, where the fires of heaven were rippling to life. The twisting sheets of eerie light pulsed green and blue across the first of the evening stars.

Another thunderous boom from the ship behind her. On instinct, Bela took a deep breath to gather herself. The cold air stung like sharp knives. She coughed for a few seconds, then forced herself to take her breath in smaller doses, more directly through the scarf she'd bunched around her neck. She wanted to close her eyes against the cold and the despair and the exhaustion, but instead she turned back to what was left of her crew.

"We'll need a fire," she said. "We're soaked through, and it'll be a cold night. Oni?"

Her shipmaiden blinked, then shook her head as if waking herself from a dream. She'd shared Bela's helm and her bed; a steady, strong anchor. Before they'd left, Bela had offered her a chance to take the vows and the wave above her gray eyes, a chance to become a shipmistress herself. She'd chosen instead to come along on this one final mission. Bela feared she'd chosen her own death, but the maiden's eyes still had hope in them. "Yes, mistress?"

"See to the gear. Let's move everything up to the cover of the outboats, clear of the fissures. We don't want to go down with her in the middle of the night. I'll want a full account of what we've managed to save."

"Aye."

Oni took one more look out at the disappearing ship, then hurried over to the piles of boxes and bags. When the others turned to Bela, she could see nothing in their faces but despair.

It wasn't becoming of the women, but it was hard to blame them. Bela felt it too: the sense that they had no path forward that didn't end in death. Her only hope was that their duties would move their minds from what faced them—herself included.

It was something she learned on the night that the Windborn came, the night she'd saved the ships and gone from Bela to Belakané, Hero of the Harbor. Despair never saved a woman. Duty and hope and trust could.

"Neka, Eshe—give her a hand," she said. "Mal and Sanyu—I want you readying those boats for good cover. Give us a secure camp for the night. It's calm enough now, but we can't doubt that the wind'll come up again. Be quick about it, while we've still got some light. Moon's rising already. Mal, soon as you can, give us a fire and a small bite to eat."

The four of them nodded and, to Bela's relief, shuffled off to their tasks. There was still enough of a sense of duty to move them, even through the despair, and Bela thanked the Mother for it.

That left only the young scriptkey. He looked up with expectation. Not for the first time in recent weeks, Bela wondered how much warmer Tewrick would be if he had hair upon his head and cheeks.

"And me, shipmistress? What is this man to do?"

Her gaze returned to the frozen sea and the exposed belly of the boat. The *Sandcrow* had rolled over completely in the pack now, and Bela saw the terrible gashes across the underside of her hull and the broken remnants of her tattered keel. A terrible sight, but it also meant they could reach the parts of the hold that were sealed off when the first of the floes had broken through the ship's flanks.

"You're with me, Tew." Bela smiled grimly. "You can swim."

His eyes were wider than usual. His bald head swiveled from her to the ship and back again. "Swim, mistress? Those waters are just shy of freezing."

"Then let's hope it doesn't come to that, reader." Bela smiled down at the young scholar. He was more out of place than ever among the hard salters and the harsh elements. "But all the same, there's at least one more thing we should try to retrieve before she goes all the way under."

"What's that?"

"Your books, Tew. What's a reader without his books?"

8

The King's Word

As they frantically tried to prepare for the king's arrival, the manor of House Mar was, as Kayden had predicted, in chaos. Lady Mar, Kayden's mother, was seemingly everywhere at once—directing the firing up of ovens, the preparing of rooms, the setting of more tables in the hall. Lord Mar was hastily calling in retainers to make a show of his authority in Felcamp. And everyone was washing up, the cold water from the well leaving faces red and bright.

One of the servants brought Shae a change of clothes after she'd run the frigid water over her skin. Dark-blue leggings and a black dress with silver buttons, long-sleeved and high-necked against the chill in the air.

She tried to stay out of the way after that, conscious of her foreign status as she watched them preparing foods or fretting about the positions of various esteemed people for the meal.

Still, she wasn't surprised when she was eventually hurried into the manor hall—long and wide, with a high, timbered ceiling. Benches and tables filled the space, with an open path between them. She'd once told Kayden that it reminded her of rowers' benches, but he'd not understood what she meant. At the far end of the room there was a dais, only a couple of steps high, where the lord's table usually sat. They'd moved it away at word of the king's coming. Only the lord's seat remained in the bare space, tall and waiting. Lord Mar, who'd filled the seat on the day Shae first arrived with Kayden, and all the days since, was standing in front of it now, just ahead of the first row of benches. All the household was arrayed behind him, row by row. The servant who'd summoned her led Shae to the front, too, but to the opposite side of the aisle from Lord Mar.

After a moment, Kayden arrived, as well. He took his place and stood beside his mother, who was at her husband's side.

No one spoke. The air in the room was taut with expectation.

A servant in the back coughed lightly, and someone shushed her.

And then, at last, footsteps. Shae wanted to crane her neck to see, but to care about the rulers of this place seemed a betrayal somehow. She wasn't about to give them the satisfaction.

After a few moments, six guards appeared from the aisle between the benches. They were wrapped in plates of silver armor, their faces hidden behind full-visored silver helmets, and while no one else was allowed weapons in the presence of the king, they had silver spears in their hands. They were meant to look, Shae was sure, like the dead aluman in the river. It was probably intended to be intimidating, but to her eyes, it was a laughable comparison, like a little girl wearing her mother's clothes.

The armed guards arrayed out across the front of the hall, and from the moment they took position, they seemed still as statues, though Shae could see their eyes through the slits in their visors, moving across the crowd in the hall, ever watchful.

What kind of leader would need such protection? Certainly no Bone Pirate did. The woman who wore the mask wore it because those who followed her believed that she should wear it. The idea that the king would need protection from his subjects seemed to make a mockery of his rule.

Next came an assortment of fine-dressed people that Shae assumed were members of what Kayden called "the court"— advisors and powerful attendants who jockeyed for the king's ear. Whenever Kayden had spoken of them, he'd always seemed to need to spit, as if admitting their existence left a distaste in his mouth. They fanned out behind the guards, turning to examine the good people of Felcamp. Many leaned at each other's ears as they watched and whispered, and Shae understood at once his urge to spit.

Sylverlyn was the last of them, one of the most beautiful women Shae had ever seen. Kayden's sister seemed to float down the aisle, straight-backed in an emerald-toned dress, the picture of elegance. Sylverlyn had been the Windborn emissary who'd come to the Spire for the negotiations, an ocean away from this place. She'd been there when the evoker Mabaya had attacked them all. She'd fought Kayden when he insisted on bringing Shae aboard the airship to save her life, and Shae would never forget how she'd laughed at her when they'd approached the Pillars that first time. They were lifting higher and higher in the airship, and Shae had asked what stone made the line of peaks such a soft white. She'd simply never seen snow. Sylverlyn had also mocked the light in her eyes just minutes later, when the first flakes of it drifted across the deck. "Gods forbid," the woman had said in her achingly superior tone, "that she might ever face a walk in winter."

Sylverlyn, Shae had long since concluded, was a bitch.

Kayden's sister reached the rest of the court gathered at the foot of the dais. When she turned to take her position among the others, she did not meet her parents' eyes, or those of her brother. She looked straight ahead, and Shae thought there was a darkness upon her.

And now came King Mark, walking alone. There was no doubt it was him. He wore a thin golden circlet around his head, and the cloak over his shoulders was a luxurious white fur that shone in the light of the oil lamps, brightening the room itself. He was middle-aged, with a trimmed beard along a strong jawline, and he looked at the room as if he owned it—which, from what Shae knew of things, he more or less did.

Each row in the hall bowed as he came down the aisle. When he passed forth into the front of the room, the first row did the same—Lord and Lady Mar, Kayden, and all the rest—but Shae did not.

He strode into the middle of the open space, turned, and immediately landed his gaze upon her. His eyes moved up and down her body in the same way a butcher might examine a pig for the slaughter. "So you're the Seaborn witch," he said.

Every eye in the room followed his. No one had been standing exactly close to her, but the nearest ones seemed to back away ever so slightly. "I'm a pirate," Shae said. "I'm not a magicker."

The king glared at her so fiercely that it took a sheer force of will for her not to look away. She could feel the stares from the others in the room, too, not anger so much as shock that she'd dared to go against his word.

After a moment, the king's mouth curled into what might've passed for a smile. He rolled his gaze from her to Lord Mar. "All these months, and she's as wild as an unbroken stallion."

The idea that she needed breaking—and what she assumed that was meant to entail—made Shae's face flush hot. Her fists clenched.

"Your Grace," Kayden suddenly blurted out, "she speaks true. She's a pirate, not one of their evokers."

Lord and Lady Mar stiffened visibly at their son's voice, but it was the king who spoke. "Ah, but you've been well broken, haven't you, Lordling Mar?"

A number of the court members arrayed in the hall laughed at the obvious joke. It suddenly occurred to Shae how the hall, seen from above, might've seemed split in two: the king and his court at the front, and the leaders of Felcamp with Lord and Lady Mar all standing before them. The spears of the guards suddenly seemed to take on new meaning.

Kayden's shoulders sank. Beside him, his mother's hand found his and gripped it tightly.

She looked to his father, who twitched for a moment as if he wanted to come to his son's defense—then bowed his head in a deferential nod. The sight of it made Shae's stomach twist in knots. She hadn't known her own parents—the Bone Pirate had found and taken her young—but she still knew the truth of parental love. She'd seen it again and again when they'd captured Seaborn vessels and listened to the pleas of the condemned. What kind of man wouldn't defend his own son?

King Mark smiled and turned away. In slow steps, he walked toward Lord Mar's seat at the head of the room. "But we know all this," he said over his shoulder. "We've read the reports. The Seaborn girl isn't one of their magickers, but the … Bone Pirate, was it?" The members of the court were all looking at her again. "And we know something of that too. A skull-faced woman who rides with the dead, who sits on a seat of bones and beats war drums of human skin." He climbed the steps to the chair and turned around as he settled himself into it. "Is this so, Shaesara?"

Shae smiled—the way that she would look at a pig. "Every word."

Whispers ran through the court around him. His eyes didn't leave her. "Then, as we said, a witch."

"I'm not Seaborn."

"Ah, yes. You think you're not one of them because you prey on their ships. You're a cat, chasing mice, but you live in the same house."

Shae's fists wouldn't unclench. He liked this game, whatever it was, and she wanted to pummel the superior smile off his face. It was a good thing, she thought, that she didn't have her pouch of fangs on her. He was close enough that she wouldn't even need the blowreed; she could probably have thrown one of the darts into the vein at his neck.

"What you fail to understand," he continued, "is that the hunting eagle sees no difference at all between them."

"This cat killed one of your eagles."

For all her rage, Shae smiled as she said the words, proud to think that her near-capture of one of the Windborn airships might've diminished this man. But in the instant her words echoed against the high timbers in the hall, she wanted to take them back. She knew what the king would do with them, and he didn't disappoint. "A loss for the eagle more than a win for the cat, we think." His eyes shifted back to Kayden. Once more, the court snickered and whispered.

Kayden's eyes were hollow, his head low. He had the look of a beaten man.

"The Seaborn will be making more of the weapons I used," Shae said. It wasn't anything that the Windborn wouldn't have guessed on their own, but it would at least turn their attention back upon her and not Kayden—though for the moment she didn't want to think about why she cared.

King Mark's smile only broadened. "We can only assume. Which is why our invading fleet will have a ship in the waves for every ship in the sky."

The court stared—it was clear they knew this was coming and were anxiously waiting to see the reaction—but not all of them were staring at her. Shae followed where many were looking, and she saw that Lord Mar was wide-eyed in shock. "Your Grace?" the old man said. "A fleet?"

"We've been preparing for months now," the king replied. He leaned back into the Mar family seat. "We thought it best not to inform you, Lord Mar. We had to decide what to do with you all."

The old man's confusion was evident. "What to do with us?"

"The loss of an airship isn't something taken lightly." The king stared down at Kayden. "When you lit the line of powder, when you decided to kill every man and woman aboard the ship, did you think how many of them might be noble-born?"

Kayden swallowed hard. His shoulders shook a little, as if the air had suddenly grown colder. "I thought only of my duty, what I was supposed to do. I swore an oath that the ship couldn't be seized."

"Only its captain, apparently."

"I... I didn't abandon them. I was going to stay, I—"

The king raised his hand, cutting Kayden off. "You were seized by this Seaborn witch. She captured you, took you prisoner. And then you bartered with your life, tried to negotiate a peace with these savages."

Kayden shook his head. "With respect, my king, we were sent to find a new home across the sea, safe from the alumen. I thought if I could negotiate a peace, if we could come to terms with them, then we could resettle in their isles without more bloodshed."

The king's eyes narrowed, an eagle seeing its prey. "Their isles?"

Kayden stammered for a moment, trying to think of how to recover what he'd said. "The isles that are theirs now, I mean. Your Grace would rule, of course. But with less killing, I thought—"

"It's not your place to think, lordling."

"Your Grace, would you have preferred that the entire crew was captured? And the airship fallen into the hands of the enemy?"

"We'd prefer we didn't lose a ship at all." King Mark

let the words hang over the court. An accusation and a judgment both.

Shae wanted to say something in Kayden's defense, something to help the poor man who'd saved her life, but what was there to say? She'd helped to design the harpoon ballistae that they'd used to catch hold of Kayden's ship. And after she'd sensed that he was going to destroy the ship—though she didn't understand exactly what the lit firepowder was at the time—she'd jumped overboard with him into the sea. She'd captured him, before they both were captured by Belakané in turn. And he had indeed tried to negotiate with them. It was all true.

"And so the only real question is just what to do with you. And with House Mar. You should know that the disgrace of your failure was enough that we considered tossing you all out, installing a new lord at Felcamp." Kayden's mother gasped audibly at that, a sound that the king acknowledged with a twitch at the corner of his mouth before he continued. "You should know it was our counselor, Sylverlyn Mar, who voiced her objection. What was it you said?"

Kayden's sister opened her mouth to speak, but no words came out.

"Speak up now, Sylverlyn. The hall didn't hear that."

"Ten generations," she said. Her voice was audible now, but her gaze was fixed on the hall's floor as if she dared not look up. "Felcamp has been held by House Mar for ten loyal generations."

King Mark nodded, and his voice was solemn and grave. "Ten loyal generations. She is right. A long hold to toss away, though one generation beyond the tenth, it was another family that sat on this seat. Felcamp came to House

Mar when another line failed, and now its line, too, stands in failure. It has but one heir"—the king's gaze fell upon Kayden like a hammer upon a nail—"and he will not sit upon this seat of his father."

Kayden's mother buckled at the knees. Lord Mar caught her and held her upright.

Kayden himself looked as if he'd been physically kicked in the gut. "Your Grace," he said, and then he stepped forward and knelt. "Your Grace, I beg you. Let me bear my failure alone. Expel me. Strip from me my family name if you must. But my guilts are mine, not theirs."

The king let the moment linger, let everyone see how small Kayden had become. Shae hated him more with every heartbeat.

At last, the king looked to Kayden's father. "Have you other children, Lord Mar?" Lord Mar was fighting to hold his head high, even as his wife tried to compose herself.

His voice trembled. "Only my daughter, Sylverlyn, our Grace."

King Mark acted as if this was new and unfortunate news as he looked back to Kayden. "Then yours is no solution, lordling. There is no male born to House Mar who can rule. So the line will end here."

"What if there were, your Grace?" Sylverlyn suddenly said.

Whatever game he'd been playing, the king seemed genuinely surprised by her entrance into it. "What if there were what?"

"Another male born to House Mar."

The king looked back to Lady Mar as if confirming something. "She's past childbearing," he said.

Kayden, alone in all the room, seemed to sense what his sister was about to say. "Syl," he croaked, "don't—"

Sylverlyn closed her eyes, nodded. She swallowed hard. "But *I* can still bear a child."

So much was happening so fast—so many things being said and implied—that Shae hadn't been able to keep up. But *this* she understood. *This* cut her to the core.

Lady Mar gasped; she stepped forward, as if she would reach for her daughter across the open space in the hall that had been hers. Her husband's hand pulled her back. "Sylverlyn," he said. "Please—"

Sylverlyn took a breath. She turned from her parents to face the king upon the seat that would have been hers had she been born a man. She knelt. "I offer myself to the king's pleasure, if he should choose. If it pleases the gods that I bear a son, allow the boy to continue the line of House Mar and hold the seat of Felcamp as my father has, in the name of the king." She swallowed hard. "Just spare my brother's life and preserve my family's name."

King Mark stared at her. Somewhere in the back of the hall, a servant—an older woman, Shae thought, perhaps the girl's nurse when she'd been a babe—cried out and was quickly shuffled away from the hall by frightened companions.

"Agreed," the king finally said. He turned to one of the silver-encased guards. "Escort the Lady Sylverlyn back to my ship."

Her mother both sobbed and choked at once, and Kayden started to get up to reach for his sister, but the king's hand made everything stop. "Let it be known that Kayden Mar has no claim to title in Felcamp, but that we grant him one mercy. We give him title to the Blue Keep, with orders that he leaves in the morning. We hope he holds it well."

King Mark strode from the hall. Sylverlyn stood. Her eyes to the ground, she followed in his wake, a guard on either side. As he passed up the aisle, each row bowed. All but Kayden, who knelt, in the increasingly empty hall, his eyes fixed where, moments earlier, his sister had stood.

Shae didn't bow either. She simply watched them all go: the king, Sylverlyn, the guards, and the court. When they were gone, she watched the household move to their tasks and chores with the silence of a house in mourning. Kayden's mother was weeping, quietly, but trying to appear strong. His father stared down at his son for a few moments, like he was searching for something to say. Then he turned away, his fists tight over his wife's arm, holding her upright as he led her from the hall.

In a minute, they were all gone.

Kayden still knelt. Shae walked over to him, took a deep breath as she tried to think of what to say. She didn't understand all that had just happened, but she understood enough. She understood he was alone.

And that meant she was alone too.

When he looked up at her, his eyes were red with the tears he'd held inside. "Shae, I—"

"There was a storm once," she said, cutting him off. "Probably the worst storm I've ever seen. We were crossing the western reach, and it rose up out of the west like a wall of darkness. Beating rain and howling wind. Waves like mountains crashed over the ship, scattering the crew belowdecks. My mistress stayed at the wheel. I was young. It was one of the first times I was put on watch, and

I remember seeing those storm walls breaking over her. I remember seeing her living smile behind the death-smile of the skull mask that she wore. I thought we would all find the Mother's Embrace that day, and I thought my own moment had come when a wave took out my feet and swept me across the deck toward the side. I caught myself, only barely, and when I looked up, my mistress was standing there, with her hand out. She said I had a choice."

"What choice?"

Shae remembered it as if she were upon that heaving wet deck even now: the Bone Pirate looking down at her through the spray, down through the dark eyes of the skull. "'We were dead in the beginning,' she told me. 'We are dead even now.'"

Still on his knees, Kayden rocked back and turned his eyes to the high window behind the seat that might once have been his. "Despair," he whispered.

"Not despair. Acceptance. Life comes from death, and the only thing we know about our lives is that they will end. So what matters is what we choose to do with that time. The mark we leave behind."

Staring at the seat itself now, Kayden almost laughed. "He just took my mark away, Shaesara."

She shrugged. "Wasn't your seat, so it wasn't your mark."

"My mark is blowing up my airship, all those men and women, and not going down with them."

"No, Kayden, that mark is meeting me."

He blinked up at that, as if a thin ray of light had cut through the storm clouds. "Meeting you?"

"And everything that you choose to do from this point forward. We make our marks with every choice we make.

You can't have this seat. Neither could anyone else in this room, but we all make our marks anyway."

"You don't understand."

"There's one other thing my mistress told me that day," Shae said. "'Just because we're already dead doesn't mean we're not going to fight like hell to stay alive.'"

The floor wasn't pitching beneath them. There was no slashing rain upon their faces. Shae didn't have the skull mask. Yet Kayden, she thought, was every bit as close to going overboard as she'd been that day—and he was the only thing close to a friend that she had in this place. "Stand up," she said. "Stand up, and I'll come with you."

She held out her hand. To her relief, he took it.

9

The Mission

The moon had long since chased the sun beneath the edge of the frozen sea, and clouds had risen up from the west to pass over the assembly of stars. Beyond the meager fire that Malaika had started, the world was shrouded in darkness.

They hadn't lit fires on the ship, for obvious reasons. But as the *Sandcrow* had splintered apart, Bela had ordered the survivors to gather what wood they could. It meant a night or two that they wouldn't have to use their precious stores of oil.

She hadn't expected that there'd also be a comfort in the open flames, a comfort to the familiar crackling of the wood as they all circled close around it, chewing their hard biscuits and talking quietly.

Not that it was familiar to see the cold air freezing the snow under the fire to ice almost as soon as it melted.

"Five days' food, then," Oni concluded.

Bela tried not to betray what bad news that was. "What else?"

"Six wool blankets," her maiden replied. "Three tarps, two small casks of oil to go with the lamp, one cask of frozen water, and three fifty-feet of rope."

A skiff of wind stirred the lighter snow into a swirl that danced delicate jigs around the circle before the heat of the fire consumed it.

"Weapons?"

Oni shook her head with a sad grace. "Only the two swords and the two harpoons you and the reader salvaged, mistress. There's a chance more stores will break through with a shift in the ice pack, but anything heavy is beneath the breakers, carried deeper by the swirl."

Bela nodded. Their attempt to retrieve the reader's bag from the inside of the overturned and breaking ship had nearly cost Tewrick his life. It was only the young man's quick reflexes and sheer force of will that had kept him from being sucked into the icy depths when one of the floes punched a new breach in the hull beside him. Even then, Bela had been forced to dip into the cold waters to help pull the scholar out. The mission had nearly cost them a hand, but it was successful: the bag, with its precious ancient books, sat upon the crusted snow beside little Tewrick. He was only just beginning to cease his shivering.

Bela had refused to chance another attempt to retrieve goods, no matter how precious they might seem. Anything else in the *Sandcrow* would have to be consigned to the deep, along with the rest of the crew.

She stood and stared out into the darkness where the ship had gone under. It was nonsense, she knew, but she swore that she could still hear the waves moving against the ice beneath them, pumping rhythmically like the pulse of the sea itself. The same part of her still awaited the cries of the dead women.

Mother help us, she thought.

"What else?" she asked. Her voice seemed small against the night.

"Extra boots, one each," Oni continued. "And some extra clothing. Six coats. Wool liners and such. Little to make it through a winter."

"If it comes to that," Malaika said, her voice gruff.

Bela turned back to her crew and the little fire. "You've a fine plan you're not telling us about?"

The older sailor shrugged. "No, mistress. Was just thinking we might try to make it back to the Fair Isles before—"

Bela cut her off with a wave of her hand. "Who said anything about going back?"

Neka looked up from shifting the fire. "Well, aren't we?"

"I don't see why we would," Bela said.

Neka stared, as if the reason were self-evident. Finally, she held her big hands out, as if her empty palms were proof enough. "We've only five days of food," she said. "Nothing for a winter's stay. It's our only choice."

"I could've done more to hold the ice out of the ship." Sanyu's voice was quiet. A short, stocky woman, she was the finest hand at repairs that Bela had ever met. She'd kept them afloat longer than they deserved—they all knew that—and yet she continued to blame herself for not doing more. Her depression, Bela thought, was a tragic reversal of her laughing disposition when they'd sailed the open waters.

"You did more than any two of us put together," Bela

corrected. "We wouldn't have made it this far if not for you."

"I could've moved more of the supplies," she muttered.

Bela put a hand on her shoulder and gripped it hard. "No one could have known. The break was too quick. You did well to save what you did. You *all* did well. No one will speak ill of what anyone here did. I'm proud of you."

"A fine crew," Oni agreed. She didn't say it, but Bela knew she was thinking of the ones embraced by the Mother in the depths below.

"Truly spoken," Malaika said. "We've done what we could. Now we head south, dragging the outboats 'til the ice breaks on open water. Make a sighting for the Isles and keep warm with rowing, aye?"

Neka voiced her agreement, as did, more tentatively, the long-haired Eshe. Sanyu said nothing. She just stared into the fire, her face unreadable. Tewrick stared at the fire, too, trying to prevent his teeth from chattering out of his skull.

"We have a mission," Bela said.

"Begging pardon, mistress," Malaika said, "but we *had* a mission. She's gone to embrace now. Even if we did manage to survive long enough to find Ealond—and you well know I don't think such a place exists—and even if we did manage to find, on that island, some ancient portal"— here she looked squarely at Tewrick, who didn't seem to be listening—"even then, we don't have a way to get back to the Isles."

"Malaika's right," Neka said. "If the High Matron still wants us to get there, she'll outfit another ship. A bigger one, with an even stronger hull. Then we can come back and try again. In the meantime, we head south."

"Can't make a stronger hull than what the *Sandcrow* had," Oni said. Her voice was distant with memory. "Three timbers thick on the prow, and Furywood at that."

"Then the High Matron would at least see fit to send another weaver or two. If Onyeka was here—"

"She's dead," Oni interrupted. Bela could feel her maiden's ire raising. Part of it was the natural tension between the salted and the evokers, but a greater part of it, Bela knew, was her desire to defend her shipmistress. "Talking of her won't bring her back."

"But if we had another weaver—" Eshe started to say, her voice pleading.

"No," Bela said. "We lose too much time going south."

Eshe looked up with sad, hurt eyes. She recognized her own weakness. Bela knew it, and not for the first time she wondered at what woman's feet she'd knelt to be given salt instead of a more suitable duty on the shore. Bela couldn't imagine her being good for much more than looking after men.

Malaika was still bristling, though. "How do we lose too much time?"

Bela turned to the chartkeeper. "How long did we drive north from landfall, Neka?"

The big woman frowned, but she knew to answer. "Two weeks and a day before the floes locked us fast."

"Driving upwind," Malaika pointed out.

"True enough," Bela said, "though it was also under sail, with full-stocked larder and full strength of crew and hand. This time we'd be rowing, going only as fast as we who survive have strength to pull. I think it would be safe to think at least a three-week return trip?"

"That's pushing it," Oni said quietly. No one disagreed.

"We have five days of food. And should a storm rise on the open water ..." Bela allowed each woman's personal experiences over the past weeks to speak for her.

Eshe made a quiet noise in the back of her throat. "Then what do we do, shipmistress?"

"We go north. Try to complete our mission."

Malaika opened her mouth to say something, then shut it as rank at last seemed to get the better of her. Neka, too, seemed to still herself after an initial reaction of shock. Eshe stared down at the fire, and her voice was again weak when she said, "But what if we don't find Ealond? What if we run out of food?"

Because she couldn't think of another response, Bela shrugged. "Then we die."

"We die trying," Sanyu whispered.

It wasn't how Bela would have said it, but it was the truth. *Helm to the end.* "That's right. We make it, or we die trying."

10

The Greensward

Shae had watched Kayden hold himself together through the night as he'd prepared what they would need for the journey. She'd seen him keep a strong face this morning as he'd said his goodbyes to his family in the courtyard where the two horses were waiting. His hands had trembled as he'd helped Shae get into the saddle, but he'd hidden it quickly by cinching down the saddlebags and the sword that were strapped across her horse's back.

Only now, when they started off—when they passed through the gate of the Mar family's home—did his tears begin to fall.

They came in silence, and Shae pretended she did not see them. She kicked her horse forward a few paces and led the way down the road through town to the bridge over the river. She hadn't the slightest notion where they were going—the Blue Keep meant nothing to her, though she'd heard members of the household whisper it like a condemnation—but she knew that at least the first part of getting anywhere from the manor meant going downhill.

Shae didn't understand everything about how power was wielded here—though seeing what the king had done to Kayden had been an education—but from the beginning, she'd known that there were those who had it and those who didn't. She had no love for such power structures—a woman, she felt, ought to be free to cut her own wake across the sea—but she at least found comfort in the familiarity that those who had power here, as in the Fair Isles, could always be found uphill. "The reason," an older pirate had once told her, "is their shit runs downhill."

In truth, so much was familiar here. If she could in her mind take away the defensive ditches and the lumicklines—those metal cables, glowing pale blue, that were strung around the perimeter of the town where water couldn't go—the whole town of Felcamp really wasn't all that different from a Seaborn town. It made sense, given what she and Bela had learned from Kayden Mar—back when he was their prisoner—about how the Windborn and Seaborn had long ago been one people.

There were little differences, of course, and Shae took note of them as her horse carried her down the cobblestone street. The roofs were taller, more sharply pitched. The doors were heavier. The windows had thick curtains. All of it, she knew, because they needed extra protection from the cold when it came—something foreign to the Fair Isles.

Winter. It was the reason there was a brown, bear-fur cloak draped over her shoulders. The reason she was wearing a heavy shirt and warm woolen trousers that seemed to resist every movement she made. Back home, her clothing was light and loose. Here, the chill in the air meant thick cloth that fought every action. Halfway through town, she was already tugging and twisting at the restriction.

"Too tight?" Kayden asked from behind her. His horse trotted up, and Shae saw that he'd wiped his face dry. He sat straight-backed in the saddle, ignoring the occasional stare from the townspeople here and there on the side of the road. Word would've traveled quickly through Felcamp, she supposed. They knew why he was riding out.

She sighed in exasperation. "Don't know how you fight in these."

He shrugged. His fur cloak was a beautiful glossy black, and she wondered whether it was a sign of wealth to have such a thing. Perhaps his family had insisted that he take with him that small sign of what he'd once been. "Easier than fighting without them," he said.

"I assure you, it's not."

He smiled at that, glancing over with an eyebrow raised. "Is fighting naked a tradition among the Seaborn I didn't observe?"

Shae wasn't sure if he was amused or interested. "A pirate reality now and again," she said. It was the truth.

He pursed his lips thoughtfully, then once more looked down the road. Shae wiggled the cloth around her hips, and finally got everything where it felt right—just in time for her sleeves to bind up at the elbows. "Will it get much colder?" she asked.

"Assuredly." Kayden nodded to a man unloading barrels by the door of a house. "Folks are stocking up for the winter. They say it'll be a cold one. Heavy, hard snows are already falling up north." He sniffed the air. "But we wouldn't really call this cold yet."

"This isn't cold?" Shae said.

"Brisk, we'd say. Cold is when it runs your toes and fingers numb."

"To'whir's hand," she cursed.

"As you say," Kayden said. Then, after a moment, he shifted in the saddle so he could look at her more directly. "To'whir is your god, yes?"

"A god." Shae held the reins with one hand so that she could rub the other across her thigh, both to straighten the wool and to warm the skin beneath it. "There are nine."

"Nine gods?"

"Yes. Nine. To'whir is the god of storms."

"That's a lot of men in the sky, Shaesara."

"Only a man would think the gods are all men."

"Some of them are women?"

"And some are neither."

"Neither?"

"Or both."

"I … I don't understand."

"I'm not the least bit surprised," she said.

He smiled at that, and it seemed to her that it was genuine amusement. *He'll be all right*, she thought. *Maybe he'll even be better for all this. Maybe losing everything would be a way for him to get a fresh start.*

It was a clear day. High clouds and bright, cold light. Far off to the east, she could see the sleek, swordfish shape of the king's airship, its triple-rotored engines churning it through the air back to Silverhall.

Engines.

Rotors.

The words were still new to her, the technologies strange,

but she nevertheless felt a kind of comfort in knowing a bit about how these things worked. For years, the Windborn airships had been a frightening mystery: where they came from, how they stayed aloft, how they sailed through the sea of the sky. Now, alone of all the Seaborn and pirates in the Fair Isles, she knew. The ships came from here in Aionia. Their great bags were filled with a kind of air that came bubbling through the waters of a lake near what Kayden called the Heron Marshes. And the ships sailed the sky using the turning rotor, driven by lumick engines.

Lumick.

On the night she'd fought with the magicker Mabaya atop the Spire—the night Kayden had spirited her away from the Isles—she'd learned about the soulglass that powered the alumen. The strange crystals, she'd learned, connected to the Stream, a power that bound everything and everyone together, accessible through a portal that the ancients had opened in Ealond, the ancestral home of both the Seaborn and Windborn. The power of the crystals gave life to the metal men. But stripped from their bodies, it could be used to fight them. Shae had often tried to imagine the act as she sat on her rock by the river: the men wading through the water, desperately tugging at the frozen thing's silver panels so they could reach in and pull out its still-glowing heart of soulglass. She tried to imagine their elation, despite their losses, their excitement when Felcamp sent out its call for the nearest roving lumicker to come and use that crystal to power more humming lines that alumen couldn't cross, the engines of another airship, or some other wonder not yet devised.

It was extraordinary, even if she still couldn't fathom the

inner workings of such things. Not that Kayden could either. This was why lumickers existed, he'd laugh. Just the same, he'd told her that what drove the airships was a machine, like the ballista that she'd help build on the deck of her own ship to take down Kayden's. A machine. Pieces and parts.

It wasn't magick, and she'd taken comfort in that fact. Things that weren't magick could be destroyed.

"Thinking heavy thoughts," Kayden said from beside her.

Shae had been looking up at the airship for too long, she realized. Staring, like an enraptured child. "Nothing."

Kayden followed her gaze with his own. "Oh," he said, seeing the airship.

"What's going to happen to Sylverlyn?" Shae asked.

Kayden brought his attention back to the road and made a point of straightening the reins in his hand. His horse shook its head in response. "I thought you didn't like her."

"Why would you think that?"

"You'd think a pirate would be a better liar."

Shae chewed on her lip, thinking. "I didn't," she said. "It's true. But then yesterday, what she did—"

He nodded. "Yeah. But, look, I know Syl. She didn't do it just for me. She knows what she's doing."

"Even when it looks like she's adrift, she's got a rudder in the water."

Kayden thought for a moment. "Sounds about right."

They'd reached the end of town, where the cobblestones gave way to the wide, weathered stones of the bridge over the river. Shae pulled rein and looked upstream. The metal man was there in the distance. Same as he ever was.

"Everything all right?" Kayden asked.

"I've never been across the bridge," she said.

"We've got a long way to go," he said. "A lot farther than this. Come on."

Their horses set forward again. There were farms across the river—the farms, she supposed, that the aluman had attacked before it walked into the water—and threading around them were the ditches fed by the river. Not just irrigation, she knew, but lines of defense against more metal men. Not far ahead, where the ditching ended, a stone archway had been built over the road, wide and tall enough for a large wagon. Extending beyond it on both sides of the road, she could see, were the metal cables, the height of an aluman's chest. In the bright light, she could barely see their blue glow. The twin lines reached a pair of support pillars in the distance, then turned out of sight as the road bent around a tree-covered hill.

"A long way to go," she said.

Night had fallen, and the campfire was crackling when Shae realized that Kayden hadn't once looked back. She wasn't sure if he would regret it in the end, but she was nevertheless glad for it. It was a sign that he was moving forward.

He'd had his moments of quiet, of course. But he hadn't wept again. And when something did break the silence, he wasn't sullen or grave. He was just a man—an Aionian man, she corrected herself, since no man in the Fair Isles would carry himself so freely.

Camp was made upon the road itself. She'd expected that they'd set up beside it, in case other travelers came along, but Kayden assured her that this was how things were done in Aionia. Between the lumicklines, they'd be safe from alumen.

And besides, they'd seen only a single tradesman's wagon during the long day of riding. Traffic on the Greensward Road wasn't likely to be much this time of year, Kayden said. As they'd seen in Felcamp, people were preparing their homes for the winter, not traveling between towns.

Kayden had a tent, but the bugs were down with the chill, and there seemed little chance of rain. So, while he'd rolled out their sleeping mats on the packed earth of the road, Shae had built a fire to bring warmth to their hands and hot food to their bellies. Watching the flames grow had been strangely comforting, and she'd wondered, sitting in the blue glow of the strange lumicklines, if it was because the fire felt like something familiar from back home.

The cured pork they'd packed had sizzled and popped over the flames, and they'd both chomped it down quickly. She hadn't expected to be so hungry, but the day in the saddle had left her famished. And sore, she was realizing. Her crotch felt like it was bruised from the hard saddle, and the insides of her thighs were chafed raw.

"How many more days?" she asked.

Kayden was poking at the fire with a stick. "What's that?"

Shae stretched, then winced at the movement. Her back hurt too. "I never asked how far it was."

"You didn't have to come," he said.

"If I hadn't said I was going to, I think the king would've taken me with him and tried to get more information out of me—though I don't have any."

"My father might've protected you." Kayden said the words, but his heart didn't seem to be behind them.

"I wouldn't have been welcome in Felcamp. You know that. I wasn't really welcome before, and now—"

"Now you'd be seen as the reason I had to leave."

"Exactly."

He looked up at the sky. There was a strip of stars between the glowing blue cables. "A week if the weather stays like this."

"Will it?"

He grinned his way back down to the flames. "I doubt it."

She had to smile. "Figures."

"To'whir's tit, right?"

The image in her mind was so sudden that she laughed out loud.

Kayden frowned. "What?"

Shae wiped at her eyes. "To'whir doesn't have tits."

"A man?"

She nodded.

He sighed, and used his stick to quash an ember that kicked out when a log popped in the fire. "Well, I tried."

"You did," Shae said. "Thank you. Truly. I suppose it must be confusing for you. From the union of To'ma and Ta'wa—sky and sea—came two children. Their son is god of storms. Their daughter is Ta'koa, the earth."

"Union?"

"For the one thing a man can provide a woman that another woman cannot."

He seemed to chew on the thought for a moment. When he opened his mouth as if he wanted to say something more, Shae had a feeling in her gut that she wouldn't like what it was. "So the Blue Keep," she blurted out. "Ever been there?"

He closed his mouth, tossed his stick into the fire, and watched it burn. "No," he finally said. "I haven't."

"What is it?"

He pushed back from the flames, shifting to his side and stretching out on his blanket. "It's a fortification in the Pillars. Guards one of the passes."

"Passes?"

"A low spot where it's easier to get from one side of the mountains to the other." He grinned again. "I guess you don't really have those on the sea."

"Not really," she admitted.

"A pass is like"—he thought for a moment—"like a channel between islands."

"Somewhere you can get through."

He seemed to be pleased that she understood his analogy. "That's right."

"So, what's on the other side of this pass?"

One of the horses huffed, and Kayden rolled over to look at it. Both animals were tied off to support poles that held up the lumicklines. One of the beasts was twitching its tail, but it looked like they were just settling in. Kayden turned back over. "The other side of the Pillars," he said, "is what we flew over when we came from the Fair Isles. It's mostly empty land. No one lives there."

Shae's eyes narrowed. "So why fortify it?"

"Sorry?"

"This pass. If there's no rival kingdom on the other side, why guard it? Are there pirates?"

It was Kayden's turn to laugh a little at an image. "On land, we'd call them bandits. And no, don't get your hopes up. There aren't bandits on the other side. Just alumen."

"Alumen?"

"That side is where our people first came ashore after

we left Ealond. So it's where the alumen first came ashore too. We fled west, pushed up to the mountains. Some of us found the passes and got through, though, and came down here into Aionia. We fortified the passes behind us."

"So the Blue Keep holds back the alumen."

"There are other keeps at other passes, and now and then the alumen find another way around. But yes."

"And now you will be in charge of the Blue Keep?"

Kayden's face was tight. "As the king wishes."

"This is a high honor."

"I'm afraid not."

"I don't understand. You'll be protecting all these lands."

Kayden leaned back and looked up at the stars. "I suppose it looks that way. But no one gets much honor for holding the Blue Keep. I honestly can't tell you the name of the man I'm replacing. I don't think I can remember ever knowing the name of the man who held it."

"Why not?"

He took a deep breath and let it out at the sky. "No one lives long enough to have their names known, I suppose. The alumen don't ever really stop trying to get through, Shae. And not just one here and there. Not like what happened in Felcamp. They come in waves. So, no, holding a Pillar keep isn't really an honor. It's a death sentence." He thought for a moment and then looked over at her with a tight smile. "We are dead even now."

11

Rain and Fire

Alira crouched to the earth, trying to pick out the Bloodborn tracks, but the sky had opened up in a downpour. The footprints filled, then overfilled and bled into one another. They dissolved into the muddy rivulets that snaked across the jungle floor.

Within seconds, they were gone.

She stood and pulled her hood tighter to keep the rain from dumping into her clothes.

Then she stared in the direction the Bloodborn had been going. She might've been able to track them through bent leaves and broken branches, but those, too, were being erased in the chaos of the storm.

The noise of the rain slapping through the trees was a roar. She'd been on a hunt with Whéuri the first time she'd experienced a jungle stormbreak. The huntress had made her stand in the middle of it, exposed to the noise and the wind and the wet and the fear until it was over.

Alira had thought it was like being stuck between competing waterfalls.

Kora dropped down from the branches and stood beside her. The girl's eyes were hidden in the darkness of the hood. Alira imagined hers were, as well.

"We could just keep going in this direction," Kora said over the splashing.

Alira was pleased that Kora had so quickly seen the problem. She'd be a great huntress one day. "Their path took several turns to get here. One more turn anywhere ahead, and we'd be off their trail for good."

"What do we do?"

Alira frowned behind her face guard. She knew what they needed to do, but she didn't like it. "Head home," she said. "Get dry. Get help."

Kora nodded. Then they both tightened down their gear against the rain and the coming run. Alira glanced up at the sky, took stock of the wind, and then set off at a steady pace along the jungle floor.

She wasn't sure what she'd hoped to accomplish by tracking the Bloodborn. She might not be the scared girl she'd been when one of them had attacked her and Bela on that fateful night, but she still doubted she was much of a match for one. They had magick. She'd seen that with her own eyes, and the Stormborn here talked of it. Shadows in the jungle. Screams in the night. Scorched marks upon trees that weren't made by a woman's fire. She and Kora were good with their bows, but it probably wouldn't be enough against a single Bloodborn magicker, much less the many they'd seen.

She wanted to find them anyway. They'd taken Whéuri and Bryt. It was the only conclusion she could make. But why? Bryt was dying when she and Kora had run. There was no saving him, not with the amount of Char he'd inhaled. Char killed mundanes. Everyone knew that. Alira suspected that when Whéuri took out her knife, it wasn't really to defend herself against the Bloodborn. It was to spare her love more pain. And then she'd heard Whéuri's scream through the jungle. That had surely been the moment when the Bloodborn had found the huntress. The scream had been the sound of her death. So why take the dead?

It didn't make sense.

Nothing did. How did the Bloodborn have Char plants? Why had they grafted them to a Furywood tree? And did any of it have something to do with soulglass?

The rain had no answer.

After perhaps an hour, Alira spotted a slanted rock outcropping and routed toward it. To her relief, the slab of rock had enough of an overhang that the two of them could duck under it.

The storm's wind still whipped around and under the rock, but it offered a chance to get out of the rain for a few minutes.

Alira shook the water off her shoulders, then pulled back her soaked hood and unclipped the face guard so she could breathe easier. Kora did likewise, taking in deep breaths.

Alira pulled out her water bag and took a long drink. Kora turned it down when it was offered and instead pulled out her own. Alira nodded, finished hers, and then walked over to the edge of the overhang, where the rain was running down and shedding off the rock in little streams. She held out the uncorked bag, filling it up.

"Why did she say that to you?" Kora asked.

"Say what?"

"The Song of the Black Hand."

Alira pushed the cork back into the bag, made sure it was firm. She turned around. "I don't know what that is."

"What Whéuri said. I know those words. My ... my mother used to sing them to me." She closed her eyes as she remembered:

A shattered tree, a hearkened sea,
a tattered sail, a hardened gale,
and the gale scattered sail and sea.
A scattered hour, a sharpened power,
a battered land, a blackened hand,
and the hand shattered land and power.

It was true. They were the same words Whéuri had said. Alira didn't think she'd ever forget them. But it didn't mean she understood them. "What does it mean?"

Kora let out her breath. "It's a Stormborn tradition. My mother's mother sang it to her. My father's parents, too, I suppose. Growing up, I didn't think it really *meant* anything. The words keep repeating like that, making a kind of circle. But Whéuri clearly thought it did. And we saw the tree."

"What tree?"

"The 'shattered tree,' just like the song says. The one that killed Bryt. 'A shattered tree, a hearkened sea.'"

"It's just a song," Alira said, but her voice was quiet, and the waves of an open sea were in her heart.

"Maybe it's a prophecy," Kora continued. She gestured at the sheets of drenching rain. "Maybe it foretells something. The gale. A storm. Something great happening."

"It could mean anything," Alira said. "'A tattered sail'? It's nothing, everything."

"It could mean you. You came from a destroyed ship of the Seaborn."

Alira shook her head as she, too, gazed out at the sodden jungle. "We've got miles to run."

Kora, thankfully, said nothing more of the song. She looked up at the sky. "It isn't going to let up soon."

"Ready to get wet, then?"

Kora pulled up her hood and cinched it tight. "Ready."

Alira did the same. Then, just before she dove into the rain, she paused. There was something on the air. A scent, just barely apparent amid the heavier smells of the falling rain and the dampened vegetation around them. She sniffed, trying to catch it again, to make it out.

"What is it?" Kora asked. The girl was beside her, looking out into the downpour.

"Thought I smelled something."

"Smelled what?"

Alira's eyes narrowed. Her nostrils flared. She turned her head side to side, scenting the rain.

There. Just a wisp of it. But enough.

Smoke.

And it was coming from the direction of home.

12

Tewrick's Story

They broke camp early. Malaika and Neka grumbled about their desire to go south as they were turning over the outboats that they'd used for shelter overnight, but they said nothing more of it when Bela faced them to the north. After that, their energies focused on preparing for the back-breaking labor of dragging themselves and their supplies across the craggy, snow-strewn ice fields that were determined to bar their passage.

Sanyu, ever practical, rigged the outboats into two rope-drawn sleds. Bela led the first boat, taking turns on the point with Sanyu and Eshe. Tewrick, smaller and weaker than the rest, tried in the early going to take his own turn at breaking snow up front, but he was as ineffective in the task as they'd all guessed he would be. He was quickly and permanently relegated to the second position in the line, though not everything was lost in the experiment. Despite the darkness of her mood, Sanyu actually managed to smile at the cut-man's expense. "A chicken is more useful than an egg," she said. "But having no eggs is more useless still."

The women laughed, and Bela laughed too.

Oni led the second team with Malaika and Eshe. Each team had been assigned one of the two swords, carried by the person at the point and used to forge a path forward if drifts needed to be breached.

The floating ground beneath their feet shifted and buckled with disturbing regularity, moaning in response to the pushing and pulling of unseen physical forces that sent angry tremors beneath the snow. From time to time, Bela imagined that she saw, in the corner of her eye, other things moving upon the white, but when she stared out, it was only the stretching expanse of snow-covered ice. Nothing else. The feeling of solitude was overbearing, and she wondered if anyone else felt it too.

Every couple of hours, great snapping sounds could be heard, the thunderous cracking of the ice as fissures opened and closed. Now and again, sheared edges rose up as if struck from beneath by some angry hand. More than once, Bela heard the others whispering prayers to the Mother, asking for her mercy.

As they trudged ever onward into the cold, Bela wondered what mercy would be at this point.

At midday they found their way blocked by a ridge of ice. It glimmered white-blue, starkly beautiful, but they lost three hours finding their way around it before they were moving north again.

A good day, though. No fissures opened beneath them. No blizzards arose in the west.

As night fell, they pulled their boats close together and unloaded them. Turning them over, Neka and Bela leaned the shells against one another and held them in place while the others packed snow around the wood, trying to keep the boats in position against any wind that might arise. Then they put their supplies inside, while Sanyu and Malaika covered the gap between the boats with canvas tarps. Bela was pleased that everyone lent a hand, that the work was done quickly and well. Soon enough, they were inside the makeshift shelter, and Malaika lit their single lamp.

The food they had wasn't much, but it was enough to relieve their aching stomachs. As Bela looked around her, she saw smiles, even from Sanyu. No one was grumbling.

Bela motioned to Oni, and her maiden obediently came, her warm body nuzzling close.

The young woman let out a breath against her chest. It felt like a smile.

"A story," Eshe said.

Bela looked up from the fire with groggy eyes. "Not from me. I'm too tired to think."

The delicate-faced girl appeared to be crestfallen. She peered around at the others, but no one seemed to be willing to come up with a tale. At last, her gaze fell on Tewrick, who was huddled back against the hull of the boat he'd been pulling.

"What of you, reader?"

The fact that she'd addressed him surprised Bela enough to rouse her from her half-slumber. She could see that it had the same effect on the others, who were all looking over at the bald figure in the semi-light. Even Oni raised her head.

If they were surprised, Tewrick was more surprised still. His eyes met Bela's, and there was a question of uncertainty upon them. "This man doesn't know many stories," he managed to say.

Bela shrugged. "A tale from one of your books, perhaps?"

"From one of my books?"

"Yes," Eshe said.

She sounded hopeful, almost begging, and Bela thought it was a disgrace for her to address a man in such a way, but she knew this wasn't the time or place for reprimands. Perhaps it was the time for a lesson, though. "A tale of what we seek," she said.

Oni's body was close to hers, and the younger woman squeezed her hand in approval.

The fact that the maiden understood her mind was one of the many reasons Bela had thought her ready for her own ship—and one more reason that she was selfishly glad she hadn't taken the vows and was instead here with her. Breath to breath. Soon skin to skin.

"A tale of the power," Tewrick repeated. He was timid, scared. But he was a man, surrounded by his betters, so Bela was not upset.

"A tale of what we're fighting for," Oni whispered. Her fingers slipped inside the seams of Bela's clothes. Cold at first, but warming fast.

"A poem, then," Tewrick said, and then he nodded his bald head. "Of what came before."

He lifted a book from his bag: rough-hewn pages in a red leather binding. He opened it carefully, turning pages as he looked through the ancient markings that only he could read. At last, he found what he was looking for, and he took a breath. He was a little man when he opened his mouth, but he seemed much bigger as his soft voice filled the void beneath their overturned boats.

When magick summoned madness,
Its desire that endless dream,
Fearful men made folly:
Power and portal pristine.

A hundred hundred lives are lost,
A thousand souls still thrive.
Loud the winds blow, loud the waves roar,
And woe to the broken shore!

The machines and metal men
Fight with flame and ice and fire.
Blood and bodies broken,
Men sail for the open sea.

A hundred hundred masts set sail.
A thousand souls outcast.
Loud the winds blow, loud the waves roar,
And woe to the broken shore!

The city lies in silence,
Frozen when families fly.
Thirteen are its towers,
Watching over the western sea.

A hundred hundred halls behind.
A thousand lives in thrall.
Loud the winds blow, loud the waves roar,
And woe to the broken shore!

As the reader finished his poem, Oni was purring against Bela's chest.

"Men?" Malaika asked.

Tewrick's eyes widened a little. "I'm certain they use it to mean all people."

"But why not say 'women'?" Malaika said.

"I don't know," the reader said. "They say it the other way."

"Women give birth," Sanyu put in. "We're stronger in all but our backs. It should be 'women' to refer to all people … and men just along for the sail. Not the other way."

Tewrick opened his mouth as if he were going to reply, then seemed to think better of it and shut his jaws again.

"I agree," Bela said. "But it must have seemed different to them. The Windborn man I knew was the same way in his speech. It is how it is among them, I suppose, and I think they hear the same strangeness in our speech."

The reader nodded his head, both in apparent agreement and relief. "It is as you say, Belakané."

Bela winced a little at the formal title, but decided not to respond to it directly. "What I wonder, scriptkey, is how it says that they sail but also fly. Do you think it means the Windborn airships?"

"And Seaborn sea ships. I do, shipmistress."

"A testament to how we were once together," Sanyu said. The shipbuilder's voice was quiet. "How we came from the same people."

Neka scoffed. "We've always been Seaborn," the big woman said. "And we've no stories of airships. Not before the Windborn came. You know that better than anyone, shipmistress."

Bela tried to smile in the way that seemed most fitting to whatever stories they believed about the night the Windborn had arrived, the night they'd bombed the harbor and she—young, foolish, neglecting her duties and seeing something she wasn't supposed to see—had witnessed the attack and famously saved several ships from destruction. "None of us knew," she said. "But how quickly is the truth about the past forgotten? I thought of the Redwave War as just a story, the stories about the Bloodborn nothing more than tales for children, but then I was attacked by one of their magickers on Myst Mahaki. I saw her kill an evoker. I'd have thought none of it possibly real, but I saw it with my own eyes. And the Redwave War was only ... five generations back? Six?"

The women were staring at her with rapt astonishment. Neka nodded slowly.

Bela sighed. "Point is, even looking back at my own childhood, I remember so little. As far back as this poem talks about, as far back as the portal goes ... I can believe that we'd all forgotten."

"Like the portal," Eshe said. Her voice was higher pitched than usual. Fear, Bela suspected.

"Yes," Bela responded. "The portal that gives the metal men life, that has them attacking the Windborn in their homeland. The portal that must be closed."

"The portal we *will* close," Oni whispered.

Bela smiled.

"Didn't anyone ever try to close it?" Malaika asked.

"The ancestors we share with the Windborn tried,

using terrible magicks," Bela said. "They only succeeded in breaking their land."

"They turned it cold," Tewrick said, nodding. The wind outside seemed to howl louder in response. "Frozen."

"So they fled," Bela continued. "The Seaborn and Windborn broke apart from one another. The Windborn only attack us now because they're attacked by the metal men that the portal made. Close the portal, and our seas are free once more."

"But what about the Windborn?" Malaika asked. "Do we know if they ever tried? Their airships can cross the seas."

Bela looked to Tewrick, who closed the book in his hands and stared at it. "If they tried," he said, "then they failed."

Bela opened her mouth, but it was Oni, nestled in her arms, who spoke. "*We* won't," she said. "We won't."

13

The Lumicker

The Greensward, as Kayden referred to it, was a sea of grasses. He called it a plain; a level flatland with the smallest of gently rolling rises, washed over with knee-high grasses that in warmer days would have waved under the brushing touch of the wind. The grasses were brittle now, shades of brown and gold, but Shae could imagine how, in summer, the landed sea would have rippled green.

The road cut across it like a ribbon untied and flung out across the landscape: a cart-wide path where the passing of horses and wagons had trampled and broken the grasses into submission—paralleled on either side by the lumicklines running between stone pillars, their blue glow pale and faint in the daylight.

For the greater part of the chilly morning, she and Kayden followed that road east.

Ahead, the broad surface of the Greensward gave way to larger hills lined with tall trees. That's what Kayden assured her, anyway. For all the hours they rode, Shae could see nothing beyond the sweeping plain but the high mountains of the Pillars upon the horizon, that wall of sharp peaks as tall as the sky. Somewhere at their distant feet, she assumed, hidden from view by the curvature of the world, hid the promised hills and forests.

They rode mostly in silence under the cold sun, trailing a fog from the mingled breath of horses and riders. A few birds chirped and twittered up from the grasses—little things, fast and sure—but there were not many. When Shae asked why there were so few, he told her that most of the birds had flown south to spend the winter in the Heron Marshes. It was warmer there, he said. On some days it would be like they didn't even have a winter.

Winter.

It had seemed so strange a concept. In the Fair Isles, there were months of summer and months of rain. Here in Aionia, it was months of summer and months of such cold that mountain creeks would seize up and cease running, as still and stiff as streams of stone.

At least that's what Kayden said. She'd laughed, thinking it some kind of Windborn joke, the first time he'd said it. Water was water. Rock was rock. But Kayden hadn't been jesting.

Water would indeed *freeze*, he insisted.

Shae had felt cold, seen snow, when she'd first come over the Pillars in the Windborn airship that had brought her here. But only now, when every hour pushed the cold deeper into her flesh, every mile brought more chilled stiffness to her bones, did she begin to understand what winter might mean.

It was unnatural and wrong, and it frightened her.

They stopped for lunch on a grassy rise that was no

different than any other on the Greensward. No fire for the brief rest. Just a chance to stretch their legs and relieve themselves before breaking off some chunks of the bread that Kayden had brought from the kitchens at Felcamp. There was a rock not far from the road, a flat boulder like an island in the grassy sea, and the two of them sat down upon it while the horses grazed free, sniffing out any remaining bits of greenery in the brush.

Shae watched them for a time, but after a few minutes, she found herself staring at the lumicklines. "They'll really stop an aluman?" she asked.

Kayden had been studying a bank of clouds that was growing along the western horizon behind them. He turned back when she spoke, and he quickly saw what she was talking about. "That they will."

"How?"

"I've told you before," he said. "I don't really know. The power shuts them down somehow."

"Are the lines always blue?"

"That's the lumick. Or at least that's what I've been told."

Shae took another bite of her bread and chewed on it slowly, sucking out the flavors as she thought. "Is that why the place we're going to is called the Blue Keep? It has lots of lumicks there?"

Kayden nodded, picking at the lichen on the rock beside him. "They say the lumicklines run across the walls and gates of the pass to keep the alumen at bay. A lumicker there wouldn't have title to the place like I will, but I assure you he'd be thought far more valuable to the Blue Keep than I would ever be."

"There's a lumicker there?" Shae couldn't help but be

interested in the possibility of meeting someone who could tell her how these Windborn wonders really worked.

Kayden looked up. "Don't get too excited, Shae. Even if there is, the lumickers don't share their secrets. Not even much with each other, I'm told."

"Oh."

He smiled. "Not that a lumicker has ever faced down a Bone Pirate."

Shae thought about throwing the last bite of her bread at him, but she ate it instead. If the first day of their travels had been any indication, there were many hours to go before they'd stop for the night and eat dinner.

Still savoring the bite, she stood and stretched before she resettled the warm cloak about her shoulders. When she looked back, Kayden was once again staring at the clouds to the west, which had definitely moved closer. "We should get going," she said.

Kayden did not disagree. He swallowed the last of his own bread, stood, then wiped his hands on his thick woolen trousers. "Mount up," he said. "By sundown tomorrow, we should be getting close to Homilden, a village on the edge of the Greensward. This time of year, there should be plenty of space at its inn. Good food and a welcome bed."

"I'll take that," Shae said.

"As will I," he agreed.

It was only a couple of hours later, as they came over a slight rise in the road, that Kayden reined in his horse. What light there had been was behind them—they'd been chasing their growing shadows since lunch—but the clouds looming over them had set a gloom upon the plains. Nevertheless, Kayden shielded his eyes as he stood up in his stirrups, as if it would make him see better.

Shae tried to follow the line of his gaze, but she could see nothing. "What is it?"

He pulled his hand down and chewed on his lip before answering. "I think it's a wagon." Shae stared again. She still couldn't see anything. Then, sighing at her own forgetfulness, she felt inside her pockets and retrieved the brass spyglass that the Bone Pirate had gifted her when she'd been made a shipmaiden—one of the few things of her old life that she'd had with her when Kayden took her aboard his airship. She extended it, then peered through its magnifying lenses, fighting away the strangeness of searching out a wagon on the road instead of sails on the sea.

It was indeed a wagon, stopped upon the road itself; a hard-sided wooden box on four wheels, its two horses unhitched and grazing as lazily as their own had at midday. "It's not moving," she said.

Kayden made a sound of agreement. "Might be it's broken down. Might also be bandits."

Shae pulled the spyglass down. "Bandits?"

He sat back in his saddle, smiled as he looked over at her. "Land pirates, remember?"

Shae cracked her neck, thinking how good it would feel to be doing something again if they were attacked, but at the same time missing the skull mask and the steady beat of the skin drums and the waves that should've been filling her ears. "Are bandits likely on the road?"

The first specks of a cold rain began pocking the dirt around them. Kayden glanced up at the clouds overhead, then shrugged. "Can be. We could go around, but I'd rather not leave the road. And maybe it's someone who could use some help." He started his horse forward at an easy pace.

Shae put the glass away and followed close beside him. The raindrops were starting to fall harder. "To'whir's spit," she muttered.

"Spit?"

"To'whir is the god of storms, remember?" Shae said. "He arose from the union of Mother Sea and Father Sky."

"So the rain is his spit?"

They had a steady pace, so she was able to use one hand to pull up the hood of her cloak to ward off the coming rain. "His spit. His tears. It is him himself, for he is the Storm."

Kayden narrowed his eyes, then seemed to shrug. "Sometimes I think I can understand you," he said. He pulled up his own hood. "Sometimes I think I never will."

"Oh, I suspect you don't understand a lot of women," Shae muttered. If Kayden heard her, he did not respond.

The road dipped down into a long, shallow low. Only when they broke over the next rise did they see the features of the wagon clearly.

It was like nothing in the Fair Isles—longer than it was wide, with tall wooden sides sloping slightly outward from the wheels. There was a window in the side wall that she could see, no different from the windows she'd had aboard ship. The roof above was curved planks, like a boat flipped upside down, and it extended out over a bench seat at the front, where a two-horse team would normally be hitched. The wooden wheels were tall enough that a ladder was needed to get down from the door at the wagon's back end.

Another ladder looked to be permanently affixed to the wood beside the door, running up from the back step to the roof. The sides were all painted in bright-blue paint, the wheels and window trim an even brighter yellow.

"A lumicker's wagon," Kayden said as they rode on.

The sight of it was bewildering to Shae. It was a house on wheels. "They all look like that?"

"More or less."

Shae thought of how the Bone Pirate had a sea chest filled with the flags of different houses, which more than once they'd used to slip closer to their unsuspecting prey. "Could it still be bandits? Using a lumicker's wagon?"

"Not a chance," Kayden said, picking up his pace to close the distance to it. "No bandit would attack a lumicker."

"Because the lumicklines protect everyone?"

"That, and the lumickers have things that make my handcannons look like toys." A gloom passed over him, but he physically shook it away. "Anyway," he continued, "you can see it's a lumicker since he's working on the lines."

Sure enough, as Shae looked closely, she could see that the wagon was beside one of the stone pillars that held up the lumicklines along the Greensward Road. Now that she knew where to focus her eyes, she could see that the lumicker himself had climbed atop the wagon. He was kneeling upon its roof and appeared to be working on a pillar on the north side of the road. She could see, too, that the lumickline beside him was unlit; it glowed blue going into the pillar, but it was a lifeless cable on the other side.

"Hello there!" Kayden called out when they were close.

The man atop the wagon glanced up, saw them, and stood to meet their approach. He wore a wide-brimmed brown hat, peaked at the ridge, and a knee-length brown coat with leather patches on the elbows and hips. There were silver tools in his hands and at his belt that were unlike anything Shae had ever seen. He was gripping a pipe between his teeth.

"Lumickers aren't the trusting sort," Kayden whispered over at her. "Probably shouldn't mention that you're a pirate."

"Bandit."

"That too."

Closer now, and Shae could see that the man wore a thick, grey mustache, its ends curling up against his cheeks. He eyed them warily, and when they were a stone's throw from the wagon, he held up a tool that looked like it was part blade. "That's plenty far right there, you four," he said around his pipe.

Kayden reined in his horse and pulled back his hood. Shae did the same, trying not to look confused by the inclusion of the horses in his counting of their party.

"We're just passing by, sir," Kayden said. "Would've given you wide berth but didn't know if maybe you needed help."

The lumicker lowered the tool in his hand, but he didn't appear to relax. His stare, coming out from under his wide-brimmed hat, seemed to be measuring them as the rain fell. "You got a silver turn-knuckle?"

Kayden blinked. "A silver—"

The lumicker puffed on his pipe. "Turn-knuckle."

Kayden shook his head. "I don't know what that is."

The lumicker chuckled to himself, and Shae was glad to see that Kayden was just as confused as she was. "Reckon you can't be much help, then."

Kayden gave a half-bow, then wiped rain off his face with what looked like an embarrassed smile. "Should've realized that when we got close," he said.

"So," the lumicker said after a moment, "you're heading to Homilden?"

"We are," Kayden said.

The lumicker pulled his pipe, looked at the bowl, sniffed, and then used it to point down the road. "It's another day, day and half."

Kayden glanced over at Shae. "That's … that's what we figured. Camping on the road tonight."

The man gave a single nod of his chin, apparently aimed at their saddlebags. "Got yourselves tent and supplies?"

"We do," Kayden said. "Can I ask, how far is the line out?"

"Just here to the next pillar. You'll be fine beyond that."

"Thank you," Kayden said.

The lumicker put a hand to his hat in what looked like a kind of farewell. He put his pipe back into his mouth.

Kayden nodded, then lifted up his hood again and signaled to Shae to start forward.

They trotted their horses around the wagon, keeping as much distance as they could. Shae felt the lumicker's gaze as he watched them pass by and continue on down the road in the rain.

After a minute she started to turn in the saddle to look back at the wagon, but Kayden's quick hush stopped her. "Don't look back. He'll think it's suspicious."

Shae stiffened up, locking her gaze on the road as it cut through the grass sea ahead. "You think he's still watching?"

"I know he is. Like I said: they aren't the trusting sort."

14

Furywood Flame

The world came in flashes as Alira ran through the jungle. Branches. Vines. Fallen bramble and brush. She darted through it all, with no effort to be patient or quiet. She'd smelled smoke on the rainy wind—smoke from the direction of home. All that mattered was getting there.

Anjel was a village woven between the limbs of mature Furywood trees whose tops pushed against the dome of the sky itself. And as Alira cut out from one stretch of jungle into the open, she could see the smoke curling amid those very treetops—streaks of angry dark against the grey sky.

"Oh gods," Kora gasped from behind her.

Alira didn't answer. Nor did she cease her mad dash. A tall, timber palisade ringed the Furywood grove of Anjel, and she angled left toward the nearest gate, picking up speed now that she was in the open.

Her mind raced faster than her feet. Fire was necessary. For warmth. For food. For safety.

But the Stormborn she'd lived among for these years were as careful with open flames as the Seaborn she'd been born into were with blazes aboard their wooden ships at sea. There was a chance, always a chance, of an accident. But it was a small chance.

And in a rainstorm? How could flames have broken loose in the wet?

The wall, bending away from her, brought one of the gates into view. It lay open. Blown open.

The wide hinges were shattered to splinters, the slabs of thick wood thrown to the ground like children's playthings, as if a horrible wind had blasted them in.

Alira and Kora skidded to a stop. They stared.

Beyond that open wound, inside the wall, there was a bare expanse where nothing was meant to grow. Storage huts and livestock pens peppered the distance between the gate and the ship-wide trunks of the Furywood trees. In other days, even under the slanting rains, there would have been women and men and children walking and working the grounds. Today, it was in flames. And the only people still walking were Bloodborn.

If Alira hadn't known them by sight, not recognized them from when she'd seen them from the high branches that morning, she'd still have known them by their laughter. The pelting rain and the thickness of Anjel's walls had kept the sound from her ears, but there was no mistaking the otherworldly cacophony now that she and Kora stood in the magick-blasted gate. It was animal screams and high-pitched laughter, and for a heartbeat she was back at that abandoned temple with Bela and the evoker Tukaha, facing a Bloodborn woman who had almost killed them all.

Alira took in her breath in a gasp. As the air flowed into

her chest, she was back at Anjel, and there was not one Bloodborn woman before her. There were dozens.

They were magickers. All of them. Like the evokers, their hands wove invisible threads of power. But where evokers breathed their power in golden Char, the evokers laughed their power in red blood.

It was streaked upon their faces, congealing to splotches and hideous strings. Some of it belonged to the Stormborn who'd not reached the ramps that ran into the mighty trees. Some of it belonged to themselves. Alira could see the bite marks that they'd driven into their own shoulders. She could see it as clearly as she'd seen the same half-moon shape in the shoulder of the Bloodborn magicker who'd almost killed her and Bela—a curve of blood the very shape of a woman's jaw.

Behind her, Kora reacted with a scream of her own. But Alira's hands had already found Whéuri's bow. She'd swung it into her hands, nocked an arrow. By the time the nearest Bloodborn woman had turned in their direction with a red-streaked smile, Alira was already loosing the string.

The arrow leaped away as the string went taut. Time slowed into one long exhale. She held the bow steady while the fletching cleared, and the arrow flew straight and true through the rain, cutting through the Bloodborn woman's long, lank black hair to bury itself in the base of her neck.

The woman was kicked backward by the impact, blood spouting, her laughter turned into a scream.

Alira was already pulling another arrow, searching out another target.

An arrow whistled over her shoulder. It was Kora's shot. The panic and horror with which the young woman had reacted to the Bloodborn had been set aside. This was a hunt, and her instincts had clearly kicked in; her arrow pierced the back of a Bloodborn woman who'd been standing above a fallen Stormborn man. She went down.

It was chaos, but flash by flash, Alira took it in. The magick of the Bloodborn had destroyed the gates. A sudden assault. Only a handful of the fallen watch had weapons in their hands. The Stormborn had fled for the ramps that led up into the great trees—the safety of height and home. Some had made it. The Stormborn in the Furywood branches above would've waited as long as they could for their friends and family. Then they'd sliced through the counterweight lines, and the ramps had snapped upward like closing jaws, cutting the village in the trees off from the Bloodborn below.

Bows were singing from archers moving in the shadows of the great canopy, but the Bloodborn were weaving their threads. The winds they wove swept the arrows away like annoying insects and cast down the archers they saw, breaking bodies against broken branches. Others of the Bloodborn were weaving fires, as Tukaha had, a magick that spat flame against the rain.

Furywood would not burn easily. But against such magick—

"Alira!"

Kora shouted in the same moment that her faster reflexes had nocked and loosed another arrow. Alira's eyes snapped around and saw that, while she'd been looking ahead, the young girl had looked to the side. There was a small building not far away. Little more than a shed, but it had windows. There were Stormborn crowded inside, their faces terrorized. Two Bloodborn women were fighting against the barred door. A third stood behind them, her hands weaving in red mist—but whatever magick she was making of the blood, it was shattered when Kora's arrow punched into her shoulder and spun her down into the mud.

Alira nocked the arrow she had in her hand and loosed a shot of her own at one of the other Bloodborn, but Kora's shout had already made her target flinch and turn. The arrow splintered against the wall just above her head.

Their prey was aware of them now. Surprise was gone. And standing together, they'd be easier targets for whatever magicks the Bloodborn threw at them.

"Separate!" Alira shouted, and she darted out into the open space between the wall and the great Furywood trees, closing the distance on the shed even as she drew another arrow. To her right, Kora was running parallel along the base of the wall. She, too, had her hand to her quiver.

In just a quick glance, Alira saw, above the young woman's face guard, the redness of her eyes. She read it against the murder of her family. This wasn't just a hunt for her now. It wasn't just a defense of Anjel. It was vengeance.

Alira pulled her sight back to the Bloodborn ahead. The woman Kora had hit was rolling, trying to get up. The one she'd tried to hit had ducked away and was caught with indecision between the two advancing huntresses. The third was already weaving.

Running, feeling the lift and fall of her feet against the wet ground, the in and out of her heaving chest, Alira aimed and loosed. In the same moment, the woman's fingers gripped and twisted on a mist of blood she'd spat into the wet air.

Where there had been nothing, there was a wall of air,

shimmering in the rain. The arrow hit it and bounced away. Then the wall hurtled forward, sweeping through the wet.

Alira dove to her right, curling the precious bow to her chest to protect it. The wall clipped her feet, spun her across the ground. Mud smeared up against her face guard.

She didn't dare stop to get up. She didn't know where the Bloodborn's magick might fall next. Instead, she let her momentum carry her forward, bending at the hips, allowing her natural roll to bring her feet to the ground. Then she crouched into her toes, digging them into the ground as they slid and her body came upright. Her bow was already forward, but her other hand was outstretched for balance. Her mind counted the precious moments, straining for that point of enough control when she could reach back into her quiver for another shaft.

She felt the magick wall to her left, felt it swinging toward her. She saw the Bloodborn woman laughing—and a heartbeat later, an arrow slamming into the side of her head.

The wall burst apart, drenching water over Alira's hood. She blinked the splash away from her eyes, moved her focus to the next target: the one she'd nearly hit.

Too slow. The woman had recovered and was weaving. But she wasn't looking at Alira.

"Kora!"

The Bloodborn thrust her palm forward, and for an instant, the air compressed against the rain in front of her. Then it burst forward, spinning, kicking spray. It struck Kora squarely in the chest, like the punch of the storm god, and hurled her backward through the rain.

Alira's fingers had another arrow now. Cursing, she brought it to the string and pulled. She loosed it, but a heaving gust of wind struck her from behind. The arrow went low and away. It was no natural burst of wind. And coming from behind, it meant that she and Kora now had the attention of the Bloodborn around the Furywood grove too.

Good. Every moment the Bloodborn were focused away from the trees gave those in them a chance to regroup. It could mean dozens of lives saved—at the cost of two.

She and Kora had managed to take out less than a handful. One day, perhaps, it would be sung about among the Stormborn, just as Belakané's glories were sung about among the Seaborn. The difference would be that Bela had survived the attack that made her famous.

There were dozens of the Bloodborn inside the walls. None of them would be surprised now, and Kora might already be down. Only seconds might be left.

If there was one thing a huntress learned early, it was that a moving target was a harder target. So Alira sprang to her feet as the wind passed by. She ran left again, toward the shed. The woman who'd taken an arrow to the shoulder was up to her knees. She was spitting blood and weaving. An unmoving target. Alira almost grinned as she lifted the bow in mid-stride and loosed a shot into the dead center of the woman's chest and dropped her backward into the rain.

That left one at the door of the shed. What good it would do to take them out now, when so many other evokers were probably converging on them, Alira didn't know. But it was something.

Her feet were eating up the ground. The woman still standing was between one of the fallen and the shed door. She was weaving; another fist of air, presumably. There would be no time to pull for another shot. So Alira passed the bow to her off-hand and unsheathed her long knife. And when the punch was loosed, she was ready. She bent backward, letting her feet slide forward in the mud. The wind shimmered over her, just inches from her face, and then her feet struck the dead Bloodborn's body and caught. Her momentum flung the rest of her upright and over the corpse. Her bow hand hit her target's face. Her knife plunged into the woman's gut. As the rest of her body crashed forward, it drove the woman into the door. The knife went through, sticking into the wood on the other side.

The last time she'd been so close to a Bloodborn had been the night Tukaha had been killed by one. In nightmares, Alira could sometimes still see the wet point of the dagger sticking out from the evoker's chest, the pale skin of the Bloodborn's face behind her shoulder in the darkness, just visible through the veil of her long, black hair.

Feeling the last breath of the magicker pinned against the door felt like payback now.

She tugged at the blade's hilt as she pulled away, but her hand only slipped on the bloodied grip. Sensing more Bloodborn closing in, she let it go.

She turned and dodged away from the shed, away from Kora, and saw three women looking at her, their backs to the Furywood trees. All of them were weaving.

She ran. No destination. Just away from the shed and the innocents within.

The first and second weaves were punches. Both missed and landed behind her. One cratered the wall of the shed. The other clipped the corner of it, blasting bricks and wood into a shower of debris.

The third was a punch too. It caught her in the hip.

Alira screamed from the sharpness of the pain, and then she was spinning through the air, careening through a world that was upside down.

She hit the ground, skidded, and tried to get up. Her leg revolted, a shocking agony in the joint—was her hip shattered?—and all she could do was rise to her elbow in the mud, her one leg stretched awkwardly out to the side. She'd dropped Whéuri's bow. It was a dozen feet away.

Alira tried to crawl to it, her fingers clawing into the rain-soaked earth, drawing her closer, fist by fist. Then something—magick or metal, she couldn't tell—struck her in the back of her head.

She collapsed. The world shifted and spun, threatening to go dark. She saw feet. Gaunt fingers lifting Whéuri's bow from the mud, then dropping it back down in two useless pieces. The feet moved away. And there were many of them. She lifted her head up, saw through her reeling vision that the Bloodborn were all pulling back. Retreating toward the open gate, abandoning the attack. The fires beneath the Furywood trees were going out.

She almost had time to smile.

But then she saw, too, that there were Stormborn captured by the attackers, being herded by magick and fear. Kora was among them. Her bow was gone. Her hood had been pulled back, and the rain was falling on a face that was bruised and bloody. Her arm hung wrong from her shoulder.

Then strong hands lifted Alira up. A burst of wind pushed her forward, stumbling painfully in their wake. And she knew that she was being taken too.

15

The Aluman

Shae saw it first.

They hadn't gone a mile beyond the lumicker's wagon when movement caught her eye.

She'd been thinking of the Bone Pirate, of her ship, of the throne of bones, and then she'd glanced to the side, out across the great sea of browning grasses to the north. It was there, out in the distance, that she saw the metal man beneath the shade of the rain-heavy clouds.

She couldn't count the number of times she'd wondered what it would be like to see an aluman move. Since the moment she'd first seen the one frozen in the river, so many months ago, she had imagined the long arms swinging, the wide legs driving forward, the crystal eyes aglow with what passed for its life. All that time, and she'd imagined that its steps would be slow. Powerful, but a careful, cautious, lumbering power.

The truth was nothing like that. The aluman she saw now, the metal man running across the dried grasses of the Greensward, was moving swiftly. Not a sprinter's pace, but an easy run, its metal arms pumping. What light there was glinted off its silver head and body.

She pulled her horse to a stop. "Kayden," she croaked.

Kayden reined in, followed her gaze. "Gods," he gasped. "It's headed for the open part of the line."

"Where the lumicker was working?" Kayden nodded.

"If it gets onto the road ..."

He didn't complete the thought, but he didn't need to do so. Shae could imagine it all. An aluman that got through that gap in the lumicklines could go wherever it wanted—to Homilden or Felcamp or some other village on the roads they'd not taken. There'd be no water-filled ditches to stop it. The only thing that would stop it would be blood.

"Warn the lumicker," Kayden said. He lifted his reins as he kicked his horse forward, ducking the working lumickline and entering the open plain beyond.

Shae drove her mount into his wake. "What are you doing?" she shouted.

Kayden was picking up speed across the grasses. "I'm going to try to slow it down!"

"How?"

"I don't know! Warn him! Get the line up!"

As Kayden pressed farther ahead, Shae angled back toward the road. In seconds, she was ducking under the lit lumickline once more. She turned in the direction they'd come, and her heels pinched into her horse's flanks, urging it to move faster.

The grasses rolled by in a blur, like the shimmering that slipped past a ship's hull at sea.

The rain had slowed up, but her speed nevertheless made it hit hard upon her face. The wind pushed back her hood and let her hair fly behind her. If she closed her eyes, she thought, she could've imagined she was astride the deck of the *Pale Dawn*.

But, of course, she wasn't. She was a world away from her ship, from her seas, from anything she really understood. She was a world away, trying to warn a man who worked mechanical magicks about a metal man that was coming to kill him.

If the aluman didn't frighten her so much, she would have laughed at the utter strangeness of it all.

Her horse carried her up over a rolling swale. She saw the wagon, and the lumicker still at work atop it. She opened her mouth to call out, to warn him of her approach, but in that same moment, a shot rang out across the plain to her right.

There was a time she wouldn't have known what it was, but she'd heard it before—when Kayden had killed one of her shipmates aboard his airship. And again at the top of the Spire on that final fateful night, she'd heard it twice— once when she'd pulled the trigger, and once when Kayden had. It was the sound of a handcannon.

It meant Kayden was fighting the aluman.

The lumicker stood up at the sound, looking north. Shae shouted, waving one arm as best she could while still speeding her horse down the road.

The man raised something from his belt. It was like one of Kayden's weapons—a tube atop a handle—but it was a brighter silver. And it had two tubes, side by side, instead of one. He raised it up and pointed it at her.

Mother, Shae thought, *he thinks I'm a bandit*.

The weapon in his hand flashed blue—lumick blue—and

an instant later, her horse made a horrible sound and buckled forward, catapulting her out of the saddle.

She tucked in the air, curling up so that she could take the impact on her upper back and roll with the momentum. Even so, it was only the fact that she hit the ground between the main ruts of the road, where there was patchy grass and rain-softened earth, that kept her from snapping her spine.

Bruises blossomed down her body as she skipped to a stop.

For a moment, the world was spinning, and all she could hear was the sound of her fallen horse screaming. She didn't think she'd broken any bones, but her mount had.

There was a thump from the other direction, and Shae let the sound of it focus her eyes and her mind. She sat up, saw that the lumicker had jumped down from his wagon. He wasn't far away. His long coat swung behind him. He had the weapon up as he approached. He no longer had his pipe.

The weapon flashed blue again. There was no sound from it, but she felt something streak over her shoulder, whistling as it cut through the air. Behind her, the horse fell silent.

The lumicker moved a lever on the weapon, then pointed it at her chest. He squinted as he stared down it, one eye pinching toward his big grey mustache.

"Next one goes through your blood-pumper."

Shae lifted her hands, a gesture that she hoped he would understand. "Aluman," she said. She gasped, suddenly realizing how much it hurt to breathe, much less talk.

His footsteps stopped. "Aluman?"

A second shot from Kayden's handcannons echoed over them. Louder. Closer. Shae pointed. "My friend, Kayden. He's slowing it down."

The lumicker stopped squinting. His gaze snapped from her to the lifeless lumickline beside them. Then he cursed, turned, and ran back toward his wagon, his long coat whipping in his wake. He hurtled himself onto the ladder that ran up the back of the wagon and threw himself up onto his tool-strewn roof.

Shae groaned as she heaved herself onto her feet. Everything hurt, but the pain could wait. The aluman was coming, and it had to be stopped.

And if they didn't stop it, the pain wouldn't last long.

She limped back to her horse. There were bloody holes in its chest and head. It was dead.

There was a sword under the saddlebags, and the straps holding it in place had been mercifully loosened by the horse's writhing and fall. Shae pulled it out. She couldn't imagine what good it would be against a metal man, but it was surely better than her fists or the little fangs she had at her hip. She slapped the scabbard belt around her waist and cinched it tight.

She hurried as fast as she could—her right ankle and left knee were sprained, she was certain—and reached the base of the wagon.

"What can I do?" she called.

There was a clang of metal. "Get up here."

Shae climbed the ladder. There was a cloth rolled out across the wet roof, and various tools were lined up on it. She recognized none of them. The lumicker was kneeling at the stone pillar beside the wagon, which came up to his knees. She could see now that there had been a metal cap atop it, which he'd removed to access whatever was inside.

"Sorry about your horse," he said once she'd joined him on the roof. He didn't look up from his work.

"Wasn't mine."

He lifted himself up to look back at her. He saw the sword at her hip. "That all you've got?"

"And fangs," she said.

His thick mustache lifted in something that might've been a smile, and there were wrinkles at the corners of his blue eyes. He thought it was a joke. "Here." He reached to his hip and pulled out the weapon he'd used on her horse. He tossed it to her. "Point. Pull the trigger. Give me all the time you can."

"Like a handcannon?"

His eyebrow lifted up at that. "Yeah. Like a handcannon." Then he bent back down into the pillar.

Shae nodded at his back, gauging the weight of the weapon. "I'll try to draw it to me."

The lumicker didn't reply. He only muttered something to himself as he leaned over to swap tools.

Shae eased herself down the ladder, taking care not to slip on the wet steps, then walked down the road where the lumickline was unlit. She fit her hands on the grip of the lumicker's weapon. Felt at the trigger and what she thought might be the lever he'd used. Then she looked north.

Kayden had fired two shots. There was no way he could reload his handcannons while he was riding and fighting. What, then, did he have against it? His sword? What if he was already dead?

Shae heard it then. The sound of metal plates sliding against one another. The sound of metal wheels turning against one another. The sound of the earth shaking as each mighty footstep struck the ground.

The aluman.

It came into view suddenly. Its eyes were a pale blue, and lumick glowed, too, from the seams between the plates on its chest, thighs, and arms. It was still running, but then it saw her—she *felt* it see her, a cold shiver of fear that ran down her spine—and it stopped.

For a moment, they faced each other. Then the aluman's upper body turned slightly from side to side, taking its eyes from the gap in the lumicklines to the lumicker's wagon and back again. Its arms made sounds as they shifted. Its clawed hands flexed in and out.

Then it came for her.

Shae took a step back out of instinct, and she felt ashamed. *What would the Bone Pirate think?* she wondered.

I am the Bone Pirate, her mind replied.

She stepped forward again. She raised the weapon in her hands and tried to line it up with the coming monster.

There were two pipes, and the lumicker had taken two shots. If the lever reloaded it, she might have more. But she couldn't be sure.

So two shots. She'd need to make them count.

The metal man got bigger with each massive step. The pit of her stomach sank.

And then Kayden's horse came over the ridge behind it. There was blood smeared across his face and chest, but he was alive, and he was racing after the aluman.

The head, she decided. She'd shoot for the head.

She glanced up. The lumickline was above her. It was still dead. It probably wouldn't be alone soon.

The aluman was only a ship's width away when Kayden caught up with it. He brought his panting, frightened horse up alongside it—how he had the animal under such control, Shae couldn't fathom—and when the aluman reached out to swipe him away, he ducked under the arm just as he'd ducked under the lumickline along the road minutes earlier. Then he yanked the reins of the horse to the side, darting into the path of the mighty legs.

The animal was no match for the metal, but it was enough to entangle it. The aluman went down over the top of horse and rider, crashing with a horrific sound.

Shae screamed for Kayden and ran forward. But already the aluman was getting up with a grinding of metal; its hands made fists into the dirt, lifting its upper body off the ground. She stopped, aimed the weapon at its head, and pulled the trigger.

Kayden's handcannon had roared and then kicked like an angry mule in her hand when she'd fired it. This did neither. It flashed, and she felt the wind as whatever it expelled rushed out from one of the tubes and plinked off the aluman's plated head no differently than the rocks she'd thrown at the one back in Felcamp.

The aluman leaned to one side, letting its weight off one hand long enough to swipe at her. Shae jumped to the side, just in time, but tripped on something in the grasses.

As she fell down, the aluman stood up. There were wet sounds when it came upright.

Shae didn't dare to look.

It came forward again, ignoring her as it walked past her toward the still-dead lumickline.

Shae got up, stared at its hulking back. For a moment, in

her despair, she thought of trying to fling one of her fangs at it, but it was no use. The lumicker's weapon was far more powerful, and it had done nothing against the armored plates of its head.

The armored plates.

Shae leapt at it from behind, planting her left foot on a plate at the back of its leg and using that to boost herself higher onto its back. It lurched in response, twisting at the waist as it tried to wrest her off. Her grip started to slip, but she managed to lift the lumicker's weapon up to the back of its stump of a head. There was a seam there, the lumick glowing blue between the plates. She placed the pipe that hadn't fired against that line. She pressed into it with the last of her fading strength. She pulled the trigger.

The weapon shook, reverberating off the aluman, out of her grip, and down into the grasses. Shae fell with it, bouncing down the metal man's back and onto the ground.

Above her, the aluman shuddered. Ripples of light snapped around the hole she could see in the back of its head. There were crackling sounds, like the tiniest of twigs snapping.

It stepped forward, more hesitant now. Almost halting. It leaned against the lifeless lumickline, pressing forward as if it meant to snap the cable with its weight.

And then pale blue fire raced out from the pillar by the lumicker's wagon, lacing along the line. It hit the aluman.

There was a buzzing sound. A loud crack. And then the lumickline was glowing steadily, pillar to pillar, and the aluman was still.

16

Into the Storm

Madness.

Bela felt it, gnawing at her mind, darkening the eyes of her crew, drawing in their cheeks, trembling their limbs. Whispers carried on the relentless wind of the blizzard that pounded against the shelter they'd made of the overturned boats.

Four days the storm had battered them. Four days they'd huddled here in the shadows of the feeble protection they'd made.

Madness.

They'd tried to pass the time with stories, but the stories, like their supplies and themselves, were thinning out. Bela knew it was her responsibility, that she ought to do something to fight the shadow back, but what could be done?

Oni, huddled up against her side, shivered and then stilled. Bela managed a smile as she ran her fingers along the furs that covered her maiden. Of them all, Oni seemed the only one who wasn't teetering on the edge of despair. With every passing hour, it seemed she was the only warmth left in the world.

"Belakané," Sanyu whispered from across the darkness.

Bela shifted a little within the icy seat her body heat had made over the days. "Yes?"

"I'm worried about one of the straps."

Some of the other women moved, seemed glad to be listening to something more than the horrible roar of the wind and snow.

"You tightened it before," Bela said.

A shipwright without her ship, Sanyu had been the one to direct the building of their shelter. And of course, she'd been the one determined to go out for repairs on the second day when a flap of the canvas strung between the shells of the boats had come loose. At Bela's direction, they covered her with all that they could spare of their garments before she braved the whiteout conditions. It was very nearly a disaster. Three wrong steps, and she lost her bearings, nearly walked off to her death, wearing their heaviest clothes. The next time someone had needed to go outside to check things— Neka this time—they'd tied a rope around her waist first. It would help her find her way back. And should the worst happen, should she succumb to the cold, they could also use it to pull her body back inside the shelter to strip it. Mother's grace, there'd been no such need.

"I think it's loosening again," Sanyu replied. "I should go out."

Bela shook her head. "We talked about this last time. We take turns."

"Then let the reader go," Malaika suddenly said.

Bela almost smiled, thinking it a joke that they would entrust their safety to a man, but then she could see from her face that the grizzled woman wasn't joking. "Each takes a turn but the reader," she corrected herself.

"That's not fair." Eshe's voice was a whine.

Bela felt a tight tiredness in her jaw as she nodded. "I agree. It's not."

"It's okay," Tewrick said. The little man started to cinch up his wool overcoat and wrap.

Bela shook her head. "You will not go, and that's an order."

Sanyu grinned. "Eggless runt wants to go."

"Let it," Neka said. "Did my own time in that storm."

Tewrick's fingers paused at the top buttons of his coat. He looked from the other women back to Bela with uncertain eyes. "It's only right that this man should go."

"You can't," Bela said. "You're the reader."

"The reader!" Malaika was forced to yell to be heard over the din as a particularly strong gale of wind buffeted the outside of their flipped outboats. "And what good is a reader out here? What good are his books now? What good against all this?"

"It's his books that brought us here," Neka said. The tone in her voice brought a fresh chill to the air.

"That's right," Malaika said with rising anger. "We wouldn't be here if it wasn't for him."

Malaika's face was flushed with hot ire, but Oni, shaking herself up, cut her off before she could yell again. "You know damn well it was your lust for coin that brought you all here. You and the others who heard the High Matron's call for able hands. You knew the risks. So did all the rest—those we buried on the way and those who went with the *Sandcrow* to the deep. We all knew."

The mention of the dead temporarily draped a respectful silence over the crew's anger.

"They're still right," Tewrick whispered. "This man

found the book of the Eldrin, found the maps to Ealond. This man translated the description of the portal. If it wasn't for me—"

"The Isles would have far less hope," Bela finished. "And our mates died for that, Tew, not for you."

Neka and Sanyu looked at the white ground, but Malaika still wasn't ready to back down. "Doesn't mean the reader can't take a turn."

Bela nodded toward the shipwright who'd been with her since she'd first become a shipmistress. "You call me Belakané, Sanyu. The Hero of the Harbor. But a hero for what? A few ships saved from burning. But think of how many I could not save. How many were destroyed? How many girls went to the Mother's Embrace that night? I was there. I heard the screaming. And that was the attack of but a single airship. The Windborn will come with many. A great fleet. What little time the Isles have is built on hope. And that hope falls upon us. It did the moment we left harbor." Bela paused to take a deep breath. She looked around at her meager crew, trying to push strength into their weakening hearts, hoping it would make her own stronger too. "A hundred Heroes of the Harbor back in the Fair Isles cannot stop them. But we can. We can reach the portal. We can close it. Without the power of the Stream, their airships will fall from the sky. We can keep the Isles free."

Oni, beside her, smiled. "Heroes of the Storm."

Bela wanted to kiss her for that. She softened her voice, softened her face. "If we find Ealond ... *when* we find Ealond, we will need to follow the maps, to understand the descriptions. I read waves, but I cannot read books. We will need to record what we find there, but I cannot scribe. Perhaps we will need an ancient tongue to close the portal. Perhaps we will need to learn that language. Can any of the rest of us do this?" Her eyes moved around the shelter, marking each of them in turn. "The High Matron was wise to give us someone able to read. Wiser still to provide us with a scholar able to read any scripts we should find or speak any tongues. He's the one person of our number who cannot be replaced. All of the rest of us—even me—are replaceable." She took a deep breath and let it out. "So stay warm, Tew. I'll go out again."

The storm struck her like a great slap, and Bela buckled to her knees in front of the canvas flap of their shelter. Her eyes were shut against the sheer rage of it, her teeth gritted as she absorbed the relentless buffeting upon her back. She flexed her jaw as she breathed into her scarf, trying to keep the moisture she exhaled from freezing too quickly into the cloth.

After a moment, she unsealed her eyes to a squint. The world was a spin of sheeting white, but she focused on the things she could make out. The dark gash of the canvas flap. The mounded shape of the snow-covered boats protecting them. The line of the rope that would let them pull her body back inside if she died out here.

Straining, fighting to keep her balance, Bela stood. Then, with slow, heavy steps, she walked away from the safety of the canvas flap, drawing out the rope, before she swung around toward the other end of the huddled boats, where Sanyu thought a strap was coming loose.

Halfway there, Bela stopped and stared out into the storm, beyond their meager shelter.

There was a white mound out there. Half as large as one of their boats. A drift, she thought.

Then it moved.

It took a moment for her mind to recognize what her eyes saw. She wasn't alone in the snow. The beast that had taken Mabaya had hunted them. It had returned.

The bear, white as the sky, rose up on four legs. In the slashing snow, Bela saw its heavy head swivel toward her. Its black eyes were blank, but she could feel that it saw her, that it knew what she was. What she was made of.

The bear opened a maw as big as Bela's head. It was filled with sharp teeth. It roared, though she couldn't hear the noise in the storm.

Then it lumbered forward.

Bela, too, was screaming. But even as her shouts were ripped from her throat, she knew they were useless. Her crew would hear her no better than she could hear the savage beast's rage.

She tried to back away, tried to turn and run, but her feet caught against a crusty ridge in the snow. She fell.

The bear caught her.

It charged into her with its head down like an angered bull, tossing her away like flotsam off a wave. Pain turned the white world a sudden orange.

Bela sprawled. Ribs broken and sharp at her side.

She tried to scramble through the agony, and for a moment she thought she might get away. Her feet caught and held on the snow, and she was up.

Then the rope around her waist went taut and yanked her backward.

Her crew. They must think she was lost. They were trying to get her back inside.

Bela turned, and the white beast was there. Mouth open and hungry. Her arm went up out of instinct, and the bear's jaws crashed down upon it.

She tried to twist away. The beast thrashed its neck, teeth grinding. Her body whipped like a storm-shaken palm. Then it tossed her out and away through the air.

She hit the side of one of the boats, and where she hit the ground, the snow was red with blood. The rope around her waist pulled still. It inched her along the cold, smearing it. Her arm was in front of her. The bones were splintered through the ravaged meat. Beyond it, the bear was coming fast. Its muzzle was pink.

Hands grabbed her. Big hands. Neka's hands. They were uncovered, and through the haze of Bela's shock, she wanted to tell her to get inside. She was going to get frostbite.

Neka was yelling. Bela could hear it distantly. And there were answering shouts.

More hands. Pulling her. The bear was there too. The world going black. Malaika had one of the swords. Oni had the other. They were slashing in the torrential snow, freezing to death as they tried to fight off the blood-hungry beast.

Blinking, fading, Bela saw Sanyu. She was the other one pulling at her. They almost had her into the flap now. Like Neka, she was screaming back at the boat. Screaming for Eshe.

And then, just as the world mercifully went black, Tewrick burst through the canvas, leaping over her. There was a harpoon in his hand, and a look in his eyes that Bela had never seen before.

17

The Wagon

Even before she was sure that the aluman was dead, Shae was crawling through the trampled grass to the heap where Kayden and his horse had gone down under its massive bulk. She hurt in ways she hadn't in a long time. She ignored it.

"Kayden? Kayden?"

He didn't respond. Through the wet grass, she could see the flank of the fallen horse. It wasn't moving.

"Mother, please," she whispered.

It looked like Kayden had tried to jump off the horse after he'd entangled it with the aluman's legs. But he hadn't made it all the way off. When the horse went down, he went down with it. And then the metal man had fallen atop them both. The horse was crushed. Dead.

Beneath it, Kayden was still breathing. The rain was smearing the blood and dirt on his face.

"He's alive?"

Shae looked up. The lumicker was standing behind her. He'd picked up his weapon from where it had fallen in the grass.

Shae nodded. "He's hurt bad."

The lumicker frowned, then scanned the scene around them. "Both your horses are dead."

"You killed mine."

He didn't respond. He was looking back at the aluman, which was frozen against the lit lumickline. "Homilden's a ways off," he said. His voice sounded absent.

"You have to help us!"

The man turned around. "Reckon I don't *have* to do anything," he said. "But I will." He put his weapon into the holster at his hip. "Let's get him free of the horse first."

He squatted down beside her, put his hands under its bulk and his shoulder to the saddle. "Grab his arms and pull," he said.

They heaved—him upward on the horse's dead weight, her outward on Kayden's limp body. The lumicker was an older man, but he was surprisingly strong. Even so, it took three goes to get Kayden pulled out. His right leg was clearly broken. His breathing was ragged. He didn't open his eyes.

"Kayden!" Shae wiped grime off his face. "Kayden, can you hear me?"

"He's out surer than a fish in hay," the lumicker said. He looked back toward the road and sighed. "Help me get him to my wagon."

They tried to carry him together, but Shae's pains were beginning to get the best of her. One of her legs felt nearly immobile; her sprained knee had swollen like a grapefruit. So in the end, she could only help hoist Kayden onto the lumicker's back, then hobble ahead to open the wagon's door.

The inside of the lumicker's wagon reminded her of

nothing so much as the Bone Pirate's cabin aboard the *Pale Dawn*; it was both a house and a work space, packed with things, yet somehow well organized. And like a ship's cabin, everything was locked or strapped down. The shaking of the road was like the shaking of the sea, it seemed. On the left side of the interior was a small iron stove for cooking and heating, surrounded by pots and pans, pokers and plates, all hanging or contained in one space or another. Beside that, below a window, was a workbench.

Tools were set in slots upon its surface. Rope-secured shelves all around the window held various metal parts, a few of which she was certain came from alumen. On the right side, below a window, was a long couch with storage beneath it. And at the far end was a bed, waist-high, with cabinets below it. Above the bed, there was a hatch against the wall, leading, Shae assumed, to the driving bench up front. Running the whole length of the ceiling was a kind of indentation, only a couple of inches deep, whose sides were made of glass. She'd not seen it in the moments she'd been on the roof before, but she could see from inside how it cleverly let in the sunlight in two long strips. The walls, where they weren't covered with shelves—there were metal parts everywhere, it seemed—were a richly polished oak, ornamented with delicate designs of silver wire.

With Shae helping as best she could with one good leg, they lifted Kayden onto a red rug just inside the door. Then they slid and hefted him into the bed at the far end. The lumicker checked him over quickly. "If he lives, he's gonna be sore the likes of which he's never been, I think." He looked at Shae. "Go strip your horses. Pile things up outside here while I figure out what to do."

Shae, tired and hurting, didn't argue. She limped out of the cabin and went first to her own horse. The rain had mercifully stopped, and the air was filled with the sweet scents of the wet grasses. She would've enjoyed it, she thought, if she wasn't so worried about Kayden.

The fact that she was worried about him worried her too. What did it mean that she cared?

Shaking such questions away, she focused on the tasks at hand. She unstrapped the saddlebags first. They were easy enough to get to the wagon, but the unwieldy weight of the saddle was harder on her sore body. By the time she'd dragged it to the foot of the wagon's ladder, the lumicker was already hopping down out of the interior.

He blinked up at the sky. The sun was peeking through the clouds to the west. "I've set the broken bones. Probably for the best he wasn't awake for it. You said his name is Kayden?"

Shae nodded. "That's right."

"And yours?"

"Shaesara. Shae. We're from Felcamp."

"Shae," he repeated. "From Felcamp."

Beneath the shade of his wide-brimmed hat, his blue eyes narrowed. Had she said too much? Not enough?

"I suppose that'll do for now," he said. He pulled out his pipe from the inside of his coat, and started to fill it from a pouch. "My name is Aro Lanser."

She nodded and tried to project a comfortable confidence. "From?"

His fingers paused on the bowl. He looked up at her like she had shrimps in her hair. "From this wagon, Shae. You don't know much about lumick-folk, do you?"

"I ... no, not really."

Aro shook his head, but whether it was in pity of her personally or disappointment at Felcamp generally, she couldn't tell. "All right, we'll start simple." He finished packing the pipe bowl, and pulled out a cylinder lighter like she'd seen Kayden use. "You'll never tell anyone about what you see in my wagon."

"Never tell anyone?"

"No. And no questions either. If you want your man to live—if you want yourself to live—you'll do exactly as I say. And that begins with you never speaking of what you might see in my wagon. Understand?"

The idea of being told what to do instinctively twisted at Shae's gut. He was a man. His only use ought to be his back for hauling and his cock for breeding. Lumicker or not, he'd have the Mother's Embrace if she'd seized him aboard a ship at sea.

But she had no ship. She had no sea. And the one person who she could hope to help her in this strange world was— surely to the trickster Ti'nay's delight—another man. A man who was unconscious and badly hurt.

So she swallowed her pride and nodded. "I understand."

"Good," Aro said. "Now get the other horse stripped. Then lie down on the couch inside. You're not in the best shape yourself."

"What are you going to do?"

He set fire to his pipe, puffing it to life while he gave her a look that indicated how little business it was of hers. Finally, exhaling a cloud of smoke, he nodded toward the aluman. "I'm going to strip down our friend here."

"What? Kayden needs help! He needs—"

"There's no help he can't get right here," Aro said, cutting her off. "And even if there weren't, I'll not be leaving a prize like this behind. An aluman is worth four Kaydens and Shaes from ass-water Felcamp all put together."

Shae opened her mouth to object again, but Aro had already turned his back, hopping onto the ladder to the roof to retrieve his tools. "Or you can walk and drag your friend along, if you'd prefer," he said over his shoulder. "All the same to me."

Shae peered down the road toward Homilden, where her dead horse was already gathering flies. Dropping her head, she limped her way to strip Kayden's mount too.

Whatever else she could say about Aro Lanser, the older man was efficient. By the time she'd stripped the second horse, he'd gathered up his own team of horses from where they'd wandered off onto the Greensward. He'd hitched them up and put her saddle on one of them. "No place else to carry it," he said. "Gonna be tight enough in the wagon as is."

He put the second saddle she'd brought on his other horse, after which he helped her up onto the couch so she could rest. As she lay down, she felt the slow roll of the wheels beneath her as the lumicker carefully coaxed the wagon into a new position directly beside the tall metal man.

She fell asleep to the sounds of him stripping it down for parts.

Night had fallen by the time she awoke. Her head hurt. Everything else did too.

Aro Lanser stood at the stove beside her. He looked to be even older than she'd thought.

He'd untied his long gray hair, and it hung loose—and probably more sparsely than he would like—about his shoulders. His long coat was hanging on the back of the wagon's door. So was his hat and the leather holster of his remarkable weapon. A small lamp in the upper corner of the interior, right beside the door, was glowing with a soft white light, tinged with the telltale pale blue of lumick at work. Warm scents rolled out from a stew in the pot he was stirring. At a whiff of it, her stomach grumbled loudly.

The lumicker looked back at the noise. His thick mustache lifted in a smile. "Awake," he said. "And it sounds like you're hungry."

She lifted her head to get up, but it immediately throbbed her back down.

"Easy now," he said. "I think you hit your head pretty hard at some point. Not the worst injury, but that kind of thing can catch up with you."

Shae brought a hand to her forehead, as if she could stabilize it against the pulsing pain. "I guess so."

"It's probably from when I shot you off your horse." Aro's smile was wide now. "Sorry about that."

Shae groaned but got herself upright. She looked to the other end of the wagon. "How's Kayden?"

Aro continued to stir. "Asleep. He's in worse shape than you, but it looks like he'll live."

"Thank the gods," Shae said.

For a moment, the man hesitated, then the stirring commenced again. The big spoon he was using made slow circles around the bottom of the pot. A smooth, rhythmic sound, like oars moving through water. He looked over his shoulder at her. "Do you work for Rumin Perle?"

"Who?"

"Rumin Perle. King Mark's lumicker. Stole my gun design."

Shae shook her head as much as she dared. "No. I don't know who that is, but I don't work for anyone."

Aro nodded. He turned and pulled two bowls from a shelf. He ladled one with broth and handed it to her. The bowl was warm, filled with meat chunks and bits of carrot floating in a hazy soup that smelled of something Kayden had once called sage. "Thank you," she said. Her stomach rumbled again. "It smells good."

"My mother's recipe," he said, as he ladled another bowl for himself. "Good for sore muscles after a long day."

Shae sighed. "A long day."

From a drawer, Aro pulled out two spoons, but when she reached out for one, he held it back. "I'm hungry too," he said. "But before you eat, I need to tell you that I made one change to my mother's recipe. What do you know of the gold-flock flower?"

"I've never been interested in flowers."

The lumicker nodded in understanding, then carefully set the spoons down on the edge of the stove, as if they were prizes to be won. "It's not a terribly common plant. Also not terribly pretty. But those who know how to prepare it correctly call it the truth flower."

Shae glanced down at the bowl in her hand. "And you know how to prepare it."

"I very much do," he said, looking proud. "And to answer your suspicion, yes, it's in the stew."

Shae's eyes narrowed. There was a game being played, she was sure, and she didn't like it. "Go on."

He fastidiously used a rag to wipe up the stovetop and its surrounds while he talked. "Gold-flock has two main effects on people. One is that it makes you sleep like a baby. The other is that it makes you tell the truth. Thus its other name, you see."

Shae wanted to frown. Instead, she tried to seem merely curious. "For how long?"

"Until you sleep like a baby. Which for most people isn't long." The lumicker finished cleaning. He hung his rag off a hook over the stove, then leaned back against the wagon door to look at her.

"You want me to take it." He knew she wasn't from Felcamp. That much was clear. But what else did he know? What else could he find out?

Aro nodded slowly. "I do, but the choice is yours. If you refuse, I'll make something else. Shouldn't take too long."

Her stomach growled, making its position clear. She pretended to ignore it. "Why would I choose to take such a thing if I don't need to?"

"For one thing, because you need the sleep. Truly. For another"—he looked pointedly at the other bowl—"well, because I'll take it too."

Shae blinked. If he was telling the truth, then she could ask him about the workings of lumick. She could ask him so many things. But what would he learn? What would he do with it? "Why would you take it too? Why even tell me about it? You could have just given it to me."

He tilted his head at that. "A person could have, I suppose. But *I* could not have. I'm an honest man, Shaesara."

Shae grunted, then looked over at Kayden, who was still sleeping peacefully. "He told me that lumickers are distrustful."

"And he's absolutely right."

"Honest but distrustful. Why don't you trust anyone?"

The lumicker grinned. "That's a question that Shaesara of Felcamp shouldn't need to ask. Just like Shaesara of Felcamp would've never heard of anyone—living or dead—who could speak of what had been seen in a lumicker's wagon, because no one but a lumicker is allowed in one."

Shae swallowed hard, but she looked to the remarkable lumick weapon beside him, and then to the bits and pieces of aluman parts perched and hung around the interior. Mother, she wanted to know how it worked. How *any* of it worked. "Then you're taking quite a chance already."

"Curiosity has the best of me," he admitted.

Shae looked back to Kayden again. Then, shrugging, she reached for the spoon. "Me too," she said. "Eat up."

As she dipped her spoon into the broth, he took the other bowl and spoon and began to sip it down hungrily. "Thank you," he said. "I'm terribly hungry, and I really didn't want to cook anything else."

Shae nodded as she, too, attacked it. "Well, it's good. Whatever gold-flock tastes like, I can't sense it."

"That can be the danger of it." Aro wiped soup off the edge of his mustache. "You did well against the aluman, Shaesara."

She nodded gratefully. It was true, after all. For a moment, she thought of how it might have been better if she'd had the bone mask for the fight. But she didn't suppose it would've mattered to the metal man, much less anyone else. No one here knew what it would mean.

"Thank you," she replied. "Just trying to help."

"Well, it worked. You and your friend held it off just long enough. I owed you a debt over this. It's the only reason I let you into my wagon."

"You wouldn't otherwise?"

"You're the first people to be in here since—" Aro scrunched up his face. "Well, I think you're the first."

"Then thank you. We're taut at the rope."

Aro's face wrinkled. "Taut at the rope?"

"Neither of us pulling the other."

"Ah. We would say 'even.'"

"Even." Shae suddenly yawned. Was it the gold-flock already? Or had the fight taken more out of her than she realized? The stew seemed to be filling her hungry stomach at least. And her head wasn't throbbing like it had been before. "I'd never seen an aluman moving before today," she admitted.

"All the more remarkable. Truly." He nodded to his weapon, hanging in its holster at the door. "You did mighty well with my boltgun too."

"A boltgun," Shae repeated, glad to know what it was called. She yawned again. It was getting harder to keep her eyes open. Her body was definitely spent. "I'd never seen one of those either."

Aro smiled. He'd finished his own bowl. He let her finish up the contents of hers and then took it and stacked them both. "Well, you're a fair shot," he said.

Shae shook her head. As she did so, the room moved slowly from side to side, like the world was taking a few moments to catch up to her movements.

"Drunk without drinking," Aro said. "That's how I described gold-flock the first time I tried it."

"A good description." When the words came out, it was as if they'd come from someone else. They were distant and muted.

"I'll let you go first," he said.

Shae's thoughts were like a drifting cloud, but she pushed and gathered them into something coherent. "How does lumick work?"

Aro Lanser laughed, and for a moment she feared she'd been tricked. "Straight to the greatest secret of all!" He pulled from his pocket a crystal and held it up to the lumick light in the cabin. It glowed with its own pale-blue shimmer, but behind this there was a darkness, like an endless smoke pooled inside of it. He looked at the crystal approvingly. "I took this one from our friend today."

"Soulglass," Shae said.

"Very good. You know that, at least. What do you know of it?"

"Kayden told me that on Ealond, a man named Kolum wanted to destroy death. So he used a machine and dark magicks to open a kind of gate. A world behind the world. He used this to pull a person's soul from their body and into the crystal. Then the crystal would give the person new life in an aluman. But instead, the alumen went mad."

"Well, that's the story. I wish I knew more. Especially how the alumen got here from Ealond when they can't move in deep water. And for that matter, how there have come to be so many of them. Mysteries even to lumickers. Don't tell anyone, but all we know is how to pull the power of the lumick and use it. Gears. Wires."

"So tell me about how that—" Shae said, cutting herself off with a yawn.

Aro yawned in response, then shook his head as if to clear it. "Ah, but it's my turn, I think."

Shae frowned but nodded. "Fair enough."

"Your friend there was born in Felcamp. I don't doubt that. But you weren't."

"Is that a question?"

"I have an ear for these things. But you—I've not heard someone talk like you. Not anywhere in Aionia." The lumicker rubbed at his eyes, but when his fingers came away, she could see he was trying hard to study her, his face full of curiosity. "So my question is this: Where are you really from, Shaesara?"

Shae opened her mouth to lie. Instead, she told him everything.

18

Step by Step

From a dream of bloody teeth, Bela gasped awake.

Hands met her shoulders. Firm hands. Both strong and warm.

"Mistress," Oni said. "Stay still."

Bela groaned. There was a taste in her mouth, like old leather, and she tried to swallow it away. Her mouth was dry, her lips parched. "Water," she rasped.

"Of course." One of Oni's hands was under her back, lifting her up. "Tewrick," her maiden said, "the waterskin."

Bela blinked as she leaned up. The world seemed reluctant to come into focus.

Everything was dark. Was she under the boats still?

Oni had a waterskin to her lips. The water was like ice against her lips and throat, but it felt good. "Easy. You've been asleep for two days."

Bela forced her eyes wider. She saw the little man first. They were indeed still under the boats. After handing Oni the skin, he was pulling back to the same spot where he'd always been. He saw her looking at him, and he averted his eyes.

Her maiden was closer. Bela turned to her, looked into her eyes. She smiled. She started to lift her right hand to touch the girl's worried face.

Oni caught her arm at the elbow. The touch sent a jolt of … something up into her shoulder. Something that didn't feel right. "Lie down, mistress," Oni said. Her voice cracked.

Bela shook. Something was wrong. "What—?"

"We did what we could," Oni said. "We didn't have a choice."

Bela read it in her maiden's eyes. She remembered the blizzards. The bear. She didn't need to look down. But she did.

There was a space, a void of cold air, where her right forearm had once been. The stump that remained, just below Oni's fingers at her elbow, was a bundle of bandages.

"I'm sorry," Oni whispered.

She was fighting tears, and Bela knew why. She'd never helm again. Not one-handed.

The fact struck Bela with such a remarkable clarity that, for a moment, it stopped her breath in her chest. But then she saw something else behind Oni's emotions, something that started her heart moving again. Devotion. Loyalty. Love.

With a conscious effort, Bela forced her right arm to relax. She lifted her left hand—her only hand—and brought her fingertips to Oni's cheek. It was an unfamiliar thing to touch her like this, but Bela was grateful for it. "You did well," she told her. It was true, though her jaw was tight as she fought to keep from weeping herself. "I would've ordered the same."

Oni closed her eyes and held Bela's hand to her cheek as she nodded.

I'll never again stand behind the wheel of my ship, she thought.

Your ship is gone, a voice replied.

The canvas flap at the other end of the shelter shook. Only then did Bela notice that they were alone beneath the boats.

At the sound, Oni opened her eyes and quickly wiped the tears from them to compose herself. "She's awake," she said over her shoulder.

The canvas split open, sending a blinding beam of light into the darkness. Bela gasped, instinctively tried to shield her eyes. But the nothingness where her hand had been did nothing to obstruct the brightness.

Fortunately, a moment later, a face blocked it out. Sanyu. "Good. We're ready to start."

At Oni's nod, Sanyu disappeared, and the flaps closed again. The maiden turned to Bela. "You need to try to get up, mistress."

"The blizzard broke?"

"Yesterday." She moved her hand to Bela's back again, to help her get moving. "Go slowly. It was a hard fever."

Sitting in the snow, Bela watched her crew break down the shelter. The morning sun was bright, but her thoughts were dark. She was their weakness now. As weak as a man.

No, she corrected herself. Weaker than that. Tewrick had two arms, and he was putting them both to use in helping the other women flip the two boats and reassemble their supplies in them. She had only one arm, and the difficulty of her ordeal had left her too weak even to walk.

And more than that, the man had saved her. He might've saved them all. When they had been screaming for Eshe to help during the attack, the girl had held herself and cried. So it had been the reader—the forgotten little man—who'd picked up the harpoon and charged out into the blizzard. With his help, they'd held the bear off long enough for Neka and Sanyu to pull her back inside. Then the bigger woman had grabbed the second harpoon, strode back out into the storm, and buried it in the beast's thick neck.

The bear's fat had made a fire hot enough to sear Bela's bloodied stump and fight back her fever. The truth was that they'd done well in that. Bela hadn't lied when she told Oni that she would've ordered the same.

The bear's fur skin was big enough for two cloaks: one for Neka, and one for Tew, who wore his with a pride that was strange to see. More important was what was beneath the skin: pounds and pounds of fresh meat. A welcome feast for the starving women, with enough to feed them for days to come.

The beast that had taken Bela's ship, her crew, and now her hand had also given them a chance at life.

Looking around, she noticed little sign of her struggle with the white monster. The storm had wiped it away. Beyond the bloodied pile of bones, all that she could see was a white blankness that reminded her of the dried sheets of parchment that made up the reader's books.

But where those pale sheets were covered in the black marks of ink that he could turn into the sounds of words, the vast plane of ice and snow was featureless, and the only sound was that of the wind.

It was almost as if the god of storms had wiped the world clean while they'd been beneath the overturned boats— erased it of people and their squabbles and their bloodshed, of everything but their small, forgotten troop, clinging to the barren, cold edge of the earth. Nothing else remained.

Oni ran a shadow line to determine the direction they needed to go. No one spoke of going anywhere but north. There was nothing behind them now. They all seemed to understand that. All that they could do was move forward, step by trudging step, until they found their place of rest.

The boats loaded, north known, Bela's crew hoisted her into a boat with what was left of the meat.

They began to walk.

19

The New Trees

Alira sat in the shadows, away from the bars of her cage, counting. When a hundred seconds had passed since the last of the Bloodborn footsteps, she unstrapped her face shield as quickly as she could and set it to the rope lashings that held her prison together. The Bloodborn had taken her weapons before they'd locked her inside, but they'd left her the flip-up fence of woven branches meant to help protect her, to help her blend into the forest. It was, for them, a mockery. One more sign of her failure to protect her people.

But while the tightly lashed pieces of cut wood were far from a weapon, Alira had discovered they could work as a kind of rudimentary saw—a blunt and fragile saw, but a reason for hope nonetheless.

Working it back and forth against the lashings, she could see, now and again, the smallest of fibers fraying.

It had been days. It would take days more.

Looking through the bars to Kora's cage, she saw that the younger girl was doing the same thing with her own face guard. Slower, though. The attack had snapped something in her shoulder, and the Bloodborn had no reason to help mend it or even provide her with a sling to ease the pain. With only one good arm, there was only so fast and so hard that she could move the wood.

No matter, Alira thought. Once she was out, she'd let Kora out too. The cages were simple things. The front opened by swinging up and was only kept from doing so by a single pole driven into the ground in front of the door— too tall and heavy for a prisoner to lift from inside, but simple enough to pull by a person standing on the outside.

The only question was whether she'd have enough time. It seemed clear that the Bloodborn—wherever they were taking their prisoners, whatever they were doing with them—were saving the two huntresses for last. Making them watch, helplessly, as the rest were taken away, not to be seen again. Mockery after mockery.

Alira sawed even harder against the lashings.

After she let Kora out, they'd open the rest of the cages together. Most of the other prisoners huddled in silent despair inside them—stares blank, unresponsive until they broke into panicked wails the moment they were pulled out and dragged away. But Alira had to believe that they would wake up, snap out of the clouds that lay heavy upon their minds, if she and Kora managed to open their cages and set them free. They'd fight. They had to.

After that—well, after that, there were a lot of unknowns. All Alira knew was what they could see from their cages and what they'd seen being dragged in.

It wasn't much.

They were upriver. That much seemed clear. After the attack, the Bloodborn had driven them uphill in the rain, herding them with fear and magick. It was a winding path, through some of the densest jungle Alira had seen on the island, but eventually it led to a village huddled at the foot of the interior mountains, up against the gorge of a river that could only be the one that ran down to Anjel. The initial part of the village could have been a twin for the one that she and Bela had found, so long ago: wood-walled homes perched on wooden stilts, lining a simple central road. Back then, the village had been abandoned, save for the Bloodborn evoker and the strange crystals hidden in a stone-built temple at the end of that road. Here, now, the village huts housed dozens of Bloodborn women, who smiled with sharpened teeth as they watched the new prisoners pass by. An old stone bridge arched over the river at the end of the road, then made two switchbacks up the higher bank on the other side to reach a great building of stone half-swallowed by the vines and trees of the jungle. It looked like part of the river had been diverted through the enormous building: a chute extended out through a rough-hewn hole in its side, and a weak stream trickled down from the end of it into the running waters below.

Whatever the strange building had been, it was a ruin now. The prisoners, taken inside, were led down a short corridor into what might once have been a great hall but was now a kind of large, open courtyard. A few rotting timbers, hung with moss and speckled with fungus and ferns, reached across the open space above them—skeletal ribs that whispered the memory of what had once been a roof.

The first things that had caught Alira's eye when they'd corralled her into the great hall were the two long, wooden planters that extended down each side of it. The planters were filled with dark dirt and a line of trees in various stages of growth. Cages for the prisoners—so many of them faces she'd never seen before—were lined up against either side of the planters, four rows in all. The cages were simple but effective: poles of wood lashed together with cords of rope, their back walls hanging over shallow trenches that pooled stinking piss and shit against the base of the planters.

Alira's initial thought for escape from her cage had, in fact, been the toilet trench itself. But it hadn't taken long to realize that there was stone beneath the excrement. It couldn't be dug deeper, and it was too shallow to serve as anything but a way to pass something from one cage to the one beside it—which could already be done through the open bars anyway.

The only way out would be to cut the ropes holding the cages together.

So Alira and Kora moved their face guards back and forth. Back and forth. Back and forth.

The building went on beyond the great hall, but when prisoners were taken into those farther corridors, only their screams returned. What was there, Alira didn't know. But she felt it was evil. Whatever it was, she was determined to destroy it once she escaped.

And the trees too.

As she'd sawed at the thick ropes during the stolen minutes between the passing of the guards, Alira had found herself staring at those trees in the planters. And every time she looked at them, she grew more fearful. They were upright, straight as arrows, like mature but impossibly shrunken Furywood trees. That alone was enough to summon memories of terror, but their leaves were unmistakable: white under green, but veined with shimmering gold.

They were the same kind of tree that she'd seen in the clearing where Whéuri and Bryt were lost.

A picture was emerging. Somehow—Alira suspected it had something to do with the power of the crystals they were collecting—the Bloodborn had grafted the Char-producing plants of the evokers to the Furywood burl. That's what they'd stumbled across, what had killed Bryt.

The Bloodborn had created a crossbreed: the strength of the Furywood made compact and small, then infused with the magick of Char.

She'd seen what a small band of the Bloodborn could do with their blood magick. What greater power these new trees could give them, she didn't want to contemplate.

She only wanted to see it destroyed.

A prisoner in another cage—one of a handful who were still awake, still willing to fight to survive—whistled quietly. Alira stopped sawing. She scooted to the other side of her cage and fastened her face guard back into position. To have it off would only raise suspicion.

Looking over, she could see that Kora had done the same. Cradling her bad arm, the younger woman gave her a single determined nod.

Moments later, one of the Bloodborn came into view. Alira, trying to seem as lifeless as the rest of the prisoners, watched her through the corner of her eyes.

It was someone new. That was clear at a glance. Most of the Bloodborn wore rag-like clothing, but this woman wore the sandals and red-orange robes that Alira instantly recognized as the clothes of a Seaborn evoker. She even had the same kind of small leather satchel at her hip, its strap crossed over to the opposite shoulder, which evokers used to carry the golden dust of their Char. For the briefest of heartbeats, Alira felt a surge of hope that somehow, word of the Bloodborn had reached the Spire on faraway Myst Wera, and that the High Sybyl had sent a powerful evoker to destroy them. But then she saw how the woman walked past the cages, indifferent to whether they were empty or occupied with broken prisoners.

And there was her hair, Alira abruptly realized. Every evoker she'd ever met or seen had been bald—a result, it was said, of their use of Char—but this woman had long, greasy, brown hair.

Had she somehow killed an evoker and stolen the woman's robes? More frightening, was she an evoker who'd joined the Bloodborn?

Whoever she was, the woman walked slowly down the path between the cages. She wasn't as old as Mabaya had been, but she carried herself with the same intimidating confidence of the *Black Crow*'s magicker. Everything about her made Alira's skin tingle with fear.

When the woman came close beside her cage, Alira focused on the satchel. Every evoker she'd seen had a mark branded upon the leather flap, denoting the school of her magick. The ember's triple flame of fire. The delver's mark of earth. The forger's of metal, or the drifter's of water. The Bloodborn women who'd attacked Anjel had been weavers of some sort—the rare evokers who could bind air. But they'd done it using blood, not Char. They'd not had satchels. This woman did. And it was marked with the five-limbed tree of a tender. She was an evoker of wood. Just like Mabaya.

Alira stared, uncomprehending, and only just managed to turn away when the Bloodborn woman seemed to sense her eyes and looked over.

It was only a moment. And then the woman stepped through a small path between two cages farther down the row. Lifting the forward edge of her robes almost daintily, she hopped over the stinking trench of refuse and up onto the tree-filled planter. Then she began walking carefully along its edge, examining the strange trees.

As slowly as she could, Alira shifted positions so she could better see what the woman was doing.

She had a knife in a sheath at her side, on the opposite hip from her satchel. Alira could see it now, as the woman pulled it free. A sliver of the thinnest blade she'd ever seen, it glinted as she moved past the trees, slicing a leaf from each as easily as it cut the air itself.

With every cut, there was a pale-yellow flash. Like the gold of Char, but less a physical dust than a shimmer of power being released. The woman smiled, a look on her face that Alira remembered from the faces of women just back from the sea, finishing their first mug of rum.

Now the woman paused in front of one of the most mature of the trees, not far from Alira's cage. She stared at it. Her lips moved in something that might have been a prayer. And then she raised her hands and wove in the air. No blood. No Char.

The tree's leaves shook and parted. Its branches spread, a sight that seemed almost obscene.

In glimpses past the woman's elbow and arm, Alira saw the trunk of the tree. At first, it looked like there was a thick knot there, the wound of some cutaway limb. But it was too large to have been the seat of a branch. And as the woman moved, Alira made it out more clearly. The tree was cracked open, split. The woman reached into that gaping wound, the exposed heart of the tree, and delicately pulled from it a single seed.

She waved her hands again, and the wound closed up, the branches relaxed, and the leaves—less luminous, less alive—sighed back into place.

The Bloodborn magicker, holding the seed between her fingers, brought it up into the light. Then, satisfied, she slipped it into the leather satchel.

Twice more, she took seeds from the trees. Twice more, they seemed to be dying in her wake.

And then her thin knife was at her side again, and she was gone, back into the farther recesses of the ruin, where prisoners were taken to scream and be silenced.

Staring at the trees, not understanding what she'd seen, Alira counted to a hundred. Then she pulled off her face guard and once more began to saw.

20

The Pillars of the Sky

As astonishing as they'd been from the air, the Pillars of the Sky were far more extraordinary from the ground. As the great mountains had grown closer, rising higher with every turn of the lumicker wagon's wheels, Shae had given a lot of thought to how she would describe them to her fellow pirates back in the Bay of Bones.

Picture an axe, she'd finally decided, driven through a plank. The blade blasted through the wood as hard and deep as a woman could drive it. Picture it stuck there. Now turn it over, blade to the sky. The plank, she would tell them, was the earth. The wall of that axe blade, sharp edge to the sky, was the line of the Pillars.

Now deep into the mountains, she still thought it was a good image, though the reality was that the Pillars were hardly a single wall. They were mountains rooted in mountains, an axe edge notched and chipped into a hundred great knives all pointed at the stars.

Ever since they'd left the open expanse of the Greensward, the road to the Blue Keep had been steadily climbing into those knives, twisting its way into them, higher and higher—a line of white-dusted gravel along loosely treed valley bottoms between the blades of the peaks and the noise of a tumbling river. For all the ice that clung to the mountainsides and the snow that covered their feet, the cascading water was still unfrozen.

Sitting beside Aro Lanser on the bench seat of his wagon, Shae shivered and pulled her wool-swaddled hands to her mouth to blow heat onto them.

"Told you to get full gloves," Aro said. "Fingerless gloves lead to fingertip-less fingers when winter comes this high up."

"So you've told me," Shae said. "And I told you that I feel better when I'm able to use my fangs."

Aro humphed at that, then moved the wagon team's reins to one hand so he could fish out a pipe with the other. "Ah, well, thank your gods we've had them at the ready."

Shae tried to glare at him, though she knew he was right. Not once in the many days they'd been together had anyone so much as shot a disapproving glance at the lumicker and the company he kept. What Kayden had said about how much people feared their weapons was true. Passing through some towns, she'd even seen people afraid to look the old man in the eye.

Aro passed her the reins, then used two hands to stuff his pipe with bits of loamy black weed before he pulled a metal cylinder from his pocket. A fire starter, he called it. Shae had seen Kayden use one to light the firepowder that destroyed his airship, and she'd stolen it from him. She watched Aro cup his hands around the bowl of the pipe, then pass the cylinder over it. The weed sparked to life, and he puffed it to health before pocketing the starter and taking back the reins. "Truth be told, I reckon you could use those fangs to get these hags moving faster, though."

Shae wasn't sure if he meant it as a joke or not, though it was true. The slivers of metal would put a kick in the animals' steps if they stuck into their backsides. Unless she dipped them in killing or sleeping poison, of course. And from this distance, she wouldn't even have to use her blowreed. She could pinch the fang between her first two fingers and fling it home.

"Thinking about it, aren't you?" Aro asked. He was smiling between the clenched teeth on his pipe.

Shae sighed, then nodded toward the river in the snowy valley. "Everything else is frozen. Why not that?"

"Hard to freeze moving water. Dead of winter, it'll go solid, though."

"You've been up here in winter?"

Aro puffed, nodded. "Been just about everywhere at every time, I think. But I'm glad to go back."

That the lumicker had decided to take her and Kayden to the Blue Keep had been a surprise. At first, he'd only agreed to take them to Homilden—he said he had business in that direction anyway—but once he'd gotten them to the town, he'd announced that his business, in fact, was at the Blue Keep itself.

It was quickly clear that the older man was simply too fascinated by her to leave. After that first night, when he'd learned the truth of what she was, there seemed to be no end to his questions about the Fair Isles and her place within them.

What were the Fair Isles like? Islands in a warm ocean, she decided.

Was the mask she wore as the Bone Pirate made from a real human skull? The front of one, yes.

What did the Bay of Bones look like? Like a river falling from a forest into a huge stone bucket with the ocean at the bottom.

Were there truly no men among her pirates? No, because cocks aren't useful for piracy.

On and on it went.

And, to his credit, he was more than happy to answer her questions too. Shae learned a great deal about the lumickers that "Shae of Felcamp" ought to have known. It was true that Aro didn't have a home beyond the wagon. No lumicker did. He'd been born in a small town called Crippledove, the fifth son of a fifth son of a farmer. Nothing about that made him special, but it did mean that he'd inherit the smallest share of his grandfather's small share. So Aro left, and time and chance—he was vague on the specifics but particular in his wording—brought him to Blackleaf, the Lumickers College. They took him in as someone to help in the kitchens, but he worked his way into an apprenticeship and then into a wagon of his own. He'd been making his random way through the land ever since. Lumickers, he explained, were like fallen leaves pushed about by the wind. The threat of the alumen meant there was always lumick work to be done somewhere. Locals paid them for repairs or for upgrades, if a lumicker had figured out something new that could be done with the crystals and the aluman parts.

Something new was, near as Shae could tell, his life's mission. Whenever his questions came back around to magick and what she knew of the Char, which was precious little, she suspected it was some foreign insight that he was after.

Even without such secrets from her, though, Aro claimed to be the finest lumicker in Aionia on this side of the Pillars. When she asked if there were lumickers on the other side of the Pillars, his only response was one side of his bushy grey mustache pinching in a lopsided grin.

"The Blue Keep is coming up soon," Aro said. "Best wake him."

Shae nodded. Sliding open the wooden half-door behind them, she peeked into the wagon's interior. Kayden was in the bed, just below, sleeping. While her own injuries were nearly healed, he still spent most of his time asleep as his body recovered.

She turned herself around and then shimmied her legs and hips through the opening. Arching her back, she managed to land her feet on the far side of the bed. Then she lifted and pulled her upper body through. Balancing through the bumps of the road that the wagon's mechanics couldn't absorb, she slid the door shut and then hopped down onto the floor of the wagon.

Aro had been generous in letting Kayden take the bed while the two of them rotated their nights between the bench and floor. It was a wagon built for one, which made it painfully cramped with three. She and Aro tried to spend as much time outside as the cold would let them. Even Kayden had been trying to come out more and more, as much as he could manage before the pain grew too great or his strength simply began to give out.

He was incredibly lucky to be alive. Half his ribs had been shattered, and an arm and a leg broken. He'd taken enough blows to the head to leave him dizzy for days even after he woke up.

But Aro had set the bones well, and he'd fashioned metal braces with straps to stabilize the arm and leg: a set for sleeping, and another set with gears that helped Kayden manage what mobility his body could stand.

He'd live. He'd be her Kayden again.

Her Kayden.

Looking at him in the dark, she wondered about that. How she'd begun to think of him as belonging to her somehow. It was an uneasy feeling, but she also couldn't deny that every time he managed to make his way down from the wagon to join her and Aro by a roadside fire, her heart whispered something that might be a song.

After hesitating for a moment, she reached out and touched his shoulder. He'd lost weight, but it was still a firm mass beneath her fingers. "Kayden," she whispered. "Wake up." She waited for a few seconds, then shook his shoulder more firmly. "Come on. Wake up."

When he groaned and shook his head, Shae let go of his shoulder and quickly stepped back with her hands at her sides. "You need to get up."

His head raised, his eyes blinking. "What?"

Shae rolled her eyes, then reached over to one of the shelves, where they'd taken to storing Kayden's mobility braces. She grabbed the arm one first. "Aro says we're getting close."

Kayden yawned, nodded, and then gingerly pulled himself up into a sitting position with his good arm. The blankets fell away into his lap, exposing his bare chest with its layers of bruising.

"They're looking better," she said. It was true. The bruises were still bad enough to make him look like he'd gotten into a fight with cups of paint—yellow and green, black and blue—but the splotches were clearly fading.

He tested the ribs with a deep breath, winced. "Still hurts on the inside," he said with a smile.

"Broken ribs don't heal quick," she said. She sat on the edge of the bed beside him. "Arm out."

Kayden helped her lift his broken arm away from his body so she could swap out the braces. "You've broken some?"

"Fell off the main mast beam once." Shae smiled at the memory as she carefully tightened the brace straps. "Landed on a barrel right next to one of the skin drums. Broke three ribs. Bone Pirate told me if I'd have broken the drum, she'd have used my skin to repair it."

"What?"

Shae blinked up at his shock. "That was a joke," she explained.

"Good. I was going to say—"

"The drums are far too large to stretch with a child's skin."

She finished the last strap, then stood up and got the leg brace. When she turned around, he was staring at her, his face caught between horror and amusement. "I keep saying I won't ever understand you. I keep hoping it won't be true. And yet ..."

Shae shrugged, and she held the leg brace out to him. "I'm the Bone Pirate," she said, as if it were the only explanation needed. "I was dead—"

"In the beginning," he said, completing the mantra for her. His eyes were kind, a look that seemed something like pity. "I know."

He reached out, his hand laying over hers on the leg brace. He gripped it. She didn't pull away.

"I just wish you'd give a shot at living too," he said.

Shae opened her mouth to speak, but then the wagon abruptly rumbled to a halt.

"You'll need to be coming out here," Aro said from up front. "Best to use the back door."

Shae nodded. Kayden was still touching her, his eyes fixed on her. "Both of us?" she asked.

"Kayden most of all. And if you could move slowly when you come on out, I'd appreciate it. We have guests."

Kayden smiled and moved his hand to another part of the brace. She let it go and turned to a different drawer as he started strapping the brace around his broken leg. "I'll set out some clothes," she said. "I don't have to tell you it's cold out there."

21

The Far Horizon

Bela had spent so much of her life running from the songs that had grown up around what she'd done as a girl—the deeds of Belakané, Hero of the Harbor—that it felt strange to be sad to know there'd be no songs of future deeds. No matron would give a ship to a woman who couldn't even turn its wheel, after all. No Seaborn girl would look upon Bela One-Hand and dream. What could she do now that was worthy of honor and memory?

She was so weak, so useless, that when she gave up her seat on the second boat to begin walking, it felt like a triumph.

Oni, of course, had pleaded with her to remain seated, to let them keep pulling her along with the supplies. It had only been a couple of days, she insisted. Bela had lost so much blood, and she didn't weigh that much to begin with, so ...

Bela had nodded and gotten out anyway. She'd walked to the lead of the first boat and taken hold of the rope with her one remaining hand. She'd tried to pull. She was determined to prove—to her crew, to herself—that she still had strength enough. That she wasn't useless.

But she was. The crew said nothing. They pulled alongside her and let her feel she was helping. But by some unspoken signal, they took their next breather early. And when they rotated positions to begin anew, there wasn't a free spot to pull. Even Tewrick had a place on the lines.

So as they pulled ahead, she fell behind, trudging along on the smooth band of snow that the passing boats had packed down.

Even then, it took all her willpower to keep moving one foot in front of the other, to not just lie down in her exhaustion and let the blowing snow cover her over in a blanket of white.

Step by step.

Minute after minute.

Hour after hour.

Two days later, around midday, Bela was so lost within the cold stillness of her mind that she nearly stumbled into the boat ahead of her when it stopped unexpectedly.

She shook herself as if waking from a dream, trying not to weep at the imbalance of her missing arm. It was a day of little wind, of blue skies and bright snows. Bela blinked against the light, trying to make out her crew ahead.

They'd dropped the ropes. And they'd all gone forward to stand in a kind of line around Sanyu, who'd been in the lead of the first boat.

As Bela looked up at them, Oni was turning back around to look at her. The maiden's face beamed with joy. "Come quick!" she shouted. And then, before Bela could respond with even a single step, Oni was running back to help her shipmistress make her way forward through the unbroken snow around the sides of the boats.

"What is it?" Bela asked.

"You'll see," the younger woman said. "You'll see."

The crew parted when Bela came up to them, gave her pride of place in the middle of their line. Sanyu pointed, as if to help them believe.

At the horizon, cutting into the blue sky like icy teeth, were the crisp edges of sharp peaks.

"Ealond," Tewrick said, and his voice broke the spell of their astonishment. Neka began to laugh, a deep and rumbling sound. Malaika did too. Oni, her arm already around Bela to help hold her up, pulled her into an embrace that seemed to go on for minutes. Even Tewrick got a hug from Sanyu.

"Let's push hard today," Bela said when they finally began to quiet down. "Try to get only a few miles offshore and then stop for the night. The ice may be fissured and broken as we get close, so we'll want full light and a full day for the final bit tomorrow."

To her relief, no one argued. Whatever she'd lost when she'd lost the arm, they still listened to her for now.

The next day, Bela didn't walk behind the boats. Though she didn't have the strength to pull them, she was determined to guide them. So she walked ahead, watchful for any sign of fissures, listening for any hint of cracking or shifting ice.

To her relief, the only thing she could hear was the growing sound of braying, a cacophony of untuned horns.

"What is it?" Oni was leading the pull on the first boat, closest to her mistress.

"Is it another bear?" Eshe asked.

Bela tried not to cradle the stump of her right arm. "The one that attacked me didn't sound like that."

"Seals," Malaika called up from the second boat. "I think it's seals."

Bela nodded, then waved them on.

Only an hour later, they crossed over what seemed like a swale in the icy landscape. And then they were there.

Ealond.

To the left and the right, the land abruptly rose up from the frozen sea in jagged escarpments of fierce stone, cragged and broken, with menacing shadows and hanging ice, that quickly built to the towering mounts they'd seen the previous day. But here, where chance or the Mother's mercy had led them, there was a shoreline rough with rocks and drifted with snow, yet more welcoming than the impenetrable walls of the land that they could otherwise see. And on the stone-beach shoreline, massed in a noisy herd, were hundreds of fat, braying seals.

They'd been sparing with the bear meat, so the sight of so much potential food made Bela's stomach speak up with sudden, sharp pangs. And the thought of the warmth of the oil in their blubbery hides made her one remaining arm shiver.

"Mother bless us," Oni said, looking at them and surely having some of the same thoughts.

Neka laughed, saying she was ready to eat one raw. Bela wasn't certain it was a joke.

"All right," Bela said, trying to focus them away from any immediate hunger, "let's get the boats ashore. Then let's see about a good meal."

Her crew needed no further encouragement. They quickly had the two outboats pulled up onto the shoreline, the wooden hulls scraping across its rough, rocky sand. A few bulls trumpeted at them, but the reaction of the beasts was otherwise one of annoyance at being disturbed.

"Why don't they try to get away?" Eshe asked.

"I don't think they've ever seen people," Tewrick replied. "They don't know to fear us."

"Don't know *yet*," Malaika said. She was weighing the sword in her hand and grinning. Bela cleared her throat, still intent on maintaining the order in the group.

"Neka, Tew, Sanyu, Eshe—let's get these boats as far up the shoreline as possible. Malaika and Oni—the two of you take the swords. Head downwind. Go as far as you can, to the most distant and isolated beast you can find. Don't split up, and don't get greedy. We don't want our food to get the idea of fighting back."

"Aye, shipmistress," Oni said. "It'll be quick and quiet-like. These pups here won't know what happened."

"Good. Step to it, then. Don't know about the rest of you, but I'm starving."

Oni and Malaika headed down the shoreline while the rest of them maneuvered the outboats up through the maze of noisy animals and then sat down on the rocks.

It wasn't long before Malaika was back.

Bela, despite her exhaustion, stood to receive the veteran woman's report. "Find one?"

Malaika grinned and held up the sword. The edge was

still wet with blood. Someone's stomach rumbled loudly, and Bela wasn't sure whether it was her own or not.

"That's not all we found," Malaika said. "Come see."

The animals shuffled around them as Bela followed Malaika down to the far end of the shoreline, where a sheer cliff of granite cut across the beach before crumbling into black boulders in the white of the frozen sea. The two women had done as Bela ordered. Near the base of the cliff, far from the other animals, lay the carcass of a freshly killed seal.

But Oni wasn't beside it. She was instead standing some yards away, leaning back against the stony wall, smiling. Malaika nodded Bela toward her before going over to their kill.

Bela cocked her head, confused, but as she got closer, she saw that there was a jagged rift in the rocks beside her maiden. Tall enough for a person to pass through, and wide enough at its base to fit an outboat. "A cave?" she asked.

Oni pushed off the cliff wall and gave a nod. "Wait until you see inside, mistress."

The two of them stepped through, blinking at the sudden dark after the bright light of the sunny ice outside. Not far inside, the cut in the rock opened up into a roomy cavern almost fifteen strides square with a floor of coarse sand.

Looking up, Bela saw how the outside rift was a jagged crack across the ceiling. She reached up with her one hand and felt the air circulating in through the entrance and up to some higher point in the rocks above them.

"Are you thinking what I'm thinking?" Oni asked.

Bela nodded. "Good airflow. And wherever this crack leads, it looks bent and broken."

"We can clamshell the boats against the entrance," Oni said. "Then tie the canvas rigging across the hulls to form a door. A bit more upright than we had out on the ice, but Sanyu will figure it out."

Malaika walked in, holding the first cut of the still-steaming seal meat. "Nice place, shipmistress?"

"It is."

Oni was still looking up at the crack. "We think it'll work for a chimney."

There was blood on Malaika's teeth as she grinned and held up the blubbery, oily chunk of flesh in her hands. "Then let's try it out."

22

The Blue Keep

As soon as Shae stepped down from the wagon, she understood why Aro wanted them to move slowly. It wasn't just worry for Kayden's health.

There were two men behind the wagon, dressed in snow-dusted furs and armed with bows. Two more stood on either side of the wagon. All of them were watching her warily. Glancing around the rear corner, she could see that there were four more men across the road in front: two on foot, and two more on horseback, carrying long spears. One of them, older and taller, wore armor under the fur at his shoulders. Long-faced and lean, he had a black eye patch over a scar that ran from his thinning white hair into the white beard of his chin. From the way he held himself and the way the others looked at him, he seemed to be the man in charge. Shae took note of that.

She also took note that the wagon had been stopped where the road turned in a stretch of closely packed pine trees. An excellent place for an ambush, and she chastised herself for being inside with Kayden instead of being outside where she might have been able to help somehow.

After a minute, the wagon creaked. Kayden appeared at the rear door, wearing the wool clothes and the wide fur cloak that she'd laid out for him. The thick garb already hid his injuries well, but when he saw the armed men, he visibly straightened his back, as if he had no pains at all.

"Gentlemen," he said, nodding at the two men. They didn't respond.

Shae reached up and offered her arm to help Kayden manage. Face tight—she could sense his pain—he accepted the help only to the bottom of the stairs. Then he shook himself free of her and tucked his cloak behind the sword strapped to his side. It brought the handle of the blade into easy reach. Perhaps more important, Shae thought, it exposed the handcannon that was also strapped to his hip.

The brace on his leg was hinged at the knee—Aro wasn't boasting when he said he could do amazing things with aluman parts—but it still gave Kayden a slight hobble as he made his way toward the front of the wagon. Shae walked beside him, ready to defend him if they attacked—or to catch him if his strength gave out.

When they reached the front of the wagon, Shae saw that Aro Lanser was leaning back in his seat, his long coat over his chest, his left hand nursing his pipe. His wide-brimmed hat was cocked back on his head as if to give him a better view of the men in front of him. Relaxed, he puffed a cloud of smoke, then pulled the pipe out of his mouth to use it as a pointer. "Kayden Mar of Felcamp," he said, "may I introduce the sneaky bastards of the Blue Keep."

Ignoring Kayden and Shae, the older man with the eye

patch looked over to the lumicker. "Sneaky bastards that snuck up on you, old man."

Aro's mustache twitched; then he used his pipe to push his cloak aside. His boltgun was firmly in the grip of his other hand, and the barrel of it was clearly pointed at the other man's chest. "That one's Oth Marek, Kayden. Captain of the keep's guard. You'll want to keep an eye on him, since he's missing one."

Marek's smile bent the line of his scar. "What brings you back here, Lanser?"

The lumicker settled his boltgun back into its holster and pulled his furs close as he crossed his arms under them to get warm again. "Just bringing your new lord."

The captain turned his one eye back to Kayden. His face was unreadable. "You're Kayden Mar of Felcamp?"

"I am."

"Had word you were coming." Marek looked him up and down. If it was an appraisal of worth, he did not seem impressed. "Our latest lowland lord."

A couple of the guardsmen to the captain's left didn't even try to hide their amusement, and Kayden turned to them. "You have a problem with King Mark's commands?"

The two looked uncomfortable. "Begging pardon, my lord," one of them managed. "We just—"

"You just go through a lot of lords," Kayden said.

"Yes, my lord."

"And the last one? Was there anything impressive about him?"

The captain answered for them. "The last one could scream loud enough to set loose a snowslide. Found that out when an aluman ripped him into several pieces."

Aro made a scoffing sound. When Marek looked over at him, Aro pulled something from his pocket and tossed it down to Shae. "Hold it up now," the lumicker said.

Shae's stomach lurched when she saw the crystal in her palm, but she held it up for them to see.

"Soulglass," Marek said. "Blue Keep has plenty powering its defenses. You've helped fix some of them, Lanser."

"So I have," the lumicker said. "Which is why I know the keep doesn't have what this crystal will power."

"What's that?"

"Something new." Aro's eyes twinkled with almost childlike excitement.

"New?"

The lumicker nodded. "And all thanks to Lord Kayden here. And Lady Shaesara. They're the ones who killed the aluman whose heart she holds before you."

The men surrounding the wagon seemed to be looking at them more closely now. It made Shae uncomfortable.

"And you're Lady Shaesara, I take it?" Marek asked.

Shae opened her mouth to deny it—she was the Bone Pirate, by Ti'nay's tricks, not a *lady*—but the lumicker cut her off.

"A lady she is," Aro said. "But no need to stand on ceremony. Shall we head up to the keep, Lord Kayden?"

Kayden looked between the lumicker and the one-eyed man, then nodded. "Yes. Much to see and do. You'll take us to the keep directly, Captain Marek."

"As you wish, my lord."

Marek and his fellow man on horseback turned their steeds to head up the road. The other guards around them pulled back and quickly disappeared into the snowy woods.

When Kayden turned and headed to the wagon, Shae stayed close beside him. To her relief, he only needed help when he made it to the steps. She assisted him as best she could without appearing to do so. There was no question that they were still being watched.

With Kayden inside, Shae climbed in to join him and shut the door. As soon as it was closed, Kayden's energy gave out. He braced himself against the stove, and Shae reached out to help take his weight. She led him up to the bed, where he sat down heavily.

Beneath them, the wagon's wheels began to turn again.

"You did great," Shae said. She helped get the fur cloak off his shoulders.

"You, too, my lady."

Kayden was smiling despite his pains. Shae just rolled her eyes and pushed him back into the blankets. "We'll talk about *that* when we get there. Which might not be long. Rest while you can."

Kayden nodded, and closed his eyes.

Shae set his cloak to the side, took one last, lingering look at him, and then climbed up and through the half-door to join Aro on his bench seat up front.

"Well," the older man said, "I'd say that went well."

"It did?"

The lumicker puffed at his pipe. "First impressions are important. The lad did well. He's resting now?"

Shae nodded.

"Good," he said. "Proud of you both. Almost enough to bring tears to the eyes. Those of us with two of them, anyway."

He laughed through his pipe, and Shae laughed too. The

sound felt good. A kind of warmth against the cold. Captain Marek and his companion, riding ahead of them, looked back at the noise, but they didn't say anything.

"Oh," Shae said, reaching into her pocket and finding the crystal. "This is yours."

The lumicker took it with a nod, placing it into a pocket of his own somewhere under his heavy cloak of fur. "Meant what I said, you know."

"What's that?"

"I've got special plans for this one. Something new."

"I'll look forward to it."

Aro Lanser smiled around the pipe in his teeth; then his grey eyebrows raised up toward the rim of his hat. "And there it is."

Shae followed his gaze forward, past the wagon team and the men riding ahead.

The pine trees were giving way in an arcing line, like an army whose march had finally ended. Beyond was a narrowing flat, framed by slab-like walls of mountain that hung their heads in cloud. The river, dwindling to a stream, still twisted its way along the floor up toward a saddle between the peaks. There was a stone wall there, grey and black, reaching into the faces of cliffs on either side of the valley. The road they were following switchbacked to it, then bent as it got close and cut into the angular walls of a keep nestled on the south side of the pass. A single tower climbed free of the fortifications, a square with high buttresses like spurs at its corners and a tattered red banner hanging down its side. At its top, the long, sleek shape of an airship floated at a mooring tower.

"The Blue Keep," Shae whispered.

"So named for its lumick defenses," Aro said. "Can't see them from here, of course."

"They all face the other side?"

"The lands where the alumen live." He pulled deep on his pipe. "Folks call it lots of different names, you know. I call it death."

23

The Dreamthief

A girl who expected to become salted learned early how to tie the four knots of the sea. Every woman aboard a ship was expected to know them, to be able to tie them without thinking, as easy as breathing. Most girls learned to tie them blind.

For days now, in moments when she thought the other women weren't looking, Bela had been trying to tie just one—it didn't matter which—with her one remaining hand.

Not once had she succeeded.

She sat with her back to the warm stone wall, knees up to hide what she was doing, holding the untied line of cord in her lap.

Bela took a deep breath and forced herself to look away from the cord, to think beyond darkness and loss. She looked up at her crew.

It was remarkable how quickly the cave that they'd found had become a home. They'd dug a trench for refuse, running out to the shore. They'd collected two oil barrels full of fresh fuel and pounds of new meat. They'd brought in fist-size rocks to enclose a small burning pit dug into the middle of the chamber. They'd brought in larger stones to serve as chairs surrounding it. Her crew sat around on them now, talking and laughing at old stories and older lies, their faces glowing with the steady, radiating heat of the fire between them.

Bela tried to smile at the sight. She'd led them here. She was still their shipmistress, even if she didn't have a ship. Even if she didn't have two hands to helm one if she did. It was her duty. Her honor.

And thinking of it helped keep the darkness at bay, as long as she didn't dwell upon the faces who hadn't made it, or her uncertainty of what to do next.

Her gaze crossed the room to Tewrick, who was sitting farther away from the fire—close enough to still have light to read by, but far enough to keep the thick black smoke of the burning fats from staining his books.

Gripping her cord, Bela stood and walked over to sit down beside him. "Are you well, Tew?"

His face seemed to redden beyond the glowing red light of the fire, as if he were blushing. Had he never had a woman ask after his well-being?

"I'm well, shipmistress. And you?"

Bela saw how his eyes glanced to where her shirt sleeve was tied off just below the elbow. She tried to pretend like she didn't notice. "I'm fine, thank you, reader. Just wanted to come check up on you."

He looked over to where the women were laughing. "I don't really fit in," he said.

One of his books sat beside him on the floor. Bela knew the rules about non-readers handling scripts, so when she picked it up, she did so with careful movements. It was heavier than she expected as she turned and rotated it in her one hand like the foreign thing it was. Finally, she sighed and gingerly set the book down. "I think you're right," she said.

Smiling, the reader picked the book back up and flipped it over, opening it up to the middle. "I can teach you, you know."

The words were matter-of-fact, as if he were talking about the weather or his shoes, but Bela's eyes winced and darted to the other women, instinctively fearing the idea of being caught thinking about such a thing. But none of the crew was paying any attention to them. And there were no Spire guards around to arrest her anyway. "No," she said, trying to keep the nervousness out of her voice. "I'm too old. You need to start young."

Tewrick shrugged. "You don't need to, but it helps. Most readers do."

Bela thought for a moment, not quite sure how to ask what she wanted to know. "How long ago did you …?"

Tewrick smiled at her uncertainty. "I struck another boy when I was seven. They cut me shortly after that. Thanks be to the Mother, I was sent to the readers, not the bent-men."

"The bent-men are important," Bela said. "We all have a role." It was an almost involuntary reflex to repeat the dogma she'd learned in her youth. "The tenders help the zambaru plants grow. The bent-men quarry their taproots for the Char. And the Char is necessary for the magick of the tenders."

"Yes, shipmistress."

Bela frowned at his sudden deference, realizing he must

have thought that she had rebuked him. "But I agree that it's better to be a reader," she said. "Safer."

"That it is." His body seemed to relax a little. "Anytime I felt tired or uncertain about my work as a scriptor, I would think about those men in the rootfields: bent double, scraping Char, trying not to breathe their death of it. A terrible life, I think."

"You were really seven?"

"Seven."

"And you were … cut for striking someone? Isn't that …?"

"I hit him with a rock. I was angry."

"Oh."

"And anyway, things were harsher at Kol Bannok, where I grew up. I just count myself lucky to have survived the cutting. Many don't. And I've done well as a reader, I think. I was lucky there too: Kol Bannok had the biggest scriptorium in the Isles before it burned, and becoming a scriptor is why I wasn't there when the Windborn came. I was already at the Spire."

"A reader once told me the biggest scriptorium was in Kol Mithtor."

Tewrick grinned mischievously. "Then he lied."

Bela laughed a little at that, for a moment forgetting her own anxieties and hesitancy. "So what are you reading now?"

"This? It's a book of old stories."

"Stories of this place? Stories of our ancestors?"

"The stories are old," he said, "but not so old as that. They're after the people came to the Isles, I think. At least some of them are. This one I've been reading is called 'The Weaver and the Dreamthief.' It's set in the Isles."

"I've never heard of it," Oni said.

Startled, Bela looked up and saw that her maiden had come over to join them. Behind her, the others were still talking. Oni smiled, and Bela felt suddenly aware of how she hadn't brought her into her bed since the bear's attack.

"It's about the danger of delaying payment," the reader said.

Oni's hand found Bela's leg. A gentle touch. But Bela felt the longing behind it. "Is it a good one?" the maiden asked.

"It is," Tewrick replied, looking at the book.

Oni slipped into the embrace of Bela's good arm and settled against her. If she was disgusted by the weakness of what remained of the other—or disgusted at the mere sight of it—she didn't show it. She cuddled up against Bela, her back to her chest, and Bela wiggled her nose into her hair. Oni pinched her playfully in response. "So, delaying payment," she said. "Is that like promising to pay for something tomorrow instead of doing it today?"

The reader smiled. "Exactly so," he said, and he opened his book.

There was once a weaver who had a great desire to be initiated in dreamthievery.

Hearing a whisper that a woman in Borhays knew more of this forbidden art than anyone else, the weaver came to Borhays in secret, hoping to learn from her. On the day she harbored, she walked at once toward the house where she'd learned the woman was living. It was raining, but she so feared being recognized that she dared not even raise a weaving to drive the water from her face.

She found the dreamthief sitting in her rooms. The woman greeted her most graciously, asking only that she hang her wet coat before dripping on the rugs. Then she offered her a chair and tea to help her warm up from the rain. At last, the weaver told the woman the true reason for her visit, begging that she be instructed in the art.

The dreamthief worried that the weaver might betray her, so she was reluctant to admit her powers. But the weaver was insistent, and earnest in her desire to learn.

"Very well," the dreamthief said. "But there is something that you must do for me in return."

"Name it," the weaver said. "Name it and I swear it will be done."

"You are a woman who could come to power through my knowledge," the dreamthief said. "But I fear that you are also a woman who would forget the one who gave it to you."

The weaver swore that this could never be, and so the dreamthief assented to teach her of her powers. It was near the evening meal, and the dreamthief called her servant boy and told him to prepare some rich fish for her and her guest, but not to cook them until she gave him the command. The boy agreed and left. Then the dreamthief began to tell the weaver how she practiced dreamthievery.

No sooner had this begun than word came to the house that a sybyl not far away had fallen gravely ill. The letter grieved the weaver greatly, not only for the fact that the sybyl was someone she knew, but also for the fact that leaving to pay her respects would bring her new studies to a halt. In the end, the weaver decided to stay in Borhays with the dreamthief.

A few days later, another letter managed to find the weaver, informing her that the sybyl had died, and that a successor was soon to be chosen. According to the letter, she herself was foremost among those under consideration by the Sybyl Council. The weaver was sad for the loss of her friend, but she took some comfort in her potential advancement.

A week passed, and two finely dressed women arrived in Borhays. The weaver went out to meet them, and they honored her as the new sybyl of Pallennor. The weaver was very happy, and word of this turn of events quickly spread through the town. So it was that the dreamthief came to her, joyed at her great fortune, and asked her if she remembered their agreement.

"I swore that I would not forget," the weaver said.

"Then I ask that as sybyl, you make my daughter the weaver of Borhays," said the dreamthief.

"If only you had come sooner with this request," the weaver said with a sigh. "I have already set aside this position for another. But I'm a woman of my word, and I will find another position for your daughter. We will continue our studies, and my new place as sybyl will reveal an even better post for your daughter."

The weaver and the dreamthief left Borhays together. The new sybyl was received with much honor at her new home, and she proved a good and able leader. The dreamthief continued to teach the weaver of her forbidden arts, and she daily asked her to provide some appointment for her daughter, but the weaver always found a reason not to do so.

It was not long before messengers came from the High

Sybyl. The former weaver had succeeded so well in her role as a mystic that she had been appointed to the Spire. Furthermore, the High Sybyl entrusted her with naming her own successor.

When the dreamthief heard this, she reminded the weaver of her promise, urging that her daughter be named the new sybyl. The former weaver declined to do so, but she assured the dreamthief that there would be an even greater future reward for her services. The dreamthief felt she was unjustly treated, but she agreed to accompany the weaver still further.

No sooner had they reached the Spire than the High Sybyl died. The Sybyl Council gathered, and they elected the newly arrived weaver to this greatest position of power. Great celebrations and revelries were held. She was seated as High Sybyl over Land and Sea, and she was pleased at how much she had managed in so short a time. She quickly forgot about the withered old woman from Borhays.

So it was a surprise to the former weaver when the dreamthief, hunched and broken, slowly approached her gilded throne one day. The tapping of the old woman's simple wooden cane in the great throne room seemed a mockery of the splendid jeweled scepter in the weaver's hand.

"What are you doing here, old woman?" the new High Sybyl asked.

"I've come for my payment," the dreamthief said.

"I don't know what you're talking about," the weaver said. She waved her hand, crafting a weave of air that pushed against the older woman.

The dreamthief took a step backward, but she did not

leave. "We made a bargain, and I desire my daughter to take your former position in the Spire."

"You know that I cannot do this thing for you," the High Sybyl scoffed.

"But you made a promise," said the dreamthief.

"Hastily made long ago. I owe you nothing, and I've tired of your presence and your constant requests. Perhaps you should leave."

The dreamthief did not move. "I've learned not to have faith in your words."

"You can have faith in these," she replied. "You're a heretic. You'll leave this place, or I shall call out the guard."

The old woman's face sank, and at last she turned to go. But she took only a few hesitant steps toward the door before looking back toward the throne.

"The journey to Borhays is a long one," she said in a tired voice. "Would you at least provide me with some food for my journey, in return for the services I have rendered?"

"You've done nothing for me that I couldn't do myself," the High Sybyl said with a scornful laugh. "I'll give you nothing but death if you remain."

The dreamthief straightened her back, no longer the withered woman. "In that case," she said, "I believe I shall have to eat the fish that I ordered for this evening."

No sooner had she spoken than they were once again in Borhays. She was no longer the High Sybyl. She was still a mere weaver, sitting in a chair by the dreamthief's fire. Her wet cloak was still hanging from the bronze hook on the wall. What was left of her tea was still warm.

Thus, it is said, the weaver's promise was proven a lie,

and a lesson was left: For the one who repays ungratefully, the more she has, the less she'll give.

"I like that story," Bela said when the reader finished. "A good lesson."

Bela was holding Oni tight around the waist, but her maiden craned her neck around to look at her. Her gray eyes were clouds that Bela knew she could lose herself in. "Agreed," the younger woman said. "Which is a good time to remind you of a promise you made earlier. A reward for finding Ealond."

The shipmaiden winked, and then she was slipping out of Bela's arm and moving back to Bela's bed of sealskins.

Bela, turning back, saw that the reader had been watching her go too. He caught her eye and immediately lowered his gaze to the ground. "This man is sorry," he stammered. "Your pardon is—"

"Oh, stop that," Bela said. "She's a beautiful woman."

There was a crinkle of a smile on the edge of Tewrick's face, but he erased it before he looked up. "It is not a man's place."

"It's a man's place if she says it is."

"It's not this man's place," he said.

"Because you're cut?"

Even as she said the words, Bela wondered if she shouldn't be so direct. But the reader managed a smile. "The cutting takes away much of the desire," he said, "but I can still perform if called upon. It would simply be fruitless, which is the reason for a man and woman to be as one. There is nothing I can offer a woman that you cannot offer each other—and without the soil of being with a man."

It was the way of things. A truth taught across the Fair Isles. Being with a man was an act of necessity, the burden of being a matron. Not one of the women here would have ever been with a man. They had each other for such needs. No breeding of children among them. Just the breeding of loyalty, of the connections that made one woman wish to sacrifice for another. For good reason, every shipmistress had her maiden.

Bela knew this. It felt right.

But she also knew that there'd been a time when she'd had other thoughts—the very thoughts that had made her pull away from her friend Alira in the moments before a Windborn bomb had destroyed their ship. Those had felt right too.

"You're a good man," she finally said. "You're worth more than you believe."

"I'm just a—"

"No," Bela said. "You saved my life. I'm in your debt."

He seemed to catch the look of seriousness in her eye, as he didn't object. "Thank you, shipmistress."

"Good. Now, I want you to take care of these books of yours."

Tewrick looked down at the book in his hand. "The journey has indeed been hard on them."

"Hard on us all."

"True," he said.

"And it'll probably get harder," Bela said quietly.

The reader's eyebrows lifted, but he said nothing.

It was now Bela's turn to grin with a glint in her eyes.

"You didn't think I'd make it all the way to Ealond just to stop here, did you?"

24

The Lumick of the Keep

Shae stood on a wide stone wall between worlds. The sun was setting down the long valley that stretched behind her to the west—back down the road they'd come—and it cast the black line of the wall's shadow across the valley that stretched forward to the east, toward the wide lands where only wild beasts lived with the alumen.

The chill of the mountain night was growing with the darkness. A wind rolled down off the icy cliffs, pushing snow dust along the paving stones at her feet. Shae pulled her furs closer to her body, but she didn't leave. Not yet. She couldn't stop staring at the foot of the wall, at the graveyard of metal men, washed in eerie blue light.

Aro had said that the lumick works were impressive on this side of the Blue Keep, but she was still stunned by what lay before her. Cables, humming with pale blue light, were bolted across the face of the wall. Still more ran between poles rooted across the ground, a maze of lumicklines above a crisscrossed tangle of trenches whose waters were frozen into flat vines fingering across the valley floor. And everywhere—slumped in the trenches, awkwardly caught in the web of cables at the base of the wall, or rising higher upon it where piles of the dead had been used as steps—the metal shells of monsters gleamed in a blue light that seemed to grow brighter as darkness fell.

"Quite something," a voice said.

Shae shook her eyes away from the valley and turned to see the captain of the guard, Oth Marek, stepping out from the door of the rising keep itself. On foot, he somehow seemed even taller than he'd been on horseback. His white hair, which had been tied back, was now loose around his shoulders. When he joined her at the wall, he set his black-gloved hands to it and looked out over the scene. The pale blue reflecting up from the frozen alumen made the lines of his face look like black canyons.

"I've never seen anything like it," she admitted.

"Few have."

"Not a lot of visitors? I'm surprised, given the scenic view."

Marek grinned. "You can come to enjoy it."

"How long have you been here, Captain?"

"Three decades and more." He seemed to take a sniff of the cold air as it breezed by. "I came here young."

Shae looked around at the high walls of the peaks around them. "A hard place to grow up."

"Same could be said of any place," he said. "This one is just a place where you die if you don't. And sometimes you die even if you do. The Blue Keep isn't for the weak."

Something about his tone made her look back at him. "You're worried about me?"

"You? No, I think you can handle yourself." He shook his head, then looked back down across the detritus below the wall. After a moment, he pointed a long finger toward an aluman that was splayed face up across a patch of snow, its chest ripped open. "See that one? It came about a month ago. Sometimes they come in twos or threes. Years ago, there was a swarm of them, a dozen, climbing over each other as they came at the wall, ripping through the lines with their dying breaths—or whatever the accursed things have for breath. That one there, though, it came alone. It wasn't like a lot of the others, which blunder along to their death. This one was careful. It watched where it went. It seemed aware, and that made it the most frightening thing I'd ever seen."

"But you killed it."

Marek reached into the pocket of his cloak and pulled out a crystal of soulglass. "Lanser isn't the only one who carries a charm like this," he said. For a moment, he sounded boastful, but his remaining eye was dark, his face grim. "This one came at a heavy price, though. It got close enough we mounted boltguns to the wall. Shot it. Tried to pin it down or knock it off into the wires or the water. Eventually it fell, went down and didn't move. A few of us went out to pillage it. Our latest lowland lord went with us. But the aluman wasn't dead. When we got close, it attacked. Killed my men. Ripped the lord in two."

"You're worried about Kayden, then?"

He shrugged and slipped the soulglass back into its pocket. "I know a proud man when I see him, my lady. Tell him his pride will get him killed here."

"He's a good man, Marek."

"That may be, but he's no good to anyone dead. And you least of all."

"Me?"

"My men are good fighters," he said. "They know their place. But there's not been a woman at the Blue Keep since before my time. If Lord Kayden were to fall—"

"You're worried about some cock getting between my legs?"

The old man's jaw dropped. However he expected her to respond, it clearly wasn't with such direct speech. "My lady, I—"

"Look, Captain, you don't need to worry about me if it comes to that. One of your boys comes after me, and it's him you'll need to worry about."

Marek looked at her, Shae thought, with something like respect. "I'll be leading a short hike tomorrow," he said. He nodded north, toward the icy mountains. "A check of the lines around the northern reach. I'll be asking Lord Kayden to join me. We'd welcome you coming, too, if you'd like."

Shae looked up at the cold cliffs in the dark. Kayden couldn't walk the length of the wall in his current condition. There was no way he could make a climb up into the peaks, but she was beginning to get a feel for how wrong it was to show weakness among these men of battle. It felt surprisingly like home to her. "I'd like that, Captain. Thank you."

Marek pushed himself off the wall. "Ah, anyway, I'd forgotten what I came out to tell you. Aro Lanser was asking for you. He's taken up shop down by the courtyard. Should be easy to find: just keep taking the stairs down, and you'll get there." He turned and started to walk away. "But if you do get lost, ask anyone you run into, and they'll point you the way."

Shae had known few buildings before Kayden brought her to Aionia. What time she hadn't passed on ship she'd spent in the cave-like rooms cut into the sheer walls of the Bay of Bones. Finding one's way there wasn't hard—if it wasn't on one level, a girl took the lift beside the waterfall to the next one.

Aionia's buildings were, in contrast, a jumble of rooms and halls and stairs. Perhaps not too different from the Seaborn buildings in places like the Merchanter's Maze on Myst Wera, but she hadn't really known such places as a pirate.

Oth Marek was nevertheless right that the Blue Keep was simple enough to navigate. The levels of the building were separated by stairs that doubled back on themselves—one set to the north and one to the south. And the levels themselves seemed sensibly organized: barracks and baths above a hall, and kitchens for eating atop storerooms and work rooms. It wasn't hard at all for Shae to find her way down to the open courtyard—a square space surrounded by stables and workshops. From there, the familiar sight of the lumicker's wagon showed her the way.

Opening the door to the shop beside the wagon, Shae was met with a wash of welcome warmth. It was a large room, deep and wide, packed with shelves and tables that were jumbled with the metal pieces of alumen—far, far more than she'd seen tucked away in the wagon. In the back, against the rear of the space, a ready forge glowed with heat.

"Close the door!" Aro called out.

Shae startled at the sound, but she closed the door against the cold. Walking around a particularly crowded shelf, she saw the lumicker hunched over the dismantled remains of an aluman's head. His hat and coat were nowhere to be seen. Despite the night air outside, the forge had the shop warm enough that Aro was wearing only a worn leather tool apron over his short-sleeved tunic and pants. At the moment, he had a couple of his strange metal tools in his hands, and he appeared to be focused on prying off one of the monster's eyes.

"Aro?"

He looked up, and his mustache went lopsided in his welcoming grin. "Glad you could make it, Shae."

The aluman's head, she could see, had wires and cables hanging out from its neck. It seemed almost obscene. "Where'd all this come from?"

"From the attacks." He spread his arms at the abundance of parts. "The keeps are a fine place to try new things."

"So all this belongs to you?"

"In a manner of speaking. Alumen, by law, belong to the lumickers guild. And by guild law, we can, each of us, only carry what our wagons will hold. The rest is left in places like this, waiting for the next wagon to come along, the next lumicker to fiddle with it all and then take what he can carry when he leaves."

"We had something similar. We called it a cache," Shae said. "If we couldn't carry everything back to the Bay, we'd stash it somewhere on some deserted islet. It was there for us to come back to, but anyone else could've taken it too."

"A cache." Aro nodded. He brought his tools back down at the glass eye and began straining. "I like that."

"You should build a bigger wagon," Shae said, looking around.

The eye finally popped loose. Aro pulled it away from the head, his tools separating a bundle of wires behind it. "What's that?"

"A bigger wagon. You could carry more things away, keep more of the best parts for yourself. Not let Rumin Perle at any of it." She grinned, knowing the hatred he had for his lumicker rival in King Mark's court.

Aro paused what he was doing and looked up at her. He wiped his brow. "A fine suggestion," he said. "Making life harder for the high and mighty Perle sounds splendid, to say the least. But I'm afraid the guild has thought about that. There are rules about wagon sizes. And I'm not one to break the rules."

"I thought it was a rule not to let non-lumickers in your wagon."

He shrugged. "Perhaps that was more of a suggestion."

Shae laughed a little at that, then stood back as the lumicker slipped his tools into the slots of his apron, picked up the eye, and stood. "So why did you send for me?" she asked.

Aro walked across the room to a large table near the forge. There were other parts already there: tubes, gears, another eye. Two stools were set beside the table. The lumicker sat down at one. "I've been thinking about something you told me. About the ... Spire, was it?"

Shae nodded as she took the other chair. "That's right. The home of the evokers on Myst Wera."

"As lumickers, we knew about Asryth, of course. An aluman that wasn't mad, that didn't kill. An aluman that could speak through the Stream that binds the soulglass crystals together. The Stream that binds us all together, I suppose."

Shae remembered how Onyeka had combined a soulglass with Char and her own blood to open a portal to that source—how the evoker had nearly killed them all with its power, how she herself was here, in Aionia, only because of that fateful night. "The Stream is dangerous," she said, unsure what he was thinking.

"I know," Aro said. He looked around at the parts strewn before him. "Just using the soulglass to run our lumicks, I've known I was only brushing the surface of the power they held. And those depths, that power ... it should be beyond the reach of men."

"And women too," Shae added.

"And women too."

"And so? What of Asryth?"

"She lives," he said. "And she's there, right in the middle of the Fair Isles that King Mark plans to invade. Right in the heart of your Spire."

It was hardly her Spire, Shae thought, thinking of how out of place she was within a stone tower that was as tall as the Mother's Mount. Then it occurred to her what he was thinking. "You want to communicate with her."

"So I do."

"To do what? Surely you don't want to warn the Seaborn about the coming invasion. You're Windborn."

"Aionian," the lumicker corrected. "But maybe I do. War will mean the end of your Seaborn. That's not a path forward. And besides that ..."

"Besides that what?"

"Besides that ... well, I've always been fascinated by her, by the one aluman who wasn't a killing thing. I did some reading in the guild about her. Old books that most of us ignored. Long ago, she'd talked about another like her, it turned out."

Shae frowned. "Why didn't you tell me this when we were sharing our secrets?"

"I did, as a matter of fact. But I'm afraid you were snoring at that point. I spilled my guts long after I laid you down and pulled a blanket over you."

"You were respectful," she said. "I am glad for that."

"I couldn't do otherwise."

"I know. It's why I took the soup."

"You were also hungry enough to lick a wagon wheel."

Shae wrinkled her nose. "Ta'koa's feet!"

Aro chuckled. "That, too, I reckon. Anyway, when she was first found, Asryth talked about another aluman. Kolum."

"I've heard that name before. I think Kayden mentioned him."

"Surely he did. Kolum was the man who started it all, long ago on the lost isle of Ealond. He opened the portal, made the soulglass, and built the first of the alumen."

"That's right," Shae said, thinking of what Kayden had told her. "'Doomed to die, we deal out death.'"

"Kolum's conclusion," the lumicker said, nodding. "So if he could end death, by putting human souls in metal bodies, he could end suffering. He made himself one of them. And Asryth too."

Shae remembered her horror at the idea when Kayden had first told her and Bela of it. "A path of madness."

"True in spirit and true in form as the alumen went mad," the lumicker said.

"Except Asryth?"

"And, I think, Kolum himself."

Shae shook her head. "I don't follow."

"These old books I was talking about. They said that when she spoke of Kolum, it was as if she could still communicate with him."

"And no one asked her more of this when she was still here?" Shae asked. "Before she came to the Fair Isles and was broken into pieces?"

He shook his head. "She stopped speaking early on, the books say. Refused to answer questions. No one knew why. But listen, here's the point: if we could talk to Asryth, we might prevent the war. But what if Asryth wasn't alone? What if Kolum is still out there somewhere? What could he tell us today? And more than that, what if they aren't even the only ones? What if there were other alumen, ones who could help us defend ourselves from the others of their kind? For all we know, it may be that an aluman, given time, can recover from its madness and learn to be human again. What then?"

"Then you've killed many a soul," she said.

He blinked at that, and, for the first time, she saw sorrow and regret in his eyes.

"I'm sorry," she said. "I shouldn't have—"

"No," he said, "I'm not so much of a fool that I haven't thought of it. I know what I might've done." He spread his hands over the parts on the table. "I know what it is I might be doing. But it's worth doing to protect the rest of us today, and to maybe save more of us tomorrow."

"Maybe," she said. "So what's your plan?"

The lumicker pulled out the soulglass that he'd tossed to her on the road. "Well, I want to build an aluman."

"Sorry?"

"The head and heart of one, anyway. No arms or legs that it can use to rip us apart. But something we can maybe talk to. Something that'll maybe talk back."

Shae stared at him for a moment. "In that case, don't use that crystal. Marek just told me a story about an aluman who seemed more aware than the others. The one who killed the last lord, actually. It seemed to be thinking its way through the keep's defenses. Maybe it was nothing. But ..."

"But maybe he was coming to talk," the lumicker said.

"I certainly never got the idea that the one we met had anything in mind but death," Shae said. She picked up the piece of soulglass and put it in her pocket. "I'm in no hurry to meet it again. Arms or not."

25

The Decision

Bela stood atop a snowy ridge, at least three grueling leagues away from the open beach and the warmth of the cave that had become their home. Whenever the weather allowed it, she'd been sending the crew out in teams to take stock of their surrounds, telling them that they needed to determine the long-term viability of their shelter, or whether something better could be found. One of their first discoveries had been that there was no sign of a beachhead among the cliffs for many leagues to the east or west. They'd been most fortunate indeed to approach the beach they'd found so directly. A sign of the Mother's kindness, many of them said. Bela, for her part, had taken it as a sign that if they were going to get farther north, they'd need to begin looking for a direct route inland. There would be no going around the ragged mountains along the shoreline. They'd need to go at them. And to even begin to do that, they'd need to forge a path through the tangled maze of frozen cliffs and broken crags that rose up around the beach.

And here, it seemed, it looked like they had.

Ahead of her, Bela saw a broad valley of snow and ice that sparkled in the sun between twin ridges of icy rock.

There was nothing there—around every corner, she'd hoped to find an ancient city, a crumbling ruin, something to give her hope that she'd found the fabled Ealond—but it was still something. A path forward.

The sound of crunching snow brought Oni up to stand beside her. "Well," her maiden said, panting in the cold air, "that's a sight."

Bela stared up at the low point at the head of the valley. "That pass can't be that far away, can it?"

It was a bright-sky day. Oni squinted. "Distances are deceiving out here."

Her maiden was right. The smoothness of the snow erased so many of the markers on the landscape that could've given them a sense of scale and distance. It didn't help that the same snow played havoc with their eyesight, especially on bright days like this.

"Could be two days," Bela said.

"Or two weeks," Oni suggested. "We don't know how deep that snow is. How solid it is. What's under it. How long—"

"I know. I know."

"I'm sorry, mistress."

Oni reached over and wrapped an arm around her waist. Even through their layers of clothing, Bela imagined she could feel its warmth there. Bela wanted to reach down and grip Oni's hand against her hip, but the maiden was on the wrong side of her: she didn't have a hand to reach to that hip. Instead, she leaned her head over to touch Oni's. "Thank you," she said.

Oni turned to her, smiled. They kissed with cold lips.

"You know I couldn't have made it this far without you," Bela said.

Oni pulled away and smiled. Then she turned and looked back south. The path they'd made quickly disappeared into the fractured terrain, but in the far distance they could see the flat expanse of the frozen sea—at the shore of which the rest of the crew waited with a warm fire. "Of course you would've," she said. "Look at how far we've come. Against all odds. I know you don't like to hear it, but you're Belakané. The one thing we all knew of you in the songs is that you don't give up. You keep going. You keep fighting. Even if we were all gone, you'd still walk on. You'd find Ealond alone if you had to." She turned back to Bela, and there was something like adoration in her eyes. "That's the reason I follow you, mistress."

"Oni, I—"

Her maiden reached out to hold her shoulders. "You'll keep going. You'll find it. Promise me, mistress. You'll make this worth it."

Bela nodded. "We will. Together."

Oni smiled, kissed her again. "Even better. Now let's get back, warm up so I can actually feel those lips, and then we can convince the others."

"But we've good shelter here," Eshe said. "Plenty of food and oil. We have snow to melt for clean water. Why leave?"

The women were all standing around the fire, their faces red with the flames—and with the heat of the argument.

"Because our good mistress still thinks she can save the Isles," Neka said.

Oni narrowed her eyes on the bigger woman. "I don't like your tone."

"Always the dog, maiden?" Malaika asked.

"Always above you," Oni hissed.

Malaika started to move, but Neka reached out and stayed the woman with a big hand on her chest. Bela reached out to do the same to Oni.

"Stand down, both of you," Bela said. "We need to work together in whatever we do. Separated, we die."

"Orders ain't working together." There was none of the amusement that sometimes lilted in Sanyu's voice.

"Which is why I keep saying I want us to talk about this," Bela explained, using the most diplomatic tone she could manage. "Each of us must make up her own mind about going on or staying here. And we must then take the next step together. All six of us. Agreed?"

Malaika, Sanyu, and Neka exchanged long looks. Finally, Neka nodded. "Agreed. But we'll have a straight cast on it. No hand above another. As you say, we're in this together."

"Fine. All of us get a cast. Agreed, Oni?"

Her maiden nodded, though her eyes were still hurling daggers at Malaika. "At your command, shipmistress."

"Good." Bela took a deep breath and let her hand fall away from Oni. "Good. Then it comes to this: I want to begin hiking north through the mountains. Not because I want to save the world, but because those are my orders. And I swore upon the staff of the High Matron that I'd do my part to fulfill her commands, come difficulty or death. I gave my word upon my honor. It's my duty, as it is yours.

We can stock up well for the journey, with plenty of oil and meat and water. We can leave behind one of the outboats, dragging only one for supplies. We've already trodden a path to that valley. We should be able to make good time beyond that and see what lies ahead. And if we find the mountains impassable, we can simply come back here."

Oni nodded. "I agree completely."

"To what end?" Neka looked like a woman speaking to untested children. "There's nothing to be found in this forsaken land. No great cities, no long-lost peoples. Certainly no great secret power. There's only death up in those mountains, *mistress*."

"How can we know?" Oni asked. "We need to be sure. What if there *is* a city? What if there are still great vessels there, ships we can take back to the Isles? What if there really is a portal? The books say—"

"The books!" Malaika motioned toward Tewrick, who was sitting apart from the others. "How do we know? He's the only one of us who can read. So, what if he's lying? How can we know he speaks truth? And how can we know to believe the books, anyway? Can they not lie too?"

"They can," Tewrick interrupted. "And they do."

His sudden entrance into the argument—the fact that he was daring to speak among his betters at all—cast an uncertain silence over the cave for a few seconds.

"You see?" Malaika finally managed to stammer, seizing on what the reader had said rather than the fact he'd spoken. "Lies."

The reader took a long, deep breath, as if he were bracing himself—though Bela couldn't tell if that was because of what he was about to say or his realization that he'd spoken out of turn. "I didn't say that all books are lies. I didn't say that these books"—he held up one of his tattered, soot-stained tomes—"are lies. I admit only that scripts are written by people, and as surely as people can lie and cheat and withhold and betray, so, too, must their books always be viewed with caution. You all have heard, no doubt, that there are three lessons taught to every member of my guild. That books can lie is the second of them."

Such was the secrecy of the reader's guild that Tewrick's free admission of one of the three lessons draped a quiet awe over everyone. Bela found herself staring at the scholar, wondering if, at this moment, she knew more of the scriptors than her mother had. How many in the whole of the Isles were so privileged?

Across the fire, Eshe shifted on her feet. "What's the first lesson?"

"That books can tell the truth," Tew replied. "That they can heal and bond and record and give hope."

"And the third lesson?" Eshe looked like an anxious puppy, and for once Bela didn't feel the need to rebuke the weak-willed girl. She was certain she looked the same.

Tewrick shook his head with a smile. "The third lesson dies with me."

Bela let out the air she didn't know she'd been holding in her lungs. Others did the same. "But I want to say this," Tewrick said, looking over at Eshe. "You're right to wonder why we should leave here. We have food and oil and fire and shelter and water. We thought that we'd die aboard the *Sandcrow*. But we survived. Then we thought we'd die on the frozen sea. But we survived. By fate or luck or the warm winds of the Father, we survived. And now that we have safety, there is no one who could blame us for refusing to give it up. Not even the High Matron to whom we swore our oaths."

"Aye," Neka muttered, staring over at Bela. "Not even her."

"So I understand the reluctance we all have to leave," the reader continued. "I, too, am reluctant to go."

Neka and Sanyu exchanged hopeful glances. Malaika's eyes narrowed in suspicion. "But you've something more to say," she growled.

"I do," Tewrick said. He stood and walked to the back of the room. Tracing his hand up the rock surface, he pointed to a thin white line that ran horizontally across it. "There's this problem."

"What is it?" Eshe asked.

Oni narrowed her eyes across the space. "It looks like a waterline," she said.

Tewrick nodded. "I think it is."

Malaika made a scoffing sound in the back of her throat. "Are you saying this room is normally under water?"

"When the sea isn't frozen," the reader said, "I think the tide probably comes in this high. If so, when the cold melts back a bit, we might be standing up to our chests in the Sea of Ice."

Neka looked doubtful. "It's dry enough for now. You've proof of this?"

"No," Tewrick admitted. "I do not."

Neka grunted, waved her hand dismissively. "It's dry enough for now. I cast we stay."

"Me, too," Malaika said.

Oni shook her head. "I cast we go."

Bela nodded. "As do I. Two to stay, two to go. Sanyu?"

"Stay."

"That's three. Tew?"

"The boy gets a cast?" Malaika's face was aghast.

"As you said, we are all in this together. Men and women."

Malaika seemed ready to spit. "He's not even a breeder. He's cut. He's not a man."

"Ridiculous," Bela snapped. "His eggs wouldn't make him a man if he had them. We are valued for what makes us useful. Whether it's timekeeping or reading the winds."

"Or reading books," Oni chimed in.

Bela smiled over at her maiden, glad for the support, and gave her the slightest of smiles.

Oni smiled back, though Bela could see a hint of redness on her cheeks that she didn't understand. "Or reading books," she repeated. "What is your cast, reader?"

Tewrick came back from the wall and sat down with his bag of books. "We've nothing to lose. If we find nothing and I'm wrong, we can come back. So I cast we should go."

"That's three and three. Eshe? Stay or go?"

Eshe looked from Tewrick to Malaika to the fire and back again. "We can come back if it doesn't work?"

"That's the plan," Bela said. "But we can't know."

Eshe stared at the ground for a long moment. "Then we should try it."

Malaika kicked at the sand. Neka groaned. Sanyu's jaw tightened. But none said anything more. They all knew they'd agreed. They'd given their word.

Bela crossed her arms, hiding her missing hand in the hope it would make her seem stronger. "Then it's settled. Four casts to three, no one counted more than another. We go."

There was a minute of silence as the crew mulled things over in their minds. Bela tried to think of something more to say, but no words came to her.

"We'll need to slaughter a few more seals, shipmistress," Oni finally whispered, her eyes fixed upon the low fire. "For meat."

"And as much oil as we can manage," Bela agreed, ever grateful for her maiden. "There's much to do and precious little time to do it. We need to leave while the weather is good."

"That could change tomorrow." Eshe's voice was even more timid than usual, and she didn't look at the others.

Bela nodded, but she said nothing more. Eshe's gaze returned to the sandy ground.

Oni ran her hands along her legs as if she were dusting them off. "Then I suppose we should get started."

26

Tracks in the Snow

Shae was dressed more warmly than she'd ever been. Between the layers of wool and the furred cloak that fell around her shoulders—this one so thick she could hardly move her head from side to side—she felt like an overstuffed fool. But Kayden, looking on from the chair in her room, seemed to approve.

"You won't catch cold in that, I can assure you."

Shae frowned, tried to move and flex. Everything was tight. "I don't think I can reach my laces," she said.

Kayden spread his legs and patted the chair between them. "Give them here."

Just lifting her first boot up was exhausting. "Are you sure I should go?"

Kayden had the laces of the fur-lined boot in his hand. He began looping them and drawing them tight up the front of her shin. "It's been clear since the day we met that I'd never get anywhere telling you what to do, Shae."

She twisted at her hips, seeing how far her arms could

rotate. "You know what I mean. It's all right with you if I go, yes?"

He tightened the last stretch and carefully set the knot. "I'm getting stronger," he said. He patted her foot to let her know he was done. "But we know I'm not strong enough yet. I can make an excuse for not going, but neither of us going looks like we don't care. And yes, that's bad."

"So I can go in your place."

Kayden patted the chair for the next one. "Right."

Shae lifted the other boot, watched the care with which he made sure the laces were secure but not too tight. She saw, too, how he concentrated through the pain that even such fine movements were causing his arm. "I don't know much about how things work here," she finally said, "and I know it's very different from where I come from. Men and women and everything. But unless I'm wrong, I can only go in your place if they believe that you and I are, well—"

"Lord and lady," Kayden whispered. His fingers hesitated on the knot, as if he were expecting her anger.

Shae instead looked up at the bed behind him, the one that he'd tried to give to her before she'd insisted that he take it, and she would sleep on furs upon the floor. "And that's why we share a room," she said. "And why Aro doesn't. Because they think you and I are … together."

Kayden finished the knot. "Married," he said.

Shae pulled her foot back down. She was still staring at the bed, still working to get her head around it. All they had was each other. It had been that way since Felcamp. In truth, it had probably been that way since she'd almost died on the Spire. "Like your parents," she said. "Lord and Lady Mar."

"I think Aro thought when he said it that maybe it would—"

Shae cut him off by reaching forward to put her finger to his lips. His eyes were wide in shock. "It's fine," she said. "Married. We can pretend if it's for the best."

There was a knock at the door, followed by Marek's voice. "Lord Kayden? My lady? We're ready for you."

Kayden opened his mouth to talk, but he'd apparently been struck speechless. "I'll be with you in a moment, Marek," Shae called out. "Just saying goodbye to my lord."

"Yes, my lady," came the reply.

Kayden blinked. "We … well, usually you'd say 'my husband.'"

"I'll try to remember." She held up the soulglass from Aro's workshop, then pulled it into her fist. "You have things to do."

He nodded. "If you get it."

"I will." She leaned forward and gave him a kiss on the cheek. "And then I'll be back, my husband."

She straightened up, smiled to see the bright redness of his cheeks and the sheer elation in his eyes as she turned back toward the door. Just before opening it, she suddenly paused and looked back. His braces were clear to see. She gestured for him to cover them up, and he quickly and sheepishly obeyed.

Satisfied, she opened the door. Oth Marek was there, filling the hall, his one eye watchful, looking past Shae to Kayden. "I'm sorry to hear you can't join us," he said.

"Soon enough," Kayden said, quickly recovering some sense of himself after his surprise. "Aro Lanser is at work on something that needs my attention. And I've letters to draft to the king."

"Of course," Marek said. "My lady? It seems the extra furs we sent are suitable?"

"They're excellent," Shae said. As she started forward through the doorway, she stumbled. Marek reached for her, and she caught herself by crashing against him. The tall man reeled but held her up.

"I'm sorry," she said, standing up and making a show of brushing her furs down once Marek let her go.

"Everything all right?" Kayden asked from the room.

"Fine now." She tried to look as sheepish as Kayden had been moments earlier. "It'll just take me a minute to get used to the new boots." She gestured for Marek to lead the way down the hall.

When the captain of the guard turned away, Shae reached back to close the door to the room. "I'm in good hands," she said, smiling as she tossed Kayden the soulglass that she'd stolen from Marek's pocket and replaced with the one of her own. "Tell Aro good luck."

It was bitter cold on the mountainside, and for once Shae was entirely, unquestionably grateful for the thick Aionian clothes. Movement be damned, she was certain she'd be a block of ice under the heavy grey sky without each and every piece of it.

Not that each step wasn't exhausting as a result. Between the weight of all the extra layers, the steepness of the trail they followed, the thickness of the snow through which they pushed, and her increasing sense that there was simply less *air* in the mountains, Shae felt certain she'd sleep as hard tonight as she had on the night she took Aro's gold-flock stew. She'd sleep, she thought, like the dead.

Marek, for all his years, seemed entirely unaffected by the climb and the cold. She wasn't sure if she admired or hated him for that.

The captain of the guard was crouched up against a snowcapped boulder ahead of her, where the path they'd been following made a switchback on its way up the slope. His spear was set against the rock beside him. He looked to be waiting for her to catch up.

She took a deep breath—the air cold even through the wool wrap around her face—and pushed forward, trying hard not to look as tired as she was, trying not to look like she was relying too heavily on using her own spear as a walking stick.

He pulled down his face wrap when she got close. "A long way up," he said.

Shae nodded, leaning on the spear and not yet trusting herself to talk without panting.

"Path goes on up that way," he said, pointing to where it continued climbing up behind her. "But I'm thinking we might go around this way."

She followed his nod around the boulder, but there wasn't much to see. The hillside was dangerously steep, and it turned away out of sight after only a few paces. There was a reason that the path had switchbacked here. "Why?" she asked.

Marek pointed down at footprints in the snow beside him. "This," he said.

To her shame, it took her exhausted mind a moment

to recognize that the tracks weren't theirs. Nor were they human. "Animal," she said, hoping that the surety of her tone would make up for her complete ignorance of what kind of animal could live in such a craggy, cold world.

"Mountain goat," Marek said. "Wouldn't want to pass up a meal like that. A welcome prize for our new lord."

Now that she knew what to look for—and had a bit of breath back in her lungs—Shae squatted down to look closer at the tracks. They were hardly filled in, despite the occasional wind that had been pushing skiffs of snow across the path as they'd climbed. "Fresh. It can't be far."

Marek smiled. "Good eye."

Shae thought of what Aro might say about having two, but she kept it to herself as the older man stood and looked around the boulder with his remaining one. "Let's get it," she said.

Marek nodded. "Hard to see it, but there really is a thin path around the knee of the mountain here. That's what the goat's on. Widens out around the other side. Follow me. We need to be careful."

Pulling his wrap back up, Marek stood. Probing the snow ahead with his spear, he cautiously picked his steps as he followed the goat's trail—slow enough that Shae, to her body's relief, had no trouble keeping up.

The path was hardly as wide as her shoulders, and the downside was a worryingly precipitous slide of snow and ice and rock down toward the alumen-strewn valley, but Marek was indeed careful. Keeping her focus on matching each footstep that he formed in the snow, she made it around the turn of the slope.

The rise ahead was indeed less steep, and Shae found

herself looking down the widening valley as it opened up to view from this height. It looked so pristine, she thought. Untouched and unspoiled. For all that she missed her seas and warm winds, she was beginning to recognize a kind of beauty in such sights. It was easy to picture chimney smoke rising from a cabin beside a little farm. Somewhere on the flats by the river that ran east to still more open, free lands. A good place, if it wasn't beyond the walls in the lands of the alumen.

But for what?

A life with Kayden? What could she have with a man? What did she even feel for him? She'd kissed him, not knowing what to expect. It hadn't been horrible. It had just been … confusing. She felt like she was at war with herself.

Shae was so lost in her thoughts for the moment that she nearly ran into Marek, who had stopped and crouched in the snow. She got down, too, and followed the focus of his gaze.

The goat. Perhaps fifty yards ahead. She was amazed Marek had seen it. The animal's pale white coat was a perfect match to the snowfield on which it stood, and it had its nose down in the snow, digging for some unseen vegetation underneath.

"By rights, the first throw is yours, Lady Shaesara," Marek whispered. His hand tightened on his spear. "But I can take it, if you like."

Shae stared out at the goat for a moment, then looked around at the movement of the wind. She shook her head. "I'll take it," she said. "A prize for my lord, as you said."

He seemed surprised at that, but he was clearly in no position to object. "Keep small," he said.

Shae nodded, then set her spear in the snow.

"What're you doing?" Marek whispered, looking at the weapon.

She looked back at it, then smiled at him. "I'd rather use my fangs," she said, and then she started forward, proud to be leaving him in complete confusion.

Shae had never hunted a mountain goat in snow, of course, but she'd taken enough animals like it—in jungles, on beaches—to know the soundness of his advice to keep small. Small and slow and ready.

So she stayed as close to the ground as she could, moving through the snow in a low crouch. And all the while, she kept her eyes locked on the grazing goat, ready to freeze into stillness at even the slightest twitch that the animal made. Just a bump in the snow, she thought. Just a bump in the snow.

As she got closer, she watched the twinkling of the flakes drifting in the air, assured herself that the wind wasn't shifting to send her scent at the animal. Few things could spook an animal like smell.

Closer still, she paused—a bump in the snow—watching the goat closely as she worked one hand out of its glove. The cold air bit at her exposed skin, but it was a necessary evil. She certainly wasn't going to work a fang in mittens.

Despite all the layers of clothes Kayden had made her wear, she'd made sure that the two halves of her blowreed were at her hip as they'd always been. With practiced fingers, she pulled the hollow tubes loose now, seeing in her mind the dark burgundy wood, the leather straps, the red-dyed threads, as she blindly fitted the two parts together.

The goat snuffed at the snow, pawing at a patch of ice.

The blowreed in one piece now, Shae brought her exposed fingers up under the wool over her mouth and breathed onto them, trying to maintain feeling in the tips for just a bit longer.

Then she reached down into her belt pouch, felt along an edge until she found one of the tiny feather-backed metal darts that had been coated with the secretions of a blue-and-white lizard a world away from this barren landscape. She pulled it free, slipped it into the back of the blowreed.

Ready.

She moved forward only a few more paces, checking and rechecking the drift of the wind. Then she pulled the wool away from her mouth. She took a deep breath, lifted the reed to her mouth, and in a single burst threw the air from her lungs into the tube.

The fang slipped through the air in silence. The animal suspected nothing.

The goat spurred when the fang slipped into its neck, jumping out of the snow like it had been booted from beneath. Shae watched it kick three times across the snow, shaking its head, before it buckled and sank down into the cold.

Smiling, she undid the blowreed and reattached the two pieces to her belt. Then she pulled her glove back on, using her teeth to help get it into place, before covering her face once more.

She stood, looking back in pride to Marek, expecting him to be in awe at what she'd done.

But he wasn't looking at her. He was standing, and he was staring down the long valley to the east, where she had imagined a little cabin sitting by a lazy stream.

Shae turned and looked again. The valley wasn't empty. Not anymore.

In the distance, just at the edge of her sight, things were moving. A line of men, but, of course, that couldn't be right.

And then a shadow passed over them, making the pale-blue light of their eyes seem to twinkle along the horizon.

Alumen. Hundreds of them.

and Alira saw that they had the prisoner's arms draped across their shoulders so that they could lead her between them, half-carrying her weight. They were smiling.

The prisoner tried to lift her head, tried to look where she was going, but her strength gave out. Her head fell, her matted hair draping her face out of sight as they turned and bore her out of view.

But Alira had seen her face. She'd seen.

Whéuri.

Mother's mercy. The older huntress had been here all this time. "Whéuri!" she shouted. The name ripped through her dry throat.

Heads in other cages turned her way. Several shushed her. Kora had come up to her bars, looking confused.

Alira ignored them all. She swung around onto her back to kick at the poles of the cage, desperate to force the partially cut lashings.

The door bounced, absorbing her feeble kicks, refusing to break loose.

Alira spun, flinging dirt, shifting so that she could wedge the strength of her body against a single corner of the door. Her feet bracing against the side bars, she shoved her back against the front. No bounce this time. Just a constant push, straining with what she had left.

She heard one of the remaining cords pop. Then another.

She repositioned, took a deep breath, then slammed herself back into it again.

The last of the lashings snapped and gave way, and she flopped out sideways around the big locking pole, out onto the stone pavement. The impact drove the air out of her lungs, but even as she gasped, she was turning over onto her stomach and crawling to get her feet under her body, to get *moving*, to get free.

Kora's cage wasn't far away. She was crouched at the front of it, her one good hand gripping the bars. Hope in her eyes.

Alira, coughing, shaking a dizziness from the lack of food and movement, stumbled to her. The pole keeping the cage closed was heavy. But, heaving, she got it out.

The shaft of wood clattered to the ground.

Alira blinked at it, wondering if the noise was a problem, knowing she had no strength to muffle the sound if it was.

Kora scrambled out as best she could and embraced her.

"No time," Alira rasped. Still swallowing against her dry mouth, she pulled Kora toward another cage, and together they freed an older woman whom Alira had known only in passing back in Anjel. She'd known her name once. Maybe even a few days ago. But she couldn't remember it now. It was hard to think beyond each footfall.

"Open more." Alira nodded to the older woman. Vayra— that was her name—braced herself on the cages as she started toward the next one that was occupied.

Alira turned to walk away, but Kora's hand on her elbow stopped her. "Where are you going?" Her voice sounded like sand rubbed on rough bark.

"Whéuri," Alira managed.

"I could help you—"

Alira glanced at the girl's limp arm and shook her head. "Free the others."

"Then what?"

Alira nodded toward the strange trees. "Then burn them, Kora. Burn them and run."

The girl nodded, hugged her once more, and then hurried to help Vayra. There were so few prisoners left. With the Mother's luck, Alira thought, the ruined hall would soon be roiling smoke and flame toward the sky.

The trees, whatever they were, would be destroyed. Whether that meant she couldn't get out this way, she didn't know. It probably didn't matter. One thing at a time.

Whéuri.

Still getting her balance, Alira hurried to the other end of the hall. Bracing herself against the doorway, she looked back and saw Kora and Vayra helping a man out of his cage. She smiled, then she ducked into the dark.

Alira was lost in the maze of unlit corridors and stairs and rooms when the screams began. She recognized it at once. She'd heard it before. It was Whéuri. It was death.

Using the stone walls to keep herself upright, she hurried through the building, turning for wherever the sound was loudest. To the right. Now left. Now down the stairs and across.

There was a new sound of rushing, running water, mixing with the cries of panic.

Down another set of stairs, and Alira saw light spilling out from an open door ahead. The rumble of the water was louder now. So were the screams.

Alira pulled herself off the wall so she could stand free. She blinked to focus her eyes.

She had no weapon, she suddenly realized. Nothing but her hands.

Good enough, she thought.

She crept up to the doorway. She looked inside.

It was a large chamber, windowless but for the light that came in between holes that gaped like wounds on either side of it. Between them ran a chute—surely the same she'd seen from outside—that was rushing with water flowing through an open gate close to the door. There was a kind of platform there, made of wood, with the gate's lever on one side and a desk overlooking the lower part of the room at the other, just beside the stairs leading down. The tender—the one she'd seen cutting the trees—was sitting at the desk beside an oil lamp. A handful of small pots were lined up in front of her, with the tiniest, gold-veined saplings growing within them. The woman's little satchel of seeds was there, too, sitting near her hand on the desk. She had her back to the doorway. She was looking down on Whéuri and the machine below.

The machine.

The rolling waters down the chute were turning a splashing wheel and an axle running to a bewildering assembly of gears and cables and wood. All of it was turning, and all of it, in turn, was spinning two metal rings—one inside the other, flat like the hoops around a barrel, but made of a bright silver like she'd never seen—over the surface of the table on which Whéuri was strapped down. The huntress was bleeding from wounds on her arms and shoulder. Three Bloodborn stood around her. The two at her sides were weaving magick, their mouths awash in blood that was not theirs. The third held an empty crystal in metal blacksmith's tongs. Full crystals—*soulglass*, Tukaha had called them— sat on shelves behind her. Hundreds of them.

In the center of the spinning rings, a blue disk was beginning to appear. Glowing. Like the light of another world.

Whéuri pitched and struggled against her bonds, screaming at the sight. The woman with the tongs began lifting the crystal forward. It looked like she was going to bridge the gap between Whéuri's chest and the blue disk that was glowing brighter and brighter.

Alira, not knowing what else to do, threw the lever beside her forward. The gate over the chute crashed down. The water stopped. The wheel stopped. The rings stopped. The portal snapped shut. Whéuri's screams choked off into sobs.

Heads turned. But Alira had not stood still. Bouncing off the pads of her feet, as Whéuri had taught her among the tall Furywood trees, she'd already leapt to the desk, had one hand on the leather satchel full of seeds. The tender gasped, trying to turn, to reach, to get up—but the movement only helped Alira pull the woman's knife free from its sheath at her other hip.

Alira didn't hesitate. Didn't think. Her arm shot forward, slicing a red line across the side of the magicker's neck.

The woman screamed and gurgled at the same time, her hands grasping at the wound even as the blood inside found the path of least resistance and began to spray between her fingers—across Alira, across the desk, across the gentle saplings in their pots. The flame atop the oil lamp sputtered, but it kept its life.

The Bloodborn below made an inhuman scream, a sound that had frozen Alira's heart when she was younger. But she was too tired and too angry and had seen too much to be scared now.

She held the satchel of seeds over the fire of the lamp. "I'll burn them," she said.

"Alira?" Whéuri gasped.

The Bloodborn women hissed, seemingly uncertain what to do. The tender was on the floor. She twitched.

"I'm here," Alira said. "It'll be over soon."

"Over," Whéuri said. She managed to lift her head. They locked eyes. Alira knew.

"We'll grow more," one of the magickers said. And they came for the stairs. There were knives in their hands. The same kind of knife she'd seen burst from the chest of Tukaha that night. Right before she'd thrown her fire into the soulglass and—

Alira lifted the strap of the satchel over her head and let it drop onto her shoulder. In the same moment, she leaned back and kicked the oil lamp out and into the shelves of soulglass below.

Flames splashed out across them, catching fire to the wooden shelves. But the crystals didn't explode. They simply glinted and flashed, reflecting the light of the flames. Tukaha's fire had been magick. Char-fire from the hands of an ember. Stronger.

The Bloodborn laughed. High and horrible. The first two of them were nearly up the stairs.

Alira had always wanted to be an evoker. But the few grains of Char she'd been tested with had nearly killed her.

She was certain, then, that this would too.

She swiped the tender's blade, shining like new, across the first of the saplings, cutting it in two.

Gold flickered in the arc of the cut, tracing the line through the air and into Alira's hand. The power flashed through her. It was a swirling, golden fire, spilling through her veins, just as the Char had been so many years before.

But there was no pain. It was the opposite of pain. It was life.

The life of the tree. Now hers.

It spilled into tired muscles, and they were strong again. It fired through her aching bones, and they were whole again. It opened her eyes, and she could see again: Whéuri's anguish, the dead tree, the last feeble heartbeat of the tender at her feet, the magickers almost upon her, and the screaming torment of a hundred voices locked in the crystals below.

"No!"

She swiped her hand at the women on the stairs, and the air in front of her exploded outward at them. They flew back. One crashed into the lever, throwing it open and lifting the gate. The other went over the fast-filling chute of water, crunching against the rock wall behind it.

The great wheel started turning. The machine came to life, and the rings began to spin.

"No," Whéuri cried out. "Let me die! Let me be with Bryt!"

Alira, angry, swatted at the wheel itself. The flaps that were hitting the water crumpled and splintered away, one after another. The wheel stopped moving.

Then the power was gone.

Alira panted, buckled to her knees, and dry-heaved into the tender's blood.

"There's only so much Life in a little tree," the remaining Bloodborn woman said from below. Her voice lilted in something like a song. "The Stream alone lasts forever."

Alira shook, weaker than she'd been before. She'd used the magick of the tree—the Life, the Bloodborn called it. But she'd used something of herself too.

Whéuri whimpered.

Something of herself, Alira thought. But not *everything*.

She pulled herself up to the desk.

The knife was still in her hand.

So was another potted sapling.

Gold flashed. Death. Life.

Alira stood. Across the room, she reached out to the shelves full of soulglass. She closed her fist, and the air closed around the crystals, the wood, the flames. She squeezed. The crystals broke in an eruption of power that she could barely contain.

And so, just before she used the last of her strength to dive for the chute and the running water, she let it all go.

28

The Breaking Point

The wind was a constant presence. No matter where Bela and her crew went, its roar was a blurry, vibrating noise that rasped in their ears. No matter where they looked, it met their faces with a slapping chill—spinning up in cloudy waves from the far white sea below, raging down from the far white heights above, or churning in drift-forming gales that wrapped around the sides of the mountains as if to grasp the slopes in its cold embrace.

For days they'd been fighting against those winds. Just seven black dots, dragging a single supply-laden outboat up into the valley Bela and Oni had seen from below, trudging in silent file during the day and sleeping shoulder to cold shoulder beneath the overturned hull at night. Storm and terrain had pushed them back again and again, but at last they'd found a path that carved across the lee slope of one of the higher peaks. They'd made good but tiring progress, steadily climbing higher and higher as they'd wound around the slopes of the great mountain, angling across icy chutes that led out into chasms filled with nothing but snowy, roiling cloud.

The crew was tied together in two teams as they labored, attached to each other by the same familiar lines of rope that they'd used coming across the frozen sea. Everyone knew that a long plummet off the edge of the mountain was only a false step away. More than once, a slipping woman had been grateful to be tied to the others.

To help protect their stores, Bela had attached their remaining length of rope to the single surviving harpoon. The other end of the rope had been tied to the end of the pulling line, just behind the harness-loop of the lead woman on the boat. This gave them an extra line that could be anchored hard to the ice if needed. Since the lead woman of the pulling team was now carrying the harpoon, both swords were given to the free team, who used them to cut a path through the larger drifts they encountered in the frozen terrain.

Put together, it was a good plan, Bela had thought.

The only problem had been the teams. She'd wanted the crew to remain in their two previous teams: Neka, Sanyu, and young Tew alongside her, and Oni, Malaika, and Eshe in the other. But from the day they'd set out from the cave along the shoreline, Neka, Sanyu, and Malaika had insisted on tying themselves to one another, leaving no room for a fourth.

It was a small defiance, and Bela had waved Oni off when her maiden wanted to enforce her will. But it was a defiance nonetheless.

So Bela wasn't surprised when she heard the wind carrying the grumbles of Neka across the wide, smooth chute of ice and snow that they were trying to cross. The big woman was in the lead of the free team out front. Bela, too, was at the head of her team, using her one remaining hand to carry the harpoon-anchor ahead of those pulling the supply boat behind.

Bela had been watching Neka and Malaika as they'd been digging hard with the blades out front, trying to scratch and claw their way past a crusted bank of snow that barred further progress off the dangerous slope. They'd been taking turns chipping into the impediment, but now they'd stopped, exchanged a couple of words with Sanyu, and turned back to face the others.

"That's it," Neka said across the chute. The big woman's face was flushed and sweaty despite the cold. "We'll not go farther."

The three of them started to come back across the chute, and Bela walked carefully on the sloping ice to meet them, mindful of the reach of her line. "We'll switch off," she said. "You've been in the lead all day."

"No," Malaika said. "We're done."

"We want to go back," Neka said.

Bela glanced back toward the others. Tew was tied behind her and had made it about halfway across the chute. Oni and Eshe were behind him, their hands guiding the outboat. None of them appeared to have any idea what was going on. They just looked tired. "We've been pushing too hard," Bela said. "We'll slow down. Or find another route."

Neka stepped around Sanyu. "We'll push no more," the big woman said.

"We're done," Malaika repeated. "We're going back."

They were only a few long steps away. Tewrick was

halfway back to the outboat. Bela glanced down the slope to where it disappeared into the yawning chasm of foggy space. "I don't think we should make rash decisions," she said.

"Rash?" Malaika, standing behind the other two women, was incredulous. "Rash was sailing north before full spring. Rash was packing our way across the ice sheet with no hope of supply or rescue. Rash was coming up here to die like fools when we had food and shelter and warmth enough at the cave."

"I don't like your tone."

"We don't care anymore," Sanyu said.

"You're under my command."

"Your command is under the ice with the dead," Neka said. There was genuine hatred in her voice and disgust upon her face.

"You can join them for all we care," Malaika said.

Neka's grin was feral. "Join them now," she said, and she came forward, swinging her sword with both hands.

Bela stumbled backward across the ice, but she managed to get the harpoon up to block the blow.

Neka was bigger. Stronger. And she had two arms. It was a fight Bela knew she couldn't win.

Somewhere behind her, too far away to help, Oni screamed.

Neka's blade rose up and slammed back down against her defense, and the best Bela could manage was to deflect it down and away. But it spun her off-balance. And Malaika had shoved her way up, too, passing Sanyu and swinging with the other of their two swords.

Bela twisted away from the second strike, contorting her

body in the small hope that Malaika would miss. But the woman was a fighter, experienced in arms.

Bela gasped as the blade scythed through her sealskins and the thick wool layers beneath them, running a line across her ribs. There was a sudden new chill as the frigid air met her torn skin. Instinctively, she rolled with the blow, arching and twisting her body as she shifted her weight away. For a moment, the move, more instinct than controlled thought, was successful.

The blade didn't carve deep into her side, and then Malaika's swing was free and moving away, the danger passed for a moment.

The next heartbeat, though, Bela's weight had shifted beyond the grip of her boots on the smooth terrain. Her feet kicked out from beneath her. She began to slide.

The others were yelling and shouting. The ground shook. Bela thought she could hear a distant rumble as she skittered down the ice, arms flailing as she tried to dig the harpoon into the cold. The line that tied her to Tewrick and the others repeatedly jerked and kicked, and each time she could feel the weight of her body bucking against the line. But it didn't stop. She was skidding toward the emptiness below. Faster and faster.

There was a noise above her. Like the roar of the breakers that she remembered from a youth long before she became Belakané, the curling waves that crashed like falling trees into the black rocks protecting the harbor. Only louder. And far, far more angry.

In desperation, Bela kicked herself onto her side and lifted herself off the speeding ice just long enough to plunge the harpoon into it with every last measure of strength she had. It stuck and was ripped out of her hand. Slashing down the ice, she looked back up the slope, and she saw it receding away at the end of the rapidly uncoiling rope that was attached to the pulling line. She saw, too, the spinning, twisting forms of Tew and Oni following her down the chute.

And behind them, moving faster than they were sliding, already having swallowed Eshe and the boat and all the others, was a wall of snow that blocked out her sight of the great peak above.

Bela saw her maiden for only a moment before she disappeared into the white. A half-second later and Tew was gone. She started to shout something, started to curse the Mother and the mountain and even the books that had given them this pointless, fruitless mission, but then the roaring wall hit her, too, and her screams were swallowed up by the cold dark.

29

Life After Life

The ruined building was roiling with smoke, flame, and screams when Kora stumbled out and into the full light of the sun.

The flames and the smoke were the death of the unnatural trees. The screams were the death of a woman.

Whether it was Alira or Whéuri, she did not know.

Most of the free prisoners had already disappeared into the jungle, taking their chances that they could scatter fast enough that at least some might survive the Bloodborn. But Kora could see that a handful, in their exhaustion and their terror, were going in the only direction they knew. They were running down the path itself, across the bridge over the river and then through the village of wooden houses on their wooden stilts.

They would be the first to die.

Already, Bloodborn were floating out of their doorways, only just beginning to realize what was happening.

Vayra, coughing smoke, came out of the hall. They two were the last of them. Except for Alira and Whéuri, somewhere deeper in the building.

The older woman saw the prisoners crossing the bridge. At a glance, she could tell there was no way to save them now. She and Kora would be lucky if they could save themselves. She pulled Kora's good arm toward the jungle. "Let's go!"

Kora rocked in place. "Alira," she said. "What if—"

They both flinched as a Bloodborn woman in the village began to laugh in high and piercing glee. She was facing the prisoners limping across the bridge. She wove the air in front of her. A Stormborn man on the bridge was thrown backward. His head bounced on its stones. He did not move again.

"Now!" Vayra shouted, and she pulled Alira toward the jungle.

Alira took a step. Then another. The screaming was very loud, very close. Was it Whéuri? Mother, was it Alira?

What if she could help them?

Suddenly, the screaming in the building stopped.

Kora tried to call out Alira's name, but she choked on the sound.

Vayra was pushing into the thinner part of the jungle where it met the front of the building. She was pulling Alira by the arm, and Alira's feet were moving in stumbling steps, instinctively preventing her from falling forward to the ground.

The world dissolved into flashes.

The pain of branches whipping against her broken shoulder. The desperation on Vayra's face each time she looked back. The screams that began again.

A crashing noise.

Vayra was pulling her down an embankment of rocks and vines. Kora stumbled beside her.

The river was streaming ahead of them, brown and white.

They should swim, Kora thought. But before she could speak the words, there was another sound of rushing water. Overhead.

She froze, looked up, saw a wooden chute above them belch a great heave of water out into the river.

Then the world exploded.

Trees. Glorious and tall as the clouds, with branches that opened out from wooden spires into a fullness of shimmering green that seemed to cover the sky.

Floating on her back—feet downstream, one arm folded around Alira's chest—Kora saw the Furywood coming. A stand of mature, ancient trees, webbed with wooden walks strung between the branches, homes and shops and halls hung tightly to the great trunks of wood.

She hugged Alira up, making sure her face was still out of the water. "Almost there," she whispered. "Almost home."

Alira blinked and coughed weakly. Kora took it for a nod.

"Do you see it?" Vayra was floating behind. They'd been taking turns carrying the barely breathing huntress.

"I do!" Kora called back. She tried to kick against the stream, tried moving toward the slower currents nearer the bank. "I'll need help."

The older woman splashed from behind, grunting in the exhaustion they both felt. The trees grew larger. They'd be upon it soon.

Not long after the river had pushed them free of the village and its screams and laughter and flames—not long after they'd found Alira facedown in the water and saved her—she and Vayra had talked about floating past Anjel in silence, on the chance that the Bloodborn were still there. If they weren't, if familiar faces still walked the hanging paths of Anjel, then they could come ashore and hike back.

But they knew soon enough that neither of them had the strength to walk more than a few feet. They'd come ashore beside the Furywoods of Anjel. They'd simply pray the Bloodborn were no longer there.

Vayra reached Kora as the river made its last turn above Anjel. The older woman wedged up alongside her, bumping her broken shoulder and making Kora glad that the cold of the water had left it numb.

They spat, splashed, and then had hold of each other, Alira between them as they struggled toward the shore.

There were boats there. And people. *Stormborn.* Kora called out, tried to wave, but then dunked under the current. She kicked, strained, managed to get her head up.

"Kora!" Vayra called out.

Kora pulled at the older woman, at Alira. She swallowed water and coughed it out, but her legs didn't stop.

Her feet suddenly struck bottom. Rocks that were slick but solid. She pushed. She heaved.

And then there were shouts. There was splashing all around them. Hands—strong hands—had hold of her and were pulling her through the water. They tugged against her broken shoulder, but she was too spent to do anything more than moan. She felt her weight fall back into them, and she let whatever fight she had left drift away, past her feet, down the ever-flowing stream.

She was home.

30

The Rope

Weightless. Swinging.

In the hazy first moments of waking, Bela remembered rocking on an old wooden swing that was hung from the oak outside a Merchanter's house in the Maze. She remembered how it felt to hang loose as it swung, her hands gripping only enough to let go. Free. Like a bird, she imagined.

A childhood moment, forgotten for years, now remembered, now real—until a sharp gust of wind raked across her body, probing the open wound at her side with icy claws.

Bela gasped in shock and pain. Her eyes came open.

She was hanging in her harness-loop off the taut harpoon line, swaying in the wind, bouncing around the pulling line that ran down to the others in her team. Looking up toward the swirling sky when she opened her eyes, she saw how the harpoon line—the rope that was holding them all—was already deeply frayed by the sharp edge where it bent up and over the ice-covered precipice above.

Bela twisted in her harness to look below her, and the

sight almost made her pass out. Tew, Oni, and Eshe were all dangling in their various loops off the main pulling line. Beneath them, pulling them all down like a leaden anchor, was the outboat. And beyond it all was the cliff face, etched with clinging ice and deep scars. It curved away into blank nothingness. They'd fallen off the edge of the world.

Bela closed her eyes to fight back the urge to vomit.

"Mistress?"

It was the reader's voice, coming up from below. Bela opened her eyes. Her stomach heaved no matter where she looked, so she concentrated on his face. "Tew?" she called down. "All safe?"

"We are," Tew shouted back. "Thought the sword or the fall had killed you, mistress!" Farther below the reader, Bela saw Oni twisting to look upward, shouting something to Tew that she couldn't hear through the wind.

Tew nodded, then waited for a lull before he turned back toward Bela. "Oni and Eshe are banged up, but they're alive. But Eshe says the boat's empty."

Bela nodded, then actually managed to hear Eshe shouting from below: "They're all gone!"

Tew ignored Eshe's distant shouts. He fixed his eyes on Bela's. "Should I tell Eshe to use her knife to cut it loose?"

Another gust battered them for a few seconds. When it cleared, Bela nodded. "Do it. We've got to get up."

"The rope?"

Bela nodded again, her face grim.

Tew exchanged shouts back and forth with the women below, then turned back to Bela. "Eshe's lost her knife, mistress. Can't cut loose the boat."

Of course, Eshe had lost her knife.

Bela fought the sudden urge to smile at the sad fate of it all. A Seaborn woman without a knife was about as useless as a shipmistress with one arm. It seemed like the punchline to a joke told over cups of rum.

Bela glanced back up to the taut rope above them. It looked like it was even more frayed now. It was her imagination, she was sure, but a part of her was certain she could see the strands snapping away from the sharp ice. She tried to lift herself along the rope, but it only took a moment to recognize that the weight of the three other crew and the boat was too much, even if she had two working arms. She couldn't climb up. She couldn't do anything.

When she looked back down at the others, all she could do was shake her head. With the howling of the wind, she couldn't even tell them she was sorry.

Bela closed her eyes and tried to imagine that swing again. That peaceful memory. She'd hold it for as long as she had.

Not long now, she was sure. A snap. Then a fall.

Shouting made her open her eyes again, made her look back down at the others on the line. Tew and Eshe were the ones doing the shouting, she could tell. The reader was yelling in a pleading tone as he looked down. Eshe was screaming in misery and horror as she looked up.

Both of them were focused on Oni, who was moving her hand back and forth across the rope above her.

Eshe might not have a knife anymore, but Oni did.

"What's she doing?" Bela called down. But then, with a sudden and unmistakable horror, before anyone could answer back, she knew exactly what her maiden was doing. She was using her knife to cut the weight of herself, Eshe, and the boat off the line. She was trying to save her mistress.

"Don't!" Tewrick yelled.

A strand in the rope shook, and Bela didn't know whether it had come loose from above or below. "Oni!" she cried out. "Oni, stop!"

But Oni didn't stop. She cut with more speed, more determination. Eshe's wails were terrible. Even at the distance, Bela could actually see the strands of rope popping loose from Oni's blade. The line below her cutting started to sway to a different rhythm in the wind.

Tewrick stopped his pleading and just stared. Far below, Eshe ceased her cries and wept, pleading with a mother that might have been a god.

Then, for a moment, the wind was gone. And Oni, holding back her final cut, looked up.

She caught Bela's eyes. She smiled. "Keep going!" she shouted. "Find it!"

Before Bela could reply, Oni took one more slice across the rope. Then, as she was drawing her hand back for one final stroke, the last strands snapped with a crack. For a heartbeat, she, Eshe, and the boat were frozen in air. Then they were lost to the swirling mists below.

It took a second or two longer for Eshe's quaking scream to fade into the wailing of the wind.

Bela stared at the cloud for a moment, as if she expected to see them come back. But they wouldn't. And if the clouds parted, she knew she didn't want to see.

Tewrick was crying, but Bela knew there wasn't the time for that. Tears could come later. It was a time to do her duty. Oni's sacrifice had bought them minutes. Nothing more.

Bela reached up with her one hand and gripped the rope. Without the weight of the boat and the other women pulling it down, she was able to wrap the cord around her forearm. Then she lifted, inch by inch, until she could grip the rope between her booted feet beneath her. That, in turn, was enough to let her loosen her grip so that she could let the rope pass through as she stood up against it, resetting her hand higher up.

What remained of her right arm flailed and flexed at her side, mimicking the movements it had made in pulling her up lines since she was a child. It was all the help of a ghost, and Bela ignored its futility. She focused on her one remaining hand.

Grip by grip, she rose. It was slower than she could ever remember climbing before. But she reached the rim of the chasm.

Secure on the ice, she pulled up the rest of the rope, heaving Tewrick up and over the edge.

The sun was going down. Night was approaching. They did not speak.

31

Departing

The river was loud in her ears, but Alira wasn't in it. She wasn't wet.

She blinked awake. She was in a boat. She was wrapped in blankets. The boat wasn't moving.

Moaning at muscles that seemed to object at every movement, she turned and pushed herself up a little. The boat was drawn up on the shore.

There were people around—Stormborn, faces that she knew—and they were piling things up on other boats nearby. And there were trees above them. Great and glorious Furywood trees.

She was home. Anjel.

"Awake, I see," came an old but familiar voice. Amaru. One of the elders who'd long been her friend.

The older woman came into view, hobbling on her familiar cane. When she reached the side of the boat, she lifted the cane and set it inside, then slowly started to climb over the edge.

Alira tried to push herself up into a sitting position to

help, but Amaru shooed away her hands. "Lie back and rest," she said. "For once, I'm in better shape than you. I want to savor it."

Alira did as she was told and settled back against the side of the boat. "Elder," she said. "How—?"

"Did you get here? Kora brought you." The elder finally clambered over the side and onto a bench seat just beside her. "See? Spry for my age."

Alira leaned up again to try to look for Kora, but once more, Amaru waved her back down. "She'll be along in a moment. She's gone to fetch water and food for you. Then we'll talk."

Not a minute later, Kora appeared. She was thinner than Alira could ever remember, her eyes sunk into her skull and her cheeks hollow. She walked with a limp of exhaustion, but someone had fashioned a proper sling for her arm and shoulder, and she was smiling as she carried a skin of water over her other shoulder, and a bowl in her good hand. "Alira," she said as she climbed into the boat and sat beside the elder. "You're awake."

Kora's voice was ragged. Alira assumed her own was even worse. She nodded in thanks as she took the bowl— filled with a simple warm broth—and the fresh water. She devoured the one and drank down the other.

As she did so, she looked around at the village. Everything was scarred by fire. The walkways in the trees were empty, some dangling, broken.

The Stormborn were on the ground, and there were so very few of them. "What happened?" Amaru asked them when Alira set down the empty bowl.

Alira and Kora told the elder everything that had

occurred after they'd been taken. How they had labored to escape. How the Bloodborn had begun growing new kinds of trees—fusing Furywood and Char—that might possess terrible dangers. Then Kora told how she'd burned the trees and escaped, before Alira told them about Whéuri and the strange machine with its magickers and its portal. She told them about how she'd used something of the magick in those trees, how she'd sent the fire into the soulglass crystals and blown them apart—the machine and so much else with them. Then she pulled out the pouch with the seeds.

"I don't know what to do with these," she said.

The elder had listened most intently at the end of the story. "Alira," the older woman said, putting a hand on her knee, "the magick in these seeds—however it was made—is beyond all knowledge of the Stormborn. It will be up to you to decide its fate. But I do not need to tell you the dangers of power. We heard the sound of the destruction you wrought even here, though we did not know what it was."

"I survived."

The elder seemed to shake a little at that. "I think the magick was still with you."

Alira felt numb. "I'm so tired. I was tired before, but the magick … it was so different from Char, but it still almost took the life from me. How long was I asleep?"

"A day," Kora said. "You had a terrible fever."

"I feel I could still sleep for a week."

Amaru made circles with the tip of her cane against the bottom of the boat. "We do not have a week, Alira Stormborn. I worried that we waited too long already, but we did not dare move you in your condition."

Alira now knew why the boats were pulled up onto the

riverbank. The survivors were loading them. "You're …
leaving?"

Amaru sighed. "I told you once, not long after you came
here, that people were like the trees. Do you remember
that?"

"You said they needed to put down roots to grow."

The elder nodded and smiled in a way that reminded
Alira of her mother. "It was a long time ago."

"I was just getting good with my bow."

"Whéuri was training you," Amaru said. She smiled in
shared pain. "I remember. I think it was the day you took
this young one into your life."

"It was," Alira said. Her voice was quiet, but she smiled
over at Kora.

The young woman responded by reaching over and
gripping her hand. "A good day for me," she said.

"You needed to hear what I said about taking roots," the
elder continued. "You need to hear this too. We can't fight
the Bloodborn. You killed many. But there are more. And
we're too few to stand against them here."

Alira wanted to protest, wanted to fight, but in truth
she was too weak to do either. "I'll do as you say, elder.
Is there word from other trees?"

"None. Kora said the Bloodborn had captured women
you did not recognize."

Alira nodded. "It's true."

"Then we must fear the worst."

Alira took a deep breath. "But if not to another tree …
Where would you have us go?"

The elder turned her gaze up into the damaged limbs of
the Furywood high above them. "I'm thinking of another

day now. The very first day you came here. I told Whéuri to take you to the height of the tree. Do you remember this?"

"I do," Alira said, looking up. "It was the day she showed me the bay where the Bone Pirate lived. The day I knew my friend was dead and there'd be no going back to Myst Motri, no leaving here, no going back to the Seaborn."

Amaru's gaze came back down, and their eyes met.

After a moment, Alira suddenly realized what the elder was suggesting. "Wait, the pirates? That's where you want to go?"

The old woman's smile was gentle. "The Bay of Bones, yes. And I need you to lead us there."

Alira shook her head in disbelief. She wanted to get up and storm off, but she wasn't sure she even had the strength to stand. "I loved Bela," she said. "Loved her. And if she lived beyond that night, the Bone Pirate murdered her. Now you want me to go there?"

Amaru straightened up and gestured toward the people moving around them on the shore. "Look around you, Alira. There aren't many of us left. We can't stay."

"But the pirates—"

"The people here look to you, Alira. Those of us who live, we saw what you did." The elder turned to Kora. "What you both did. We saw your bravery. We see you survived. Many now live because of you."

Alira shook her head. "But so many are gone because I—"

"No." Amaru hit the tip of her cane against the bottom of the boat. "This is not the way forward, Alira Stormborn. You fought hard, and you fought well. You live. As do we. None of us gets to choose where the lightning comes down.

It strikes where it will. Some trees it will destroy. Other trees—the Furywood—are strengthened by this. The bolt struck here. It struck hard. We who were struck are left to decide whether we will be stronger for it."

Alira opened her mouth to argue, then thought better of it. Amaru was the wisest woman she'd ever known. "The Bay of Bones," she repeated. Then she shook her head again.

The elder shrugged. "I think it is a fight either way. We can stay and fight alone. Or we can go down the river and hope the pirates fight with us."

"It might work," Kora said. "You were Seaborn. You can talk to them, right?"

Alira wanted to laugh at the notion. The Bone Pirate preyed on the Seaborn. Salted women, veteran hands, would wake screaming from nightmares about meeting the *Pale Dawn* at sea. But she heard the desperation in Kora's voice, and when she looked around, she saw that others had been listening in. All of them were looking for something.

Hope.

"I absolutely can," she said. And then, because she couldn't think of a reason to wait to find out whether they were floating downriver to their deaths, she lifted herself up a little to talk louder. "We should leave right away," she announced.

32

Together Alone

The sky was just beginning to lighten when Bela got up.

She hadn't slept. She'd spent the night staring out at the snow and sky: the familiar moon passing over the stars; the strange green fires dancing among them. She and Tewrick had taken what shelter they could against a rock outcropping, sharing what warmth they could beneath their sealskins and the reader's overstretched white bear-fur cloak.

There'd been no snows or great winds, at least. The god of storms, she supposed, saw fit to give them that reprieve.

But she knew the sun would bring no real warmth.

The world seemed so much emptier than it had ever been before.

In silence, she wiped frozen crystals from her cheeks. Then she began to check the few supplies they had. The reader still had his bookbag to carry. She had a pack with a container of oil and two seal-meat bundles that had fallen off the outboat before it careened over the edge and then somehow managed to float their way to the surface of the snow as it spent its energy and settled out.

Not for the first time, a distant voice in her mind told her she ought to thank the Mother for such a miracle.

Not for the first time, she did not.

The avalanche had swept enough snow and ice from the side of the mountain that it had been possible to make their way across it with far more ease than before. The two of them had made a fast pace. This morning, the ridgeline was only just ahead.

For this, too, she'd not said thanks.

Tew stirred, and she broke loose some pieces of the frozen meat for them to chew on cold. What little oil they had needed to last.

Neither of them spoke as they ate. Without a word, they cinched up their packs and began trudging toward the ridgeline.

There was, Bela thought, nothing else to do. She'd given her word.

The ridgeline wasn't far. In less than an hour, they crested it and saw, at last, the full extent of the land they'd reached. Tew pulled one of the maps from his bookbag, and together they held it under the bright morning sun, talking for the first time since the others had died, trying to find comfort in pointing out various possible landmarks and surveying Ealond.

The maps showed a massive but largely flat land, laid out like a great saddle between a line of southern mountains— the divide of which was beneath their feet—and a line of mountains out of sight farther north that were, according to the map, even taller than those in the south.

Bundled up against the cold and having difficulty catching their breath from the altitude, Bela and Tew found such an idea difficult to believe. The southern mountains, after all, were taller than anything they'd ever seen. But the map left no room for question: the more northern range was far taller, far more foreboding.

Pointing to the odd shapes of scripting on the map, the reader told her that their ancestors called the northern range the Bordweall. The peaks there were like a boundary wall for the hospitable lands of Ealond. Beyond that range, according to his books, was an inhospitable and frozen land, filled with little more than icy wastes.

Bela looked around them with disbelief. "This is hardly hospitable."

He shrugged. "The Breaking," he said, as if it were all the explanation needed.

Perhaps it was, though for all the stories she'd heard about the great war in these ancient lands—of ancient magicks and the breaking of Ealond that left it a frozen wasteland overrun by metal men and the spirits of the dead—it was jarring to see that anything of it was actually real.

But here it was. The icy wastes had crossed over the Bordweall. They'd swallowed the whole of Ealond. That meant, maybe …

Bela shook, holding back tears.

Tew quickly folded the map away. "Mistress, are you well?"

"It's real," she whispered.

He looked back and forth between her and the cold landscape ahead. He didn't seem sure what to say. "Yes, shipmistress," he finally managed.

"All of it, I mean. Ealond. The Breaking." She swallowed hard. "The portal, too, I guess."

He nodded. "If the map is right, it isn't far. The city of Niwdraca, they called it. Nestled at the base of these mountains, where a river meets the sea." He pointed toward the west. The mountains swung slightly northward in that direction, cutting off a direct line of sight to where the ancient city might have been, but they could see the frozen ribbon of a river in the valley below. And every Seaborn girl and boy knew that all rivers, frozen or not, led to the sea.

"I'm not sure how to feel," Bela said. "I guess ... I'm not sure I really ever expected to find anything."

"Not even from before, when we left?"

"Not even when I swore before the High Matron," she admitted. It was the truth of it. She didn't see why she should lie.

"So why did you come?" Tew asked.

Bela looked down at the cut-man. His eyes were red. She imagined hers were the same. "I told you before," she said. "Hope. If not for me, then for the Isles."

The reader nodded in understanding, gripped her arm for a moment, then walked off a few paces, leaving her with her thoughts. And when she began to weep, he pulled out one of his books and pretended to read.

Going downhill was far easier, and far faster, than climbing uphill. Even so, the shadows of evening had grown across the snowy valley by the time they'd reached the river at its bottom.

Less than an hour later, the river was a cascade of glittering icefalls, plunging toward a deepening, narrowing canyon of shorn black rock. They decided to camp there, to face the canyon in the morning. And as they searched for a place to shelter, they found the wall.

Or at least it had been a wall once. It was little more than a short line of ragged blocks now, just the top of it protruding from the ice and snow. It was unnatural, though. A man-made thing. And it hinted at far more both beneath the ice and up ahead.

The structure's appearance after such a long journey, after so many months of seeing nothing but storm and sea and desolation, felt like a dream, and the two of them touched it repeatedly, even taking off their gloves to run their bare fingers into the cold seams between the stones, as if to reassure themselves that it was real.

"We were so close," Bela said.

The reader didn't need to ask what she was talking about. "She was a good woman, shipmistress."

Bela looked up at the ribbon of sky that was visible above the canyon ahead. The stars were many, filling even such a small space. "Bela," she said.

"Shipmistress?"

"My name, Tew. It's Bela. Oni called me that. You should too."

The reader was silent for a moment. "Bela is a beautiful name," he said. "This man … I am honored to speak it."

Bela smiled through a long sigh, watched her breath float upward. "I miss her. She was, indeed, a good woman."

"So are you," he said.

"I've no right hand. I'm hardly a woman."

"I've no eggs," he said. "But you said yourself that I'm still a man."

She looked over at him. "You are."

He shrugged. "Then you're still a woman."

"We're worth the use we have." She reached out and touched the white fur of his cloak. "Being cut didn't stop you from saving my life against that bear."

The reader hesitated for a moment and then reached up to grip her hand against the fur. "And being one-handed didn't stop you from pulling me up that cliff, Belakané."

33

Fire from the Sky

Once, when she and a handful of other pirates had been looking for an old cache that a previous Bone Pirate had left on an island, Shae had kicked open a mound full of ants. They were fat black ants, not little fiery red biters, so she'd stopped to watch them for a while. It was fascinating, she'd thought, how what first looked like a chaos of the little creatures was, when she watched closely, an intricate dance. There was order to it. The players, though they were scrambling in seemingly every direction, all seemed to know their part.

The Blue Keep was like that now. Men were rushing everywhere she looked, all of them busy, all of them intent, and she hadn't any idea what was going on.

The boot that had kicked them all into action was what she and Marek had seen from the mountainside: an aluman army was approaching the wall. Something he'd never seen. Something that scared him. And whatever order there was to the seeming chaos now unfolding in the keep, Shae felt certain that the men knowing what parts to play was all that was holding panic at bay.

She and Marek had run into outriders on their way back down the mountain, and they in turn had sent the word flying ahead of them. Soon, a great bell was ringing in the keep, pealing off the mountainsides.

Marek was swarmed the moment they entered the courtyard, and he hurried off, shouting orders amid the streaming men. Shae stepped aside and tried to catch the breath stolen by the hike and the cold and the fear.

The lumicker's wagon wasn't far away, and the workshop where Aro would be was close beside it. His door was shut, but he'd be hearing the bells. There was no way to miss the bells.

Shae thought about going to him, thought about telling him to … what? Run? Bring his guns to the walls?

Shae was so far from anything she knew or understood that her greatest despair was her ignorance.

She looked up at a darkening gray sky. In only a few hours, it would be dark. Would the alumen get here in the night? In the morning?

As her gaze fell, she saw figures on the wall, outlined against that sky, running to and from the towering keep. She saw Kayden there, speaking with some men, pointing up toward the airship on the mooring tower high above.

Taking one last look at the lumicker's door, Shae hurried across the courtyard to the wooden stairs that led up to the wall. Ducking between running men—some with weapons, others with boxes, even one hurrying with a bag full of nails—she took the steps two at a time.

Kayden had just finished directing the men, who rushed off. He was leaning against the half-wall of the parapet, she could see, using it to help hold up his weight. He had no business being out of bed, no business—

"Shae!" he cried out.

She hurried to him to keep him from moving. He reached for her, and she embraced him, feeling his weight unfold in relief. "Kayden, you shouldn't—"

"Thank the gods—whichever gods—you're all right."

Shae let him go, gently pushed his weight back into the wall. "You need to rest."

"I'm the Lord of the Blue Keep." He tried to smile, but he could read the look on her face. "That bad?"

"Marek's never seen anything like it," she said. "There were more than we could count."

Kayden nodded. "Maybe they're going somewhere else?" He laughed to himself at the absurdity of the thought.

"Kayden," she whispered, keeping her voice low so none of the passing soldiers could hear. "Marek was scared."

"I got that impression."

"We can take the wagon," Shae said. "You, me, Aro …"

"And go where, Shae? If this wall falls, there won't be anywhere to go. We hold the Blue Keep, or we hold nothing at all."

"But with so many … Kayden, you can't fight. You can barely stand."

"I can point," he said indignantly.

"And what am I to do?"

"You?" He looked up at the top of the keep. "You're going to take the airship."

"The airship?"

"Don't argue," he said, and he took hold of her shoulders so he could look her in the eye. "Just listen. It won't be a lot different than sailing your ship. Read the winds, turn the wheel. You'll figure it out. I ordered some men to grab provisions from the kitchen stores. A few weeks' worth. But take whatever else you want too." He pointed out, over the metal graveyard, out toward the coming danger. "Sail right over the alumen, Shae. Head for the rising sun. Might take a while, but you'll reach the Fair Isles. You'll get home."

She stared out where he'd pointed, felt the yearning in her heart. The Bay of Bones. The *Pale Dawn*. Her crew. They were all out there, waiting. "Kayden, come with me."

He shook his head. "I can't. I wish I could, but I'm the Lord of the Blue Keep. When it falls—"

"If it falls," she corrected.

He smiled, and it was a smile she remembered from the first day they'd met, aboard his airship high above the ocean. It was the smile he'd given when he lit the firepowder fuse to blow up his ship and his crew and himself in order to keep it from falling into the enemy's hands. "My family means something, Shae. I know it's hard to understand that, after everything that's happened. But it's true. I can't leave. I've got to stay and fight."

"Then I'll fight too."

"No," he said. "You'll go in the airship. It's already being loaded. I'll order you dragged there and cut loose if need be."

"Let these boys try," she said. "Only way I'm getting in that airship is if I'm going to rain fire on the alumen."

Kayden had been smiling at her—a look of love, she suspected—but then his face seemed to freeze, and he simply stared at her for a moment.

"Do what?" he finally asked.

"Rain fire on them. Like you did to our ships for years."

His eyes widened. "Ta'koa's tit," he gasped.

She grinned, tried to tell him that he was finally getting it right, but he'd turned and was looking past her.

"You!" he shouted at a young man hurrying by. "Come here."

The young man, hardly the age a Seaborn girl could be salted, looked frightened to be addressed by the lord of the keep. "My lord?"

"Does the keep have a store of firepowder?" Kayden asked.

The boy blinked. "Of course."

"Where?"

"Southern storeroom, my lord. First floor." He pointed down and through the keep. "Under the mountain."

"Good," Kayden said. "Good. Find Oth Marek and tell him to meet me there. And tell him to bring two men with strong backs who need something to do."

"Yes, my lord."

"Go!"

"What are you doing?" Shae asked as the lad hurried off.

"Making a plan," Kayden said. He looked back up to the mooring tower and let out a long breath that rose toward it like a cloud. "You're getting on that airship, Shae, but you're going armed."

"Are you serious?"

"I am. Now, come on. That storeroom is a ways away." He grinned and gripped her hand. "Decent chance I might need you to carry me."

★

She and Kayden had only just reached the heavy oak door of the storeroom when they heard more footsteps approaching. Kayden lifted himself from the wall he'd been leaning against. Shae held forward the lit torch in her hand as if it would give them a better view.

A moment later, the long face of Marek appeared, marching down the corridor. "Lord Kayden," he said, "there are duties—"

"It'll be quick," Kayden said. As he limped back from the locked door, he saw the two men behind the older captain of the guard. "Good. You brought help."

"May I ask why?"

"Open it up," Kayden said.

There was confusion on Marek's face, but his lord had given him an order. Producing a ring of keys, he fitted them to the lock and pulled the heavy oak door open.

Kayden stepped inside. Shae started to follow him, but Marek's heavy hand caught her in the chest and stopped her in her tracks. When she looked at him, surprised, he glanced up to the burning torch and shook his head.

"There's more than enough in here," Kayden said.

Satisfied that she wasn't going to take the fire into the room, Marek pulled his hand away. "Enough for what, my lord?"

Kayden came back into view. "Enough to rain fire."

"The firepowder is for the cannons mounted along the wall," Marek said. "The guild brings it to us in carefully counted—"

"Do you think you can stop them?"

Marek blinked. "Lord Kayden, the Blue Keep has stood for generations upon generations. Never once has an aluman reached—"

"An answer," Kayden said, interrupting him. "Not a lecture."

"I've never seen anything like it. It may be that …" His voice trailed off as Kayden just stared at him. The old man swallowed hard. "I have doubts, my lord."

Shae saw the two younger men look at each other in shock. If he saw the same thing, Kayden ignored it. "Then we're agreed," he said. "We'll need the cannons and the lumicks and the bravery of all who have held these walls before. But we'll need something more too."

"What would you have us do?" Marek asked.

"I want three barrels of firepowder taken to the airship."

Marek gasped. "Three? We've only got—"

"Ten," Kayden interrupted. "Unless anyone has any hidden under their beds somewhere. And if you do, you'll want to pull it out. Because I want three on board that ship. Two cases of oil. A pallet of burlap sacks, big enough to hold at least ten pounds of powder."

"But my lord, I don't—"

Kayden looked over at Shae and winked—she could've punched him—before he answered. "We're going to rain fire on the alumen," he said. "But even before that, we're going to rain it on the mountain."

Marek just stared for a moment, then realized what Kayden was planning. "Start an avalanche."

Kayden nodded. "Water takes them out. Enough snow should too."

"That may be brilliant," Marek said. There was, for the first time, respect in his eyes when he looked at Kayden. "Who will fly the airship?"

"I will," Kayden said. He pushed aside his cloak to show

the braces he'd been hiding. "I can hardly stand, Marek. I'm no good in a fight. But I was an airship captain once. And I've strength enough to stay upright at the helm."

"Then who will lead—?"

"You know this place better than any lowland lord ever will."

The old man's one eye blinked in disbelief. "I'm just the captain of the guard."

Kayden looked past him, to the two men watching. "Gentlemen, would you follow this man? Even to the end?"

"Yes, my lord," one of them said.

"Gladly," said the other.

Kayden nodded. "I don't know much," he said, and for an instant he caught Shae's eye. "But I know leaders when I see them."

"Lord Kayden," Marek stammered. "King Mark gave defense—"

"To me, yes. And now I'm giving it to you. If this doesn't work out, I don't think either of us will be in a position to care how angry he is. And so, Captain Oth Marek"—Kayden stood as straight as he could manage, spoke as formally as he could manage—"until I return, I give you charge to see to the defenses of this keep. Hold these walls, lord. Whatever it takes. However you see fit."

34

A Pirate's Song

They saw the steam-like mist of the bay, rising above the jungle, long before they heard the roar of the great waterfall that caused it.

Alira had never seen the Bay of Bones, though she knew that the most experienced Stormborn huntresses, like Whéuri, had long kept tabs on the Skull, as they called the feared pirate. But Alira was the most experienced of them left now. And all she knew about what awaited her were the tales she'd heard of the strange place: a river sinking to the sea, moving mountains, pirates who floated up a waterfall. Fantastical but fascinating images.

So while she was fairly certain that going to the Bay of Bones meant she'd die at the hands of the Bone Pirate—perhaps within the next hours—she was grateful, at least, that she'd see the truth behind the stories before the end.

Assuming the pirates didn't fill her with arrows at the gate, of course.

As the noise of the waterfall grew louder, and its mist drew nearer, she directed the Stormborn to bring their boats closer to the bank of the ever-widening river, where they'd be able to beach before the current carried them over the edge and down to their deaths.

When the river turned and at last they saw that dreadful plunge, Alira's breath was taken away by the enormity of it. The noise was so loud that she felt it like a rumble in her chest and bones.

There was a tall palisade of upright logs built right up to the river's edge on either side, close to the falls themselves, and a bridge spanning the gap of the river beyond it, so Alira motioned for them to beach the boats well before that.

Then she told them to wait, to make no moves of any kind while she went ahead alone. Anyone keeping watch from the walls would know they were there, but a single emissary would surely be less likely to provoke an immediate fight than the dozens of them who'd made it out of Anjel. Kora wanted to stay with her, of course, in case there was trouble. But the truth was that neither of them was in a condition to fight. They could hardly walk. And it would be weeks, if she was lucky, before Kora's shoulder was well enough to once more draw a bow. So Alira asked her to stay and protect Amaru specifically. That seemed enough to satisfy her.

And then Alira walked on, crossing a wide zone where the jungle had been cleared, approaching a large, double-doored gate in the wall.

Wearily limping up to it, Alira could see that the wall, and even the gate itself, wasn't greatly different from what had enclosed Anjel. It was both a comfort and a fright to know that the pirates weren't as secure as they might've thought.

"That's far enough!" a woman said from somewhere

inside the gate—a high-pitched voice trying to sound deep and imposing. A younger woman, Alira suspected. That could help.

Alira stopped and held up her hands, though she doubted that anyone seeing the condition she was in could imagine she was a threat. "I am unarmed," she said. "I've come to talk."

"Who are you?"

"My name is Alira, from Myst Motri." She let her arms down, knowing she didn't have the strength to keep them up long. "I was stranded here by the sinking of my ship, the *Black Crow*." It felt wrong to Alira to say that she was Motrian—she was Stormborn now—but in discussions with Amaru and some of the others, they'd decided to begin with this. The truth was that none of them had any idea what the pirates knew of the Stormborn. They clearly knew that someone was with them on the supposedly deserted island—they protected themselves with a wall, after all—but it could be that the Bloodborn had been attacking them, too, and that they'd think that the Stormborn were that enemy. Far better, they decided, that she first present herself as something familiar. As Seaborn. As prey.

There was a long pause. Longer than Alira expected. Her mind began to imagine bows being drawn behind unseen arrow slits, the points aimed for her chest. Or a knife being sharpened as they prepared to use her to replace one of the Bone Pirate's fabled skin drums. Or perhaps it was true they were cannibals, and they were—

"What ship?" the voice was so high it was almost a squeak.

The voice wasn't angry. It sounded, if anything, confused.

Alira's brow furrowed. Hadn't she been clear? "The *Black Crow*," she repeated, speaking more loudly. "It sank."

Again there was a long pause. But this time, Alira could hear the whisper of hushed voices in disagreement. That was good. And bad.

Feeling that something was teetering on the other side of the wall, Alira decided to push her luck. "The Bone Pirate is in danger," she called out. "I need to speak to her."

The disagreement hushed. Only a few seconds later, Alira heard the sound of a bar being pulled away from the gate. Then hidden hinges creaked, and one door of the gate was pulled open. There was a small, young, brown-haired woman standing behind it, and for a moment Alira was stunned by how normal she looked. Alira hadn't given much thought to what a pirate ought to look like, but it still surprised her that this one could've passed for a young hand aboard a Seaborn vessel—no different from how Alira and Bela had been when they'd come here aboard the *Black Crow*.

"You are being watched," the young woman said.

Alira nodded in understanding. It was a warning not to make sudden moves, and even if she wanted to do so, she certainly couldn't. "I mean no harm to you or your shipmistress," she said. Then, for an instant, Alira wondered if she'd made a mistake in assuming the Bone Pirate was referred to in this way among her crew.

The woman, though, didn't even blink at the reference. "She may mean you harm," she said. "No one enters here and leaves."

"I'm willing to take that chance."

The girl nodded at that and signaled for her to approach.

Alira hobbled forward, unable to hide her exhaustion.

There were other pirates inside the gate, she saw. All of them women—most of them older—and all of them looking at her with obvious curiosity. "Thank you," Alira said as she stepped inside.

"My name is Tai," the small woman said.

"I'm Alira."

"So you said. Alira of the *Black Crow*."

Alira nodded.

Tai frowned. "Follow me."

Alira heard the gate shut and barred behind her, but she didn't turn to look. Even if she knew someone planned to stab her in the back, she wouldn't be able to stop them. So better to keep her eyes ahead, to see the truth about the Bay of Bones.

And what a truth it was.

Tai led her down a path between wooden buildings. Storage, Alira suspected, though she couldn't be bothered to look at them closely. Her every sense was fixed on what lay ahead. The cliff that the river fell off curved ahead to the left and right, reaching so far around that the walls nearly touched each other far ahead on the other side of what seemed a great hole in the ground.

As they got closer to the edge, Alira could see that those high walls embraced a circle of deep ocean waters. "Ta'koa's bones," she whispered. "I've never seen anything like it."

The path led to a wooden structure along the cliff's edge, directly beside the waterfall. The bridge over the river leapt across close beside it. Smiling at Alira's amazement, Tai led her there and stepped out onto a platform of sorts—a kind of open-faced box, sized for multiple people—that was hanging from ropes over the terrifying drop.

Alira looked up before she stepped on, saw pulleys and lines of ropes thick and thin that ran from the structure into the waterfall itself. "What is this?"

"A lift." Tai fiddled with two smaller ropes that hung down into the interior of the box. "Get in."

Not knowing what else to do, Alira got in. The pirate pulled a lever, and the floor sank a few inches—Alira gasped in shock—before the ropes caught and held. Then the lift began slowly creeping down along the face of the cliff. Tai pulled at another of the ropes for a moment, and the lift picked up a small amount of speed.

Wooden landings steadily passed by, and Alira, looking out, saw that the landings led to wooden paths bound to the cliff walls around the bay. Other pirates were moving along them, walking to and from cave-like holes carved into the stony earth. They were like the paths and homes of the Stormborn, Alira thought, only instead of weaving around and upon Furywood branches, these were clinging to the rock walls. Turning to look out the other way, out onto the bay through a window on that side of the box, Alira could see that where the ocean squeezed through the gap between the arms of the high cliff wall, the pirates had built a massive gate, painted and formed to look like the rocks themselves. Moving mountains, Whéuri had said. Alira smiled at the description.

And this lift, of course, would explain the floating pirates.

But where was the *Pale Dawn*? The Bone Pirate's legendary feared ship was nowhere to be seen.

"You've had a rough time of it," Tai said.

"What's that?"

"Looks like you can barely stand."

Alira smiled. Befriending Tai surely couldn't be the worst idea if her meeting with the Bone Pirate didn't go well. "That obvious?"

Tai grinned. "You don't look like you could jump a rat."

"Probably not," Alira admitted.

The smooth surface of the bay was getting close. Alira's nose was suddenly filled with the thick, briny scent of it, and it occurred to her that she hadn't smelled the sea since the days after Bela's death. Sensing it now, she felt an ache of loss and wondered if a part of her hadn't wanted to come back. No elder had told her that she couldn't go to the island's shore, after all. She just hadn't.

Tai pulled on one of the lines, and their descent slowed to a crawl. Just a few feet above the water, a wooden landing rose into view, and the pirate pulled the lines to stop the lift when the floor of the platform met it. Then she moved the lever-locking mechanism back into place and stepped out.

Alira followed, her head swimming with thoughts. Wonder at the strange lift and how it might work. Fear at the feelings in her heart. Fear at what the Bone Pirate might do to her.

The wide walkway—hard against the base of the cliff, roofed against the wet of the waterfall close beside—bent back into an enormous cavern behind the streaming wall of water.

There were dockworks there, and two ships at anchor in the half-light. She couldn't see anything of the second ship beyond its masts and rigging, but it probably didn't matter: Alira couldn't imagine anything that would've taken her eyes away from the ship in front.

Brig-built, with two masts rigged for square sails, she

was a large but sleek ship with wide Furywood cladding running over the darker oak planking of her sides. Her bow was bleached white, and beneath it a fierce Furywood ram, pointed with iron teeth, sat at the waterline. Everything about her screamed speed and maneuverability, strength and power. Alira didn't need to see the bone-pale flag atop her mainmast to know what she was.

The *Pale Dawn*. The most feared ship on the seas.

There were pirate women on her decks and in her rigging doing the familiar work of maintenance. As Tai led Alira closer—deeper into the cave and farther from the noisy waterfall that had become a glimmering sheet of sunlight over its mouth—she heard that they were singing as they labored. It was a song she knew:

Come all you young ladies who follow the sea,
Step up, pay attention, and listen to me:
On a dark as black midnight, came fire from on high,
Sails all turned to cinder, ash choking the sky.
Then an unsalted lass, brave Bela did cry:
Come quickly, cut anchor, to the waves we must fly!
They followed that maiden, the ships she did save,
And she helped them along with the point of her blade!
Oh she helped them along with the point of her blade!

Hearing them sing, Alira, for a moment, set aside her fear at the sight of the *Pale Dawn* and at the thought of that nightmare who lived within it. Instead, she smiled. Bela hated that song. She well and truly despised it—which was one reason that their shipmistress aboard the *Black Crow* had encouraged the crew to sing it whenever she or Bela had been slack at their duties. The embarrassment inevitably made them work harder.

There was a wide plank from the dock to the ship's deck. As the pirate women began another song around them, Tai led her across the plank and onto the dark-wood main deck of the *Pale Dawn*.

So much was familiar to Alira—the lines of knotted rigging, the brass cleats, the rails, and even the buckets and mops—that her eyes went immediately to what she'd never seen before. There were three strange contraptions like horizontal bows mounted to the foredeck where they had come aboard. As tall as a woman, with metal arms and gears and what looked like mighty harpoons in the place of arrows. Piles of rope were carefully coiled up at their feet.

Alira didn't have time to look at them long. Tai turned her onto the main deck, toward the rear of the ship, and she saw what could only be the drums. One on each side of the deck, mounted facing forward, they were covered with waxed canvas sheets. But their shape was clear. And so was their size: large enough to take the skin of a woman.

Tai, looking back before she opened the door to the lower deck and cabins, saw how Alira stared. "We were dead in the beginning," she said, as if it were all the explanation needed. "We are dead even now."

35

City of Towers

Bela and Tew stood on a bridge at the edge of a bay, staring out on an ancient city that felt like a dream.

For all that the place was in ruins—the scars of the distant war frozen in time—it was still a beautiful sight. It was haunting. It was what Oni had died for. What they all had died for.

Guilt and elation wrestled in Bela's mind, twisting at her gut. She took deep breaths to steady the pounding beat of her heart.

"The city," Tew said.

The reader's voice distracted her from the weight of memories, allowing her to push it all down and focus on the task at hand.

"Is it the right city?" she asked.

"The city where the portal was had towers. From the poem, remember? 'Thirteen are its towers, watching over the western sea.'"

"'The city lies in silence,'" Bela remembered. "'Frozen when families fly.'"

"Good memory, shipmistress Bela." The reader smiled approvingly, then gazed around the bay, counting off the towers that ringed it. Some were more whole than others, but there were indeed thirteen of them. All of them, like the city and the wide bridge beneath their feet, were fashioned from cut blocks of grey-white stone, the color of dusty pearls, tinged with light flecks of pink and green, roofs tiled in a sheathing of flat red and black rock. Even from here, Bela could imagine that a main avenue connected them, a ring of paved road, cratered in places, that ran over their bridge, spreading out of sight to the left and right like a great crescent. Soaring arches, many now broken by decay or forgotten fires, spread from building to building across the avenue and the smaller, narrow paths that branched off from it, leading to structures closer in against the landscape or farther out onto local quays and stone piers that jutted into the foggy waters of the bay.

"Why doesn't it freeze?" she asked, looking out over the glassy surface of the sea.

"Hot springs under the bay," Tew replied. "The old books talk about them. I think they're all over this area."

It was certainly true that the river they'd been following had grown less frozen as they'd followed it. Here, where it opened itself up to the bay around which the city was built, the river's surface was loose slush. And the bay itself was free of solid pack altogether, scattered with only a few lonely bergs that drifted away from the incoming river of ice or the outgoing frozen sea in the distance. The shrinking chunks of ice floated like little white isles amid steamy wisps that danced like ghosts across the bay's surface.

There were fish rising on the open water, and birds were

soaring out from nests on the towers or in the crumbling roofs, turning in reels above the sea as they looked to feed.

In the distance, in a haze of swirling fog and snow, they could see where the arms of the city ended in great, skeletal towers that might once have been lighthouses marking the way home. Beyond them was the world of snow and ice— her ship somewhere beneath it.

"So," Bela said, trying to focus herself, "where's the portal?"

Tew pulled a small book from his bag and opened it. His mouth moved as he silently read a few pages. "South side, I think. It'll be a big building. We have the Spire for our High Sybyl and the Stone for our High Matron: one place for magickers, and one place for mundanes. They had one place for both. They called it the Citadel."

"So an evoker could lead them?" The idea worried her.

"I guess so."

Bela shook her head and began following the road to the south. "Glad we changed that. Magick unchecked is exactly what Mabaya was after: one woman to rule everything."

Tew kept pace beside her. "Though it's worth remembering that she nearly got it. If not for Shae and Kayden …"

He was right. Bela had been there. She tried not to think about what she'd done in those moments. The blood on her hands. "Yes."

"I wonder where they are?"

"Who?"

"Kayden and Shae."

"She was almost dead when he took her on the airship. If she lived, I guess she's with him. Somewhere across the sea, where the Windborn live. Unless he helped her get back to her pirates."

"Why would he do that?"

Bela actually smiled at the question, remembering all the times she'd caught Kayden looking at the pirate while they'd all sailed together to Myst Wera. "Because he liked her."

Confused for a moment, Tew suddenly opened his eyes wide in shock. "Liked her?"

Bela shrugged. "It would be normal where he came from."

"And what about her?"

"Not much place for men among the pirates. I doubt she'd ever seen a man she hadn't killed before Kayden."

"Fascinating," Tew said, and then he was staring ahead as they walked down the street.

Bela didn't think it was that interesting. Not in comparison to the city through which they walked. The ancient war against the alumen had been horrifying. She'd known that. Its terrible magicks had somehow left this land in winter. Its terrible destructions had broken the people into Seaborn and Windborn, sent them fleeing for other homes. She'd known this as well, but it had all been distant. Stories. She accepted that it had been so; she'd bet her life upon the truth of the awful portal that had set it all in motion. But even so, she was realizing that she hadn't thought of it as a physical reality.

But it was. Looking around as they walked, Bela saw the war truly frozen in time. Here in black scars of fire on a wall. There in the front of a house blasted out across the street. Doors caved in. Piles of rubble. Wagons stacked in broken barricades. Windows to flame-eaten rooms. And among it all, the little signs of human life that made it all the more tragic, all the more real. A child's toy. A splintered spear. A chair inexplicably standing alone in the middle of a square.

As a Seaborn child, Bela had been taught that the dead took the ghost boat to Ealond, the home of their ancestors. Witnessing this scarred city upon it—imagining the same violence and destruction being played out across city after city in this shattered land—Bela began to understand how such stories could come to be. It was, she thought, a city of ghosts.

Tew was likewise struck to silence at the sights, only occasionally pointing to some strange thing that caught the eye. A sign outside a building that announced a brothel. A garden of dead trees. A boat still moored at a dock.

Nearly half an hour had passed when the reader suddenly broke the quiet with a sharp gasp.

Bela, startled, followed his gaze up along the stretch of road ahead and saw, in the distance before them, a building larger than the rest. It had the same light stone walls, but it had a dome for a roof, tiled in crimson, and fronted by a colonnade of black pillars. A brilliant white tower, perhaps taller than the others around the bay—it was hard to tell from the ground—rose behind and above it, looking over the city like a sentinel.

And floating beside the tower, hanging in the air, was a black ship beneath a bulbous gray mass that looked for all the world like a spineless pufferfish.

Bela stood in shock and horror. Her heart skipped a beat. "Windborn," she whispered. By the Mother, had they come all this way only to have their enemies arrive before them?

Tew had stopped walking as well. Gazing up into the sky, he shielded his eyes with his hand. "Can't be," he said.

There were multiple docks—she had no other word for them—atop the tower. The airship was fitted into one. The others were empty. The wind was rippling the bag above the ship, but nothing else was moving.

"No," Tew said, and his tone was confident. He took a few steps forward. "That's not a Windborn airship."

Bela shook her head. It was true that it didn't look quite like one of the crafts she saw raining fire on the harbor in her nightmares, but what else could it be?

"Centuries," Tew said. His voice was almost reverential. "It's been there for centuries."

"Centuries? Are you saying that's … from the war?"

Tew nodded. "I think so."

He looked back at her, and he was smiling—but then his smile froze. His eyes fixed on something behind her. His face shook.

Bela turned.

An aluman was behind them. Twice Bela's height. Broad shouldered. Plated with metal.

It had come out from one of the buildings, and it had stopped in the middle of the street. Neckless, its upper body twisted until it was looking down the battered paving stones of the road—down at them. Its eyes were pale blue. The claws on its long arms flexed. In and out. In and out.

The aluman's legs turned now, facing them. It made a whirring sound and took a step.

Bela thought she could feel the street tremble.

She took a step back. Her one arm reached behind her, as if it would protect the reader. "Run," she said.

"Mother," Tew whispered.

It took another step. Bela saw its wide hips flexing, like a wild cat preparing to charge. "Run!"

Bela grabbed hold of Tew as she turned. She pulled him into motion.

They were running blind, but they were near a side street. Bela sprinted for it, anxious to at least put a building between them and the horrifying thing. It was coming after them, she was sure. She felt its footsteps heavy on the road.

They rounded the corner onto the smaller street. It was littered with blocks of stone from the buildings to either side. Bela jumped and swerved through them, Tew close behind, searching for someplace to hide.

The aluman made a sound like a scream or an angry roar through clenched teeth. To Bela's horror, it was echoed back. From their left. From their right.

And from ahead. Around the corner of another street, a second aluman appeared. It turned to look at them. It, too, screamed.

Bela skidded to a stop, started to back away. But then the first aluman was behind them, and they were trapped.

The alumen, as if they were of one mind, stepped forward at the same time. Tew made a sound like he was weeping.

"No," she said. "No. No."

There was a thunderous, quaking sound. The remains of a shop across the street from them shook, then broke as a third aluman burst through its wall, shattering stones like thin glass on its impact. It turned to face them, to see them, and Bela saw that it had a satchel at its side, like a larger version of the reader's book bag. It had a leather scabbard strapped around its back as well, though it was empty. The sword—as long as Tew was tall, Bela thought—was gripped in one clawed hand. Blue fire rippled along the edges of the blade, crackling and sparking like lines of lightning.

"Hide," it said.

Its voice was deep, the sound of mountains moving, and though neither Bela nor Tew understood how the monster could talk, they did not argue. They backed into an open doorway. Crouching, they hid behind the debris inside.

And there they watched, in fascination and in horror, as the first two alumen turned toward the new one. They roared. They attacked. And the third one, raising its sword, roared back.

36

The Bone Mask

The door to the Bone Pirate's cabin was thick oak, stained and polished to a deep red sheen that was the color of blood at night. It might've been beautiful, Alira thought, but for the bones that had been set into its surface: the face of a human skull, its jaws open. Staring at it in horror, Alira wanted to imagine that it was meant to be coming from the wood, like a diver just breaking the surface of the sea, gasping a breath into aching lungs. But the more she stared, the more she thought it wasn't a gasp. It was a scream. A final shout of terror before the face was pulled down forever.

Tai knocked on the heavy wood beside it. Then, after a few heartbeats, she opened the door. Alira, motioned forward, stepped inside.

The room was in the same place that the cabin of the shipmistress had been aboard the *Black Crow*—across the stern of the ship, just above the rudder—and it was roughly the same size. But nothing else seemed the same. It was ornate in a way that neither Seaborn cabins nor Stormborn homes ever were. The woods—of the bunk, of the massive bleached-oak desk, of the cabinetry—were all intricately carved. Even the wooden frames between the panes of glass in the great bank of windows across the rear of the cabin were made beautiful with twists and turns in the wood. Alira's eye wanted to go to it all, but her gaze couldn't be shaken from what stood at the center of the room, behind the broad desk, framed by those windows: the seat of bones and the skull-masked woman who sat upon it.

To stand before the Throne of Bones was to stand before death. Every Seaborn girl knew it. And every Seaborn woman upon the sea lived in fear of it.

The truth was more frightening than Alira had ever imagined: a jumbled mix of human remains, spliced together almost as if to mock the human form itself. The sides of the chair were the long bones of human arms, held together by the mortal grips of the thinner bones of hands and fingers. The fronts of its arms, leading down to the floor, were legs, ornamented with twists of human spines.

The Bone Pirate sat at ease on a seat of leather stretched over pelvis bones, her back against a pile of skulls stacked among splayed ribs. She wore a stormcoat the color of shrouds, and her long, dark hair was pulled back around the mask upon her face: the front half of yet one more skull, this one missing its lower jaw. In the shadows of the open sockets where another's eyes had once been, the living eyes that stared out were big and brown.

Alira took a few hesitant steps into the room. The door shut behind her. Tai was gone. She was alone with the Bone Pirate. Her heart was pounding so hard in her chest that she felt it in her ears.

She took a deep breath, trying to calm herself, trying to

focus, trying to figure out how to start talking to a woman who'd sent untold numbers of Seaborn women to their deaths. A woman who'd killed so many for so long that some thought her immortal. Some kind of magick, Alira had thought when she was younger. Though now, seeing the lack of wrinkles on the living fingers that rested on the throne's bony arms, she wondered if maybe the only thing long-lived was the mask.

Alira opened her mouth to speak, then couldn't decide whether to begin by kneeling or giving a respectful nod. Caught between both, she gave an awkward bow.

The Bone Pirate didn't respond. She just stared. Her mouth, visible beneath the half-face of skull, was a tight line.

"Thank you for—"

The Bone Pirate cut her off by raising her right hand, a single finger lifted up. The head tilted a little, and Alira felt like a mouse in a trap, beneath the gaze of an owl that was curious to study its prey before eating it.

"Your name is Alira?" The Bone Pirate's voice wasn't as high as Tai's had been, but it was no less surprising. It had a soft undertone. The sound of a young woman who, in another life, might have grown up to be a healer.

Alira nodded. "I was born on Myst Motri. I was shipwrecked here on the Rootless Isle."

The skull-masked face tilted the other way now, examining her. "The ship?"

Alira's face was tight. "The *Black Crow*."

The Bone Pirate nodded slowly, thoughtfully. "If you've come to seek vengeance, you should know I did not sink it."

Alira swallowed hard and nodded. So the Windborn

airship had indeed sent it to the depths. And Bela hadn't lived to be seized and murdered by the Bone Pirate. That night—that moment when they kissed, when the airship dropped its fires upon them—Alira had been thrown into the sea. Bela had met the Mother.

It was good to know. But she was too exhausted to hold her emotions in check. Her limbs shook. She wanted to sit down. If she had any tears left, she wanted to shed them.

There was a knock at the door. It opened, and someone else entered the cabin.

"Do you recognize her?" The Bone Pirate was looking over Alira's shoulder, at the door.

Dazed, Alira turned toward the open door. Tai was there, and another young woman stood beside her, almost as small. She had bright-green eyes, and they widened on seeing her. "Alira?"

Alira blinked. She knew her. The girl who'd spent so much time up in the gull's nest of the *Black Crow*, watching the horizons. A face she'd thought dead, but now standing here—alive, breathing, a little older. "Hikora?"

Hikora ran forward to wrap arms around her. Alira gasped at both the firmness of the embrace and the shock of seeing her. "We'd thought you'd gone to the Mother's Embrace!" Hikora exclaimed.

"I thought you all …" Alira choked on her own words.

Hikora pulled away, face beaming. Then she tugged at Alira, forced her to move so she could look out the windows on the starboard side of the Bone Pirate's cabin.

The other ship she'd glimpsed. Alira saw it now. And she knew it too. Whole chunks of the ship were different— repairs after the Windborn attack, surely—but she still recognized railings and hull boards that she and Bela had scrubbed clean again and again. The *Black Crow*.

Alira staggered. The world was suddenly spinning. If Hikora was alive, if the *Black Crow* hadn't sunk, then maybe—"Bela?"

"Not here," Hikora said. "But she's alive."

It was too much. The floor suddenly seemed to be rising up, but Hikora had grabbed her elbow and was keeping her upright.

"She's very weak," Tai said, coming up to help.

The Bone Pirate stood. "Sit her down."

One of them had pulled a chair to the other side of the massive desk in front of the throne.

Guided by Tai and Hikora, Alira fell into it. Her arms shook in relief.

Bela. Alive. All this time. *Alive.* Mother.

She couldn't believe it. Her mind reeled with questions. What had happened to her, where she was, how she could—

No. Safety first. Kora, Amaru, all the rest—they were here now. They needed help. "There are others on the island," she said.

Tai exchanged a look with the Bone Pirate, who sat down and stared across the bare wood of the table at her. "The Rootless. They've taken some of us."

Alira shook her head. "No. They haven't. All this time, I've been living with the Rootless—the Stormborn, they call themselves. I assure you that the same thing that hunts you hunts them. They hunted me too. They took me. I barely got away."

Hikora set a hand on her arm reassuringly. "Is that what happened to you?"

Alira nodded, smiled with as much strength as she could manage. "I lived."

The Bone Pirate abruptly stood and walked to the window at the side of the room. She stared out at the *Black Crow*. "Are these Stormborn, as you call them, the ones at our gates?"

"They are. What's left of them. They've come—I've come—to ask for your help. Please, let them inside."

Tai's back straightened up as she turned toward the pirate leader. "We can't do that, can we?"

Something about her tone made Alira blink up through her exhaustion. The Bone Pirate's shoulders had fallen, as if a heavy weight had been placed upon them. "I … I don't know," she said.

"This is your ship," Alira said. "Your bay. You're the Bone Pirate."

The Bone Pirate let out a long breath. "No, I am not." She reached up and pulled the mask from her face before turning back around. She was, as Alira had thought, a young woman. A beautiful woman, though her eyes seemed tired early. "My name is Julara."

"I don't understand."

Julara carefully slipped the mask into a bag at her side. "The Bone Pirate left here not long after you arrived on the island. She left with Belakané."

"What?"

"I can read numbers. I'm the only one left who can. So the women put me in charge to help keep track of the stores."

"Ti'nay's broken toe," Alira swore.

No one disagreed. It was, indeed, chaos.

"We all have questions," Hikora said after a moment. "But to start—"

Julara chewed on her lip for a moment, then nodded. "Right. To start, we get your people inside the walls. Tai?"

The pirate stood, hesitated. "Some of the women will grumble."

"Suggest to them that I might miscount their next meal allotment if they do."

Tai smiled, gave the slightest bow of her head, and left.

"Thank you," Alira said. "But you should know the Bloodborn will be coming."

"The Bloodborn?" Hikora asked.

"The ones who took me."

"Our walls are strong," Julara said.

"Ours were too."

Julara walked back and sat down on the throne with a heavy sigh. "Well, it's a start. A step while we figure out what to do."

37

The Lumicker's Shop

The bells had fallen silent. Everyone in the Blue Keep knew what was coming. The walls were manned. The airship was ready to take flight. All that was left was the waiting.

And for Shae, a visit to Aro Lanser, to try to convince him to leave.

Even from the doorway, Shae could see that the workshop full of strange metal parts and pieces was more of a mess than it had been before. Closing the door behind her, she made her way toward the table he'd been working at before. Alumen parts were everywhere.

"Aro?"

She heard a clang from farther in the back, a rattle of dropped metal. "That you, Shaesara?"

Shae weaved her way between piles of strewn debris, heading toward the lumicker's voice. "It's me. Did you hear the bells?"

Around a corner, she spied him. He was on his knees, sifting through parts on a lower shelf. He looked tired and sweaty, but he was completely absorbed in his work.

"Did you hear the bells?" she repeated.

Getting close now, she could see he had a tiny metal gear in his fingers, and he was carefully comparing it to other gears of similar size. "Hmm?"

"The bells, Aro. Did you hear them?"

"Oh. Of course. Yes. Distracting."

"It's an army of alumen," Shae said. "No one has seen anything like it."

It appeared that he'd found the part he wanted. He grinned over at her in victory. "So I've heard—the army, your plans ... Think you could help an old man up?"

Shae took hold of his hand and helped haul him to his feet. He staggered for a moment but caught himself on the shelf. It rattled in response. His eyes were even more sunken than she'd thought. "Have you even slept since we got here?" she asked.

For all his age, he suddenly looked sheepish, like a child caught out of line. "Well, I've just been working, and—"

"Aro—"

"Now, now, don't be lecturing your elders." He abruptly cheered up and gave her a friendly wink. "I may not have slept, but come see what I've done."

The lumicker led her back to his work table, talking as he did so. "You know, I've taken countless crystals out of them over the years. Pulled them apart bit by bit. So you'd think putting it all back together wouldn't be hard. But it really is. Seems the soulglass needs a specific system around it. It's like a person, I suppose. Take away an arm or a leg, for instance, and a person can live just fine. But take away vital organs, and they can't."

Shae thought back to what she'd seen him working on

when she'd first visited the shop. "So that's why you started with a head?"

He paused to quickly rummage through an assortment of boxes with wires sticking out of them. After a moment, he picked one out before continuing on. "Exactly. I thought I'd just route power from the crystal to the head. But it wasn't that simple." They reached his work table with its scattered parts and tools. He set the newly scavenged pieces down, and he organized them in a fashion that, from Shae's perspective, had no organization. There was a cloth in the middle of it all. He lifted it, exposing the soulglass that she'd pickpocketed from Marek. The smoke inside the crystal seemed to coil up like a threatened snake. "See, the soulglass is the heart of the aluman. It's what gives it life. I've figured out that the better thing to do is to start with that and move outward."

"Only add to it what it needs to work."

"Right," he said. "Well, only add what we need to work."

"So, like, a way to hear."

"And, hopefully, a way to communicate."

Among the parts on his table was one of the metal heads. It had no jaw that she could see. Neither had Asryth, though the stories were that she'd been able to talk before she'd been attacked and nearly destroyed. "Wait. How *do* they speak?"

Aro's mustache went crooked in a familiar grin; then he pushed through his parts before he found a silver box the size of his hand. It had a black circle on one side. "Lumickers call it a 'speaker,'" he said. "Not a terribly creative name, I know."

He handed it to her. The circle, she saw, was a rubber

ring. And the round material it framed could flex and move. "This makes sound?"

"That particular one is broken. But yes."

Shae shook her head and laughed at her own expense. "I don't understand how any of this works."

He shrugged. "Can't say we really understand, either. We know the what, but not the how—if you catch my meaning."

"I do." It was fascinating. But it also wasn't why she'd come. She set the strange object down. "Listen, Aro, the attack that's coming—"

"Ah, yes," he said. "Is it true that you and Kayden will take to the airship?"

"Kayden wants to bomb the mountain slopes and send the snows down on them."

The lumicker nodded, then smoothed his mustache with his fingers. "It's a good plan. He's a smart man, that lad."

"So, what will you do?"

He spread his hands over the table as if the answer was obvious enough. "Make this work."

"They'll be here soon, Aro."

"I know. But I'm close. I just need a little more time." He sat down at his stool and started to fit the gears he'd brought with a bundle of them that was already there. "I'm sure this will work. And if Kayden's avalanche fails, if the lumick defenses here fail, this might be all the chance we have."

"Do you think they'll fail?"

"Do I think what will fail?" he asked over his shoulder.

"The defenses."

He paused, seemed to chew on the thought. "Hard to say. As you said, no one has seen this before."

"If they fail, can you fix them?"

"While we're being attacked?" He shook his head. "No. If they fail … well, everyone here will die."

"That's what we thought too," she said. "And that's exactly why you need to come with us."

He stopped what he was doing and looked up. "Come with you where?"

"On the airship," Shae said. It was her turn to gesture to the table littered with parts. "You bring what you need. Finish it there."

"My tools are here."

"And they can be there. Listen. If the worst happens, you're no good here. But on the airship … well, there might be more time."

Aro seemed ready to instinctively object; then he saw how serious she looked and thought about it for a moment. "I suppose I've got most of the pieces ready to go. I could finish gathering them up. Haul it up and meet you there."

"Quickly. There isn't much time."

"Of course. It won't take long."

"Good." Shae smiled, genuinely relieved that Aro would be with them. "I'll try to send someone to help."

"No need. Though, if you could, I'd appreciate it if you carried something ahead for me."

When Shae agreed, he stood and pulled off his work apron. Then he weaved his way through the shelves to the door of the workshop. His familiar long coat and his wide-brimmed hat were there, as was the holster for his boltgun. He quickly put them all on and opened the door.

It was bitter cold outside the workshop, and getting colder by the minute as the sun set.

Aro walked to his lumicker's wagon. But instead of going to the door in back, he went to its side. There, he crouched down and reached for the belly of the wagon, the long stretch of wood between the large wheels. As she watched, his fingers found latches that she could not see. He moved them, and a long panel fell open.

The thing inside looked like a boltgun—the same grip, the same shining silver tube—but it was three or four times as long as the one he had in his holster. Aro carefully pulled it out and checked that it was in good working order. A thin leather strap hung down between its grip and the end of its barrel. When he was done, he held the strap open for her shoulder. "If you don't mind carrying this to the airship, I'd be obliged." He smiled as she took it up. "If things start before I get there, do use him well."

"Him?"

The lumicker shrugged, once again looking a little sheepish. "I named him."

"Do I dare ask?"

He grinned. "Perle's Eyes."

"Pearl Eyes?"

"No. Perle's Eyes. As in, Someday-I-Will-Put-A-Bolt-Between-Rumin-Perle's-Eyes."

38

Streets of Ghosts

When its left leg was nearly twisted out of whatever passed for its hip socket, the second of the attacking alumen went down hard. Its face slammed into the surface of the pitted street with a sound of crumpling metal. It made a noise like a groan. It tried to push itself up. But the left leg was useless and refused to cooperate.

It saw Bela and Tew still hiding in the doorway of the ruined building beside the street and tried to push and pull itself to them with its remaining limbs.

It didn't get far. When it was ten feet from them, the third aluman—the one that could talk—leaped up onto its back. The fallen thing made a sound like a scratching of bark on burlap canvas.

A whimper, Bela thought. That's what it was.

The aluman standing on its back had picked up the sword that had been knocked from its hands in the fight. The edges of the blade sparked with blue power. It lifted the humming blade, pushed the tip between plates on the fallen thing's back. Leaning its weight forward, it shoved the point down, through the metal man, to the stone below.

The fallen aluman shuddered. It seemed to sigh. Then it looked up at Bela, and the blue light of its eyes went out.

"Mother's mercy," Tew whispered.

The remaining aluman yanked the blade out, then turned its enemy onto its back. It stood to one side, lifted its blade, and removed the metal head in a single terrifying stroke. Then, quick and easy as a fisherman cleaning his catch, it stabbed its strange blade down the monster's neck and cut open the plates of its chest. In less than a minute, it was pulling free the soulglass at its heart. It tossed the crystal into the satchel at its hip. Just as efficiently, it did the same to the other metal man it had killed. When it was done, the blue lightning along the edge of its blade vanished, and the aluman sheathed the quieted weapon into the scabbard at its back.

Then, at last, the remaining aluman turned toward the broken doorway where Bela and Tew had cowered during the violent struggle of metal monsters. "You hid well," it said.

"You can speak," Tew said.

The aluman's torso made a sound of grinding metal plates as its upper body flexed slightly to the side, and Bela imagined that the neckless creature was effectively cocking its head to the side. "I spoke before this," it said.

The slats below its blue-glowing eyes didn't move, but Bela nevertheless saw them as the hulking thing's mouth. She could discern no visible movement causing it, but the sound of its deep voice clearly rumbled up from there.

"Yes, I know," Tew stammered. "I just didn't—"

"No time. Must go. Follow Kolum."

"Kolum?" Tew blurted the word in his shock, then turned to Bela with surprise.

She, too, couldn't believe it. For all that they'd talked of him—the man, according to the stories, who'd opened the first portal and brought about so much destruction, who'd become an aluman himself—neither of them expected him to still be alive ... if what an aluman had might be called life. And certainly neither of them thought they might meet him, might talk with him. That he was real, that he was here in this city of ghosts, was just one more shock.

But Bela was, she thought, becoming numb to shocks. They had a mission. That was what mattered. Find the portal. Close it. And Kolum would know where that was.

For his part, Kolum ignored their reactions. His hips turned, and he took a giant step away from them. "More approach," he said. "Come with me now."

He didn't wait for their response. He was already moving away. The two destroyed alumen on the paving stones rocked slightly as each step landed beside them.

Though she knew enough to understand that having a mutual enemy didn't make an ally a friend, Bela also knew that they'd be helpless if more alumen came. She stood and slipped out of the doorway, Tew in her wake. "Come on," she said. "If he wanted, I think we'd be dead already."

Kolum had nearly rounded the corner to the south, heading west, and they had to hurry to keep up with the strides of his long legs.

He led them through streets of disaster, and Bela began to see them not just as monuments to past horrors, but as testaments to a present fight. What they'd seen hadn't been Kolum's first fight against his fellow alumen. He'd destroyed others. She hadn't understood this before. Perhaps she'd been too in awe of the extraordinary size of the city or the magnificence of its architecture—or even just the impossibility that it existed and that she'd found it. Whatever had kept her blind, she saw now what she'd been missing. The metal arm caught in a pile of rubble. The lifeless aluman crumpled in a hole in a building, its chest splayed open. The line of metal heads on a wall, set up like some kind of mocking decoration.

But no human bodies. For all the destruction, for all the death that had been dealt in the stories, there were no piles of bones.

If it wasn't for the size of the doorways and the rooms and the chairs and everything that was in them—all much too small for the lumbering metal men—she could almost have thought that no women or men had ever lived in the city at all. Kolum said nothing. His only acknowledgment of their presence was to hold up a clawed hand, now and again, causing them to stop in place while he listened. Bela tried to listen too. The most she heard was the echo of falling stones, clattering down onto some distant street. Whether it was caused by another aluman's footsteps or was just one more sign of the city's slow decay, Bela didn't know. Kolum only waited a minute before dropping his hand and walking on.

It was a meandering path, but she could tell they were headed west. Now and again, she'd see, between the canyon walls of buildings, a glimpse of the mighty tower and its single strange airship. It was getting closer.

At last, Kolum turned them off the street, down a kind of path between shops, so narrow that he had to step sideways to pass through. He had no neck. Neither had the others. So

Bela watched him walk—step by step, facing the wall just a foot in front of his blue eyes—unable to turn to see where he was going or how far he had to go.

Blind faith, she thought.

The path opened into a square space big enough for the aluman to step out and turn around. Just before she stepped out to join Kolum in the openness, Bela saw that there were claw marks all along the walls of the narrow path near its exit. The buckled bricks of angry impacts. Places where the walls were cracked and bent. Another fight that Kolum must have won.

Did they feel anything being killed? Did he feel anything as he killed them? Could he?

Kolum turned to an adjacent side of the square. There was a sheet of metal leaned up there, the size of the aluman himself. His own metal parts creaking, Kolum lifted it away, revealed a hole that had once been a doorway but had been broken out—tall and wide enough for him to hunch over and pass through. He set the metal against the side of the house and turned to them.

"Inside," he said.

They entered what must have once been a communal area for a family. A table and chairs. A long chest. Everything had been pushed aside to give space for Kolum to step inside, but none of it had been thrown out of the way. It had all been very carefully moved, as if to be ready at a moment's notice for the former occupants to return.

There was a half-wall along the other side of the room, with cooking spaces beyond it. Plates. Cups. Utensils. Everything sat there still, untouched but for the dust and the spidering lines of frost upon them. Stairs and hallways whispered of ghosts.

Kolum stepped inside behind them, turning away to pull the metal sheet back into its place.

When the aluman's back was turned, Tew nudged Bela to look up. The ceiling had been pulled away, broken down, but only in a single, careful line through the middle of this living room. Through the hole, she could see other rooms. Beds. A child's room.

"Safe here," Kolum said.

Startled, Bela turned. Kolum was able to stand upright with his head and shoulders through the hole in the ceiling, but he was nonetheless squatting down to face them. His every movement was controlled, as if he didn't want to disturb even the dust. As if this was a sacred place.

"This was your home," she said. "Before you became ..."

Her voice trailed off as she couldn't think of how to speak of what he was. Tew gave her a look that she wanted to understand. Was he surprised that this had once been Kolum's home? Or surprised she'd said it out loud? But she kept her focus on the metal man. He creaked again, and his torso once more moved to the side. "My home it remains. And you are guests in it." He raised a clawed hand and swung it toward the chairs that had been pushed to the side of the room. "Sit."

Tew nodded, pulled a chair from the wall to give to Bela. They sat.

Kolum brought his weight gently to the ground in front of the door. His arms moved up to rest upon his knees. For a moment, Bela thought, he looked like the Throne of Bones on the *Pale Dawn*—a memory from what seemed a lifetime ago. Ghosts of her own.

Kolum's eyes didn't change. They glowed steadily, bathing everything in a pale-blue light that made the air seem even colder than it was. "You watch for signs," the aluman said.

"Signs of what?" Tew asked.

"Of humanity," Kolum replied.

Bela at last looked away, to nod at the reader. "He can talk. He brought us to his home. We were told they were monsters. The others were. Or seemed so. And he destroyed them like they were. But now, here—" She looked up at Kolum's face again. "Are you … alive?"

Kolum's clawed fingers flexed and fell. "I think that word has no meaning here."

"Do you feel pain?" Bela asked.

"I think this, too, has no meaning here. But I feel loss. I look into these rooms. I see what once was here. A family. I recognize the absence."

"Your wife's name was Asryth," Tew said.

One of Kolum's fingers scraped across his knee. It felt like an angry sound. "It is her name."

"I'm sorry," Bela said. She tried to smile, tried to restart their conversation. "We didn't thank you for saving us. Those others out there would have killed us. So thank you. My name is Bela. This is Tewrick."

"Bela." Kolum's finger lifted and fell upon his knee. "Yes. It is as I heard."

Tew cocked his head. "Heard?"

"Why you are here, I know," Kolum said. "Whispers on the wind. You would destroy the portal. You would destroy me."

"Does that make you afraid?" Bela asked.

"I think it has no meaning here."

"And what about death?"

"We were dead in the beginning," he replied. "And we are dead even now."

39

Taking Flight

Shae had seen how firepowder had blown Kayden's airship apart. She'd seen how it could propel an iron ball through a woman's body. It was powerful, its own kind of magick.

And now, kneeling on the deck of a different airship, she held open a burlap bag so that the two young men who were helping them could quickly fill it with scoops of the explosive, soot-like dust and a fuse.

It was more than a little frightening.

The men's names were Ragan and Tadd. Good men who worked quickly and efficiently to get the bags ready. She didn't think they needed her help, but she was glad for the movement to keep her fingers warm in the cold night air. She was glad, too, for the distraction to keep her from staring out at what was marching far too quickly up the valley below.

Bombs, Tadd called the bags. They'd made a half-dozen already. As each was prepared, it was lined up along the railing to either side of the foredeck.

Kayden had been right when he'd said that the airship

was little different from her *Pale Dawn*. Take away the bladed lumick engines at its sides, replace the massive bag of air above the deck with some proper masts and sails, and the Windborn craft might've made a passable seafaring vessel. It even had a similar deck layout to some of the ships the Bone Pirate had taken over the years. The helm for the shipmistress—the captain, she corrected herself—was on a raised rear deck over the stern, looking ahead toward the bow across the mid- and foredecks.

Steps to a single-door hatchway ran down under the helm, allowing access to the cabins and storage spaces belowdecks. The lines binding the airbag to the ship were similar to those aboard a Seaborn ship. There were even rope ladders heading upward, though they were disappearing up the side of the gray floating mass rather than into sails and beams.

The newest bomb now filled, Shae heaved it over to the port side. Coming back, she saw the lumicker hustling across the ramp from the Blue Keep's mooring tower. His long coat was flapping in the cold wind; his wide hat was pulled tight on his head. He got aboard, smiled at her, then looked past her into the eastern dark, out beyond the airship, where the blue eyes of the alumen bobbed like the rising tide of a glowing sea in the valley.

"Gods," he said.

Shae had braided her hair for the coming fight, but the cold breeze was grabbing stray strands and pulling them across her face. She pushed them out of the way. "Told you it was bad. Let's go."

The old man had several satchels around his shoulders. Behind him, two men were hauling a large box aboard.

Shae directed the lumicker through the hatchway toward one of the quarters belowdecks, but he hesitated. "I'd rather work up here," he said.

As if on cue, Kayden limped up the hatch stairs. He was doing what he could to hide his pain and exhaustion as they hurriedly readied the airship for flight, but Shae could see it clearly. "Warmer down below," he said. "It'll get colder and windier when we get going."

Aro smiled. "I'm not playing with papers, lad. And if I get this box to work, you might need my help."

"Right." Kayden pointed up to what he'd called the map table when Shae had first come aboard. It was on the raised rear deck, just behind the helm itself, waist-high, with a fixed stool for a seat and lit by two oil lamps at the corners of the stern. "Up there. Let's go."

In minutes, Aro and the men helping him had his satchels of tools and his box in place.

Behind them all, Kayden had managed to lift himself up to the rear deck too. He was holding himself upright using the pegged handles of the helm's wheel. He ordered Aro's helpers to loose the mooring lines. "Then report to Oth Marek," he said. "Hold the wall. Whatever it takes."

After awkward bows, they freed the lines before hurrying back down the tower into the warmth of the Blue Keep.

As Kayden fiddled with switches on the helm, Shae watched Aro remove the front of his box. An aluman head had been mounted inside. Surrounding it was a mess of cables and wires that ran up holes drilled in its neck or the sides of its head. The thing he'd called a speaker was mounted to the upper-left corner of the box. In the upper-right corner was a metal cradle, inside of which he'd fitted the soulglass. When she thought about it, how these were the insides of an aluman, now dragged to its outsides, the sight seemed awful and obscene. Instinctively, she looked into its eyes, expecting to see a sign of pain or anguish, but they were just empty black lenses of glass.

Aro was already spreading out tools and trying to connect the remaining wires and parts. "You spent your whole life on the waves," he said over his shoulder. "How is it that you're more comfortable on this ship than I am?"

"A ship is a ship," Shae said. "Haven't you ever been on one of these?"

"Only on the ground for lumick repairs." He laughed a little. "I'm afraid of heights."

"Ramp clear, mooring lines loose," Kayden announced. "Engines burning blue. Shae, I need you here with me."

Shae patted Aro's shoulder, then turned around and moved forward to stand to the left side of the helm, in the same place she'd stood during her many years as the Bone Pirate's maiden. Tadd and Ragan had paused their bomb-making to swing the ramp back into place against the side of the hull. That left the mooring lines still dangling down from the corners of the ship. "Shall I draw in the lines?" she asked.

Kayden shook his head. "I don't think you can do it alone. And this isn't like a ship at sea, where the water will ruin the ropes. All that matters is they're clear of the engines, which they are."

"I could help," the lumicker said from his bench behind them.

"Rather have you get that thing to work so you can tell these metal bastards to get off my land," Kayden replied.

"Besides, we'll be needing the lines when we fly back as heroes."

Shae wished she had anything like optimism for such a half-baked plan, but she was comforted that they were doing something, at least, and not simply waiting for the wave of the coming sea to wash over the walls of the keep and drown them in their own blood. Even better, if the worst came to pass, the three of them were aboard an airship now. Kayden had wanted her to use it to go home to the Fair Isles. But with Aro's help, she could surely take him there herself. She told herself that this was because a Bone Pirate with an airship and lumick weapons would own the waves and stand forever free—but in truth, her heart told her there was a far different reason that she wanted Kayden with her.

Love.

That would definitely complicate things back in the bay.

"Two things are different," Kayden said.

"What?"

"At the helm here, Shae. I'll have the wheel. That moves us on the horizontal plane, port and starboard. Same as your wheel at sea. But that's where the similarities end." Still holding tight to the wheel for support, he pointed to the closer of two tall levers to its left, standing between them. "This one is for speed. We don't have to tighten or roll out sails. Just push it forward to go forward, and pull it backward to go the other direction. Got it?"

"Do I do this?"

"To start, yes. But we're rather shorthanded on crew just now. You may need to do other things."

Shae was certain that he didn't have the strength to turn

the wheel and work the levers, too, but she was also certain that Aro would help if it came to that. Probably while smoking his pipe. "And the other lever?" she asked.

"That's the hard one. You're at least used to the idea of speed. But that lever controls what you don't have on a Seaborn ship at all: the vertical plane. Push it forward to go down, pull it back to go up."

Shae frowned. "Forward to go forward would make sense. But forward to go down?"

"Think of it like leaning forward onto the bow and pushing it down."

Shae chewed on her lip as she touched the levers and mapped the actions in her mind. "So slam them both all the way forward and—"

"And we hit the ground very fast."

"Please don't do that," Aro said from behind. A puff of smoke drifted up between them. He had indeed lit his pipe while he worked.

"Got it," she said. "Orders?"

"Slow ahead," he said. "That means to ease us forward."

Shae nodded. "Slow ahead, aye." She slipped her hand around the knob atop the lever for speed and shifted it toward the bow of the ship. It moved easily. Below them, there was a thrum in response. On either side of the deck, the swordlike blades of the lumick engines began to turn, slicing through the cold air.

Kayden turned the wheel to port, and the ship eased forward in that direction. "Well done," he said.

Shae moved her hand to the other lever. "Do I do anything with this one?"

"Not yet. Let's keep her steady-plane for now," he said.

"That means level, just as we are. Down-plane means down. Up-plane means up."

Shae took her hand off the lever and stood in what had been her ready position for orders. "Steady-plane, aye," she announced. There wasn't anyone to carry the orders forward into the rigging and the sails, but the habit of announcing the commands was a habit just the same.

"I could get used to this," Kayden said.

"What?"

He grinned at her. "You doing what I say."

"It won't last long, my lord," she said, and it was her turn to grin. "In the long run, you'll find I know a lot more about little men in boats than you do."

Kayden narrowed his eyes, confused.

Behind them, Aro laughed around his pipe.

40

The Last Man

Bela stared. "You're not the first person I've heard say those words. 'We were dead in the beginning.' The Bone Pirate—Shae—spoke them. Why?"

Kolum, sitting before them, didn't move as he spoke. "It is an old saying here. Why she speaks it, I cannot say. But surely this is not what you wish to ask?"

Tewrick leaned forward. "You said that you knew of us. 'Whispers on the wind,' you said. Does that mean Asryth?"

"I hear much through the Stream. Much that I wish I did not."

Bela gently pushed Tew back into his chair. "We have a lot of questions. You said you knew why we were here."

"What we built, you would destroy."

"What you built," Tew corrected.

"This is your story? That I alone did this?" The metal man's body flexed in what might have been a sigh if he'd had breath. "She has done her work well."

Bela took a deep breath of her own. "Let's start there, then. We have stories, Kolum. But I'm starting to think they're half-told and only half-remembered. Tell us what happened. The portals. The war. How all this came to be. Can you tell us that?"

Kolum seemed to think for a moment. "Yes. It is good for you to understand what you do."

Tew pulled a book from his bag, then a quill and a small glass bottle of black liquid that had somehow survived all that they'd been through. He put the bottle between his hands and breathed on it to warm it up.

The aluman's blue eyes watched his movements. "You will draw my words," he said.

The reader smiled. "Yes. Writing. Is it … may I write down what you say?"

Kolum's shoulders flexed. A shrug, Bela suspected. "If you copy them well."

Tew nodded. "I will. Thank you."

"Long have I thought how I would speak of things, though I have had no one to speak to."

"None of the others can talk as you can?" Bela asked. That would be one question she had answered.

Kolum moved his body to shake his head. "None here. Only to the bones I find do I talk."

"The bones of the people?" That would answer another of her questions.

"Hard is the ground. But still, I dig for them."

Bela smiled. Whatever he'd become, a part of him was still human. That had been her biggest question of all. "Proof of humanity."

"I am glad that it is found. For my story, make it read as if better said. As if spoken by yourself."

Once again, Tew nodded. "As you wish."

"Good," Kolum said. "Do you have a name for those who use the gold dust in your lands? The ones who make magick?"

Tew was frantically rubbing the jar of ink, but Bela could see that he was listening. Writing in his mind. "Evokers," he replied. "And I think your gold dust is what we call Char."

"Evokers. Char. Yes. I have heard these words." Kolum's clawed fingers flexed and moved on his knees. "I will speak when you are ready."

Tew shook the jar, looked at it, then carefully secured it between his thighs. Uncorking it, he carefully stirred his quill in its black waters before cleaning the pen's edge on the glass lip. He opened his book to a blank page and lifted the quill to it. He looked up in anticipation.

He was born for this, Bela thought. Maybe they all were.

Kolum straightened up. Then he began.

You must imagine me a man. Not this. I had flesh and blood. I had hands, and if I would have placed them on my chest, I could have felt my heart beating. I could laugh. I could cry. I was mortal. I was alive.

I did not seek power. But power came to me. None of us knows why not everyone can take the Char. Some believe there is something in us, something in our blood, that turns the Char to poison or power. Maybe. But I think it is other than this. I think it is the Char that accepts or rejects us, that blesses or kills us. It accepted me, I know. It slipped into my skin like breath into my lungs. It blessed me. It spoke to me.

I opened gates. Windows to other worlds. The things I saw were things none before me had ever seen. The things I learned were things none before me had ever learned.

The greatest, *people would say of me*. None smarter.

But I knew it wasn't the truth. Because my wife, Asryth, was far greater, far smarter. She was not an evoker. She did not take the Char.

But she made magick just the same. Magick from the sweat of her brow, the strength of her hands, and the brilliance of her mind. She grew up in the glow of her father's foundry. She knew the sheen of metals as others know the faces of their friends. And she saw in the metals things that never were—things unimagined—and she made them real. Machines to till fields. Machines to guard doors. Machines to drive airships. Machines for making machines. What others saw as limits, she saw as problems to be solved. When she needed greater heat to make greater metals— greater powers than man or magick could provide—she found ways to harness the power of the sun itself.

The foundry was quickly the largest in Ealond, and as he grew old, her father grew fat and happy. He was a good man, and his riches did not taint him. Few can say this.

I met Asryth at court. Not long after her father died. She and I were at first fascinated by our powers, I think. Each of us so far ahead of the others. I helped her see ways that magick could infuse her metals. She helped me see ways her metals could enhance and hold my magick. We became friends. And, in time, we grew to be more than that. We fell in love.

The name of our daughter was Ada. She was beautiful. I remember how we told each other that she would be smarter than the two of us put together.

When Ada became sick, when we found out she was dying, we learned we were right.

I do not know which of us thought of my gates first.

Sometimes I think it was me, but perhaps I want to spare Asryth the guilt of that. Other times I think it was her, but perhaps this is because I do not want the guilt myself.

The idea was simple. I could open gates to other worlds, but they were fleeting things. Windows opened and quickly shut. What if I could open a gate to a place without death? What if we could pass through it, with Ada? Even more, what if we could end death itself—not just for ourselves, but for everyone? To live is to fear death, and that fear drives so much that is evil in this world. We steal, we cheat, we kill, we create wars, we do all we can to ensure our survival. In the end, we create death from our fear of it.

Doomed to die, we deal out death. End death, and we could end it all.

It took both our skills—her machines, my magick—to find the Life Stream and hold open the window to it. It was dark magick. Bloody magick. It cost me much. But together, we created the portal. Shimmering blue. Perfect.

One of our assistants touched it first. I tried to stop him, but the yearning was too much for him. When he touched it, his soul left him. We saw it. He joined with the Stream and was gone.

It is our flesh that makes us mortal, you see. Flesh is death. The soul is forever. I saw it as a limit. Asryth saw it as a problem to be solved.

We did it, as you know. Two solutions. I created the soulglass, a crystal formed of the most delicate magicks I possessed, which could bridge this world and the Stream, to touch it but remain here. But an eternity lived in a crystal would be a prison, so Asryth built for us new bodies that would never get sick, never rot away. Eternal homes for our eternal lives.

I had only the power to make three crystals at first. One for each of us. And one for Ada.

I went first. I died. I lived. I became that which you see now. Asryth followed. We learned how we could speak to each other, feel each other, through the course of the power that binds together all things in this world. Through the Stream.

No two people have ever been as truly one as we were in that moment. I knew her soul. And she knew mine.

But our daughter—she was, as I said, smarter than us both put together. When she discovered what we'd done, she refused to join us. Said it was an abomination. An evil thing.

She died cursing us.

And we, having become these things, could not weep for her.

Asryth begged me to use my magicks to find a world where Ada still lived, to create a gate to bring her to us, but I refused. She pulled at my very soul, in ways the living cannot imagine. Again, I refused. Her grief gave birth to rage and hatred.

She condemned me, told others that I was trying to keep the secret of immortality to myself. I was driven out of the city, up into the mountains, where I mourned alone.

While I was gone, she used evokers to study what I had done, to make new soulglass. She taunted me with it, let me see it through the Stream. She told me it was because she did not want to suffer eternity alone with me. Perhaps this is so, but I had touched her soul. Even now, I can feel her out there, across so many seas. She speaks only in glimpses, only lets me see what she wants me to see, but I think that there is more to her than hate. I believe she mourns still. And she thought that if the other evokers could learn the secrets of the soulglass, then perhaps they could unlock my ability to open gates, and that they would do for her what her husband would not. They could bring her Ada. It is all she has ever wanted.

But the crystals they made were imperfect. Broken. The metal men they created were mindless beasts, thoughtless until she filled them with whispers of destruction and hate. Of these, she built an army.

When the fighting broke out, it was bloody and terrible. The strength of men is nothing to the strength in these metal arms. And Asryth was using the alumen not just to kill, but to bring her more and more souls for her empty crystals, more engines for the metal men that filled her foundries.

If she could keep making more alumen, all would be lost. So I tried to help those who fought. A group of evokers banded together under my banner. I taught them things I planned to take to my grave. I gave them the power to bring the ice and the cold. To blot out the sun that gave her foundries life.

If your stories say that I broke the world, there is the truth of it. These hands cannot evoke. But I told them how it was done. I told them why it must be done.

When the cold came, the alumen retreated. But war brings more war. It always does.

Asryth told the people that it was magick that had driven the alumen mad, the same magick that had broken the world. Others blamed the machines. People turned on each other. Death fed death. And all the while, the land froze and died.

A group of female evokers left first. They became the Seaborn—hateful of machines, hateful of men.

Group by group, others fled too. The largest of them

would become what you call the Windborn. Asryth went with them, to help run their machines, to help them rebuild. They did not know that her alumen followed too.

I stayed behind. I buried the dead. And then I took the single airship that was left. I went far from here. I did not plan to ever come back.

In all these centuries, I have seen glimpses through the Stream of what she has done. She has helped the Windborn learn to use the soulglass to power their airships and their weapons.

But she has also managed a secret alliance with some of the evokers of your Seaborn—they have been learning how to make new soulglass and to open new portals and gates, just as before. She made the preparations for a great gate in the land of the Windborn, and they did not suspect her treachery.

Through it all, she has been patient. Through it all, she thought she had forever. Until now.

She did not expect that the evokers would use their blood-magick against her. When they did, she was nearly destroyed. You have seen her, Tewrick, for I have seen you through her eyes. She is a shell of herself, trapped among the Seaborn. She nearly had everything taken away by the one you called Mabaya. I saw what happened. I was there, in the Stream, that night, looking out through the portal she had opened. I saw Mabaya destroyed.

But I also saw that Asryth survived. I have heard her whispers. She knows that time runs short. She knows you have been sent to destroy the portal that gives her alumen life. She knows she must act now.

She has sent an alumen army against the Windborn—to march and kill.

She has sent a Seaborn fleet against the Windborn—to take her back to the gate she has built.

She has sent out her blood-magickers—to make their final collections of souls to power it.

And she has sent a band of alumen here—to destroy you and preserve the portal that powers her metal men.

Tewrick pulled his pen back from the page. Despite the cold, there was sweat on his brow. The jar of ink was half-gone. "Here?" he asked. "To kill us?"

"This I saw," Kolum said. "For this I have come. I have protected you. I will see you do what I could not."

The reader nodded. He bit his lip and scratched more lines onto the page.

"Why haven't you destroyed the portal before?" Bela asked. "All these years it's been here. Surely you could have."

Kolum didn't answer for long enough that Tew looked up from his writing. "For centuries we have been between worlds," the metal man finally said. "Without life, we live. Without death, we die. To face that forever alone …" One of Kolum's claws scratched across his knee. "The portal connects us, just as it connects Asryth to the minds of the alumen she made. I do not want to lose her. Alone I will be. Forever."

Tew furrowed his brow. "But you will destroy it. After everything she's done—"

Bela interrupted. "I don't think he will. He said he will see us do it."

Kolum raised and lowered his finger with a click. "Yes. I will protect you. I will let you destroy it. I will see it done."

"Can I have one more question?" Bela asked. "You said the crystals in the other alumen, they were all broken. Can they be fixed?"

Kolum pulled one of the pieces of soulglass from his satchel. He held it up in the blue light of his unblinking eyes. "I have collected so many of them over the years. I have studied them. But without flesh, I cannot wield magick; I cannot see with the blessing of the Char. I do not know if they can be repaired. But I would not wish to do so. I wish them all destroyed."

Tew looked up from his writing. "Destroyed? What happens if they're destroyed?"

The fog in the crystal shimmered in the blue light before them. "I believe that the broken crystals torture the souls inside," Kolum said. "I believe, when they are destroyed, the souls are released to become whole again. They rejoin the Stream."

"To die," Bela whispered, staring at the shifting shape of the darkness in the soulglass. "At last."

"Yes." Kolum put the crystal back into his satchel. "It is for this reason I would make of you a demand, a promise that you will make here in the home where my daughter died."

Bela looked him in his steady eyes. "Name it."

"When destroyed is the portal," Kolum said, "you will help me find Asryth. You will release her."

Bela heard Tew's pen scratch to a halt, but she didn't look away from the metal man whose heart she was beginning to understand.

"And when that is done," Kolum continued, "you will release me."

41

The Last Chance

From the east side of its walls, looking over the alumen graveyard, the Blue Keep was very much true to its name. Every lumick line that laced along its stone heights had been turned on, and their brightness was enough to reduce the torch fires along the tops of the wall to mere points of red and yellow. The lumick light reflected off the high walls and the icy trenches and white snows below, bathing the mountains and the valley between them in an eerie blue glow.

The picture of it might've been beautiful, Shae thought, if it didn't feel so small and desperate.

The feet of the alumen army resounded through the valley like a thousand ceaselessly beating drums. Shae heard it, and she was afraid. She had seen the destruction caused by a single metal man. They'd survived fighting it by luck and chance. Even now, weeks later, Kayden's hands upon the airship's wheel did more than just steer the ship—they held his half-broken body up.

Ragan and Tadd, standing by the bags of firepowder at the foredeck, were looking over the side at the waves of glowing eyes swarming up the valley. They'd exclaimed their astonishment at the sight again and again. So, too, had Aro, who'd twice stepped away from his parts and his tools to do the same.

Shae refused to look. She feared it would stop her heart.

Better to focus on what she could control. Keep Kayden upright. Get the ship into position.

He was bringing the airship up along the highest of the peaks, just ahead of the swarm of alumen. The slope of the mountain below was steep. The snows appeared to be thick. If they could set them loose, they could bring down an avalanche. If the avalanche was big enough, it might sweep up the alumen. If the snow was wet enough, it might kill them.

If, if, if.

"Up-plane just a little more," Kayden instructed. "And slow us down."

Shae moved the levers accordingly. The lumick engines thrummed. The turning rotors alongside the airship slowed them to a crawl, while the nose of the airship rose toward the peak.

The slope was close enough that the engine blades were picking up the skiffs of snow that the winds peeled off the mountain's surface. The crystalline flakes shimmered across Shae's vision.

The feet echoed off the mountainside. Tadd turned back toward them from his position up front. "They're almost below us!"

Kayden nodded. They all knew the plan. If it was going

to work, they needed to set the slope loose upon the mass of the army. "Be ready!" he shouted back.

Tadd nodded. He had a metal cylinder in his hand—the same kind of device that Aro used to light his pipe, that Kayden had used to light the firepowder when he'd destroyed his own airship. Tadd would use it to light the fuses of the bags they were going to drop.

The bombs.

"Any more up-plane?" Kayden asked. He was anxious to get higher on the slope. They all were.

Shae tried to pull the lever back farther. "It's all we've got. Wind off the peak is pushing us down."

"Could give it more power," Aro said from behind them. Though he was busy putting the final touches on his reconstructed aluman, the lumicker was listening to everything happening on the ship.

"No," Shae and Kayden both said at once. She looked at him, saw that he was beaming at the coincidence. He nodded at her to go ahead. "If we did that and the wind stopped, we'd crash into the mountainside. And with all the firepowder on board ..."

"Yeah," the lumicker said. "Don't do that."

"I wish we could at least distract them," Shae said. "Slow them down?"

"Try Perle's Eyes," Aro said, and then he cursed as he dropped a tool and had to scramble for it along the deck.

Kayden looked over at Shae, confused.

"His big gun," she explained.

Kayden's face was strained with exhaustion, but for the moment, he had the ship under steady control. "Get it."

Shae had slipped the long boltgun just inside the hatchway

below. In seconds, she'd hopped down to the mid-deck, opened the door to grab it, and brought it back to the helm. Pulling the leather strap across her shoulder, she leaned over the port side of the airship—close enough that she could grab the helm the instant Kayden needed help—and looked down across the valley.

"Mother," she whispered to the wind.

Before, when she and Marek had seen the army nearly head-on, it had looked like a blue wave. Now, seeing it from above, it looked like a river. Uncountable and uncontrollable. The walls of the keep, mighty as they were, wouldn't stop it. The river might pile up its dead against that lumick-lit dam, but they'd eventually flow up and over it. They'd breach the keep. Marek would die. Everyone there would die. There'd be nothing else to stop them.

It was the end.

Shae steadied herself against a rope ladder that ran to the bag above them. She raised the boltgun and looked down the longer line of its barrel. She aimed it as best she could at what seemed like the front of the marching alumen. She pulled the trigger.

Perle's Eyes coughed blue light and kicked back against her shoulder. She couldn't tell if it hit. The alumen didn't react. But she was glad for the padding of the furs keeping her warm.

"Quick," Aro said from behind her. "Let me see it."

As Shae handed the weapon over to him, the lumicker pulled from his things a brass-tubed looking glass, almost exactly like the one she'd used to spy vessels on the horizon from the deck of the *Pale Dawn*—only his had two rings attached to the bottom of it. He slipped the fittings over the end of the weapon's barrel and carefully slid it down until it fit snugly near its base. "Now you'll see what you're aiming at," he said. Then he showed her how to move the lever to reload it. "And now you'll have another shot."

He handed it back, and again she braced herself against a rope ladder. She raised the boltgun. This time, she squinted one eye to look through the glass.

She could see the alumen now. Not just a pulsing mass of them. Individuals. She centered one in the circle of glass, then tried to think how a fang shot from a blowpipe would fall over a distance. This was much farther. But the bolt moved much faster. She aimed high. Then a little higher still. She pulled the trigger.

The boltgun coughed. Something blue flashed off the shoulder of an aluman in her vision.

Not where she'd been aiming. But close. A little to the left, she thought. And not quite as high.

"First bag!" Kayden called out. "Light it!"

Shae looked up along the railing to the foredeck. Ragan was already picking up the first bag. He balanced it on the wood of the railing, carefully holding the line of fuse out. Beside him, Tadd triggered the metal cylinder he'd been holding. He set it to the fuse, cupping his hand over the dancing flame to shelter it from the wind. When the fuse began to spark, he cut the flame off the lighter, and Ragan tipped the bag overboard.

Shae watched the bomb fall, a line of light flashing red in the blue, trailing smoke. It hit the snow, sank into the powder, and went silent.

"Damnit," Kayden muttered. "Another!"

Shae levered another round into the boltgun, then

brought it back to her shoulder. She aimed, adjusted, and pulled the trigger. This time, the bolt went true. It lashed into the side of an aluman's head, and the huge metal thing went down. Several of the alumen around it looked in their direction. "Got one!"

"Well done," Kayden said. "Only a couple thousand more to go."

The two men up front dropped a second bag of lit firepowder. It, too, sank into the snow without a sound. "The snow is snuffing the fuses!" Ragan called back.

Kayden grunted as he tried to stay steady on the wheel, and Shae threw the leather strap of the gun around her shoulder as she turned back to the helm. She helped him turn the wheel, then helped to hold it while he settled his weight on the handles again. He looked terrible. "You can't even stand," she said.

He smiled through gritted teeth. "I'll sleep tomorrow," he said. "Go help them send another. Try to hit a hard patch where it won't sink."

Shae nodded and ran to the foredeck. The two men saw her coming.

"My lady?" Ragan said.

Shae just pointed to the next bag of firepowder. "Get ready."

The wind stung at her eyes as she leaned out over the side, staring down at the snowy slope.

There. Just ahead. There was a stretch of white that reflected the distant light of the keep with a different sheen. More like glass. It ran down to a lip of ice over a snowy chute.

"We need this one to work!" Kayden called up.

Shae looked back at him and pointed. "Steady-plane! Slight to port!"

Kayden nodded. The handles of the helm turned.

They were running out of time. They all knew it. There might only be one more chance here.

"Got one ready," Ragan said.

Shae looked over at the burlap sack in the man's hand. How thick would the ice be? What if the bomb wasn't enough? What if it didn't break the slope loose? She looked around at what they had at hand. "Any of the barrels still have firepowder?"

Tadd nodded. "One does."

"Bring it here. We're pitching it over first."

The two men exchanged looks, but they didn't argue. Tadd heaved the half-full barrel up onto the railing.

Shae took over for him, holding it balanced while she pointed. "I'm going to drop this on the ice. It should slide down and then get stuck, right there at the edge. See it?"

"Aye," Tadd said.

"Soon as I'm dropping it, you'll light the fuse on that. I want it coming right on top of it. Right after."

Ragan seemed to get what she was going for. He nodded and lifted the bomb up beside her barrel. Tadd had his cylinder ready at the fuse.

"One chance," she whispered. The wind pushed snow across the glassy slope. It made a kind of scratching sound. Perfect. "One, two—"

Tadd was lighting the fuse. She eased the barrel over.

The lit bomb followed it, fuse flashing.

The barrel hit. The ground crunched, but it didn't give way. It was ice, and the barrel was sliding down just as she'd hoped.

The bomb hit, too, almost perfectly in line with the impact, and it was sliding after it, tumbling across the crusted snow.

"Gods," Tadd gasped. "No."

For a moment, Shae couldn't see what he was talking about, but then she realized that the rolling of the bag was bringing the fuse around and onto the ground. It was still lit, though.

They'd only need seconds.

The barrel rolled up to the precipice, slowed, and stuck. The bomb slid up to it, upside down, its fuse snuffed.

Ragan made a sound like he'd been kicked in the gut. "Get another ready," she said.

"But, Lady, we're past the ice," Tadd said.

"Then we'll come around again."

She turned back to the helm to shout directions to Kayden. He was slumped over the wheel. "Kayden!"

She ran for the helm. Aro, turning at her shout, got there first. By the time she leaped the steps to the rear deck, the lumicker had pulled Kayden down and set him on the stool beside the map table.

"I'm fine," Kayden said.

The air on the deck was close to freezing. His forehead was slick with sweat. "Don't think you are, lad," Aro said.

"Just can't stand." He smiled weakly, then looked up at her. "Did it work?"

Shae shook her head. "I'll try to bring the ship around. See if we can try again."

Kayden sighed. "No time. Winds."

He was right, now that she heard him say it. With the winds pushing down off the mountain, it would take them at least half an hour to work back into position. "We just need one," she tried.

There was a mighty boom from the Blue Keep.

Shocked, Shae looked down and saw the smoke rising from a cannon on the mighty walls—and the corresponding debris bursting up from the frozen earth where the iron ball hit among the alumen. A few were tossed back, but the rest pressed on. The first of them were hitting the start of the lumicklines stretched across the valley floor. There were flashes of blue light as the metal men fell over the lines and more piled up over them, charging onward.

"This isn't working," Kayden said. He shook his head, as if he were clearing cobwebs. "Take the helm, Shae. Down-plane. Hard to port. Full power."

Shae looked at the wheel, then back at him. "That'll take us right to them."

He grinned. "Rain fire, Shae. Rain fire."

42

New Horizons

Kora and Alira helped Amaru up the wooden ladder into the watchtower by the sea. The elder had insisted that they meet Julara someplace quiet—and those were in short supply now that the surviving Stormborn had joined the pirate women in the Bay of Bones.

Amaru was a little out of breath from the walk around to the far side of the bay, but she was thankfully no more worse for wear by the time they were helping her up. And Alira, for her part, felt a kind of pride—a sad pride, she had to admit—in knowing that she and Kora were now in better shape than the older woman who walked with a cane. That certainly hadn't been the case when they'd first arrived in the bay. Bed rest, and the Bone Pirate's supply of healing herbs, had done them wonders, though Kora's arm remained in its sling.

Julara came last up the ladder. The young woman hadn't stopped smiling since they'd stepped off the lift beside the waterfall to start the walk here. She seemed genuinely glad to be away from the *Pale Dawn*, with its Throne of Bones and skull mask and everything else she had to do to keep up the lie that the Bone Pirate still held sway aboard her ship.

The tower wasn't large—the four of them standing at different corners filled it well—but it held watch over the mighty sea gate that kept the bay hidden. Perched where the cliff of the bay and the cliff of the shore met—the open sea to one side and the great waterfall with its wonders on the other—the tower had a truly magnificent view.

There was a high stool in the tower, and Amaru took it. The Stormborn elder, after situating herself, tapped the point of her cane on the wood boards beneath their feet. It was a call to silence and attention. Not exactly necessary with no one else in earshot, but Alira supposed that old habits died hard.

"We must thank you and your people, Julara Skullborn," the elder said.

There were many things Alira had learned in the days since she'd come to the Bay of Bones. That Amaru called the pirates "Skullborn" was one that still made her smile.

By her reaction, it also delighted Julara—in truth, just Julara—because the younger woman smiled. "We stand united against our enemy," the pirate said. Then she nodded to Alira. "And we stand united with a common friend."

Alira acknowledged the gesture with a nod, though she still found the pirates' interest in Bela fascinating. In the past days, she'd learned everything the pirates knew of her old friend.

After the *Black Crow* was bombed by a Windborn airship, leaving Alira stranded alone on the shoreline, Bela had taken command of the floating wreck. She'd set sail with it, and she'd by chance come upon the Bone Pirate's ship as they'd fought to take down that very same airship. The Windborn vessel had been destroyed, but Bela had captured the *Pale Dawn* and killed the woman who had been the Bone Pirate. This had made another young woman, named Shaesara, the Bone Pirate, because Bela had refused to take possession of the Bay of Bones for herself.

Bela's refusal to seize what by all the rights of the sea ought to have been hers—her insistence that it was her duty to return with the *Black Crow*'s survivors to the High Matron—had become something of a legend among the pirates. They'd already heard of Bela—one couldn't live in the Fair Isles and not know the story of Belakané, the Hero of the Harbor—but now they felt they knew her better than most anyone did. She was, in their minds, one of them. And because Bela had spoken often of Alira, that had made her something special in their eyes.

The whole thing was a little bewildering to Alira, but she wasn't about to turn down the advantage it seemed to give her in negotiating for the safety and sanctuary of the Stormborn behind their walls.

"Your kindness was not expected, but it has been welcomed," the elder said. "But we know it has not been easy."

Julara seemed reluctant to speak of difficulties, but Amaru's expectant stare made her talk. Alira knew the feeling. "We were already looking to be short rations for the season," the pirate admitted. "Shaesara went with Belakané to Myst Wera to procure more supplies, but she did not return. We have heard whispers of some terrible event happening at the Spire. Magick and Windborn. We've even heard rumor that Shaesara was stolen away by the Windborn." She shivered. "Anyway, we've made a few runs to the outer islands, which has helped, but I still had things measured pretty tightly."

"And we've brought more mouths to feed," the elder said.

"You brought some supplies, too," Julara hastened to add. "And that stretches things out a bit, but … yes, it's still a problem."

"Not to mention housing us all," Alira said.

"And trying to keep everyone from killing each other," Kora pointed out. Many of the pirates were displeased at having strangers in the Bay of Bones, and many of the Stormborn, though desperate for their help, distrusted the pirates. It was a volatile mix that had already nearly come to blows in their days together. Just this morning, Kora herself had been forced to stand between two angry groups, holding out her one good arm, to keep them from coming to blows.

"All that too," Julara agreed.

The elder traced small circles on the floor with the tip of her cane. At last, she let out a long breath and looked back at the Bay of Bones, with all its wonders. "How long would it take to build a ship?" she asked. "I know nothing of these things."

"Months," Alira said.

Julara's brow furrowed. "Why would you build a ship?"

"We may need to leave these shores," Amaru said. Then she tapped the point of her cane as if she were hammering something down in her mind. "No, we must leave these shores."

Kora was aghast. "But, elder, surely—"

"Surely what, child? Surely we can wait around to die

here?" The elder shook her head. "These Bloodborn will come. It's only a matter of time. And when they do, these walls will not stand. We saw what they did at Anjel. You have seen what they can do with their magick. This place, too, will fall. It may take a long while, or it may be quick, but it will happen. Do you disagree?"

Kora wanted to object, but it was clear she had nothing to say. She hugged her bad arm to her side. She looked troubled.

"I'm sorry," Amaru said. "I do not wish it so. This is our home. But right now … I do not think we have the strength to stay."

"Where would we go?" Alira asked.

The elder turned to look out over the sea now. "I've never known another place, though I have seen ships enough to know they are real out there somewhere. Where would you have us go, Alira?"

Alira blinked. "Me? You're asking me to decide?"

Amaru's smile was kind. "Let us say an elder is asking a huntress for advice."

Alira tried not to focus on why she—still young, still inexperienced, still new to the Stormborn, even—was the most senior huntress left. But in her mind, she saw Whéuri's face anyway—the look of relief and release the older woman had in that final moment before Alira let go of the magick. It wasn't comforting. But though the memory frightened her, Alira recognized that it was proof of exactly how desperate they were. The Bloodborn could destroy them, body and soul. And if they had to leave to survive that threat, who better to guide them than the one woman of their number who'd sailed the Fair Isles?

"It is a hard thing I ask of you," Amaru said.

"It's a hard thing to ask of us all," Alira replied. "But I think you're surely right. It's not safe here. And even if it was, we have too many mouths to feed in too little room. We must move on." Alira looked over at Kora. The younger woman's expression was still troubled. "You and I came to Anjel hurt and lost, Kora. Its people welcomed us, and it became home. We can do this again. Where we go will not be Anjel. No place can be that. But in time, we can make a new place home."

Kora took a deep breath. Gathering her strength and swallowing down other things she wanted to say, Alira suspected. "Where?" she finally asked.

"I grew up in the town of Ranhold on Myst Motri. I have family there, and I know they appreciate strong hands. It seems a place to start."

"The Eye Open," Julara said. She seemed thoughtful.

Alira nodded. "The symbol of the Blood Motria," she explained to Amaru and Kora. "A banner emblazoned with the Sleepless Owl, or the Eye Open, gold on a blue field." It was strange how foreign the image felt to her, and yet how close in memory. She hadn't truly been gone that long, but it felt like a lifetime ago.

"And they will welcome us, these Motrians?" Kora asked.

"They call you the Rootless." Alira allowed herself a smile. "You steal babies in the night."

Amaru chuckled a little. "Is that so?"

"Stories told to children," Alira said. "I do not think they will be hostile. Mostly curious, to see what is the truth behind the stories. As you all were when I came."

"A Sleepless Owl," Kora repeated. "The Motria are watchful, then?"

"Ever so. Good fighters too. They would welcome your strength."

"You are not wrong to feel uneasy about leaving this place," the elder said to Kora. "It will be difficult for everyone, each in their own way. But in making the decision, we must not waver. We must be true to what must be done."

"When I close my eyes, I still see the cages," Kora said. "At night, I still hear the screams. I know we can't stay. I know it's the right thing to do." She took a deep breath, and she turned to look Alira in the eye. "Promise me this: even if we leave, it isn't forever. We will avenge ourselves on these Bloodborn. We don't leave this island to them. Not one more soul to their machines and their magicks. They must be destroyed."

Alira thought of how she'd found Kora alone in the jungle as a child. She thought of what the girl had witnessed when the Bloodborn had taken her family. Alira had only seen the horror of what was left after it was done. It was bad enough, and she hadn't had to be there to hear the screams and the begging and the despair. "I, too, refuse to lose even one more Stormborn to them," she said. "That's why we must go; staying here gives them so many more of us. But when we are stronger, when we are ready, we will come back. We will hunt them down, cut them out—no stone unturned, down to the root. I promise."

"You'd make the Rootless real," the elder said.

"I would."

Kora's face was grim but determined. "Then I will do

what must be done. You can be sure of me. I'll help the others see it too."

"Myst Motri, then," Amaru said. "How far is it?"

"Good weather and calm seas?" Alira pursed her lips, thinking. "A week, perhaps. Building the ship will take far longer."

"Take the *Crow*," Julara said.

Alira turned. "What?"

"The *Black Crow*," she said. "She was the ship that brought you here. You and Bela. Makes sense for her to be the ship that takes you away."

"But she is yours by salvage rights," Alira said.

"She was Bela's," Julara corrected. "And Bela gave the ship to Shaesara when she left. We've kept her here, fixed her up enough to make her seaworthy, but I don't know what Shaesara would've wanted done with her in the end. None of us does, I guess. But I think she would've recognized you as a friend of Bela's and a worthy new mistress."

"And will the other Skullborn think the same?" Amaru asked. "The ship has value."

"They'd gut me quick as a plump fish if I were offering up the *Dawn*," Julara said with a grin. "But the *Black Crow* is a loss they will surely accept, especially if it means getting rid of you lot and leaving more food for their plates. Their biggest question, I expect, will be how you're going to sail her without a crew. Begging pardon, elder, but I don't think any of you knows how to trim a sail."

Amaru laughed. "No pardon needed. It's quite true. You should come with us."

Julara blinked. "Sorry?"

"Have you not been listening, child? You're no safer here than we are. You must leave too."

Alira stared at Amaru, wondering how far ahead she'd thought this through. She would've known there was at least one ship in the Bay of Bones. Whéuri and the senior huntresses had probably kept close enough watch that the elder likely knew there were at least two. From the moment she knew they'd have to leave Anjel, had this been her plan?

"I—I don't think I could do that," Julara whispered.

Amaru looked down at her from her stool, pity on her face. "I don't think you can't."

"The bay is our home. Always has been. And we don't have other places to go. No one in the Fair Isles would give the *Pale Dawn* harbor. No one would welcome the Bone Pirate with open arms."

"It's true," Alira put in. "Nothing is as hated and feared as the Bone Pirate. Not even the Rootless. But this could be the way forward. The House Motria, for instance, has long been rivals with House Kubwa. Perhaps in exchange for safe harbor, you could offer up the services of the *Pale Dawn* to attack ships under the flag of the Grasping Hawk, while leaving the Open Eye at peace."

"I am not the Bone Pirate," Julara said. "It's not my place."

"The women here trust you to lead." Amaru's gaze was watchful.

"Because after Shaesara left, I was the only one who could read the accounts and keep stock. It's not because they trust me at the helm. If I tell them all to go, I can assure you that someone will challenge me for the mask."

"Enough for now to bring some supplies to your ship," Amaru said. "And we will do the same for the *Crow*."

"You can tell them you're thinking of raiding the shipping lanes," Alira added. "I imagine the hardiest of pirates will get excited about that."

"They will," Julara said. "A bed unmoved by the Mother's breath—"

"Is no bed at all," Alira finished. It was a truth of the Seaborn, who were only truly at home upon the sea. Was that still her? Who would she be in the weeks to come? Who would she be with what needed to be done?

"It's settled, then," the elder said. "Kora? Perhaps you and Julara can go to the *Black Crow*. Start thinking about what work is left to do. I'll send Alira along shortly."

Kora made a slight bow in acknowledgment; then she and the pirate were walking away.

"You want to say something," Amaru said when they were out of earshot. "I can tell."

"I just … I grew up Seaborn. But when you welcomed me, I became Stormborn. I left my old life behind, and I was at peace. I knew who I was. I knew what I was. Perhaps for the first time ever. And now …"

The elder drew circles with her cane again. "Now you're uncertain who you are."

"Yes."

"You are Alira."

"Alira what?"

The cane stopped. The elder looked up. "If I have learned you are anything, it is that you're a survivor. Stormborn. Seaborn. Skullborn, if need be. You are Alira. That is all, and it is enough. It is what we all need right now. More than ever."

43

The *Sparrow*

Shae's hands were fists: one tight around the wheel, the other moving between levers on the helm. The bow had turned and dipped, pointed right at the base of the valley, right at the battle in front of the Blue Keep. On either side of the ship, the rotors were spinning hard, driving them forward like a gale to stern. The bag overhead rippled against the wind that had sleeked the stray hairs off her face.

The air was ice itself, but there was no keeping a hood up against the wind that was a whine across her frozen ears. Beyond it, the world seemed to be full of sounds. The lumick engines, a throaty hum. The flashing cannons from the walls ahead, a roar. The noises of the alumen, a horrible scream.

And through it all, Shae was smiling.

Shipmistress. Captain. It didn't matter the title.

She had a ship. She had a boltgun on her back. She was hunting for prey. She'd never felt so alive.

Kayden moaned from behind her.

"You should go down below," she called back.

He coughed. "And miss this madness?"

She wanted to go to him, to tend to the fool man before he killed himself of exhaustion and fever. But she had a mission. A duty.

Skies to sail.

Behind her, she heard the lumicker shuffle to the rail and put his head over the side. He threw up his last meal across the slashing slopes below.

"Not usually this fast," Kayden muttered.

Shae grinned. The ropes to the bag above were taut. The cleats and buckles were straining. The decks shivered. She felt and heard it all. A ship was a ship. At sea. In the air. "She'll hold. Does she have a name?"

"Does what have a name?"

She felt a crosswind catching the bow, and her hand jumped one handle to starboard. Muscles flexed from her arm to her back to her legs to her booted feet on the deck. The bow bobbed and righted, pointed at the enemy. "The ship."

"*Sparrow*."

"*Sparrow*," Shae repeated. "Light. Fast. I like that."

Mother, she wished she had her skull mask. Let the alumen look up and see death riding down on them.

Ragan and Tadd were holding hard to the railings on the foredeck. It didn't look like they'd ever been on an airship moving so fast before, either, especially not one rushing down the side of a mountain. "Portside!" she called out. "We're going to flatten out and come right across the front of them! Be ready!"

Both men's eyes were wide. But Tadd managed to nod.

"I'll help them light," Kayden said. And before she could

stop him, he was stumbling his way forward, down the stairs, then nearly sliding his way into the other men. They helped to catch him. He crumpled against the railing, then held out a lighter with his good hand and smiled like the fool he was.

Shae wanted to slap him. She vaguely wanted to do other things to him, too, which was new and confusing.

But the Blue Keep was close and fast getting closer. So was the alumen army. So was the valley floor.

"Do you think they'll hit us?" Aro had staggered up to stand beside her. He had one of his tools in his hand, but she could see that he'd pulled his coat back off his hip so he could quickly get to the boltgun in its holster. He was looking at the cannons flashing along the walls.

Shae's gaze moved from the cannons to the airbag above. "I sure hope not. No luck on the aluman?"

"Almost there."

The crosswind abruptly died. Shae grunted the wheel one handle back to port. Then she readied her other hand on the lever to pull the bow before they buried it in the frozen ground. "Then don't waste time talking to me."

He went back to the table. She heard his metal tool clinking.

"Ready?" she called forward.

Kayden and the two men all nodded. The bags were lined up against the railing. Kayden had his lighter. Tadd and Ragan had bags on either side of them, ready to light and throw. The two young men were terrified, but they clearly knew their duty. And they seemed glad to have the Lord of the Blue Keep with them—even if he was broken.

Shae pushed Kayden out of her mind. She focused on

the wind and the engines and the ground and the straining ship. She felt it coming. The moment. "My *Sparrow*," she whispered, willing the ship to hold together.

The airship bucked on the line of wind rolling off the walls of the Blue Keep. "Up-plane!" Shae shouted. She tried to pull back on the lever, to pull out of their dive, but she was pulling against the force of the ripping wind. She threw her shoulder into the wheel to hold it in place so she could get two hands on the stick. "Hold on!"

The lever heaved backward. The *Sparrow* let out a long, loud groan. The lumick engines strained, and she moved a hand over to pull back on their power too.

A cleat on the starboard side of the ship cracked loose and clattered back and down, out of sight. The cable that it had been holding whipped up and back against the airbag above.

Aro lunged over the top of her, grabbing the wheel. "I've got this!"

She shifted, closing her eyes as she put her whole body into the levers. They complained. The rest of the lines protested. But nothing snapped. Nothing more came loose. The *Sparrow*, screaming off the mountain slope, leveled out over the valley.

"Bombs away!" she screamed.

She opened her eyes and saw Kayden with his lighter moving left and right, lighting the fuses of the firepowder bags as fast as the other men could get them to him.

The bombs were going over the side.

And, just heartbeats later, they were exploding among the alumen.

Metal men were fragmenting in the fire. Clods of frozen

dirt were scattering up into the night sky. The *Sparrow* was leveled, slowing. Bits of it all were hitting the bag, clattering onto the deck.

With the tension out of the controls, Shae could move them more freely. She pushed over onto the helm. "I've got it!" she said to Aro. He nodded and fell away, back to his work table. Handles in hand, she spun the wheel to starboard so she could angle through a thicker wave of the alumen.

Shae glanced over at the Blue Keep. Alumen were already dying against the base of the wall, contorted against the lumicklines. But more were piling atop them. The tide was coming in. Across the top of the fortifications, even with them now, the cannons had paused. The only explosions were coming from the bombs of the *Sparrow*. The men of the keep shouted in a great cheer. In the middle of them stood Oth Marek. His arm was raised in defiant camaraderie.

Ragan's voice broke through the noise. "Almost out!"

Shae looked back to the foredeck, saw that their firepowder bags were indeed getting low. "Hard to starboard! Flip sides! We're coming around!"

Tadd reached down and helped Kayden to his feet. Ragan got under his other shoulder. Together, they clambered across the deck toward the bag lined up to starboard.

Shae moved her left hand to the levers. *Steady-plane*, she thought. But this would be like letting the wind out on a tack. She would slow down, let the rear of the ship sink into the turn. That might bring the bow around faster. Then she'd speed up again and shoot out of it.

The other side of the valley loomed large, a steep wall of snow and rock. A couple of cannons on the far end of the wall behind them opened up again. The world was pale-blue light flashing orange and yellow and red.

"Brace!" she cried out, and then she slowed the lumick engines and spun the wheel as fast as she could.

The *Sparrow* groaned once again. It felt like her hull sank, and Shae's stomach with it. The bow lurched hard to starboard, for a moment pointing at the Blue Keep itself before it was swinging around along the line of the wall and back toward the direction they'd come. She could see the lines of the cannon fire hurtling out ahead of them into the screaming alumen army.

"I got it!" Aro suddenly shouted from behind her. "The eyes!"

Shae—one hand on the lever, ready to up the speed—looked back. The eyes on the bodyless metal head in Aro's box flickered blue. Then they lit and held. The speaker popped and buzzed for a moment.

Aro was stepping back from it, back into her. The blue light of its eyes highlighted the elation on his face. "I did it!"

"I see fire and war," the speaker in the corner of the box said. "And I see the Bone Pirate."

44

The Citadel

Night had fallen when Bela and Tewrick left Kolum's home and followed him out into the dead city, but the moon was high and full. They did not have far to go, and Kolum knew the way. The Citadel wasn't far.

At every turn, Bela expected another attack, another strange scream, another aluman in the street. But none came. The city was silent. The streets were empty but for the rubble. The only footsteps she heard were Kolum's metal feet falling and gripping on the pavement, stride by stride, taking them closer to the Citadel and the portal somewhere inside it.

At last, they faced the great building across an open square. Far above, beside the Citadel's white tower, the airship that they now knew to be Kolum's floated in the moonlight. Before them, at the building's front, wide steps led to a pair of shadowed doors.

For a minute, they stood and watched. Nothing moved.

"How many alumen did Asryth send to kill us?" Bela

whispered. Kolum had killed two in saving them. But they'd heard the screams of at least one more that day.

"This is something I do not know," Kolum said, then moved out into the open. He motioned them forward, and the three of them walked out across the moonlit pavement and up the wide steps to the entrance. Still, there was silence.

The doors of the Citadel were massive, made of thick planks of old wood, and there were shapes carved into the surface of the stone wall beside them. Letters, Bela supposed, though she could not read them. The snow clung to the carvings like white moss. She watched the reader brush the surfaces clean. He studied the letters carefully, mumbling to himself as he tried to make them out.

Kolum loomed over them both. "There is no time. We must go inside. I will take you to the portal. I will see you close it."

Bela looked up at the big metal man. "Do you know how to shut it down?"

"It is machine and magick. Destroy one or the other."

"But how?"

"I have not done this," Kolum said.

"Your sword?" Tew asked.

Kolum's torso moved slightly from side to side. "It is not a weapon for this purpose."

"Well," Bela said, "if you think of anything else, tell us."

"I have thought long about many things. More thoughts on this I do not think I will have. I will see it destroyed."

As Kolum turned to the entrance, Bela saw that Tew's gaze had returned to the writing on the wall. His shoulders seemed to have fallen. She patted his arm. "After this is done," she said, "we'll come back out. You can teach me how to read it."

He brightened a little. "I'd like that," he said.

The doors were closed, but Kolum had no difficulty pushing one open enough for him to get through. Bela and Tew followed inside before he turned and pushed it shut again.

A wide and straight hall stretched out before them, lit by Kolum's eyes and the moonlight coming down through glass windows in the roof above. Lining the sides of the hall, like sentinels, stood statues of ancient people, carved in gleaming white rock. The statues were mounted upon black marble bases, and each of them was crowned. Many of them, to Bela's surprise, had the trimmed beards of old men.

Bela noticed that some of the statues—men and women alike—had their hands clasped to the hilts of swords that stood point down before them. Others held open books, as if they had just looked up from reading. They reminded her of Tew, and she smiled.

The floor beneath the statues was paved with black stone. It was littered with tiny ridges of snow that had blown in through the open door. They melted quickly.

The reader had noticed it too. "I think the building is built on the same heat that keeps the lake unfrozen."

"Asryth's design," Kolum said. There might've been pride in his voice.

"It's amazing," Tew said.

It was, Bela thought. Truly so. The air was hardly what she would have once called warm, but it was far warmer than anything they had felt since leaving the cave on the distant shoreline.

They stood for a minute just inside the doors, staring at the statues. The darkness of the floor, Bela suspected, was meant to give the statues a sense of inner vitality, a light glow as if they might be warm to the touch. She'd never seen anything like it. No one from the Fair Isles had, she supposed.

Kolum seemed content to let them adjust to the warmth of the air and the scale of what lay before them. It was, Bela was certain, the biggest room in which she'd ever stood.

At last, the metal man stepped forward, and they followed at his side, walking down the hallway toward the center of the building.

There was another set of double doors at the other end of the hall. After listening at it for a moment and hearing nothing, Kolum pushed it open. They slipped through.

The chamber they entered was large, circular, and from the shape of the dome above it, the center of the Citadel. It also seemed to be a throne room of some kind. At the far end of the room, beyond a long and low firepit whose grates were still caked with black, was a simple seat of stone, set upon a small dais that rose three steps from the level of the floor. That floor was tiled with the same bright-white rock used to fashion the statues in the hall, as were the walls.

The inside of the dome was tiled likewise, and its solid, smooth surface far above them was broken with a ring of long rectangular shapes of crystal pane. The moonlight outside gave them a dull glow. A low stone bench encircled the whole of the chamber, but otherwise the room was starkly bare but for five sets of double doors around it, just like the one they'd come through.

"The court of Ealond," Kolum said quietly. "A busy place once."

"This is where you met her," Bela whispered.

Kolum stood still, a metal statue in the room of stone. "Yes."

Bela turned, saw that Tew had drifted over to the closest door to their left, which was slightly open. Walking over, she joined him and looked over his shoulder. The room beyond was walled with shelves stretched from floor to ceiling. On the shelves were piles of dust and rotting bits of leather.

"What is it?"

"A library," he whispered. "An ancient library." There was a reverential sadness in his voice.

"Do you want to look?"

Tew sighed. "Looks like it's all gone." He brought a hand to his face where she couldn't see before he turned back around. "Anyway, it's not what we came for. The portal. That's what matters."

Kolum's feet hadn't moved, but his upper torso had rotated to follow their movements. When they came back, he reached out a long arm toward Tew. The reader flinched, but he didn't run away as the clawed hand rested on his shoulder. "I have saved some of the books," the metal man said. "When this is over, you shall have them."

The reader smiled. "I would like that. Thank you."

Kolum turned and crossed the court to a set of doors on the other side of the room. One of these was open. He led them through and down a hallway that was so large that even he only half-filled it. His metal feet echoed along the warm stone floor, and Bela flinched at nearly every step.

Remembering how the swords they'd had were lost in the

avalanche, she almost stopped to ask Kolum if there was an armory somewhere nearby in the Citadel, some place she might get a weapon. But without one arm, she figured she was no more of a fighter now than she was a shipmistress.

And what good would a sword be against an aluman, anyway?

Doors and other corridors broke off from the hallway they followed. Kolum took one turn only, which seemed to carry them deeper into the great building. That hallway ran straight to one more set of large double doors, which were closed. Kolum stopped in front of them. Again, he listened. They did too.

"The portal is here," he finally said. His torso turned to face Bela. "I will see you close it."

"I promise," she said.

The torso bent slightly—an acknowledgment, she thought—and then turned back to one of the doors. His metal hand reached up and pushed it open.

The room beyond was as big as the entrance hall: a long rectangle with a tall ceiling. But unlike that room, no statues lined the walls here. And they also hadn't entered it on the floor.

Instead, they stepped out onto a metal platform at its mid-height.

The room, in fact, appeared to be divided in two. Not far ahead of them, the platform they were on gave way to what looked like a kind of checkerboard whose squares were open frames. The lines between the squares were gridded metal sheets at least three feet wide, and the squares of their intersecting paths were at least twice their width. The ceiling high above was glass from wall to wall, and though it was mostly covered with snow, there were places where the moonlight still shone through, like pillars of white light. Where they fell upon the checkerboard, the squares weren't empty. Plants filled them, clinging to the spaces. Between the moonlight and the blue light of Kolum's eyes, Bela could see that the wide fronds of the plants were still green and alive, stretching up from round and flat bulbs grown and laced to the metal.

"Taproots," Tew said. His voice echoed through the chamber.

Bela turned to reprimand him for the noise, but then she saw that while she'd been staring out across the top level, the reader had stepped forward to look down a stairway to the lower level. Even from where she stood, she could follow his gaze through the open grids to see that much of the dusty floor of the room below them was littered with the brown twists of decayed plants. But under the still-living bulbs, there were tangles of roots that hung down. They seemed to shimmer even in the dim light. Golden.

Mother, Bela thought. They *were* taproots. Zambaru. The same plants that grew in the rootfields surrounding the Spire. That meant the shimmering she saw below—

"Char," Kolum said. The metal man's voice was still quiet.

Bela shivered, thinking of how the bent-men—men like Tewrick, but ones for whom the Mother had chosen another path—made their way through the rootfields day after day, breathing through their masks to be sure they didn't inhale the powerful Char and die screaming in agony.

Tew was nodding. If he was thinking of such dark thoughts, he didn't show it, though from his rooms in the Spire, he would've heard the screams anytime one of those unfortunate mundane men had died. "The grids," he whispered, apparently having realized the degree to which noise carried in the cavernous room, "they're watering the plants?"

Bela tried to look closely without leaning closely. But she could see what the reader was talking about now: thin pipes webbed under the walkways, still audibly trickling water through the grid even after so many centuries unattended. It was remarkable, she thought. As was the system of suspending the plants to make it easier to harvest the Char from the taproots. It was far better than the way the evokers did it now, forcing the bent-men to hunch along the dirty ditches between rows.

"Yes," Kolum said. "A gift Asryth made to me. These were my plants."

Bela looked at him, wondering what emotions lay behind that truth. Pride in what she'd built? Gladness at the memory of the gift? Sorrow at what happened? Sorrow to see so many of the plants dead?

But Kolum only stood over them, unblinking. One clawed arm raised up. "The portal," he said, "is there."

Bela and Tew both turned in the direction he was pointing. Beyond the long stretch of the checkerboard with its scattered plants, at the far end of the room, there was a larger platform. On it was what Bela would have described as a workshop, with shelves and tables and chairs—but all of it had been pushed back, like the furniture in Kolum's home. Only here it wasn't to make headspace for an aluman; it was to bring one to life. In the middle of the space was a metal machine, shining as if it had just been made. Great gears were turning at its side in complete silence. They spun two rings of silver, one inside the other. Between them floated a perfect circle of perfect blue.

The portal.

Bela took in her breath, and then, in the heartbeat that followed, she heard an aluman's angry scream from the hallway behind them.

The three of them turned back. The pounding of approaching footsteps was unmistakable. More than one.

Kolum pulled the sword from his back. The edge crackled to blue life. "Here will I hold," he said.

Bela opened her mouth to respond, but before she could, the metal man stiffened and shook. "The Stream," he said. "Flashes. Somewhere."

Tew looked every bit as confused as she was. "You're seeing something through the Stream?"

"I see fire and war," Kolum suddenly said. "And I see the Bone Pirate."

45

The Shot

Shae stared at the box with its metal head and its wires and soulglass and speaker. The lumicker had done it. He'd built part of an aluman.

It was talking. And it knew who she was.

She had so many questions, but she knew they all could wait. What was important right now was whether the onslaught could be stopped, whether the Blue Keep could be saved.

Like her heart, the *Sparrow* hung in the air, poised at the edge of the battle.

It seemed that every last cannon on the walls of the Blue Keep had opened up. The valley was the flashing of fire and a single great roar.

"Tell the alumen to stop!" Aro shouted at the box. "Tell them to retreat!"

The pale-blue eyes he'd built didn't blink. "I command them not," its speaker said.

Well, Shae thought, that was that. She pushed the lever forward, spinning up the lumick engines.

"Her fight belongs to her," the speaker said. "Close the portal, Bela. Run!"

"Bela?" Shae turned physically toward the box with its disembodied aluman. Ti'nay's teeth, had it really said Bela's name?

Her hand was still on the lever. The rotors were already churning the air toward the thick of the fight. The *Sparrow* started forward …

… and then lurched to a halt that sent Aro tumbling into Shae, who caught herself against the ship's wheel. Ragan and Tadd sprawled across the wood of the foredeck.

"They are here," the speaker said.

Kayden had already been on the ground, collapsed against the railing up front. So it was he who lifted himself up first, looked over the side, and saw what it was. "Alumen!" he shouted. "They have the mooring lines!"

Shae helped Aro to his feet. Together, they ran to the edge. The mooring lines at the stern and bow of the ship, which had tied them to the keep's tower, hung low enough that the alumen were able to grab them. Three of the metal men already had hold of the rear line. More were running for the front line at the bow.

"That's not good," Aro muttered.

Shae spun back to the helm, pushed the planes upward to lift the bow and the mooring line with it. Alumen on the stern line were bad enough. She certainly didn't want to know what would happen if they got hold of the bowline too. They'd likely pull the *Sparrow* down and swarm it.

She felt the front of the ship start to lift, but it wasn't fast enough. Probably because their speed wasn't fast enough.

Shae reached over and shoved the power to full. The

lumick engines whined to speed. The airship crawled forward, dragging the alumen like anchors.

Aro was beside her. "Is that all the power we have?"

"Damnit," Shae said. It was enough of an answer. They both knew it wasn't enough power. Even now, the little bit of forward movement they'd gained was stalling out. More alumen were probably grabbing hold of the stern line. The airship physically jerked downward. "Damnit," she repeated.

"They're pulling us down!" Ragan shouted. He was panicked. Tadd was too. And Kayden, between them, was shaking in his fever. None of them was useful on deck. They were a distraction. Kayden most of all. She needed him protected. Safe. And if they went down and he was on the deck—

"Both of you: I want Lord Kayden below!" she shouted up at them. "Now!"

It was an order. They didn't disobey. Each man took a shoulder, and between them they lifted the fevered man up. They hurried him back toward the rear hatchway beneath the helm.

Kayden looked up at her like a man betrayed. He shook his head, tried to shrug himself loose. "No, Shae, let me fight!"

Ragan and Tadd paused, confused about whose directions to follow.

Shae leaned over the wheel, looking down on them. "It's not a debate, my love." Something caught in her throat. She stiffened her back against it, whatever it was, and she focused her emotions into a gaze upon Ragan and Todd that was hot enough to burn holes through wood. "I've got the helm. Get below. All three of you. Bar the door behind you. Protect Lord Kayden with your lives."

Terrified of her wrath, Ragan and Tadd obeyed. They carried him to the hatchway and opened it, began helping him down. The whole time, Kayden simply stared at her, caught between sorrow and elation. It hurt him that she knew he was too weak to fight. But he was enraptured to have had a glimpse at her heart.

Just before he disappeared out of sight, his tongue finally pried loose. "Shae," he said, "I love you."

And then he was out of view, and she heard the doors of the hatchway shut. She heard a bar being put into place.

Her hand was squeezing a handle on the wheel so hard that she feared it might crack. She forced herself to let it go, then pushed herself away from the helm so she could look once more over the side.

A mass of alumen crowded around the stern line. They were clambering over each other, jumping, trying to reach the airship. The ship jerked lower.

"Remember how to reload?" Aro asked from behind her.

She turned around. The old lumicker had his boltgun out of its holster. He seemed to be checking its two barrels. The flashes of cannon fire from the Blue Keep's walls made dark lines of the wrinkles on his face.

Shae swung Perle's Eyes down from her back. She levered the action on the handle. The boltgun was a remarkable weapon. She wished she had more time with it.

Aro held up his smaller boltgun. "This one works the same. Just in case. Ever kill someone?"

Shae thought of the men and women whose blood had dampened her blade. "Many."

"Good. You know you can't hesitate," the lumicker said. "Try for chest shots. Middle of the works, about right between where you and I got nipples. That's where the crystal is." He took two fingers and tapped his chest. "Does it every time."

Shae nodded. "We used to spread bone powder on our faces before battle."

His mustache ticked up in a half-grin. "I like that."

Shae smiled. His calm acceptance of what was coming calmed her too. They were dead in the beginning, she thought.

She gripped the handle of the boltgun, took a deep breath. "Ready?"

The lumicker shoved aside his tools so he could climb up onto the map table. He looked down at the box with its now-silent speaker. "Had a lot of questions for that."

Shae stepped up to the railing and looked over the side. Alumen were continuing to surge toward the wall. Metal bodies hung across most of the lumicklines. But hundreds more were climbing up behind them, piling up as they fell, forming a metal ramp of the dead that would soon enough reach the top. Oth Marek was visible in the distance, trying to get cannons repositioned to fire down at the base of the pile, close to the wall, rather than out at the army in the valley. He would fight to the end, and that made her glad.

Closer, the swarm of alumen at the stern mooring line was drawing near. Shae shouldered up against the rope ladder to steady herself. She aimed, waited for one to expose its chest, and fired a bolt through it. Its blue eyes went black, and it fell away, out of sight in the tumult.

Aro opened fire, too, his boltgun lashing down into the

pile. A metal man fell. Then he shot and felled another. "Two to one," he laughed.

Shae pulled the trigger to even the count, but Aro had already reloaded his two barrels and was firing again.

And so it went. Tick by tick, the airship was pulled down. Shot by shot, the pile of the dead rose to meet them.

Futile. But then, so much in life was, Shae knew. They were dead even now.

"Shae, the wall!" the lumicker suddenly shouted between shots.

She looked up. The ramp had nearly reached the top of the wall. Marek still couldn't get his cannons to fire at its base. One aluman, scrambling up, had already jumped the last reach and managed to latch its clawed hands onto the stone parapet. It was heaving itself up. The men on the walls were pulling back, trying to form lines against it.

She swung Perle's Eyes in that direction, took quick aim, and pulled the trigger.

Too fast. The airship was shaking as the alumen pulled it down. Her bolt cratered into the rock of the wall.

Shae cursed as she reloaded the weapon. She tried to imagine that it was just like shooting a blowpipe on a moving ship. Patience. Breath. Calm.

She braced on the rope ladder, once more centered the aluman in the boltgun's glass, and adjusted for the distance. The airship beneath her shook and trembled, but she gently let each bounce bring the aluman back into her sight. She watched the aluman lumber to its feet. She watched it straighten up to its full height. She watched its clawed hands ready for flesh.

Then she watched her bolt blow a hole through its back.

"Damn fine shot!" Aro said.

"Next one will be better," Shae said as she reloaded. Seconds later, she took down the next aluman attempting the ramp.

"The pile's getting tall back here," the lumicker said between shots of his own. "Not to brag." He laughed. "Got another barrel of powder I could toss overboard to reset the stack?"

Humor of the Embraced, they used to call it aboard the *Pale Dawn*. Some of those sent to the Mother insisted they do so with a joke. It was, Shae had always thought, a way that they protected themselves from the horror. And as Aro said it, she grinned, felt the urge to laugh too.

But then she remembered the barrel of firepowder they'd dropped on the mountainside.

The one that had slid onto the precipice and not gone off.

She whipped the boltgun around, tried to spot its dark shape up on the slopes. It had to be there somewhere, on the edge. She ought to be able to find it. She stared up at the mountain, trying to remember what she'd seen as they'd flown down the slope, trying to work backward to where it would be.

"What are you doing?" Aro asked.

"The barrel up there," she said. "If I could shoot it—"

The lumicker stepped up to stand on the railing beside her, one hand on the rope ladder. "Even if you could find it, you'll never make that shot. Ship is shaking too hard." He thought for a moment, then pointed above them. "Top of the bag."

"What?"

The lumicker tugged at the rope ladder, then paused long

enough to shoot an aluman below his feet. "Climb up. The airbag will dampen the movements."

Shae swung Perle's Eyes back to her shoulder, looking up to where the rope ladder disappeared up the side of the airbag. "Give me time," she said.

"All I can."

She hopped up onto the railing, saw for herself how close the alumen were piling up below. It wouldn't be long before one would make the last leap, just as the one had up onto the wall. Would they attack the lumicker on the deck first? Or would they crash through the windows on the side of the hull as she once had? Would Kayden die first?

Shae pushed back the yawning pit in her stomach and started up. The ladder stretched out over the side of the ship as it angled up toward the bag, so she stayed on the inside of it for the initial climb. It was a familiar feeling, really. Hand over hand, foot over foot. Just like running the ropes up a mast.

When her head reached the bottom of the bag, she flipped her grip onto the other side of the ladder and swung herself around in the open air until she was on the outside of it. For a moment, looking down as she hung in space, she saw the lumicker astride the railing at the base of the ladder, his boltgun flashing down at the clawed hands reaching up.

Her toes caught on the ladder again, and she was going up. In seconds, the ladder was against the bag itself, and her hands and toes were pushing into it as she climbed. Then she rounded the outside of it and sped up even faster, scampering her way up to the top on all fours.

She spun around to her belly and looked back at the mountainside, the boltgun propped up by her elbows.

Aro was right. The bag absorbed most of the movements from below. If not for the din of the cannons on the walls and the screaming of the alumen and the damnable cold, it might have been peaceful.

She tracked up the mountainside, scanning the scars on the snowy slope, rock to rock.

It didn't take long to spot a squarish shape, dark against the snow, at the top of a rocky precipice.

She measured her breaths, guessing at the drop over the distance. She pulled the trigger twice, but she saw nothing react to either shot.

That meant the bolts had to be hitting snow—which meant she must be missing high, right? If she was missing low, she'd be seeing something spark off the rocks below her target.

She reloaded. Took aim, just slightly lower. Loosed another shot. Again.

And again.

The fifth shot hit. One moment the barrel was in her vision. The next moment, the glass flashed with blinding light. Shae gasped and pulled her eye back from the weapon, blinking away the circle of brightness.

When her vision cleared, she saw the debris falling from a cloud where the barrel had been. Above it, great cracks were opening up across the wide, snowy slopes.

The slope broke up in slabs so massive that, for a moment, it looked like the mountain itself was coming apart. They slid out—one under the other, folding and piling up—and then it all gave way in a slide rushing down the mountain, growing and speeding by the second, hurtling toward the valley bottom.

Closer, a cheer went up from the Blue Keep.

Shae lowered the boltgun, got to her knees. *So that*, she thought in fascination, *is what an avalanche is*.

It crashed into the side of the metal army, an unrelenting surge of white, and blasted out across the valley, swallowing alumen whole. The wide wall of it seemed to rise up like a great wave, and Shae abruptly realized it was going to hit them too.

She heaved Perle's Eyes around to her back, then threw herself around to the rope ladder on the opposite side of the airbag. One hand gripping the rope, she was trying to weave the other around the line for a better grip when the snowslide hit.

The bag bounced into her, pushed her up into the air.

She had time enough to feel her grip give way, and then the white powder hit her, and she was flying.

46

Scattering Bones

Dawn was a few hours away, but nightmares of cages and death had Kora awake.

Thankful that she'd not cried aloud during her fitful sleep—more than once, she'd awoken herself and anyone near her—she'd crept out of her makeshift tent along the wall and walked to the rim of the bay.

She sat down on a rock. The waters below, ringed by cliffs, were a dark circle. The sparse torches lighting the ramps and platforms strung along the wall between—useful though they were for navigating between chambers and levels at night—were, from this angle, no match for the shadows.

Though she knew she could turn around and see the many tents of her fellow Stormborn, crowding the space between the rising walls of the palisade and the falling walls of the cliffs, Kora could look out from here, in the silence, and almost feel alone.

Sometimes that helped. Sometimes it didn't.

Carefully resting her injured arm in her lap, she adjusted

the sling around her neck with her good hand. At once, she was thinking only about how it showed no signs of recovery, how she might never draw back a bow again.

Deciding this would be a night when the feeling of solitude wouldn't help, Kora looked up at a sky filled with stars that twinkled in the rising mists of the waterfall.

She sighed.

Then a bell began ringing upon the palisade wall behind her.

Kora scrambled up to her feet. Turning, she saw tents rattling. Beyond them, two women stood at the watchtower near the gate. One was pointing out into the jungle. Another was ringing the alarm.

"Bloodborn!" screamed the woman at the bell. "Bloodborn!"

Another bell answered from behind her, below, echoing up from the bay itself. A ship's bell. Then another.

Panicked faces were emerging from the tents. Kora ran between them, heading for the watchtower, waving her one arm as she went. "To the bay!" she shouted. "To the *Crow*! Take the ramps!" The lifts down to the bottom were faster than the zigzagging ramps and platforms, and many of the Stormborn, like Kora herself, had learned to use them. But there were only two lifts, and each could hold only a handful of people. If they tried to take the lifts down, dozens would be standing around waiting for them to come back up. They'd waste precious time.

And if the Bloodborn were truly here, they had no time to waste. "The ramps!" she repeated. "The ramps!"

A woman was running from the watchtower. It was Vayra, the older woman she and Alira had saved from the Bloodborn. "They're here!" she was screaming. "I saw them!"

Kora angled for her, grabbed hold of her. "What? Vayra, it's me! How many? What did you see?"

The woman's face was ashen in the light of the torches that marked the paths between tents. "Run!" she said. "Run!"

Vayra pulled and twisted in her grip. Kora let her go and ran on toward the first watchtower, where the bell was still ringing.

She was nearly to it when she heard the high and horrible laughter of the Bloodborn on the other side of the wall. She looked up to the young woman ringing the bell. One of the pirates, she saw. Perhaps her own age, though she didn't know her name.

"Get down from there!" Kora called out. "Get down!"

The pirate couldn't hear. She was ringing the bell. Her eyes were wide.

The wind, when it came, threw her head against the bell. She hit it and went down.

Kora reached the steps a moment later. She took them two at a time. The pirate was dazed but alive. She was trying to get up, and Kora had to shift around her in order to get her weight under the one good shoulder she had. As she did so, she looked out beyond the palisade.

There was an open space between the wooden walls and the jungle, kept clear by the younger pirates so they could see anyone approaching. From above, it was lit by starlight and the torches of the walls. Dark figures were walking out from the darker wall of the jungle. Most of them were moving toward the great gate, slow and unhurried. They laughed. They moved their hands. The gate shook as it was battered by unseen forces. Like the fists of an invisible giant trying to pound his way in.

The pirate groaned as Kora dragged her to the stairs. Another slap of wind blasted the tower apart behind them. The debris scattered, clattering across the steps.

The pirate was hurt badly, Kora was realizing. Her head was bleeding. But there was no time to stop. "What's your name?" Kora asked her.

"Jélyn," the pirate managed.

"I need you to be strong, Jélyn." Kora almost had her down the stairs now. "Walk with me."

Jélyn moaned, and she tried to get her feet under her. It wasn't much, but it was enough to help Kora move her weight along faster.

Ahead, a man was standing where the ramp headed down along the cliff's face to the first level. He had a torch raised high in his hand. He was waving it, getting the attention of the Stormborn streaming toward the rim. As she'd ordered, he was directing them down that way.

Good, she thought. *Good*.

He looked up, saw Kora and her burden. Handing his torch to someone else, he came running. He put his arm under Jélyn's other shoulder.

The gate broke.

Kora didn't turn to see it. She didn't want to see it. She heard it give way. And she heard the laughter getting louder.

Jélyn's weight shifted, and Kora realized that the man was trying to take her in a different direction than toward the emptying ramp.

"What are you doing?"

The man nodded toward the waterfall. "The lift," he said. "We're the last ones. Can't carry her the whole way."

He was right. They'd never make it down the ramps in time. Not with the Bloodborn soon coming after them.

She nodded. Jélyn mumbled, stumbling on her own feet.

"We're almost there," Kora reassured her. "Just a little farther."

Fire bloomed behind them. It threw their shadows forward to where the rim met the waterfall. The lift was there beside the bridge over the river. Open. Waiting.

They reached it. The man took Jélyn's weight. "She's bad," he said.

"I know," Kora said as she unlatched the lock holding them in place. She tugged the line to go down.

The lift dropped, and the levels sped by. Kora was pleased to see that the first few were empty. People were getting down to the shoreline. They were getting to the ships.

She pulled the line to slow and stop them at the bottom, faster than she'd intended to. The box they were riding in shook and jerked, but nothing broke.

The platform before them was crowded with people hurrying to the two ships behind the waterfall. Many of them had bags of precious things. Kora had watched Alira and the pirates ready the *Black Crow* for carrying them all. The Stormborn would be packed in like logs, she knew.

But they'd live. Alira and Amaru were right. That's what mattered.

Kora abruptly realized that no more bells were ringing. She hoped that was because they'd all left to get down here and get on board.

She and the man hauled Jélyn through the crowds, past

the roaring waterfall, and into the torch-lit cavern. It was a swarm of chaos, enough so that her heart quaked. Did they have time to set sail at all?

The dock for the *Pale Dawn* was less crowded, and they turned toward it. One of Jélyn's crewmates saw them and called to another to help. Soon, a number of pirate women had her in hand and were hurrying her away, up the ramp, onto her ship, and into the rooms belowdecks.

Kora, panting, turned to the man. "Thank you," she said.

Wiping Jélyn's blood from his hands, he smiled. "I'm just glad you told everyone else not to take the lifts. Let's get on the ship, shall we?"

Kora nodded, and they turned to go. But there was a new crowd forming between them and the walkway to the Crow. An angry crowd. Two groups. Pirates facing pirates. Kora recognized Julara at the head of one group, trying to order the others to move. "Aboard the ships!" she yelled. "Ready the *Dawn* to cast off!"

But those in the cluster of women standing between Julara's group and the *Pale Dawn* weren't moving. "We'll not be sailing. You're not our mistress," hissed the pirate at their head. She was older, a veteran hand, with wide shoulders and a strong back.

"Shaesara—"

"Isn't here!" The woman opened her arms as she addressed the crowd around them. "For all we know, Shaesara is dead. And our oaths were not to her. They were to the ship! I am Madoka. You know my strength! By the law of the sea, I challenge for the helm!"

Madoka's supporters cheered her. Kora saw the women behind Julara hesitate in doubt.

Whatever they thought about her orders to set sail, it was clear they had misgivings about whether or not she could stand up to the looming veteran.

"Madoka," Julara tried, "please, we've got to sail out, like they said—"

"We don't listen to them! And you"—Madoka pulled the sword from her hip and pointed the tip of the blade at a wide-eyed Julara—"you gave them a ship. We should gut the lot of them. Right after you, I think."

"Stop this!" a voice shouted.

The crowd behind Julara parted, and Alira walked out to stand next to the pirate. Kora saw Amaru at the edge of the circle behind, watching what was happening.

"You've no say here." Again, Madoka pointed her blade at Julara. "You've less right than this one."

"I am Belakané's friend," Alira said.

"And we don't care."

Alira nodded over at Julara. She was trying to give the young pirate confidence, but it wasn't working. Alira could see it as clearly as Kora could: Julara was no fighter. If Madoka swung her blade, the girl would spend the last heartbeat of her life pissing herself on the dock.

"You swore an oath to the ship?" Alira asked, turning back to the angry pirates.

It wasn't what Madoka expected her to say. "We did. We all did."

Alira stood up straighter. "Then I, too, challenge Julara."

Julara looked like a stunned deer. "Alira, I—"

"Yield to me," Alira said to her.

"You've no right!" Madoka cried out.

Alira ignored the other woman and focused on Julara. "Yield," she repeated. "Yield to me and serve as maiden."

Julara, open-jawed and eyes wide as she looked between the women, simply nodded.

Alira spun back to Madoka. "Then it's me you'll fight. Yield or challenge. Be quick."

"Challenge," the pirate growled.

"And I accept," Alira said.

Without words, a circle opened up. Alira didn't draw a blade. "Last chance," she said. "I'd rather have your strong hand when we leave."

"The *Dawn* won't sail," the older pirate sneered.

Alira lifted slightly onto the pads of her feet. Kora recognized it. The same stance she'd taught Kora to use as they'd trained, dancing blades as they balanced among the Furywood branches. "She'll sail," Alira said. "But you won't."

The pirate roared. She thrust her sword toward Alira's chest. But Alira, trained in the branches to be as light on her feet as a feather on the wind, stepped easily aside and forward, dodging the blow and moving inside the sword tip's reach in a single quick movement. Her hand darted up and across Madoka's outstretched arm. Alira had a knife in her hand, Kora now saw. A tiny blade, but it was impossibly sharp. Kora had seen it cut magick from the strange trees of the Bloodborn.

It cut flesh just as easily. A bright red line sliced across Madoka's upper arm, severing muscle. The pirate screamed in agony. Her sword fell from her hand. She tried to cover the wound with her other.

Alira had the blade to the woman's throat just as quickly. There was a stunned silence. "Yield," Alira said.

Madoka spat.

Alira made another cut and stepped away from the splash.

The pirate's body fell forward, blood rushing out over the wood. Several stepped back, away from it.

"Anyone else?" Alira asked, turning around quickly. Red pulsed thick at her feet, but slowed quickly. "No? Then remember your oaths to the ship. Hikora?"

Hikora's small face appeared out of the crowd. "Yes, mistress?"

"You've helm of the *Crow* for now. Pick six from the crew of the *Dawn* to help you sail her. Lines off in two minutes. Go!"

Hikora pointed to a half-dozen crew. They hurried away, pushing the Stormborn up toward the *Black Crow*.

"Julara is my maiden aboard the *Dawn*," Alira announced to the remaining pirates. "Now as she said: all hands aboard! Ready for sail! Move!"

47

The Portal

Two things were true.

Kolum was seeing Shaesara in a battle somewhere far away. And alumen were coming to kill her here and now.

The first thing gave Bela nothing but questions, but the second thing meant that questions were the one thing she didn't have time for.

"I command them not," Kolum said, and Bela was somehow certain that he wasn't talking to them.

"Bela," Tew implored. He was pulling at her one sleeve, trying to get her to move. "Please."

Kolum turned to her. The lightning crackling along the edges of his sword made his face seem even more skeletal. "Her fight belongs to her. Close the portal, Bela. Run!"

The last word was a boom in the room, and it shocked her out of her paralysis. She turned, let Tew push her out onto one of the metal pathways crisscrossing the room. Then she was running, sprinting.

Behind them, the double doors exploded in a hail of

wood. Bela glanced back, saw two alumen charging out, one behind the other.

"They are here," Kolum said, and she didn't know if he was talking to her or to Shae. With his blue sword humming, he charged.

Time. He was buying them time.

Tew was running along a track parallel to her right. His eyes were locked on the machine and the portal at the other end of the great room.

Through the crash of metal bodies behind, Bela heard another sound from above. A pounding. She looked up to her left and saw a third aluman bent over against the glass ceiling near the corner of the room, raining down blows with its metal fist.

Two strikes. Three. And the glass gave way with a crash.

Tew screamed. The aluman fell into the room, body controlled, its legs rotating up to land on its feet. It cratered down through the metal walkways and into the dust and debris of the lower level. The entire metal floor shook, and Bela stumbled, awkwardly keeping her balance without the familiar weight of her arm at her side.

A moment later, a metal hand clawed up onto the pathway where it had fallen. The aluman sprang up after it, hips flexing like a rabbit's. It squatted, head scanning, until it saw them. Then, ignoring the fight at the entrance, it surged forward, big and fast.

Bela, looking back as she ran, saw how quickly the aluman was closing. It was leaping sideways over the wide-open spaces as it thundered forward, angling toward their path. Here and there, pipes burst and sprayed as the weight of its massive body strained the old lines. It was matching their pace.

No. Not matching their pace. Overtaking them. Closing faster than they could run.

Bela could hear Tew gasping for breath in the cold air. He didn't have much energy left. Neither did she.

They were hardly halfway across the room. The portal was perhaps a dozen squares away. The metal man was only two. It passed behind a still-living plant, then leapt across an open space. The floor reverberated, bouncing at its pounding steps.

The aluman took two great strides, parallel to her at last. Then its huge legs coiled up the strength to pounce, just as they entered one of the beams beneath snow-cleared glass. Moonlight shone down, sparkling gold on the flecks of Char that stuck to its body when it fell. The pale blue eyes were unblinking. Unfeeling. Merciless. The claws of its hands were open and ready.

It launched into the air, and Bela dove across an open square to her right, shoving Tew down with the stump of her arm—right into a living plant.

They pounded into sharp fronds, bounced off one bulb, then smashed into the side of a second. The last plant snapped free of the grid, and they fell, screaming, to slam into the darkness of the littered half of the hall below.

Bela's momentum carried her on. She slid through withered vine and crumbling leaves. Shadows and light were flashing and spinning. Above, the aluman roared in fury.

Her left hand caught on a crack in the floor. Her legs instinctively kicked her feet underneath her. She got up to one knee.

Tew was behind her. He'd hit his head. Dust was strewn all around him, but it didn't look like he'd inhaled any.

Thanks be to the Mother.

The aluman crashed down to stand beside him. Tew twitched and moaned at its feet. The metal man bent slightly to look down at the little man of flesh before him. A clawed hand flexed in and out, as if anxious to begin his dismemberment.

Bela glanced toward the end of the huge room. She could see stairs, beyond the hanging masses of still more plants, bathed in blue light. The stairs weren't far away, and not much farther would be Kolum's machine and the portal. But she knew the metal man would slaughter Tew long before she reached them.

Too many had already died. Oni. Her crew. Even her ship. If there was any chance to save him still, she had to take it.

"Here!" Bela screamed. She waved her one arm wildly. "I'm the one you want!"

The aluman looked up at her. The moonlight shone on its shoulders, which were dusted with a snow of golden Char.

"Me!" she yelled at the aluman. "I'm Belakané!"

The aluman raised one metal foot. For a horrifying moment, she thought it might crush the reader with it, but then it put it down on the other side of him, stepping toward her.

Bela smiled. "Let's race," she said. Then she turned and ran, weaving through the open spaces, keeping as close to the plants as she could without touching them and disturbing the Char that dusted their roots.

The squares of light passed, one by one, stride by

exhausted stride. Every step felt as if it would be her last. Every breath as if it would end in screams.

The aluman was behind her, feet pounding the floor, shoulders crashing into the plants she dodged, slowing it down.

She reached the steps and took them two at a time, bounding, breathing heavy. At the top, she faced the machine.

It rose up before her, shining in magnificent silver. Sweeping curves. Twirling gears. Dancing springs. A table sat before it, with straps and belts at its corners. The machine stretched two pairs of arms over it, and they held two rings between them. The rings, such a gleaming and glorious silver that they seemed nearly white, spun one inside the other, like two snakes chasing their own tails in opposite directions. They framed the portal—a glowing circle of pale blue, the color of the most perfect sky Bela could ever have imagined.

The aluman roared, coming closer. She ran up to the machine, staring at it with amazement and despair. She was sure that she'd never again see anything like it. She was also sure that she could scratch at it until her remaining fingers were bone, and she wouldn't manage to close it.

Machine and magick, Kolum had said. *Destroy one or the other.*

She couldn't do anything about the machine.

But magick …?

The aluman leaped up behind her. The floor shook from its footsteps. The great room echoed with its roar.

Alone, Bela turned and faced it. Alone, she took two steps and leaped toward its chest, reaching out with her one and a half arms as if to embrace it.

The aluman's clawed hand swung forward. It caught her in the chest and flung her across the room. She hit the ground, slid, and stopped with her back against what might have been a shelf of books at one time. Bloody lines marked the scrape of its claws across her front. And half-healed fractures from the bear attack brought fresh pain with each breath.

She'd landed facing the aluman, but she wasn't looking at it. She was looking at her one remaining hand, which was dusted with the Char that she'd wiped off its metal plates when she'd touched it. Her upturned palm shimmered golden in the moonlight.

She lifted it to her face. She said a prayer to the Mother. Then she put the dusted hand over her mouth and nose.

She inhaled the Char. She silenced her own scream.

The aluman had followed her. It was there. Clawing at her, groping at her flesh.

But she didn't feel it. She didn't even feel her own body convulsing, though she knew it was.

All she could feel was the wind, driving down from the broken ceiling. Reaching up to curl around the tower to where the ancient airship still floated, high above. She felt it stretch beyond, across the dead city, streaming up the canyon they'd descended. She felt it all the way to the mountain pass, to the deep canyon where Oni had died.

I am the wind, Bela thought. *The wind is me.*

She'd closed her eyes, and when she opened them, she saw the face of the aluman. There was blood upon it. Her blood. It made spots of darkness on its pale, glowing eyes.

The wind came to her. Between the blows of the aluman,

her one hand twitched and flexed as she focused the will of her mind, gathering and twisting the air into hammer blows that buffeted the sides of the aluman's head.

It screamed and took a step back, confused. Air filled her lungs. She could see it streaming like threads in the air, and she read them like waves, measuring their depth, their power, their motion.

Like a paddle turned against the flow, she pulled the threads back, held them between her and the aluman. She focused on them, willed them to bend, coaxed them to weave into one another.

In the eye of her mind, she made the knots that her single hand could no longer tie. The aluman tried to come at her again, but an invisible wall stood between them now.

The metal man roared and slashed, but the wall would not move.

The threads were loosening, though. The room was going dim. Her will was fading. Blood loss, she imagined.

Bela screamed in her frustration, and she threw the wall forward into the metal man.

The unseen wall smashed into the aluman's massive chest, staggered it several steps away before she lost her grip on the threads and it dissipated. The aluman had its back to the machine and its glowing portal. Its torso turned left and right, looking for what had struck it.

"Bela!"

She blinked over, saw that Kolum stood at the end of the platform. Tew was in one of his arms, cradled like a babe. Alive.

The hand at the end of his metal arm held a crystal of soulglass, one of those he'd taken when he'd saved them.

He threw it. Not at her, not at the portal, but at the space between them.

Time crawled. The crystal turned through the air in a slow tumble, end over end. Somewhere, her body was shaking. Dying, perhaps. But she had life still.

She pulled the air up from the floor, up out of her very lungs. It caught and lifted the crystal. Held it for a moment, floating. Weightless.

Such a small thing, she thought. But such great power.

The aluman had looked to Kolum when he shouted. Now it was slowly turning back to her.

She wrapped the air around the soulglass, spinning it tighter and tighter into a fist of wind that gripped the crystal like a knife. She could see it now, as specks of dust sucked into the churn.

The tightening air beat upon the crystal's facets. It, too, began to spin. Bela smiled at the aluman. She hoped it was afraid.

And if Asryth was watching through its eyes, perhaps she would be afraid too.

Bela spun the crystal forward, buried its drilling point between the seams of the metal plates across the aluman's chest.

The impact hurtled the aluman backward. Its legs hit the table with its straps and chains. It fell back onto it, splayed out, face up. Its eyes reflected the shimmering portal, blue on blue.

Bela's body was gasping for breath, but she focused the energy she had left on drawing every last bit of the air in the room down and down, into the fist of wind that still had hold of the soulglass.

She felt it crack.

And then, after the space of a single heartbeat, it broke. The soulglass exploded. Down into the aluman. Up into the machine. And across the floor to Bela, who had time enough only to see the metal parts flying and the portal disappearing before her world went black.

48

The Crash

Shae awoke in freezing darkness.

In shock, her body instinctively convulsed, but nothing would move. Her arms, her legs, her head … everything was held down.

Snow.

She was buried in snow.

She flexed and contorted, wiggling against the weight, and the snow felt like it gave way from her face. She pushed harder in that direction, straining, and then the cold seemed to be shifting around her. Her right arm lifted, broke free.

The snow was a powder, like light sand, and she clawed through it until she was rising up to kneel, coughing and shivering, on the field where the alumen army had been.

There were metal hands around her, frozen as they reached up to the night sky. A few metal heads were staring out at the snowy waste through unlit, black eyes. Farther away, she could see a few of the lumicklines still glowing blue across the walls of the Blue Keep, but the ramp of alumen dead had been kicked over by the avalanche—nothing more

than a pile of metal bodies now. Two alumen had made it
to the wall and survived, but they weren't fighting the men
there. They seemed to be fighting each other, the parapet,
even themselves. As she stared, one turned and walked off
the wall, plummeting into the snow.

Handfuls of alumen were still moving elsewhere in the
valley, somehow lifted close enough to the surface of
the avalanche that they weren't killed by it. But they,
like the ones on the wall, seemed aimlessly angry. Not far
away, one had another pinned down and was ripping it
apart, plate by plate.

There was a groaning sound behind her, and she turned
to see an aluman, swinging its clawed hands, coming at her
like a mindless drunk. She coughed and screamed at the
same time, tried to kick away through the cold—but every
time she tried to get her feet under her, they only sank and
pushed down into the snow.

The boltgun! It was still at her back. She reached around
for it, desperate, the aluman close—but her stiff fingers
wouldn't bend. They slapped uselessly at the leather strap.

The aluman made a discordant, horrible sound, like
nothing she'd heard before. It lurched. It raised a claw up
to strike.

Then a hole sparked open on the side of its head.

It turned, teetering, and a second shot struck it in the hip.
It fell backward beside her.

"Damn frozen fingers," Aro said as he walked up. His hat
was gone. Snow was packed in the folds of his long coat.
His hands were moving the lever on his boltgun. His feet
kept pushing into the powdery ground.

The aluman rocked back and forth, its arms flailing as

it tried to right itself. Shae rolled out of reach, then started trying to work her way up to her feet again.

The lumicker walked up next to her. He gave her a quick nod and then took one more careful shot into the chest of the aluman. It went still.

Shae tried to thank him as he helped her up, but her teeth had set to chattering instead.

"Never mind that," he said. "Put your hands in your armpits. If you don't warm them, you'll lose them."

She nodded and did as he said, while he punched snow out of the fur hood of her coat and pulled it over her head. There was a fresh wet and cold, but then she felt a slight rising heat in her ears.

"Let's see if the others were so lucky," Aro said.

He put one arm around her shoulders, held her close as he trudged them forward. For a minute, she could only stare at the snow in front of her feet, numb to the core, trying to keep her balance while she kept her fingers under her arms. But slowly, feeling began to return with tingling pains. "My skin hurts," she said.

"It's like you've hardly seen snow before," he said with a laugh. "Pain is good. Means all you got is snow bite, and you won't lose that part. If you don't get pain, you've got ice bite. Don't get any of that, please."

Shae nodded. Pain is good. She could understand that. The noise of the two alumen fighting each other not far away caused her to look in their direction. "What happened to them?"

"Your avalanche happened, Shae. A damn fine shot, I must say. Didn't think you'd manage it. Mostly sent you up there so you wouldn't have to see me killed."

"I mean those. They're not acting right. Neither did the one back there."

"Don't know. I think something's happened to the lumicks. Even my boltgun was acting strange. Hoping I can ask my box, if it survived. We're almost there."

Shae blinked up and saw where he was taking her. The *Sparrow* was half-buried in the white, keeled over like a ship run aground. Its airbag had been ripped open and was strewn out across the snow beside it.

"Kayden," she gasped. She pulled free of Aro, forged a path ahead through the powder.

As Shae got closer, she could see that the *Sparrow* had gone down bow first, but the force of the impact had split her hull across the mid-deck, as if the whole airship had been broken across a mighty knee. She lay open like a half-cracked egg. Both engines had been ripped off the hull and were nowhere to be seen.

"Kayden!" she shouted when she got close. The ship's wound was open to the keel, so she tried hoisting herself through the gap. She started to slip as she climbed in, but a strong hand caught her arm and pulled her up into the ship.

It was Tadd. He was badly beaten, one eye almost swollen shut, but he was alive. "Lord Kayden's in back, my lady," he said. "He's fine."

Something in his eyes made her pause. "Ragan?"

Tadd shook his head.

"I'm sorry." Not knowing what else to do, she embraced the young man.

He was startled, but then he seemed genuinely grateful for the gesture. "Thank you. He was a good man. Come on, Kayden's back here."

They climbed down a slanting hallway toward the stern, to the captain's quarters. Tadd pulled the door open for her.

The furnishings inside had all slid back into one corner. Kayden, who'd apparently been placed on the bed, had gone with it all but had ended up more or less on top of the pile. He was sitting upright, his legs stretched out under a blanket. Tadd had clearly tried to make him comfortable by drawing the mattress flat and putting a pillow behind his back.

"Shae!"

"Careful," Tadd said from behind her. "His leg is bad."

Shae nodded, carefully stepped her way down to him. Tadd closed the door behind her.

"So you went and broke your leg again?" she asked.

Kayden shrugged, looking as meek as he looked weak. "Captain is the one who sent me down here."

"So she did." Shae knelt by him. "I'm … I'm glad to see you again."

"Shae, I—"

Whatever he was going to say, she interrupted by embracing him. He seemed to melt into it for a moment, then gasped and pulled back. "You're half-frozen!"

Shae nodded, feeling the sting of the heat rolling off him in turn. "And you're more than enough to warm me up."

Pale and sick though he was, he managed to arch an eyebrow that she read as hope.

"No, no," she said, laughing a little at the thought. "I'd break you right now. I meant that you're fevered."

"Everyone decent in there?" Aro asked from outside the door.

Shae winked at Kayden. "Decent as we can be," she said.

The door opened. The old lumicker had lit his pipe, and the fire in its bowl made his cheeks glow red. "Well, my box is busted bad."

"Think you'll get it working?" Shae asked. She had questions she wanted to ask of it. Where was Bela? What was the portal?

"No time soon. And with the lumick acting strange, it's hard to say if I can do it at all." He nodded to Kayden. "You're looking even worse than usual, lad."

Kayden smiled. "Thanks, Aro."

"Well," Shae said, "it'd be a long, cold walk to the keep with two legs, and Kayden here only has one. Think we can put together a fire or something to get us through the night?"

"Reckon me and Tadd can get something going," the lumicker said. He nodded and left. They could hear him moving things around outside.

"Who put you in charge?" Kayden asked.

She looked back down at him, saw that he was smiling.

"Oh, you'll get used to it." She smiled back at him. "I'm a captain now."

49

The Gates and the Dawn

Everyone was moving, with most of those on the dock running for the *Pale Dawn*, stepping over or around the body of Madoka in its pool of blood. Kora and the man who'd helped her let the crowd push past them; then they strode up to Alira and Amaru, who were standing beside a shaken Julara. "Alira saved your life," Kora said.

Julara was trembling. "I know."

"You'll stay with me on the *Pale Dawn*," Alira said to Amaru. "It's right here."

The elder nodded and began heading for the ramp.

Julara turned to go, then froze.

"Get aboard," Alira ordered her.

"Alira—mistress, I …"

"What?"

"The gate," Julara said. "The gate of the bay."

They all seemed to turn at once. Though they could see nothing beyond the falling wall of water, each of them realized what the pirate was talking about. A massive gate stood between the Bay of Bones and the sea. It was kept closed to conceal them from the open waters. And if it wasn't opened, it would seal them in.

"We can't open it from down here," Julara whispered.

Kora saw the filling decks of the ships. Sail lines and mooring lines were being loosed. All of it would be for nothing if they couldn't leave the bay. And, at any moment, the Bloodborn would be streaming down the emptying walkways into the cavern.

"I'll go," she said.

Alira stared. "Kora, you can't get back if—"

For the first time in her life—likely her last, she supposed—Kora ignored her mentor. She grabbed hold of Julara's shoulder. "How do I open it?"

"There's no oxen up there right now," the pirate managed. "You can't."

"Tide's moving out," Kora said. "Can the ships push it open?"

Julara shook her head, numb. "It's locked. On both sides."

"I'll go too," the man beside her said. When Kora looked over at him, he shrugged. "Maybe we jump into the rigging when they sail past us."

Kora gave him the slightest of nods before squeezing Julara's shoulder hard. "Can I lift the latch? Can he?"

"Yes," Julara said.

The man took a few steps toward the waterfall. "Come on, then! We've got to hurry!"

Alira was staring. There were tears in her eyes. "Kora, I—"

Kora hugged her quickly. "Just don't forget your promise," she said. And then she turned and ran ahead before she could change her mind.

The man caught up to her at the lift. "My name is Tevlyn," he said as he stepped onto the platform. Then he seemed unsure, embarrassed. "Don't know why I told you that."

"I think I know why," she said. Looking up, she saw the Bloodborn pouring down the ramps and ladders only a few levels above them. "My name's Kora. I'll go left. You go right over the bridge."

Tevlyn laughed nervously as Kora unlocked the lift. "No need to take it slow," he said.

She grinned, nodded, then yanked as hard as she could on the rising rope.

The floor leapt upward, and they both buckled to their knees. Empty levels sped past. Then levels with the torchlit faces and the reaching hands of Bloodborn.

They sped past them all, and Kora didn't bother to slow at the top. There was no telling what awaited them. Speed and surprise were their only chance.

The lift reached the top with a crash of wood that threw them up and out onto the hard ground. Kora tried to roll, but she took the fall on her bad shoulder anyway. It made noises that she felt under the skin.

Tevlyn was already on his feet, kicking into a run. "Come and get me!" he shouted as he headed over the bridge and into the dark.

Her head spinning, fighting the urge to throw up, Kora clambered to her feet too. Cradling her screaming arm, she ran along the rim she'd only just left.

Tents were in flames, but there were no Bloodborn to be seen. They'd all gone down the ramps after their prey.

She passed the rock she'd sat upon while she'd looked up

at the stars, and it made her glance up once again. The sky was just beginning to lighten.

Dawn was coming.

She ran on, past the tents and the outbuildings, past the point where the palisade closed in on the cliffs as they rounded the bay, where there was only a narrow path for her to follow, and she stayed close to the wall for fear of getting too close to the edge.

And then the wall pushed back away, and the path opened up. The sky was glowing even brighter now, and across the leveled space, she saw the watchtower where they'd met with Julara. She saw the mighty gates close beside it. And between, in the middle of a cleared circle of trodden-down earth, sat a massive, pegged wooden wheel, lying over on its side, with the chains controlling its half of the gate wrapped around it.

As Julara had said, there were no oxen in sight to hitch to the wheel and walk about that dirt circle. And for a moment Kora despaired over how she'd find whatever mechanism she needed to unlatch the gate and give the ships below a chance of pushing through. But then she heard the rhythmic wooden thump of the gate shaking against its locks as the waves shivered the doors from below.

She followed the noise to the huge wooden hinge at the top of the gate. There was an arm of the gate beyond the pivot point, she saw, and it was caught between a thick post and a log dropped into a hole in the earth. Pull the log, and the gate would swing freely.

There were pegs stuck into the log to help lift it out. Kora squatted down, and with her one good hand she grabbed the lowest of them and tried to pull it up. Straining, she could do little more than jostle it in the hole.

There was a grunt and a loud thud from the other side of the gate. Then Tevlyn's voice called out. "Did you make it, Kora?"

She smiled and peered through the half-light, hoping to see him. "I did! And so did you!"

Tevlyn laughed. "Mine's free. Did you find yours?"

Kora strained again. Again it hardly budged. "Found it! Can't get it out!"

There was a pause, like he was thinking. "I don't think I can get to you."

Something about the way he said it made her look out along the line of the rim. She saw torchlight bobbing along the path to him. Bloodborn. They were coming along her path too. "Yeah," she said. She tried and failed again.

"A ship!" Tevlyn cried out.

She stood and walked to the edge. The bow of a ship had pierced the waterfall. It had oars out, and they were pushing it hard. "It's the *Pale Dawn*!" she called over to him. With luck, the *Black Crow* would be close behind.

The outgoing tide had already floated Tevlyn's half of the gate open a crack. The Bloodborn were getting closer to them on both sides.

Again, she squatted down and failed to lift the log.

"The other ship! They're both away!"

Kora cursed. Then she stood and pulled the sling from around her neck. Pain shot through her wrecked shoulder as it took the weight of her arm. She ground her teeth against the shock of it.

"They're coming!"

She didn't know if Tevlyn meant the ships or the Bloodborn. Either one. Both. Didn't matter.

"Kora, hurry! You can do it!"

She bent down. She hugged the log like it was the lover she'd never had. She squeezed it, letting the pain run in tears from her eyes. She flexed, pushing the surges of shrieking agony down from her shoulder into the tightening grips of her hands and the ground beneath her feet. She heaved upward.

The log shifted, stuck, and then came free at last. She fell backward with it, and it rolled over her broken shoulder when she went down. She screamed out at the last of the fading stars.

The sound seemed to echo back to her not in screams, but in the laughter of the Bloodborn.

So close.

So very close.

Kora cradled her broken arm and stood.

She could see Tevlyn standing on the other side. The Bloodborn weren't far away behind him, but he was smiling at her. Both halves of the gate between them were swinging free.

In the Bay of Bones, the *Pale Dawn* had straightened out her line and was approaching the gate. The *Black Crow* wasn't far behind. But neither ship would reach the gate before the Bloodborn did.

The ships would get out. But the two of them wouldn't.

Tevlyn seemed to have come to the same conclusion. As she watched, he turned his back just long enough to get to the other side of the log he'd pulled. He began kicking and rolling it to the edge.

A smart man, Kora thought. And though every movement hurt, she did the same. Their logs dropped down into the water far below. A small gesture of defiance, she supposed, but one that ensured the Bloodborn couldn't lock the gates back up.

The ships would get away.

"Well," Tevlyn called out, "do you have any ideas?"

Kora looked from him to the approaching Bloodborn to the too-far-away masts of the ships. She let out a long, steady breath.

Her shoulder, she thought, didn't really hurt anymore. Maybe because it didn't matter anymore. "Meet you in the middle?" she asked.

Tevlyn's face was tight, but he smiled. "Sounds good."

He took a few steps back from the edge. So did she.

The Bloodborn, perhaps sensing it, screamed and tried to close the distance.

But already, the two of them were running. And as the dawn broke over the island, they embraced in the sunlight and fell.

50

All Things Change

Bela was floating, adrift. And warm. Truly warm.

Her hand moved against the fur that enwrapped her. It felt comforting and real.

She opened her eyes to find she was on a slung bed in a room of wood. It was spare, as a ship's cabin ought to be, and for a moment she thought she'd somehow dreamt an impossibly long dream, that she was still aboard the *Sandcrow*, that they were still under sail at sea.

But then she saw that the skin around her had the pale fur of a white bear. Her right arm, when she pulled it free, ended just below her elbow.

And the cabin, though familiar in its ways, had fittings she'd never seen, like a lamp affixed to the ceiling that burned with a steady, unflickering glow.

She tried to get up, but pain shot through her. She winced and groaned. Her head was swimming, too, as if she'd had far too much of the barrel.

Glass window ports showed circles of sky, and she steadied herself by focusing on them.

Working carefully to get her feet to the floor, she realized that she was naked beneath the bearskin. Her chest was striped with wounds, but they appeared to have been cleaned and even sewn in a few places. Not the finest work she'd ever seen, but it had done its job.

She was alive.

Making it upright, standing, she scooted her way across the little room to lean on the wall and look out through one of the circular ports.

She wasn't just looking out at the sky. She was in it. Below her was a city of stone around a deep, circular bay.

Her head spun out into a wobble, and she felt the pit of her stomach rise up.

She braced herself against the wood wall of the room, focusing on its solidity, trying to push from her mind the worry that the wood of the wall or floor might give way and she'd fall, for long, horrible seconds, to her death.

When the room stopped spinning, she turned back to the bed. The scraps of her sealskins were in a corner, but new clothes had been left in a neat pile atop a nearby trunk. She went to the strange clothing, gingerly began to put it on. It took time, as she fought the pains of her body and her instinct to reach for things with her missing hand.

The garments were black cloth beneath black leather, with straps for tightening to fit. The upper garment was tight across her chest when she finally managed to get it on, but she gritted her teeth and used her one hand to pull the strap of the buckles down even farther, cinching it to stabilize her aching ribs.

Once everything was on, she pulled the polar bear cloak over her shoulders. White on black.

Then she stepped outside.

Tewrick was there. Standing mid-deck. Like her, he was dressed all in black. And he didn't seem so little anymore. He was fiddling with one of the lines that ran up to the gray shape floating above them.

"You're alive," she said.

The reader looked up. He was surprised, but he was pleased. And he didn't need to ask what she was talking about. He just raised his chin at her. "You too," he said.

It was true. She'd inhaled the Char. She'd convulsed. But here she was. "I don't understand why. I ought to be dead."

He stopped what he was doing. "We've been thinking about that for a while now."

"We?"

"Time for discussion has been plentiful," Kolum said from behind her.

Bela looked back. The metal man was standing at the helm. "So closing the portal didn't kill you."

"It did not."

"I admit, I wondered if it might."

One metal hand lifted slightly. Some kind of shrug, perhaps? "I wondered the same."

Bela smiled. "I'm glad it didn't."

"I am equally glad of this."

"And the others?" she asked.

"The Stream is closed. Asryth is cut off from me, just as she is cut off from the others she made. Much madness is there in the world now, I conclude."

Always eloquent. Bela considered for a moment how she would like to read the metal man's speech as Tew would have written it. He would surely be easier to understand that way. "Thank you for all you did," she said.

"It was not I who used the magick," Kolum said.

"That's right," Tew said. "From what Kolum told me, you not only survived the Char but were a natural at using it. Had the evokers never tested you before?"

Bela shook her head. "I never wanted to be an evoker."

"We do not always get the things we want," Kolum said, and then he turned and walked past them. There was a ramp leading to the dock of the white tower beside them, and she could see crates there. Supplies.

"He's a good man," Tew said after the aluman left. "As much as he is a man."

Bela nodded. Looking at the rope in his hands, she could see that he'd been trying for a knot and failing. "Can I help you?"

"I believe you can, shipmistress." He held up the rope with a look of exasperation. "I found a book in the library on the basics of such things, but, I confess, I don't have hands-on experience."

"Experience does help," Bela said. She came up and, with her one hand, guided his in the proper motions. "You'll have to be my hands, you know."

"I will do all I can, shipmis—"

"Bela," she said. "Call me Bela, Tew."

He blushed, but he nodded.

Bela looked around the deck. The airship was in remarkable condition for its age, but she could see that Tew had been working hard to swap out some of the old lines for new ones.

Apparently, Kolum, with his clawed hands, hadn't been any good with rope-tying either.

The reader followed her gaze. "We've been gathering supplies for a while. You slept for a few days."

"And you read books."

"There are a lot of them." He beamed. "Kolum wasn't lying when he said he'd saved some. I brought every one I could aboard."

Bela lightly patted her side. "I'm glad that some explained healing."

"Me too."

"I just—" Bela cut herself off, ashamed at her own astonishment that they'd survived. "I'm glad to see you, Tew. I'm thinking this should make for a good story one day."

"I'll teach you how to write it," he said. "If you'll teach me how to fly this thing."

"Deal."

Bela limped to the side away from the tower and looked over. Her head swam a bit at the sight, but already she was getting used to it. She remembered how the threads were like waves when she'd taken the Char. That made the sky a kind of sea, she supposed. Sailing was sailing, after all.

Tew had followed her. "Kolum gathered a lot of the Char. He said you'll need it."

Bela shook her head in astonishment. "Bela, the one-handed evoker. Not sure if that's better than the Hero of the Harbor or not."

For a minute, they looked out over the city. Seabirds were calling as they circled and dove for surface-feeding fish on its warm-watered bay. Despite the height of the ship, the air didn't seem as cold as it had been before. Bela found herself thinking of Oni's face.

"It's what you are now," Tew said. "A hero of two worlds. That's how I'll write it, anyway."

Bela grinned. "If I'm to be a one-armed shipmistress, then you can be sure I'll tell everyone you're a reader who can kill a bear."

He smiled. "I could imagine some fine songs about such a man."

"At least a few."

He laughed a little at the thought, then seemed to settle himself. His face was one of determination, and it made her wonder how much strength they had in the Fair Isles that they'd never tapped. "Orders, then?"

She peered out at the line of mists that edged the bay, and the encircling sea beyond them.

"Well, tracing the shore should be simple enough. Let's see how she sails."

"We're going back to the cave, Bela?"

He'd used her name, and she was glad for it. She smiled. "For supplies, aye. Fresh seal meat. Fresh oil. Kolum might not need it, but we will."

"Certainly easier than the fishing I've been attempting," he said. "And what then?"

"Then south to open waters, Tew." She could almost smell the salt already. "Then to the home of the Windborn, I suppose."

"The Windborn?"

"I made a promise, remember? Kolum said there's a Seaborn fleet headed for the Windborn lands, and Asryth will be with them."

Kolum had walked back across the deck to join them. "I am glad indeed this was remembered."

Tew took a deep breath. "So we're sailing into the middle of a war."

Bela nodded. "Sounds about right."

"She'll definitely need a name for that."

"What will?"

"This ship," Tew said.

Bela looked to Kolum. "Has this ship a name?"

The metal man's torso turned from side to side as if he were looking for it. "This is not something it has."

"*She*," Bela corrected with a smile. "Ships are always fine ladies." She took in the wood around them, dark against the sky, their black outfits, and their white fur cloaks. "*Snowraven*," she said. "I name her *Snowraven*."

"A fine name," Tew said.

Kolum made a kind of bow, then lifted a metal hand to point to the helm.

Bela gathered herself with a deep breath, then turned to where a brass steering wheel sat waiting on what passed for the airship's quarterdeck. It beckoned her.

Tew was at her side. She could feel his strength. "Helm to the end?" he asked.

"Together," Bela replied, looking from the reader to the aluman to the sea. "Helm to the end."

Acknowledgements

A long time ago, I had a dream. A small group of women stood on a frozen sea, the wind whipping snow across the meager fire they'd lit to keep warm. Behind them was a massive, frost-painted ship. Locked in the ice. Broken by it. A slight young man was with them, teeth chattering from the cold water he'd just escaped. One of the women—the one in charge—looked around at them all with both pity and determination. I heard the voice in her head as if it was my own. *Helm to the end*.

I don't know how it is for other authors, but a lot of my stories start this way: I wake up with a scene in my head that's viscerally real, and I have to figure out just what the hell it is. In this case, I wrote an initial short story about the desperate mission this crew was on to find a secret weapon.

Not long after the publication of my third Shards novel, my then agent was approached by Audible, wanting to know if I'd write a novella for them. As luck would have it, I'd been fiddling with my ship-in-the-ice story for a few years at that point, adding more and more depth to the world and characters. I gave it a final polishing, trimming out some story threads to make it the proper length, and it appeared as the audiobook *Black Crow, White Snow*.

It did well.

Bestseller-for-a-couple-of-months well.

Audible was pleased enough to ask if I would be interested in writing a trilogy of novels in the world. I answered "Yes"—obviously—because I knew I had a much larger story of these characters in mind. I also had a much larger picture of their world, thanks in part to the inadvertent help of N. K. Jemisin and a creative writing class I was teaching around that time. I talked about this in the acknowledgments of *Seaborn*, the first book in this series.

Writing Bela's backstory in *Seaborn* and then expanding the events of *Black Crow, White Snow* from a short novella into the larger novel you've just finished allowed me to tell a far deeper and richer story of why she and her crew found themselves on that ice and what happened to them there. So *Iceborn* is, I would say, my preferred truth of these events. But it would not exist if not for *Black Crow, White Snow*, so my first thanks here go to those who made that prior novella a reality: Paul Stevens, Steve Feldberg, Janina Edwards, and of course the many listeners who gave it a hard push on the charts.

I don't listen to audiobooks myself, and they're rather hard to put on the bookshelf. So the fact that the Seaborn Cycle is now available in this beautiful print copy is a dream come true. For this, I am enormously grateful to my agent, Georgina Capel, along with the extraordinary folks at Head of Zeus and Ad Astra: Nicolas Cheetham, Charlie Hiscox,

Sophie Whitehead, Zoe Giles, and Simon Michele—the last of whom created the stunning covers for the series.

The support of friends and family is vital to me, so as ever I owe them all thanks. I dedicate *Iceborn* to my parents specifically, however: Though this is the second book in the Seaborn Cycle, it is in some sense the start of it for the reasons outlined above. It seemed right, then, to dedicate this one to Mom and Dad, who were always unwavering in their support of my dreams—even at the start when I'm sure the stories sucked.

About the Author

MICHAEL LIVINGSTON is the author of the bestselling audiobook *Black Crow, White Snow* and the Seaborn Cycle series of novels it inspired, as well as the Shards of Heaven epic historical fantasy series. An acclaimed conflict analyst in his day job, he has twice won the Distinguished Book Prize from the international Society for Military History (2017, 2020) and is the author of numerous popular histories, including *Never Greater Slaughter* and *Agincourt*. At present, he serves as the Citadel Distinguished Professor at The Citadel. You can find Michael at www.michaellivingston.com or on X @medievalguy.